A MEMORY OF LIES

A
Memory
of Lies

Best wishes

Johnnie Gallop

Johnnie Gallop

Matador
9 Priory Business Park,
Wistow Road, Kibworth Beauchamp,
Leicestershire, LE8 0RX
Tel: 0116 279 2299
Email: books@troubador.co.uk
Web: www.troubador.co.uk/matador
Twitter: @matadorbooks

ISBN 978 1789018 516

British Library Cataloguing in Publication Data.
A catalogue record for this book is available from the British Library.

Printed on FSC accredited paper
Printed and bound in Great Britain by 4edge Limited
Typeset in 11pt Adobe Garamond Pro by Troubador Publishing Ltd, Leicester, UK

Matador is an imprint of Troubador Publishing Ltd

Cover design: Henry Hyde
Cover photograph: Deborah Grace Photography

Inspired by real events.

The footnotes are not essential and can easily be ignored. I apologise for any inaccuracies which remain despite my best efforts.

My research was wide-ranging and uncovered many photographs. Visit www.johnniegallop.com to learn more and access the hyperlinks.

Johnnie Gallop 2019

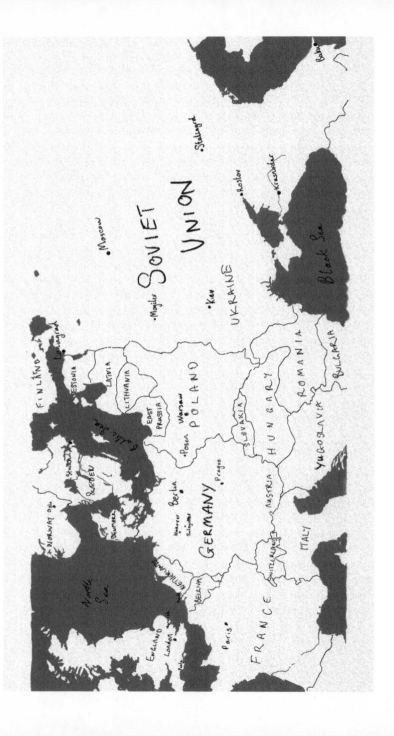

PROLOGUE

IN THE SUMMER OF 1992, AS THE NEW RUSSIA AROSE FROM the ashes of the old Soviet Union, Misha seized the moment. He spoke to his boss in London to demand a transfer. Credit Suisse was the first international bank to open in Russia for seventy years. Michael 'Misha' Cheshire was employee number three.

Misha was half-Russian and his grandmother, Baba Tanya, had taught him well. His language abilities were strong but beyond that, Tanya had nurtured within him a deep love of the country, at least to the south. She had told him of her young life on the Kuban river in the Caucasus: the early days of her marriage, his mother as a child, the privations of life within the Soviet totalitarian regime, and of course the wonder and bravery of the Kuban Cossack Host who settled the eastern shore of the Black Sea in the eighteenth century.

Misha excelled in the art of client relations. His ability with language and Russian culture, alongside his education in the manners and customs of the people and his natural ability to win friends, afforded him an extraordinary ability to matchmake between the bankers of the West and the resources of the East. While others made the deals, Misha's forte was drawing clients to the negotiating table and keeping them there even when the spinning coin went against them.

By 1993 Misha was living in a large apartment in old Arbat close to the Kremlin. Life was fine for a well-heeled

Westerner in Moscow. At Easter it is traditional for Russian families to tend the graves of their departed.[1] For Misha, Easter 1993 was time for a pilgrimage, not to tend to family graves but instead to tend their memories and the stories he had learned in his youth. The city of Krasnodar in the northern Caucasus was over a day's ride south by train from Moscow. Departing Kazansky Station in the morning, he stopped for a few hours at Rostov for supper, slept somewhat fitfully in his seat overnight and finally arrived in the city of the Kuban Cossacks at 10am the following morning. Misha had been transported in place but also in time. Gone was the bustle of the capital, the boulevards beginning to adopt the brand names of Western capitalism, the restaurants, clothes, the cars. As he walked out of the railway station in Krasnodar, life switched to the monochrome of a 1930's newsreel.

He made his way through the streets, asking passers-by and policemen for directions to a grey block of flats on the outskirts of the main centre. He couldn't have been sure that it still existed but the address had been recounted by Baba Tanya so many times during his formative years that it was branded on his brain. He walked up the steps of cracking concrete and dandelions to the first floor and along the outside landing until he came to the door – the same door described by Tanya. He knocked.

---

1   Radonitsa (Радоница) (Day of Rejoicing) is the Russian Orthodox Church commemoration of the departed observed on the second Tuesday of Easter. The name is derived from the Slavic word radost, meaning joy.

1

DEAREST PASHA, THE LOVE OF MY LIFE, WEPT AS WE boarded the train at Posen bound for Berlin. Our dreams had fallen apart.

In Russia, under the Communists, life had been oppressive and claustrophobic. Yet despite the Soviet passion for control – life, thought, and outcomes – their entire empire was beset by a lack of efficiency. Everywhere, and in every aspect of Russian life, machines were broken, the schedules were wrong, the people were untrained. Endless plans, lists, rotas, quotas, all wrong, incomplete, unread, misfiled. I hated the inefficiency even more than I hated the dogma.

Then had come the Nazis. Brutal, yes, (at that time we could not have known the full extent of their atrocities), but also logical, planned, and consistent. I had rejoiced at their arrival in our city of Krasnodar in southern Russia. Does that seem a terrible thing to say? With hindsight of course it does, but if you had lived under, and understood, the daily workings of both the Soviet and Nazi totalitarian states, you might have also found it hard to choose between the two evils at the time. Thank God we were neither Kulak[2] nor Jew. Under the Soviets we had been intelligentsia and thus always suspect to an extent, whereas under the Nazis we were Russian – the enemy – and a feared enemy at that. But the Nazis respected us as intellectuals and for most of the war years at least, that countered our Russian heritage.

I'm practical; I rely on logic, form and process. Pasha describes me as 'matter of fact' but I know others who say I'm just rude. Pasha, though, is the total opposite. He has an easy manner which removes rough edges. He makes sense of the world and smooths our way through life.

His understanding, empathy and respect for others makes everyone like him. He forms easy friendships leading to occasional extra help and little favours coming our way. Whilst alien to me, I could see how his charm and humour had shaped our life in Krasnodar. Later on, his qualities facilitated our move to Posen[3] where we enjoyed a simply amazing standard of living compared to our established Soviet expectations. We were well paid, and with our cash we could go shopping in stores that actually had goods to sell. There was coal for heating. Hot water on tap. Public baths that actually worked. Fresh meat, expertly butchered, which tasted wonderful. Superb!

I appreciate Pasha's charm but my immense pride for my husband rests on his scientific brilliance. His work as

---

2   Kulaks was the name given to wealthy independent farmers in the Soviet Union. Stalin ordered the kulaks 'to be liquidated as a class'. Solzhenitsyn suggested 6 million died during the famines of the 1930s whereas Soviet sources estimate deaths at 700,000.

3   Posen is the German for Poznan, the ancient city in the west of Poland.

an agriculturalist at the Posen Reichsuniversität and the advances that he, and others within his European network, made in botanical science and crop yields changed living conditions throughout the continent, despite the ravages of war.

But it was a war the Germans had lost. Modern historians tell of many acts of Nazi stupidity and hubris, and perhaps this was a waste product of their terror. But, for me, the most obvious stupidity by the first month of 1945 was their lack of acceptance that the war had been lost. With the Russians to their east and the Americans to their west, the blindingly obvious choice was to surrender to the US forces and invite them to occupy Germany and the annexed lands before the Russians got there. The Nazi failure to surrender to the USA condemned the majority of the German people to half a century of oppression under Soviet control. When the war was over, the wonderful cultural idiosyncrasies of German people – all those things that I respected most: the logic, the planning, the consistency – then combined with the oppression of the Soviet regime to create the uber-totalitarian state. The efficient terror of East Germany. But it is too easy to get ahead of myself.

Pasha was weeping. Sofia, then aged eight, held my hand and her coal eyes engaged mine; concern and confusion. As we boarded that train Pasha wept for the life we had lost in Posen, our hopes of watching Sofia grow within a safe and prosperous regime, his research (left behind at the university – never to be seen again), his European academic network (now in tatters), but most of all weeping for our future. We were no longer intelligentsia, to be respected. We were just the enemy. We were feared. We were hated.

I didn't weep. I never weep. I was just angry. The whole thing was a broken-down machine. It could have been fixed. It was like a musical box which Sofia had left behind. The ballerina in the box had twirled slowly in time with the music, but one day Sofia had dropped the box. After that, the entire clockwork movement rotated whilst the ballerina remained quite still. A single screw to anchor the clockwork movement to the wooden box could have fixed it. It would have meant a new screw hole, and so it wouldn't have been quite as perfect, but the ballerina would have started to twirl once more. The Nazi failure to admit defeat was an act of gross stupidity. The machine could have been fixed.

The journey to Berlin was hard. We had tickets with allocated seats but that system had also broken down. There was no way we could even get near our seats, let alone ask whoever was sitting in them to move, but at least we did manage to get aboard a passenger coach unlike some poor devils who were bundled into freight vans or even into open iron-ore wagons. Undertaking an overnight journey in January for those in the open trucks, especially the children, left survival in doubt. In our carriage we managed to haul Sofia into an overhead luggage rack. Initially both Pasha and I stood, it was so crammed full that Pasha was balanced on just one leg for many hours but gradually during the night of the train ride more space appeared as the human bodies around us transmogrified to enable them to fill every square centimetre of available space. We fitted between one another like a jigsaw. This might make it sound like there was a camaraderie between us and our fellow passengers, but there was none. All around us were Volkdeutsch, ethnic Germans who had been moved to Posen by the Nazis to colonise the

4

city at the expense of the native Poles. Now because of the Russian advance to the east they were being forced to move again. They hated us.

When the train finally left Posen, as the people in our carriage rocked from side to side, it afforded me occasional glimpses out of the window. It was late afternoon and the light was fading. It was an ethereal, mustard-coloured light, where darkness is yet to come but where the passing scenes were cast as mere outlines, caricatures of real images. A silent picture show. The railway followed the road for some miles and I could see the flow of horse carts and lines of people trudging west. There were all sorts of carts. Nearly all were overloaded, with possessions piled high and inadequately tied with string. Occasionally a case or bag would slip from its high perch and crash to the road to spring open and disgorge its contents, whereupon children would come to steal clothes as the owners cursed and sideswiped the urchins to get them away. Some carts pulled other carts in ungainly road-trains, often with a single horse, managed by an obviously inexperienced driver, straining at its harness. It was an outline of human misery and it ran for miles. It quite probably ran all the way to Berlin but then the mustard-yellow light faded to black and the train began to run a little faster as it left the city behind.[4]

As we approached Berlin's Schlesischer Bahnhof[5] in the early hours, the train kept coming to a halt during air raids. Obviously the carriages had no lighting – a blackout – but a

---

4   https://commons.wikimedia.org/wiki/File:Bundesarchiv_Bild_183-1983-0422-315,_Umsiedler_auf_dem_G%C3%BCterbahnhof_Berlin-Pankow.jpg

5   Now renamed the Berlin Ostbahnhof.

moving locomotive would shoot sparks high into the night sky acting as a beacon for enemy aircraft. I would rather we had kept going as, stationary and silent, the sweat of fear was palpable despite the clouds of steam from exhaling breaths. Urine ran along the floor, although in some places it had frozen.

The carriages were the old style, four wheels, a single door at each end with an open vestibule and steps down to meet the low-level platforms. When we eventually arrived at the station in Berlin there was a surge towards each of the doors to get out, but the doors had been locked at Posen on departure. People panicked and screamed in the dark as the wind was squeezed out of them by the mass of humanity heaving forward to escape. Eventually order was restored and silence returned, save for sobbing, as we waited for the train guards to unlock each carriage.

From the train we were led in groups through the deserted station, into the street and then to a nearby school taken over by the NSV.[6] All the party members were in mustard-coloured uniforms and there were Red Cross women helping. We weren't asked to show any documents, we just had to declare ourselves refugees. Pasha initially objected and started to say that he had papers to work at the university and was not a refugee. I told him to be quiet. We were hungry, thirsty and utterly exhausted. The NSV man just needed to tick the box on his clipboard to say we were refugees so that then we could be fed and I wanted nothing to distract him from that. We were each given a bowl of vegetable broth, some coffee (lukewarm

6   Set up in 1933, the NSV (Nationalsozialistische Volkswohlfahrt) (National Socialist People's Welfare) was the Nazi social welfare organisation.

and weak but welcome nevertheless) and offered cigarettes. We both smoked, but not heavily and so the cigarettes were carefully put away to afford future bartering opportunities. Then we slept in a classroom on damp mattresses until a cold sun shone through the windows.

Porridge and more weak coffee for breakfast, and then we set out. Our short walk, the previous night, from the station to the school had provided a vague impression of damage by the debris strewn in the streets, but that had been during blackout conditions. Nothing could have prepared us for the devastation we encountered when leaving the school the following day. The Allies had neutralised the Luftwaffe in February 1944[7] and since then Berlin had been bombed from the air by the United States by day and by the British by night. The entire city had been ravaged. Rubble was king, although where it had been cleared away remained vast wastelands bordered by tall crumbling edifices. They looked like an old Cossack's jaw: a few remaining blackened teeth, broken, sticking out at acute angles.[8]

Pasha had been told to report to the Berlin Technical Academy in Charlottenberg, which incorporated the city's old agricultural college. We made slow progress, many roads were closed off and we had to be directed round diversions. Pasha and I each carried a single suitcase containing what few clothes and possessions we had been able to take from Posen.

---

7   The USA launched 'The Big Week' (20–25 February 1944) as a series of missions against the German aircraft industry successfully luring the Luftwaffe into a decisive battle. The Luftwaffe were defeated allowing the Allies' air superiority for the remainder of the war.

8   https://commons.wikimedia.org/wiki/File:Berlin-_the_Capture_and_Aftermath_of_War_1945-1947_C5284.jpg

At least we still had our precious family photographs, safe in a cigar box inside my case. Sofia had a small satchel over her shoulder and walked between us grasping our gloved hands in her mittens. All three of us were stiff from our night on the damp mattresses but also stiff in apprehension of what lay ahead for us in this utterly unfamiliar and barren city.

There was a hard frost. The air was still. The sound was dead. Berliners dug through the debris in search of any remnants of property they could salvage. Brigades of police and the Volkssturm[9] worked to clear pathways. Bodies by the side of the road were covered with blankets, with sometimes an arm or a leg flopped into the open, and a blueish tinge to the flesh. Pasha tried to stop Sofia from seeing but it was impossible. There was no mains water and people hauled water in buckets away from standpipes in the street. Fires were just left to burn. The tooth-like ruins continued to smoulder. Occasionally, you would hear the crack of wood or masonry and a section of building would simply collapse. The noise of the fall should have been immense but somehow all was silent. A vast dust cloud hung in the air, quite still. The dust congealed in your throat and made you choke. It was only our own coughing and the spluttering of others that broke the stillness.

There were two air-raid alarms as we walked and each time we found air-raid shelters, but there were few people inside. Aircraft flew overhead but they were not very close. Most of

---

9   The Volkssturm or 'people's storm' was a German militia established at
     the end of WW2. It was not Army but established by the Nazi Party on
     Hitler's orders. Men between sixteen and sixty not already serving in the
     armed forces were conscripted to form a Home Guard. The Volkssturm
     was one of the final components of the Total War promoted by
     Propaganda Minister Goebbels endeavouring to overcome their enemies'
     military strength through the force of will alone.

the Berliners paid no attention to the raids and simply carried on their business of silently sifting through the debris.

Eventually we arrived at the Academy, clearly once the most glorious building with a Palladian front and colonnade galleries many storeys high, all approached by a vast sweeping driveway. Now it was smashed. Instead of being upright, the front of the building was stepped like an Egyptian pyramid. The colonnades left standing had lost their front stonework and existed just as blackened arches.[10] They reminded me of rows of skulls with eye sockets staring forwards. The damage was not recent and the building was partly boarded shut. In the grounds we found wooden huts manned by caretakers and they directed us to the botanical department's temporary accommodation in nearby Kantstraße.

Pasha had known perfectly well by the time we had left Poland that the academic system in Germany had collapsed. Nevertheless, Wittram, the Dean of the Posen Reichsuniversität, had told him to make contact with Professor Belling at the Berlin Academy and there was little else to be done other than try to follow this command. But on arrival at Kantstraße we found that Belling had moved away months before; long gone, to Stuttgart apparently. Instead we found his secretary, Frau Mantels, who attended to the administration of the botany department, or at least maintained the schedules of professors and the lists of students who might return to complete their

10 The Berlin Technical Academy – before:
    https://upload.wikimedia.org/wikipedia/commons/e/ea/8._The_
    Technische_Hochschule_in_Charlottenburg%2C_Berlin.jpg
    and after the bombing:
    https://www.tu-berlin.de/fileadmin/a70100710/Dokumentationen/
    Geschichte/3.jpg

degrees – someday after the war. Frau Mantels was a plump lady in her forties and seemed to be desperately trying to live a normal life in a completely abnormal world.

She stood and offered Pasha her hand.

'Herr Zayky… yes, yes we are expecting you. The Department of Botany welcomes you here to Berlin.' She gave a short perfunctory smile with a nod of her head and continued. 'But if you have made it here then I expect that you have also seen the Academy, and I'm afraid that given the current circumstances the Department grants you indefinite leave. We are most grateful to you for making the journey… please do keep us appraised of your address so that we can contact you when it is time to return to the Academy.'

'But where shall we live?' I interjected urgently, perhaps almost aggressively, whilst Pasha asked,

'… and Frau Mantels, would it be possible for our daughter, Sofia, to have a glass of water?'

Frau Mantels closed the office in Kantstraße at 3pm. We picked up our suitcases once more and she walked with us so we could see the way to her house in the last of the January afternoon light. She lived fairly close by at Justelstraße 77 but as with everywhere in Berlin her route home wound round bomb craters and closed roads. As we approached number 77 we could see a fallen aircraft resting inside a neighbouring house. A wing stuck out over the edge of the front first-floor wall where the roof had once been. Thankfully, Frau Mantels' house had suffered only minor damage. The windows were boarded and the front door off the street opened stiffly, pushing against the floor as the top hinge had come away from the frame during a blast.

Frau Mantels was obviously put out by the arrival of a professor and his family from the East, but had said we could stay with her for just a few nights until some alternative could be found. Pasha was gushing in his thanks. She acknowledged the situation curtly whilst Sofia and I said little. It was all rather awkward but we had few options and didn't want to spend another night in a school hall if that could be avoided. Inside, Frau Mantels showed us to her own bedroom and made up a bed for Sofia on the couch downstairs. Frau Mantels moved to sleep in her daughter's single room. We didn't ask the whereabouts of her daughter or indeed Herr Mantels and she didn't volunteer any information. The house was cold; there was a smell of damp. You could tell that everything had been cleaned only recently and yet, as throughout Berlin, a layer of dust from today had settled on the fresh polish from yesterday. It was, in truth, a miserable house but it was better than another night on the damp mattresses.

The following day we all walked back to the Department's office in Kantsraße. Frau Mantels had lent Sofia some of her daughter's picture books, and Sofia dutifully sat in the corner and read, honing her German language skills.

With it clear that Frau Mantels' charity could only last so long, it was time to face up to our biggest problem – we were Russian. To the Germans, we were the enemy, whilst to the Soviets, advancing from the East, we were traitors. When he had been a part of the Reich's university system Pasha had received some degree of protection. In Posen it had been through Wittram. Even Himmler had made it known that Pasha's work was vital to the German effort, but we didn't think for one second that Himmler's blessing would be of any use in our current circumstances. None of the other professors from Posen appeared to have followed us to Berlin, and apart from Frau Mantels there was nobody to speak up for Pasha from the Berlin Academy.

The grim reality we faced was that our continued life expectancy depended on solving the problem of our Russian nationality. If we were to stand any chance of survival post the Russian invasion – now surely inevitable – then we had to become German nationals; we needed to swap our old Soviet passports for new German ones. My German language skills were good but I still spoke with a pronounced accent. On the other hand, Pasha and Sofia spoke the language with almost no trace of accent, and certainly sufficiently well that, if they held German passports, they ought to be able to convince a Soviet army officer that they were German and not Russian.

And so, leaving Sofia safely in the care of Frau Mantels, we made our way to the Ostministerum[11] based near the Reichstag parliament.

The Ostministerum was in a large building with only a little damage. Following signs we eventually found ourselves in a huge room. It was, perhaps, as long and as wide as three railway carriages and its ornate ceiling was at least three storeys high. There were mezzanine floors running the circumference at various levels, and all around clerks, secretaries and men and women in all sorts of different coloured uniforms moved in between each other – backwards and forwards – bustling to destinations – clutching folders. It was as though we had entered a beehive.

---

11   The Ostministerum (Eastern Ministry) was the Nazi Party office that oversaw the eastern territories; it was a vast bureaucracy.

There was row upon row of clerks at desks, with typewriters, papers, stamps and ink pads. There were about a dozen queues and we tried to find the shortest one. Evidently, many of our erstwhile Russian compatriots had come to the same conclusion regarding the need to change their status. We were reassured that many seemed to be leaving smiling, with fresh German documents in their hands. But each application took an age. After a couple of hours we made it to the front of our queue. A man gazed up at us. The sign on his desk proclaimed him as Inspector Schmidt, but he didn't attempt to introduce himself as we explained, most earnestly, how we had helped the Reich to date and how German passports were now a necessity for the three of us. In return, he asked lots of questions, dates, places, references, affiliations, making careful note of each on a checklist (I was irritated as we could have filled that in whilst we had been waiting). In the end he asked us to wait and disappeared from the desk for ten minutes. When he returned we expected him to simply stamp the papers and hand them across, as he had with the other applicants before us, with a cursory 'The Third Reich welcomes you as new citizens; Heil Hitler!'

But he didn't stamp the papers nor did he provide us with his salute. Instead, he pointed to a wooden-panelled booth in the farthest corner of the room.

'Sit over there and wait.'

The booth had frosted windows letting in light from the main room. Its wooden sides were a couple of metres high but ended well below the level of the room's lofty ceiling. At least there were wooden chairs outside and we could sit down. But now we were nervous – why had we been singled out?

The busy room in front of us hummed away, telephones rang, typewriters clattered and clerks walked briskly past our chairs on errands, giving us an occasional sideways glance. Inside the booth we could hear voices but the noise of the main room made what was being said inside impossible to decipher.

Eventually the door to the booth opened; a tall, obviously Slavic man stepped out, turned and slammed the door behind him. Without a word, his face set hard, he strode off towards the exit door.

Should we just go in? Should we knock? The occupant must surely be able to see that people were waiting outside through the frosted glass. This didn't seem the time or place to be overly forward… we waited.

Eventually, after a further fifteen or twenty minutes, the door to the booth opened.

'Herr and Frau Zayky? I'm so sorry to have kept you waiting, would you like to step in? Please do both sit down. I am Kreisleiter[12] Jerter, Director of the Ostministerum here. Inspector Schmidt has asked me to review your application for German citizenship.'

He wore a dark suit, with no swastika armband, but I noted the gold NSDAP pin on his jacket, denoting him as either one of the original 100,000 Nazis, or as an outstanding party member. I knew that his pin would have been awarded by Hitler personally.

He was around fifty, I guessed, a little overweight, balding with horn-rimmed round spectacles, a smiling man with a warm, dry, firm handshake.

---

12 Kreisleiter was a formal rank within the Nazi Party hierarchy. Hitler was Führer (leader), whilst Kreisleiter was four ranks below.

There was a large leather-bound ledger on his desk; it looked quite new, not old and crumpled as most do. There was a telephone and blotting pad. The corners of his booth were stacked high with crates of papers. Behind him were shelves, slightly bowed from the weight of box files.

'And so, please tell me why you wish to become citizens of the Reich.'

Again, we explained all we had said to Schmidt at the desk. How Pasha had proved invaluable to the Reich by promoting new methods of arable planting and cropping; how I had worked in the research station in Posen and how Sofia had obtained remarkable school reports and played a full role in youth activities. We said all the right things.

During all this, Jerter nodded and murmured approval. He sat forward against his desk, leaning towards us, listening carefully, his hands clasped together, fingers intertwined.

'Very, very good indeed,' he said when we finished. We both looked pleased. 'But Herr Zayky, tell me about General Vlasov?' he continued.

'Vlasov?' Pasha queried.

'Yes, I have a report here that you were unable to join the Volkssturm as you were already a member of Vlasov's army...'

And in an instant I knew that we were in trouble.

Andrey Vlasov was the former Red Army general who defected to the Germans after the siege of Leningrad in 1942. He established the Russian Liberation Army, a force dedicated to fighting alongside the Third Reich to overthrow Stalin.

Vlasov, Himmler and the Führer signed a contract agreeing to a free Russia after the war. Several regions, including our old homeland in the Kuban, would be given the right to autonomy provided their tenability could be justified. In 1944, Vlasov remained a single beacon of positivity for Russian exiles and Pasha wrote to him committing to the cause and explaining how he might be able to help with a new free Russia. Perhaps unsurprisingly, Vlasov never replied.[13]

In Posen in 1944, the Blockleiter had been the Nazi responsible for the political supervision of a neighbourhood. He was a low-ranking official who actually wielded enormous power as he was charged with the distribution and allocation of ration coupons. Our Blockleiter was Hiltze, a short fat man in a tight-buttoned jacket, who smelled variously of tobacco, cabbage, or body odours. He always addressed us in short, sharp, loud bursts and repeatedly referred to the fact that we were Russian. In fact, Hiltze was the first person I remember to ever comment negatively on our ethnicity. I recall that we had been due 1,100kg of coal but we only ever received rations for 600kg from Hiltze. The winter of 1944 found us shivering and sneezing.

Then, one day in November 1944, Hiltze had arrived at our door with an application form for the Volkssturm, which he thrust at Pasha for completion.

'Fill this in, Zayky,' he had demanded.

Pasha sat at our table and read the form carefully and looked up at Hiltze slightly blankly.

'But I'm not a German,' Pasha had explained. 'This form is clearly for Germans. I'm a Russian, part of General Vlasov's

---

13   Himmler with Vlasov September 1944.
     https://commons.m.wikimedia.org/wiki/Category:Andrey_
     Vlasov#/media/File%3AVlassof.Himmler.jpg

organisation. I'm sorry but I can't join the Volkssturm as I'm a foreign national serving as a member of the Russian Liberation Army.'

Hiltze had gone purple with a mixture of rage, confusion, and pure dislike.

'I might have known that you'd be a turncoat, Zayky – your kind are the lowest form of life. Everything handed to you on a plate, job, flat, food, but when it comes to the fight you're suddenly not a German. You're a Russian after all. You're the enemy! Everyone else on this list ticked to join up; every other application form completed except yours. Well your name will stand out, and we shall just see where that gets you…'

Hiltze had been a most repugnant little fat man.

But now we were in the Ostministerum and Director Jerter was speaking again.

'I think I recall from the newspapers that Vlasov's headquarters was located in Prague, I'm not sure where he is now; but if you were fighting in Vlasov's army then you must be a Russian. If you had been German then you would have been in the Volkssturm, would you not…?' His voice slightly tailed off.

Blockleiter Hiltze, the nasty fat Nazi, had done for us. When Pasha had refused to join the wretched Volkssturm because he wasn't German, Hiltze must have filed a report. A report which, despite all the chaos of war, had filtered its way from Poland to the Ostministerum in Berlin and was now threatening our lives. In my head I was exploding with rage, although despite everything some small part of me had to admire the efficiency of the bureaucracy of the Third Reich.

'I am so sorry, Herr Zayky, but if you were not willing to join our people's militia because you were Russian rather than German in November then I can hardly make a case that you have become a German national now. As far as I can see, despite your excellent work in the past – for which the Fatherland thanks you – you are now a redundant Russian academic. Do you disagree?'

A truly harsh summary, but neither of us could disagree. Jerter did not seem a mean man, in fact, quite the opposite, but he was clearly an ardent Nazi and not willing to waiver in his ruling. We could, I suppose, have simply said that it was untrue, that some error had been made. But we wouldn't have been convincing liars and Jerter was no fool.

Our quest for a quiet family life, to seek the best for Sofia, to make best use of our personal skills, had seen us journey from Krasnodar to Posen but was now set to end. Berlin was in ruins, the will of its people broken by the relentless bombing. The German army was all but defeated. The advance of the Soviets was relentless and the fall of Berlin to the Russian horde was utterly inevitable. We had no papers to leave the city, we could not hide, and in fact the Berliners would be only too delighted to give us up to the Soviets as Russian nationals. We were done for.

Hiltze! Bastard. We had Sofia to think about. What would become of her? Could Frau Mantels adopt her? Was there time for that? Who was Frau Mantels anyway? It is amazing the thought processes that your mind goes through in such a situation.

Just a few sentences over a few minutes had caused my entire life to implode. Both my heart and my stomach had sunk to the floor and as I sat in the chair I looked down at my feet with resignation and utter despair. I was suddenly completely oblivious to Pasha and Jerter. I began to shake gently, but noticeably.

'Frau Zayky, I am sorry, I truly am. But I cannot allow this to pass. We do have an orphan programme, the Lebensborn,[14] for good Aryan children. Neither of you look Russian, and I am sure that your daughter could be taken in by them if future events dictate that you do need to go home.'

I simply could not speak. Home! What on earth was that?

The interview was over. Our fate was sealed. We rose to leave. Pasha, his face ashen, helped me to my feet, holding my arm to support my weight.

We moved to the door. Jerter jumped to his feet and opened the door for us, just a couple of paces in his tiny cell. We walked back out into the whirl of the main room. Its people were now swimming and the noise was as if it were road traffic in the fog. Jerter watched us leave.

'Frau Zayky, a moment please!' Jerter called out. Pasha, still holding me up, stopped us both. I had heard nothing. 'Please do come back for a moment. I have had a thought.'

We duly returned to the booth and sat down once more.

'Frau Zayky, I might have thought about this the wrong way,' Jerter started. 'I was thinking about your husband's profession as a botanist, which frankly is of little use to us now. But you are a trained engineer, are you not? You

---

14 Lebensborn (literally 'Fount of Life') was an SS-initiated association with the goal of raising the birth rate of 'Aryan' children classified as 'racially pure and healthy' based on Nazi racial hygiene and health ideology (Children Of The Master Race).

worked in Krasnodar within the factory there, I think you said. But you were not just a factory worker, you were on the engineering team, yes?'

'Yes, yes that's quite correct,' said Pasha answering for me. 'Tanya… Frau Zayky… did in fact receive honours under the Soviets for her work.'

'Well one aspect of my job here is to locate and redeploy those with skills useful to the Fatherland. As I say, Zayky, botanists are of no use now, but engineers are in short supply. Normally I would only consider men for such a role but perhaps Frau Zayky possesses the appropriate skills? With so many men fighting at the front, the Reich can no longer regard gender suitability as a paramount requirement.'

I was now taking notice, although still physically unable to speak whilst these men were conducting a discussion about me in my presence.

Jerter rose from his desk and dragged down one of the box files from the shelving, which groaned a little as the shifting of the remaining boxes caused the shelf to sag further. Still standing, he opened the file, and began thumbing through its contents.

'Where…? Where…? Yes! Here!' In a moment he was scribbling a note on some headed paper, which he thrust into Pasha's hand. 'Take this to Wilhelmstraße, the Ministry of Aviation.'

Pasha looked puzzled.

'You're looking for the Berlin head office of the Reichswerke Hermann Göring. The office is located within the ministry building, on the third floor. Take my letter of introduction. They need engineers at their steel foundry… in Salzgitter, south of Hanover. That's 250 kilometres west of Berlin. Frau Zayky will need to apply, and they will only take her if she is satisfactory. You won't get German passports but all three of you would get travel papers to Salzgitter. It's to the west... do you understand?'

A great curtain was lifted. Of course, we understood. The Reichswerke Hermann Göring was a massive German conglomerate, probably the biggest company in Europe before the war. But most important from our point of view was that although the headquarters was in Berlin, the industrial operation was located in Salzgitter in Central Germany. In the centre of the country we had more chance of being overrun by the advancing Americans and British from the west rather than by the Russians from the east. Jerter had given us a lifeline. But I still had to get the job.

It was now 5pm and we had been in the Ostministerum all day. We walked back to Justelstraße to find Frau Mantels reading to Sofia. They had clearly had a rather less demanding day than us. But I was so relieved; so happy to see Sofia; to hold her and to hug her...

'Mama let me go... I can hardly breathe!' How could I ever have considered Frau Mantels adopting my beautiful child? I was ashamed at the thought.

That evening we all had our soup supper at the local NSV station. Given there was no food to buy in the shops and no means of cooking it in any event, it meant that the NSV had the task of feeding the entire city. But having been fed we returned to the house emotionally exhausted after our day and slept badly, worrying about attending Wilhelmstraße the following morning... it was only a lifeline... not yet a life.

The following day, having all breakfasted at the NSV, Frau Mantels, or Hilde as she had now become, and Sofia went off to the office at Kantstraße, Sofia to read her borrowed German storybooks, and Hilde to reorder her lists of missing students and schedules for lectures that her professors would never deliver. We left our suitcases in the bedroom and set off towards Wilhelmstraße.

The Air Ministry was the most imposing building I had ever seen. It was designed to intimidate the onlooker and carried out this task admirably. It was the perfect building for an authoritarian state and ran for 250m, the full length of the block between Prinz-Albrecht-Straße and Leipziger Straße. It was seven storeys high, with 2,800 rooms, 7 kilometres of corridors, and 4,000 windows. It was the headquarters of Reichsmarshall Hermann Göring, the head of the Luftwaffe, and second in command of the Reich after Hitler. It was the home of many thousands of bureaucrats, but it was also the headquarters of the Reichsmarshall's eponymous Reichswerke.

Before the war, Göring had overseen the creation of a vast state-owned industrial conglomerate. Despite being publicly owned, Göring had the entire enterprise named after himself and bestowed upon it a corporate logo derived from his own coat of arms.[15] The main business was the mining and smelting of iron ores from the region around Salzgitter, ores deemed too low grade to be economical by the steel barons of the privately owned factories and foundries of the German Ruhr. But as the country prepared for war the corporation grew to take over munition production and a multitude of other enterprises.

---

15 Göring's logo remained the symbol of the Salzgitter complex, albeit slightly updated, right through until the mid-1980s.

Although Pasha had accompanied me to the Air Ministry we had discussed that he should probably not enter the building with me. I was the person seeking the job and he could have been a distraction. So Pasha left me at the entrance and went off to find what was left of the Berlin State Library in nearby Unter Den Linden – he had a twofold desire to seek comfort by surrounding himself in academia, and to keep warm.

My interview that day was a matter of life or death for us. It was with a deep intake of breath that I entered the Ministry and was directed to the third-floor offices of the Reichswerke.

I had used my smartest and cleanest clothes and Hilde had lent me a brooch and hat. But I must have still looked quite shabby for a job interview, especially one where I had no appointment. The receptionist stared at me and examined my letter of introduction from Kreisleiter Jerter. The letter was taken away; I was asked to take a seat. I waited for several hours.

Eventually I was advised that the director would see me soon, and after a further hour I was guided down a long corridor. My escort knocked twice on a door. 'Enter!' My escort looked at me, nodded curtly, turned on heel and left.

I entered.

'Frau Zayky, I am Paul Pleiger, General Director here at the Reichswerke. Thank you for waiting, I'm afraid I have been extremely busy. Now, Jerter at the Ostministerum advises that you are an engineer. What sort, please?'

Pleiger neither rose from his seat nor attempted to shake hands. He looked to be in his forties and his stomach slightly rested on the desk in front of him. He had prospered well under the Nazi regime. His pudgy face was topped with slicked-back hair – obviously dyed black. His lips were thin and unsmiling.[16] He was certainly not aiming to be welcoming. I explained that I was a trained mechanical engineer, and extracted my Russian qualifications. He gave them no more than a cursory glance.

'Well I'm sorry but I have no Russian so these are no use to me. They could say anything. And I confess to be rather amazed that a woman could be a mechanical engineer. It's an incredibly technical and mathematical job, I don't think that a female mind could possibly be up to the task.'

Pasha and I had discussed this line of questioning as a possibility.

'Perhaps, sir, rather than trying to convince you with foreign certificates, you could allow me to speak to another engineer. I appreciate their time is valuable but if I could speak to them directly then…'

'Frau Zayky, I am an engineer, say what you wish to me, but please be quick as I have other meetings very soon…'

And so I explained the Bessemer process in detail to Pleiger, who leaned back in his chair and began firing all sorts of questions at me. He was quick to explain that he was the son of a miner and had trained as an engineer just after the first war.

---

16 Paul Pleiger (1899–1985) was one of Nazi Germany's most influential state entrepreneurs. In 1949 he was sentenced to fifteen years for war crimes, but was released in 1951. In 1952 he founded a plastics company and expanded from Germany to the USA and South Korea.
   https://4.bp.blogspot.com/-cr0lmxEpPa4/
   V9ltLo_aKfl/AAAAAAAABWc/
   kNV4Zq9zKJofaEa1Rlp7Ow9GFISgr4P0wCLcB/s1600/
   Paul%2BPleiger.jpg

His success in business was, he told me, therefore underwritten by his own expertise in engineering. Swiftly, he moved on from straightforward steel production to other subjects, particularly locomotive operation including diesel engine technology.

Back in Krasnodar, my father, Ivan Moroz, had been an engine driver. Many might have expected my brother Pyotr to have followed in his footsteps but it was me who grew up on the footplate and in the railway's engine houses. I drank tea with the men in the maintenance shop before I was ten and by the early 1920s was helping, after school, in the locomotive yard as well as in the motor house on the fleet of lorries.

Now, my childhood at the railway works paid substantial dividends.

Pleiger explained their desperate need was for engineering competence in locomotive maintenance to enable them to shift steel around the works. Several of his key engineers had been drafted elsewhere in the Reich to try to keep the main lines operating through the bombing and shelling. Their absence left the works critically short of key personnel. If the railway yard stopped operating then the entire foundry ground to a halt.

He called for coffee – delicious, quite unlike the tepid brew on offer at the NSV. We spoke for nearly an hour, the pressing engagements mentioned at the start of the conversation having seemingly evaporated. His mood had changed too, and thankfully for the better.

'So, Frau Zayky, you have a job. My congratulations. I need you at Salzgitter straightaway, can you leave now?'

I explained that Pasha and Sofia would need to accompany me.

'Accommodating your daughter is not a problem, we have schools on site at the plant, as well as in the town, but we have no use for a botanist I'm afraid… a shame he is not a geologist… but I am sure some kind of role can be found in the office. Okay, so you can all leave first thing in the morning. Please go to see my secretary; she will make all the arrangements and provide travel papers. One final thing… I will put you on the top women's secretarial pay scale, and that will be subject to a six-month review. Obviously, we can't pay you an engineer's wage… you are only a woman.'

2

TANYA ZAYKY

Salzgitter, Germany,
January to April 1945

S ALZGITTER, 65 KM SOUTH-EAST OF HANOVER, IS
the steel town built by the Nazis. Conceived as a National
Socialist utopian dream, the reality was a bloody prison. By
the time we arrived in late January 1945, Salzgitter was a
mammoth state-run industrial complex, engaged in mining,
steel and small arms manufacture. Originally established
round a salt mine in the fourteenth century, it took 500
years for the population to reach 20,000, and then, from
1938, only seven years more to grow to 100,000. And this
number now included the three of us.

The mining of salt had very recently given way to
the extraction of low-grade iron ore. The Ruhr industrial
complex on Germany's western fringe had long imported
high-quality ore from the Lorraine. But the National
Socialist regime of the late 1930s demanded autarky,[17]and
in 1937, despite bitter opposition from Ruhr industrialists,

---

17   Autarky: economic independence – self-sufficiency

Göring ordered the compulsory purchase of the Salzgitter mineral rights: 'German soil will be drained of iron to the utmost,' he barked.[18] In 1938 the capital of the Reichswerke Hermann Göring was raised to 400 million Reichsmarks, equivalent to about $160 million.[19] From the start, the managing director was Paul Pleiger.

Such rapid expansion had resulted in such a chronic housing shortage that most workers were housed in a series of camps sited on the outskirts of the main works area. Some special camps were within the factory area itself – the *konzentrationslager* or concentration camps. It was made clear that these camps were simply designed to house workers of specific ethnicity, who were conveniently available for work within the factory complex. That's what we, as well as ordinary Germans, were told. And, in January 1945 at least, that's what I believed.

On arrival at the station we were processed and allocated vouchers to obtain bedding and cutlery. Ration books and food tokens, to be exchanged in the company food halls, were provided, but it was explained that you had to work to 'earn' further tokens. Despite Paul Pleiger setting my pay grade at my interview in Berlin it seemed that money was actually immaterial in Salzgitter. The town's economy worked on a voucher system with, as we later discovered, an advanced barter economy running in parallel alongside. With huge irony, given the Nazi

18   Hermann Göring: 16th June 1937

19   To put this sum in context, the *Chicago Tribune* of 10th June 1938 reported that Britain had ordered 400 US planes for $35m. Thus $160m might be said to have bought 1,800 planes, equivalent to the entire strength of the RAF in 1938, according to the *Tribune* article.

persecution of Communists, it was a very well-developed and efficiently run Soviet system.

All in all, about half the population in Salzgitter were non-German: Poles, Dutch, French and a large contingent of Russians. The various nationalities were segregated, as were men and women of course. Sofia and I were sent to our dormitory and Pasha to his. It was the first time we had ever been apart since we had been married. I couldn't really fathom how I felt as I watched him board the truck to the Russian male camp. The tailgate was slammed shut behind him and he turned to stare back at us. As he made his tight-lipped smile of farewell, I could see his chin quiver. It was only later on that I recognised my own emotion as fear.

Our barracks were fine, fairly new, and spotlessly clean. The huts were built in a U-shape around a small green, and there was a latrine hut with a wash house. Made of cedar with shuttered windows under a pitched roof, each hut slept twenty – ten beds down each side with a log-burning stove at either end. Sofia and I were allocated adjacent beds near the middle of the room, a locker and a small table. We put out our photos on the table. It wasn't home, but at least our photos helped us ignore our new reality.

The school secretary came to collect Sofia to get her enrolled. The Reichswerke operated many different schools in various languages for the children of the foreign nationals but I was relieved to have been able to get Sofia accepted into a German-speaking school. That had been thanks to Paul Pleiger's secretary who, when providing our travel vouchers after my interview, had asked about schools and had got Pleiger to sign off *'Deutsche schule'* rather than *'Russische schule'*. The latter would have been a retrograde step.

Outside our camp, it was only a short walk to the forest and there were rotas for gathering firewood, as well as for cleaning. It was civilised and organised, but also stark and soulless, and patrolled by guards. In reality we had become prisoners. I told myself that we had come here to escape the oncoming Soviets. It was a sensible move – the only move. The war would end soon. I prayed to God it would.

Work began immediately. The railway yard had been advised of my arrival and I was to report to the yard director, Dettmer, within the hour. The forest was in one direction, and the railway yard was just a twenty-minute walk in the other. I unpacked our suitcases into the locker and went off, following directions to the yard to meet Dettmer who had obviously received a full report on me from Paul Pleiger.

'Frau Zayky, I gather you are our new locomotive expert. We are most indebted to you for coming here. You, a Russian woman, to tell us what to do. I have many locomotive experts – they will look up to you, I'm sure…'

I ignored the cynicism, took my leave of Dettmer and went straight to the engineering workshop to roll up my sleeves. The Reichswerke's railway tracks and signalling were all perfectly standard, but in the locomotive department they had used extra capital to buy in the latest technology. They had a fleet of *kleinlok* diesel shunters.[20]

Shifting steel requires lots of shunting; moving one wagon under the crane for loading, and then pushing the loaded car along so the next one is properly positioned to take on its cargo. At the birth of the railway age in the

---

20   The WR360 C14 diesel shunters were built in the late 1930s for
     use by the German army and in industrial complexes.

mid-nineteenth century, locomotion was undertaken by steam engines (in German, *dampflokomotivs*), but shunting was always a problem. Steam engines are extremely heavy, requiring enormous energy to get them underway. On the main line, with stations set some distance apart, steam locomotives build up speed and momentum, but to use a *dampflok* for shunting was slow, laborious and expensive in fuel. Many railway yards used teams of horses to haul freight cars short distances; but horses simply didn't have the power to move wagons loaded with steel.

Rudolf Diesel had patented his combustion engine at the end of the nineteenth century and some countries, notably the USA, began using diesel propulsion on their railways in the early 1920s. Diesel engines respond instantly to start/stop work, require a single operator (rather than both a driver and fireman), and are much more economical on fuel. They are the obvious alternative to shunting by steam. Furthermore, during a war, with the constant threat of attack from the air, diesels don't shoot sparks into the sky to give away their position.

However in Salzgitter in January 1945, the steel foundry was at a standstill. Why? Because all the new diesel locomotives in the railway yard, all the very latest technology, had broken down. The lack of motive power was disastrous, and meant there was no way to shift the completed steel sheets, wire and rods. Production had just backed up and ground to a halt.

On a cursory inspection, I could see that the problem was straightforward: all the diesels were suffering from a lack of routine maintenance. They had simply coked up and died. As Director Dettmer had pointed out, Salzgitter had plenty of locomotive engineers but they were all well over sixty years old. The younger engineers at the yard, all specially trained to work on the diesels, had been taken by the army to maintain locomotives closer to the front line. The older men, who had been left behind, had years of experience in maintaining the old *dampfloks*, but had no idea how to look after diesels.

Years earlier, when I had been working in the railway yard at Krasnodar as a young girl under the watchful eye of my father, diesel locomotives were certainly not the norm. Soviet Russia was always slow to pick up new technology. But there had been one: the Lenin Memorial Diesel Locomotive. It had been built in Petrograd[21] and completed in 1924, the year that Lenin had died, hence the rather bizarre name given to both the locomotive and indeed to the city where it was built. It was an ugly beast lacking the grace of the era's steam-powered leviathans, but it worked trains on our line and was often to be seen in the yard at Krasnodar.[22]

One of the reasons it was so often seen around our yard was because of its dreadful unreliability. Almost every journey it made resulted in a stopover in the Krasnodar workshop for some problem or another. I was fascinated by the new engine – so unlike anything else on the system, and its regular sojourns in our yard meant that I was able to

---

21 St Petersburg on the Baltic coast was renamed Petrograd in 1914, then renamed Leningrad in 1924, and finally returned to its original name in 1991.

22 The shch-el-1 (Щэл 1) was Russia's first diesel locomotive. It was completed in 1924 and named 'The Lenin Memorial Diesel Locomotive'.
https://en.wikipedia.org/wiki/Russian_locomotive_class_shch-el-1#/media/File:DieselLoco_first.jpg

clamber all over it and quiz the maintenance team on the latest breakdown.

As it turned out, the locomotive's beating heart, the diesel engine itself, was also its Achilles heel. But it wasn't Russian designers who were to blame. The engine in the Lenin Memorial Diesel Locomotive had been made in the north-west of England by a firm called Vickers of Barrow-in-Furness. Originally it had been fitted in a British submarine which had then sunk in the Baltic in 1919. The Soviets had subsequently salvaged the craft, towed it to Petrograd and stripped out the engine for use by the Putilov Railway plant. The theory of diesel traction was excellent, the quality of manufacture was superb, but the design of the Vickers machine was atrocious. No wonder it was always at Krasnodar in pieces. But I understood exactly how it worked.

The *kleinlok* diesels were all lined up neatly in the yard's sidings, pushed into place by a single operational steam shunter. In the workshop's stores sat boxes of spare parts, neatly catalogued, and ready for fitting.

I arrived on a Monday. I got the first *kleinlok* shunter operational by Wednesday that week, and another two were on the move by Saturday. Dettmer said nothing but I allowed myself just a little pride. The other engineers at the yard were also sullen but gradually, as I began to prove my worth, they started to come around.

'Frau Zayky, the compression is still too low what should I do?'

'Frau Zayky, can you help with the cylinder liners?'

'Frau Zayky, do you know how I remove these glow plugs?'

And a turning point was when Paul Pleiger stopped by to see Dettmer the following week and came into the workshops to speak to me.

'Frau Zayky, my thanks for getting our works moving once more, I am glad my intuition in selecting you has proved sound.'

I couldn't help but smile.

Sundays were the best days – no work – and the only day when the three of us could get together to be a family once more. Pasha would walk round to our camp and we would go for walks in the forest, or go to the work's cinema and later all eat together in the camp's food hall. It was so sad when he had to leave us at 5pm to make his way back to his own barracks.

He was billeted in Camp 1, a Russian 'house', but his roommates were actually hard-drinking and heavy-gambling Kazakh Tartars. They were always trying to get Pasha to join their game, mainly because they realised that he had possessions to lose. One Ukrainian who entered the barracks had gambled away his boots and ended up wearing pieces of wood tied to his feet. We had been worried that Pasha would be drafted to work within the steel foundry itself, but his education allowed him to be selected for office work and he was placed within the *personalabteilung*.[23] This was a huge relief, although he found the work tedious, dealing with lists of workers arriving and leaving the complex, rostering them for their work duties and recording the fate of the huge number of workers who suffered industrial accidents.

Pasha said that the many thousands of workers who were given the most dangerous tasks of pouring the molten

---

23 *Personalabteilung*: Personnel office.

steel and working with live ammunition were drawn from the three special camps: the *konzentrationslager* situated at Watenstedt, Salzgitter-Bad and Drütte. The latter camp was sited within the works itself with its accommodation built under the arches of a road viaduct. At Drütte it was the young Jewish female workers who made the boxes of stick grenades which were in such high demand by the German troops at the front; apparently only their hands were nimble enough to carefully assemble the fuses packed inside the TNT explosive. It was obviously dangerous work. There were about 6,500 labourers spread between the three special camps but the number of industrial accidents leading to the death or serious injury of workers was very high. Those billeted at Drütte seemed to be the most at risk.

Pasha asked about my knowledge of accidents during my time at the food factory in Krasnodar. Of course, we had had our fair share of casualties, but the scale of death and serious injury reported through the Salzgitter *personalabteilung* seemed extraordinary. That said, the workers were dealing with molten metals and ammunition and we were in the midst of a war. In any event, it was the Waffen-SS who managed the rosters of the workers at those three camps and Pasha merely had to file the lists of workers, their deaths, and their replacements, replacements which were normally drawn from another camp further north at Neuengamme[24] near Hamburg.

---

24 The Neuengamme concentration camp south of Hamburg was established by the SS in 1938. An estimated 106,000 prisoners were held there and the verified death toll is 42,900. Watenstedt/ Leinde, Salzgitter-Bad, and Drütte were all Satellite camps of Neuengamme housing slave-labour workers for the Reichswerke Hermann Göring.

There was also Camp 21, the discipline camp run by the Gestapo. If you were late for work, if you claimed to be sick but the medical centre disagreed, or if you disobeyed a command, then you faced a stint in Camp 21. There were normally 1,800 inmates at any one time who rose at 3am and made ready for inspection within two minutes. They would stand outside for two hours, whatever the temperature, and then go to work at 5am. Beatings were regular, especially of the fittest inmates, and most nights each barracks would have two or more roll calls so everyone was sleep-deprived. Food was a thick turnip gruel although at least there was a full bowl each day; but before final discharge you had to spend two days in the bunker without food, light, or company. Camp 21 seemed a terrifying deterrent. Pasha's Tartar roommates were regular attendees following their late-night drinking binges, but needless to say, we were never late for work, never sick, and never spoke out of turn.

Air-raid sirens now sounded throughout the days and the nights although most of the enemy aircraft flew straight overhead in large formations en route to Berlin. There was little or no damage to the steelworks or the camps. The enemy planes were too high for the works' anti-aircraft guns, but that didn't stop the defenders on the ground from firing at the droning dots in the sky. I wasn't sure if the guns were fired to try to show the plane crews that our resolve was still strong, or just out of mere frustration, but I was quite certain that it was both pointless and deafening. The sirens and the firing just went on and on every day and all through the nights. One Sunday, whilst walking in the forest, with Sofia playing round a fallen tree looking for insects and out of earshot, Pasha confided in me.

'I don't think I can take more of this constant shooting at the planes. I shake every time I hear one of the guns go off. The sirens, the droning, the shooting, my pointless job... this bloody place. It is literally driving me mad. We have to leave, I can't take much more of it.'

'Pasha!' I exclaimed. 'This is stupid talk. The war is all but done. Keep your nerve! If your resolve fails now or, even worse, if you to attempt to get away, then we would be ripped apart. You would be sent to a KZ camp – perhaps us too. Pull yourself together, Pasha, or else I should be ashamed of you. You would be ashamed of yourself.' He said not another word as we walked that day. He kept his head bowed. Sofia danced around us, singing and swinging on our hands, but Pasha could only summon a weak smile. I kept shooting him glances but his eyes remained fixed on the forest floor that day.

As I think back to my harsh response to my delicate husband's plea, it is I who am ashamed. But Salzgitter was an unsympathetic town, a Nazi utopia which brought out the worst traits in all of us.

At the beginning of March they announced a new signal: a siren which sounded for a full five minutes to indicate the danger of troops landing from the air. My reaction to Pasha's plea for help had been wrong, but my prediction was right – the end was coming. What would it bring?

By the middle of that month food was short. There was no meat and the works' food halls served only small bowls of macaroni soup or fried potatoes with cabbage. Everyone was hungry; Pasha, in particular, looked thin and wizened. He was only thirty-eight but looked twenty years older.

I probably looked just as lined and tired although he never commented when he saw me on Sundays. My work in the railway yard began to pay off and I was given a few extra privileges including a pass to allow me to attend the factory *banya*: a large building with round sinks in the middle and thirteen shower cabins with changing rooms. I had not been able to wash properly since leaving Posen in 1944 and now, on a weekly basis, I could luxuriate in the hot steaming showers. I could see for the first time how thin I had become. My breasts, never large, had now all but disappeared and the skin on my stomach lay in folds.

We made sure that Sofia obtained extra rations by exchanging whatever goods and rations we had with others. For example, twelve cigarettes would get you a kilo of bread. But you had to be careful; cheating and theft was commonplace and hoarding food could lead to a spell in Camp 21. More than that, much of the food stowed away by others was made of sawdust or earth, or bulked out with leaves from the forest. I was just glad we were not big drinkers as the Tartars in Pasha's camp drank some terrible homemade hooch from time to time.

Whilst I had gained the respect of my male work colleagues at the railway yard I began to lose friendships in our hut. Initially most of the other women and mothers had been perfectly civil to Sofia and me but as the weeks rolled jealousies emerged, most noticeably after I secured the privilege of visiting the *banya* and no longer had to use the camp wash house with them. In any gaggle of women it is quite usual to get one domineering loudmouth, and ours was Mrs Shukova, a foul-mouthed hag, who sneered at the other women in the dormitory but always had time for any camp guard who could supply extra cigarettes in return for a quick feel, or more. She had a little gang consisting of her, Mrs Averina and Mrs Gavrikova. They bullied younger women to fulfil their rota duties, and would often enter the dormitory giggling, with their extra rations, whilst adjusting their smocks. I regarded them all as whores and slovens and although Pasha would, so often, implore me to keep my opinions to myself, I could not help but let it be known what I thought of them.

By now, if Vlasov's name was mentioned at all then it was always with negative connotations, either by Germans who mistrusted all Russians, or by Russians themselves who now regarded Vlasov as a failure at best or a traitor at worst.

Now the coven, Shukova, Averina and Gavrikova, began to tell horror stories in front of Sofia and the other children as to what might unfold. How they, in fact, as good Russians and good Communists, had always supported the Soviets. That traitors to the Russian people should be dealt with harshly, especially collaborators. The gulag was too good for such enemies of the Soviet people, they said. They would start by shooting Vlasov and then move on to all other traitors to the Revolution – it always seemed as though they were looking directly at me when they said this – and smiling too. The other Russian women in the room seemed to agree, or at least they didn't raise a voice to disagree. They were all preparing their scripts for what they would say if the Soviets got to Salzgitter first… what they would say to the Soviets about us. The bitches!

On the last Saturday of March they took away two young girls from the camp next to us who had planned to escape. That Sunday, when we met with Pasha, he said that his camp had been subject to a thorough search. Apparently, a rifle had been found in one camp and the Gestapo were cracking down. An Italian had been found with a roasted rabbit; he said it was a cat, but he was taken away along with his roasted cat. A cobbler had stowed away some large pieces of leather and was taken off. They even confiscated somebody's geography map. Everyone was nervous, the workers, the guards, the Gestapo. Mrs Shukova predicted a collapse within two weeks. She was nearly right.

Easter Day was Sunday 1st April and we all went to church. The kitchen had taken the trouble to 'blow' all the eggs rather than simply crack them so that the shells could be given to the children to decorate with wax crayons. Everything was so pretty, Sofia was delighted, and that afternoon the school organised party games. Easter that year was a happy day at a very unhappy and uncertain time; the Soviets were just 300 kilometres east of us.

On Monday 2nd April I went to work at the railway yard as usual, but it was an unusual day in terms of transport and needs. Normally I worked in the workshops to ensure that our shunters were all fully operational, but on that Monday, Dettmer said I was needed to help in the signal box at the marshalling yard[25] rather than in the workshops. All the troops in Salzgitter, the police, Gestapo and SS, were being moved to the front line to become the last defenders of the Reich and so, that day, it was workers and manpower which needed to be moved rather than raw steel and weapons. For us railway workers, the logistical problem was to summon sufficient rolling stock and

---

25 A marshalling yard is found at some freight terminals and used to separate railway cars on to one of several tracks. Coaches and wagons are stored in sidings and shunted into the yard to be joined together to make up the train required.

obtain the necessary locomotive power to get the troop trains underway. Obtaining sufficient passenger coaches was not really a problem as all normal passenger traffic had ended some weeks before; it was the main line locomotives that were in short supply. Our diesel *kleinloks* had the power to shunt the coaches but could not attain the speed required for use on the main line. The various locomotive manufacturers of the Reich were building engines as fast as they could but Allied bombing was taking a heavy toll. By this stage in the war there was simply not enough motive power available.

The marshalling yard at Salzgitter was down the line from the main station and consisted of about six parallel tracks, each around 350 metres long, and all linked at both ends by points (or switches as the Germans called them). At the head of the yard stood the signal box, two substantial concrete towers either side of the lines, bridged by steel beams, supporting a wooden cabin structure straddling the tracks. It was a huge box, completely modern, much larger than Krasnodar's with seven large windows looking down the length of the yard. The train assemblers could signal the shunters from the windows indicating the cars to move, whilst the signalmen would be busy with the mechanical frames switching the points as required. That day the box was alive with activity and I was helping to direct the *kleinloks* shunting the passenger coaches.

There were already three trains in the yard; one was empty and ready to go to the cranes at the works for loading, another was already loaded with steel, and a further one comprised closed vans full of boxes of the grenades assembled at Drütte. All were without a locomotive. By late morning, alongside the freight stock, we had assembled a fourteen-car passenger train, the longest we could manage within the constraints of the yard. The SS had immediately packed it with troops. But whilst the coaches and their passengers were all ready for the off, there was no engine available to take it away. This was a source of considerable frustration and the SS divisional commander at Salzgitter had come up to the signal box to demand that two or more *kleinloks* be paired up to pull the train. I pointed out that even though they had the strength to pull the train their extremely slow top speed would hold up all the main line traffic. Furthermore, the small fuel tanks of our *kleinloks* meant they had a limited range and given that diesels were such a rarity on the German railway system, there were limited refuelling opportunities. To take the train away with a diesel ran the probability of leaving troops stranded in the middle of nowhere with a dead train blocking the line.

Either because I was a woman, or because I was Russian (or both), but the commander didn't appreciate receiving this information from me. He turned his purple-tinged face towards the signal controller, who simply shrugged, pointed at me and nodded. 'Pah!' A frustrated explosion of sound, and the SS man stomped out of the box in disgust, slamming the door behind him. There were raised eyes and titters from the railwaymen left inside the box.

But then, in fact, a train arrived from nearby Brunswick, hauled by a large engine. It was a train of cattle vans, although as I peered through the windows of the box, I could see that the vans were full of people rather than livestock.

Immediately the SS commander ran back up the steps to the box. He made it plain to the signal controller that the locomotive was to be detached and used, instead, to move out the troop train. The engine and stock movements took place with all haste, and I arranged for one of the *kleinloks* to come and shunt the cattle wagons and their human cargo onto a spare line, running between the middle of a train of steel rods on one side and the closed vans loaded with the grenades on the other. The engine was taken off to the locomotive yard for refuelling and watering, to make ready for its next journey.

Then I was amazed. A truck drew up outside the yard and out jumped several SS staff in uniform as well as several other men in suits. As I looked down from the box I recognised Pasha among them! As I carried on watching, an entire convoy of trucks began to pull up in the street outside, each one crammed full of people dressed in striped grey-blue work clothes. The newly arrived SS officers, the men in suits and Pasha all came up to the signal box. Pasha and I exchanged glances and by silent communication agreed not to make it obvious that we knew one another, let alone that we were husband and wife.

I listened as the newly arrived SS officers spoke to the signal controller. Apparently, the cattle train from Brunswick had been loaded with a thousand inmates from a KZ camp in Büssing. Those in the lorries numbered a further 3,000, about half of the KZ workers from the camps at Watenstedt, Salzgitter-Bad, and Drütte, and were also due to be loaded onto the train. Obviously today's locomotive had been requisitioned but once a fresh engine could be made available, then the whole train would be taken on to the town of Bergen to the north-east of Hanover, to a camp called Belsen.

Pasha managed to shuffle alongside me.

'Why are you here?' I hissed.

'Not my idea!' he responded, 'I'm supposed to be helping with the roll call for these poor devils. I couldn't understand why the SS had decided to move them all, but now, having seen them, I realise that they wouldn't have wanted them to be discovered when it ends. Just look at them…'

I looked on from the signal box as lorry after lorry was unloaded. I thought that we had grown thin… but these poor people were clearly starving, their shaven heads were bowed, their sunken eyes were black. They were led by the guards in separate lines slowly across the tracks towards the cattle train, dragging their feet, tripping on the rails as the SS guards pushed them on with rifle butts.

We had all heard stories of the concentration camp inmates, the Konzentrationslager Leute, or, more simply, KZ-Leute; the Jews, along with gypsies and the Poles. We had thought that they were simply internment camps, perfectly civilised work camps, not dissimilar to the camps that Pasha, Sofia and I lived in, albeit with tighter security given the inmates were deemed as antisocial elements within the Nazi regime. But now it was plain to see that these people had been put to work at the Reichswerke as slaves. Now the penny dropped that the 'industrial accidents' recorded by Pasha at the *personalabteilung* were only in part because the KZ-Leute had been assigned the most dangerous tasks. It was Nazi mistreatment that had caused the death toll to rise so high. This was the regime we had aligned ourselves to. The regime we had welcomed to Krasnodar. The regime with which we had collaborated. They were swines. What were we?

'I had better go down there – I have to check their numbers off the roster,' said Pasha, leaving me and walking down the wooden steps of the signal box to the track below.

After an hour they were, very nearly, all loaded into the cattle wagons, which were now seriously overcrowded. We could hear the groans and cries from the signal box despite the SS banging on the wooden sides of the vans telling them to be quiet. The final groups stood around, exhausted, ready to be pushed onto the train. The Jews had all worn a cloth Star of David on their striped suits, but these others had different coloured triangles, reds and pinks.

'Political prisoners and sodomites,' said the signal controller.

The troop train had also, by now, been prepared. The locomotive had reappeared fully fuelled and watered and was finally backed up and coupled to the front of the passenger coaches, packed full with soldiers, police and gestapo, along with all their rifles and pistols. It set off.

And then, at about midday, the air-raid siren went off. Nothing unusual in that, but pretty soon the anti-aircraft guns fired up and the whole deafening cacophony started. At least it drowned out the cries from the cattle train – God forgive me. Despite the sirens and the anti-aircraft fire everybody carried on with their work. I could see Pasha down by the train with his book and pencil ticking off the numbers as the SS guards called them out and then pushing the final poor souls into the already crammed wagons.

But then a plane flew overhead; we all craned our necks to look upward through the windows of the signal box. An American bomber, much lower than usual, and then another. The anti-aircraft firing was blasting all round the sky. Then in the distance a third plane. It flew past us but this time the noise of the engines and the firing was joined by another sound – a whistle, which grew to a wail, and then finally to a scream.

'Bomb! Take cover!' We threw ourselves to the floor as a huge explosion erupted outside – all the windows of the box were covered in blast tape arranged in diamond patterns, but they shattered anyway.

'Pasha!' I jumped up, but the signal controller was next to me. A large man, he also jumped up but only to grab me around the shoulders and wrestle me back to the floor.

'Get off me, you bastard!' I yelled, but he held on to me with all his might, and I was pinned down to the floor just as the second, most almighty, blast went off. This time the entire signal box seemed to rock and part of the ceiling nearest the windows collapsed.

The second blast wasn't a bomb. It was obvious what had happened. The first bomb had caused the ammunition, those grenades loaded on the train in the siding, to go off. Now the signal controller relaxed his grip on me and I was up and off. Running for the door and clambering down the remains of the staircase.

'Pasha!' I screamed, although it didn't seem to make much of a sound. The sirens and the guns had all stopped; the bombers were gone, but my ears were ringing from the blasts; I was deaf. And then Pasha was with me, filthy and bleeding from his cheek, but hugging me, and kissing me. He was shouting words that neither of us could hear. Later I learned that as the first of the planes approached his roll call had ended, and he had run for cover to a ditch behind the signal box. He grazed his cheek against a rock as he had fallen but was otherwise unharmed.

But that was not true of most others in the railway yard. It was a scene of hell, a scene worse than anything we had seen in Berlin, far worse than we could have ever begun to imagine.

The train of ammunition vans had been in the siding next to the cattle train. The former had more or less completely disappeared, with just a few wheels and mangled metal frames remaining. The cattle vans, on the other hand, had been blown off the track and hurled, like a toy train, at least 50 metres. Some of the wagons were on their roofs, others on their sides, some had clearly somersaulted and ended upright but with their wooden bodies crumpled down onto their wheels as though a giant had sat on them. Pieces of rag and dust were raining down, all around. But it was the blood that I cannot forget. Effectively, those cattle vans had been full of blood. Now everything was dripping red and as my eyes adjusted through the smoke and the debris continuing to fall from the sky, scattered throughout the blood-soaked yard were body parts, everywhere. The SS guards who had been in the yard were gone, caught in the blast – surely everybody in the cattle train must be dead.

But then I began to see movement from the cattle trucks. The bodies had been so tightly packed inside that those close to the edges of the wagons had shielded those in the centre. And now those in the middle were breaking through the corpses, gasping for air and pulling themselves free. A superhuman effort from KZ-Leute who had been half-dead to start with. First one, then two, then ten, then fifty. More and more were escaping alive from the carnage.

First, they stood and stared at the scene around them, just like us. But then they ran. Down the railway tracks heading out of Salzgitter, towards the forest. Hundreds of them.

And then I saw the troop train, slowly backing along the line. The locomotive, now at the back, gingerly pushing the coaches rather than pulling them. The troops all hanging out of the windows. It had set off only fifteen minutes before the raid, but as we later learned, another bomb had hit the track ahead of it, and so returning to the yard was the only option.

The troops were all whistling loudly, annoyed that they had been kept in the coaches for hours while the train was assembled, only to set off and then have to return almost immediately. As the train came into sight so the troops could see the damage inflicted on the yard, the smashed cattle train, the ruined signal box, the debris. The whistles stopped. But then from the windows of their train they saw the KZ-Leute in their blue-grey striped suits. The runaways had been heading along the railway line, aiming for the forest, but now with the troop train coming back towards them they scattered in all directions.

There was a first shot from the troop train, then another. One of the KZ-Leute fell and others dived for cover. The troop train was still moving but the carriage doors swung open and soldiers began to jump down, each one taking aim with his rifle or drawing his pistol. Firing started from both sides of the train towards the men in the grey-blue striped tunics and trousers. Every so often one, or maybe a few, of the KZ-Leute would break cover and make a dash for a tree, or a ditch, and there would be a volley of firing. If a runaway was hit, then a great cheer rose up from the shooters gathered round the train.

'*Das ist ein hasenjagd!*' said the signal controller, who had by now climbed down from the smashed box and stood next to Pasha and me.

Ein hasenjagd: a hare hunt. Sport. For those troops cooped up in their train and ready to go to war on the front line, sport was just the thing to relieve their tension. Shooting down the escaping KZ-Leute. *Ein hasenjagd.*[26]

---

26 The massacre as described in the Salzgitter yard actually took place at the nearby town of Celle between 8 and 10 April 1945 when two to three hundred escaped KZ-Leute were killed in what became known as the 'hasenjagd'. In 1948 a British court convicted seven men. Three were sentenced to death and four had long prison terms imposed. The death sentences were subsequently quashed on appeal or converted to prison terms. All those convicted had been released by 1952.

3

PASHA ZAYKY

Krasnodar, Caucasus,
Southern Russia, 1937

Sometimes your mind wanders, without warning, to consider completely random matters. My lecture on agronomy had ended; I was reordering the hand-coloured drawings of plants and seeds which had been pored over by my students when images of our own precious family photographs entered my mind. Happy thoughts caused me to stop and smile.

Tanya and I are thoroughly modern people, unburdened by sentimentality or tradition, but nevertheless our family photographs are as essential to our home as the roof, the door and the bed. Some were in frames, and some with crumpled, yellowed edges were just propped against others. Our respective parents, gone, but remembered in various poses. Pictures of Sofia – of course! Formal studio portraits of her alone accompanied by snaps of us holding her; me looking wary but happy, and Tanya, with furrowed brow and dark eyes caught in the moment illuminating her concern, wonder and love for her baby child.

All placed carefully on the shelf above the stove in our flat.

One of the yellowed, unframed snaps was of two children fishing in a shallow stretch of the Kuban river. A skinny boy in shorts, no shoes, grinning as he turned to the camera, his line dangling in the water, his face caught in dazzling sun was slightly overexposed. Next to him a girl, slightly taller, in a summer dress, bony with frowning dark eyes carefully adjusting the wire on her rod. Tanya with her younger brother Pyotr in summer 1925. A moment in their early lives which both of them had described to me so often and in such animated tones that I often considered I might almost have been there too.

'Pasha, good afternoon to you, I do hope I am not disturbing?' It was the voice of the assistant director. The replay of our photographs in my mind's eye was terminated instantly. I had not seen him enter the lecture theatre from the doorway behind my desk. My shoulders stiffened, and my gaze fixed downwards. I focused hard on reordering my botanical drawings. He strode round to the front of the desk, placing his palm over the leading edge. A stance specifically intended to show his strength and command of the situation.

A tall man, handsome to some, with a square-cut jaw, in fact everything was square-cut from his hair to his suit. At one time he had been a leading Komsomol[27] member drafted in, by the party, as an undergraduate at the Institute – guaranteed a top-flight degree on the understanding that he would watch and report. Unlike so many of the

----

27 The Soviet youth wing and a natural entry into becoming a full Communist Party member later on.

party favourites pushed into a university irrespective of their academic abilities, he had excelled and remained in the education system. His speciality, however, was in the bureaucracy and organisation of university life rather than teaching, and his brief to watch and report remained intact. One day, as he rose through the party, he would leave the university and move into government, but for the moment the square-cut assistant director was in my lecture theatre, the eye of the Soviets was on me, and every move required careful consideration.

'Do you know, Pasha, I just watched your students disappearing; always so excited, your students, they leave your lectures speaking to each other so energetically – so enthused.' He paused, lightly drumming his fingers on my tabletop.

'Isn't it wonderful to think of their bright futures as we build our Soviet society? It isn't easy for us though, is it, Pasha? You and I strive so that our students can reap the rewards of the wonderful seeds we have sown.' Then, looking rather pleased with himself, he continued.

'Rather good to speak of sowing the seeds of our Communist society to a botanist like you, Pasha, is it not?' I chose to remain silent, tidying my lecture props – I knew what was coming.

'Not so much animation following a lecture from Pavel Romanovich Mishchenko, though, do you think? I often wonder if our students are the real barometer of our society. We can learn so much from just watching them; considering their reactions. After all, they were born into our society post the Revolution. For them, Communism comes from the cradle.'

Now a longer pause, demanding a response. Still looking at the table I nodded. A curt, single, jerky nod, but clearly signalling agreement. From the corner of my eye I noted that he pouted, not in a coquettish way, but rather to imply triumphalism. He furrowed his eyebrows and returned my nod, almost as an officer's return of the salute of a loyal subordinate.

'Yes, I do wonder about Comrade Mishchenko, of course he was very close to Nikolay Antonovich Lensky who, as we know, was attempting to destabilise our state and the work we are doing. Thank goodness his plotting was uncovered by the excellent detective work of the state security services. I do just wonder if Mishchenko might harbour similar thoughts, and perhaps subliminally that's what his students are picking up on. Barometers, able to detect high or low pressure in the air.' The assistant director paused again, this time, just for dramatic effect.

'Pasha, do you think our students, our young, devoted Soviet citizens, can distinguish between high and low pressure in the demeanour of their teachers?'

Once again I nodded, curtly and stiffly, and the assistant director, pouting once again, returned my nod, this time more purposefully, and with a slight twist of his torso to signify a knowing assent.

'Yes, I think so too. Good barometers. Pasha, I so value your advice; such wise counsel from a devoted citizen and teacher.'

The conversation was at an end, the assistant director turned and left. I had said nothing.

The late 1930s was a time of purges. Initially, Stalin used his secret police to rid the Communist Party of anyone who might represent future opposition to his leadership but then went a step further to demand the removal of all anti-Soviet elements in society. In true Soviet fashion the police were set arrest quotas for each district. Whenever a quota was met the next target was higher and thousands were sent to labour camps or executed.

Anybody of prominence, clergy, former members of the White Army or intelligentsia, were suspect and were wise to keep a bag of spare clothes packed and ready for a sudden departure from home. Everybody slept fitfully, listening out in the small hours for a squeal of tyres, a bang on the door, shouting, then silence. Later on, during the war, I realised that living through the purges had been like experiencing life in the air-raid shelters. A shelter protected you from a blast but not a direct hit. As you sat in the damp hole you would hear the wail of a falling bomb, listen to it getting closer and closer, freeze in terror, then hear an explosion – which would shake you and cause dust to fall from the ceiling – and thank God that someone else was hit and not you. The purges produced a similar dread: when you heard the arrival of the NKVD[28] car in the street, and froze still as a statue in your bed, you thanked God that the knock came on someone else's door.

The state assumed that the universities were hotbeds of anti-Soviet sentiment and so as intelligentsia, both I and my colleagues were suspect.[29]

---

28 The NKVD was the People's Commissariat for Internal Affairs (Народный комиссариат внутренних дел, Narodnyy Komissariat Vnutrennikh Del). They were the Soviet secret police prior to 1946.

29 Years later, in the mid-1960s, the Cultural Revolution in China proved devastating to the intelligentsia of that country, but the purges in the USSR during the late 1930s were the precursor.

As I walked home from the Institute in the late afternoon I reflected unhappily on my meeting with the assistant director. The key to surviving the purges was to trust no one and to say as little as possible. You had to know who was reporting to the NKVD and be more useful to them alive and in position, rather than in the gulag or worse. Let me say, I never actually denounced anybody, but in my 'conversations' with the assistant director my actions could be taken as a confirmation of his accusations. Poor Mishchenko. Perhaps other colleagues, in their own conversations, denounced me. But during those years, by saying little or nothing, and just occasionally providing a curt nod, it was others who vanished in the night – not us.

In September 1937 our flat was newly built and an easy walk back from the Institute in Krasnodar. A block of twelve flats over three floors, built of concrete, painted white, with green roofs. Steps led up to open landings with a toilet on each floor. Each flat had two rooms but every floor also had a shared kitchen and a wash house.

Tanya, Sofia and I lived on the first floor; it was all clean and new, with distempered walls and good log-burning stoves in each room. Only on the wettest days did the damp rise up to the first floor although bugs and cockroaches were always something of a problem. We should have had another family living with us but as Sofia was just one year old the warden had allowed us the luxury of living alone. I allowed myself a modicum of pride; our flat was, to me, a palace.

Krasnodar is a city on the Kuban river in the northern Caucasus; that is southern Russia, south-east of the Ukraine and east of the Crimea. Unlike so much of the Soviet Union it enjoys the most favourable natural and climatic conditions.

The surrounding agricultural land is fertile and abundant. Excellent river transport along the Kuban out to the sea of Azov had existed for hundreds of years and the arrival of the railway line to Moscow in the nineteenth century increased the city's strategic importance. Given the agricultural inheritance it is perhaps unsurprising that the farming institute grew to be one of the best known and respected in Russia. I was raised in Saratov, the son of a botanist, and had always been determined to study in Krasnodar. I won a place and found that academia suited me; after graduation I continued my studies, finally accepting a teaching position in the Institute's department of botany.

We met whilst at university, when she was in her first year and I was a postgraduate. The daughter of a proud Kuban family, her father, Ivan Moroz, had been a train driver and she idolised him. In the West, misogynistic attitudes forced women down traditional female lines of work, but there was less gender stereotyping within the Soviet system, particularly in the early years after 1917. It was thus a natural progression for Tanya to study mechanical engineering to gain the understanding of the science behind the practical skills taught to her by her father and the other engineers at the railway yard.

Tanya is unconventional. Tall and slim, her body has a sense of angularity. Perhaps an embodiment of her beloved engines. She feels that there is beauty to behold in machinery, in its delicacy and continuity of motion, but I am not sure I agree. I see machinery as intricate and built to extremely tight tolerances but also as a source of wonderment and perhaps inspiring a sense of awe. Properly maintained, a machine does its job to exacting standards without heed to its surroundings. This is how I would describe Tanya. She speaks when needed, remaining silent otherwise. If engaged in a task then she completes it without fault, but without interest in others around her. She never falters. In 1930 when we met, she was not beautiful but she was most certainly striking with piercing coal-black eyes and a shock of short black hair. If you said something of interest then she would hold you with her eyes and you would feel on fire as her eyes burned into you, extracting, from your audible and visual signals, every nuance of your message. Most people found Tanya hard to like, but for us it was an almost instant love which has never waned. She, just like that intricate machine, is awe-inspiring. A human embodiment of wonder.

On graduation with honours in 1931, Tanya secured a position in the engineering team at the city's vast food-processing facility. Processing the huge grain output of the Russian steppe into flour, at speed and without breakdown, was key to bread production for the whole country. In Tanya's terms it was the oil to ensure the smooth running of the entire Soviet machine. In 1936, for creating a new process leading to increased output, she was one of the first recipients of the Order of the Badge of Honour, conferred on comrades for outstanding achievements in production. As befitted her nature, she made little of the award, but I was proud![30]

---

30 The Order of the Badge of Honour was established in 1935 and was a civilian award of the Soviet Union for outstanding achievements in production, scientific research and social, cultural and other forms of social activity.
https://en.wikipedia.org/wiki/Order_of_the_Badge_of_Honour

I had beaten Tanya home; she would be collecting Sofia from kindergarten on her route back from the food factory. Now I heard voices approaching the door, quite unmistakably those of all my family. Tanya's slightly flat tones at a constant pitch, accompanied by the delighted burble of baby Sofia, and then the bassline boom of my brother-in-law Pyotr who would be, as was usual, joining us for supper that evening.

I stood and opened the door for them in readiness and all three appeared in a rush! Eighteen-month-old Sofia Zayky led the way, tottering, jabbering loudly, wrapped tightly in her brown winter coat despite the last remnants of a warm September sun. She proceeded to tell me of her day in sentences comprised of burbles and gasps, with her wonderful dark eyes emphasising every point.

Verbally she was still beyond comprehension, but her body language made total sense, and I nodded and smiled in agreement with all her utterances as I got her ready for bed. She knew what she wanted to say. She had serious points to make, and it would be frustrating for her if they went unheeded. She was her mother's daughter! Once ready, she reappeared to kiss her mother and Uncle Pyotr goodnight then took herself back to her room. I sat on the chair to read to her and she sat on my lap to listen, but only for a minute, because by then she was already asleep. I carefully picked her up and tucked her in between the sheets and took that last long look at my beautiful daughter as every parent does just before leaving them sleeping at night.

In Russia it was not unusual to have two working parents and Sofia attended the kindergarten full-time during weekdays and Saturday mornings. Westerners in the 1930s might have been surprised that mothers didn't naturally stay at home, but that was not our way. If you were qualified you were expected to work; the kindergarten was for children and was run by women who were experts in childcare. It was just the way things were. It was efficient. Tanya and I were much more effective in our work than we would have been looking after Sofia. It didn't affect our uncompromising love for her.

We might have expected to have had more children after Sofia but Tanya's experience of childbirth suggested otherwise. For Tanya, and her machines, creating output Sofia was the pinnacle of production – the straight line connecting two given points. For both of us Sofia became our raison d'être. From the moment of her birth, whatever we did was always for her sake.

Over supper that night we kept our voices low, partly for fear of waking Sofia and partly because you never knew who might be listening. The three of us were a close unit. Perhaps other than me, Pyotr was the only person who understood Tanya. She adored him for that. For me, he was the brother I never had, although visually we would never have been mistaken for siblings. Pyotr was a bear of a man and in his mid-twenties had changed beyond all recognition from the grinning skinny youth, with his fishing rod, in the yellowed picture over the stove. We were both nearly six feet tall but whereas I stoop rather and walk with a slightly shuffling gait, Pyotr strode everywhere, upright, his huge frame enhanced by his luxuriant black beard. When I was at a tender age working alongside my father in the nurseries and greenhouses of Saratov, and Tanya was in the engine house, Pyotr was already heaving sacks up to the open doors of the railway freight cars, and learning to drink his vodka with the men to keep out the worst of the winter cold.

Pyotr and I shared an ability to charm people in a way which Tanya did not. At the Institute my role went beyond simply lecturing the students: it would often fall to me to go out to visit the farms on the steppe to persuade some of the older managers, set in their ways, to put aside traditional methods and accept modernisation to achieve higher outputs. I found that I was good at convincing the old farmers to do as I asked. It came to me naturally. I would take the time to talk round a subject, highlighting their success and then gently requesting a few small changes which taken together represented quite a large shift. Put another way, I can make well-placed compliments which help people like me, so they become more willing to do as I say. On the other hand, Pyotr simply made use of his physical demeanor, his huge open smile, his roar of laughter, his arm placed around the shoulders of his listener. That worked.

And all three of us were devoted to Sofia.

'Three thousand sacks of flour a day heading north on the trains and yet no bread in the shops in Krasnodar. God knows what it's like in the country.' Pyotr's voice remained loud even when attempting whispers.

The early 1930s had seen the start of the Soviet farming collectivisation. I had been a junior botanist then and involved in the implementation. The demands of the state's five-year plans to increase output had made perfect sense. Combining small farmsteads allowed far more efficient land management; it meant more grain could be shipped north to feed the hungry and growing cities of the USSR. All went well at the beginning, and although many Kulak farmers protested over the loss of their personal land holdings, it was for the greater good of the Soviet people.

'Land and farm collectivisation was fundamentally the right policy,' I responded slightly defensively. 'The old farms were just too small; every Cossack being given his own smallholding on coming of age led to diminishing returns. It just couldn't continue.'

'Pasha, you're not to blame for what happened after '32. It was the north continuing to demand ever-increasing amounts of grain that led to the famine.' Pyotr was right: after the crops failed between 1932 to 1934 it had been the continued greed of the Soviet north which had led to famine in the south. As Muscovites buttered their bread, so the people of the Kuban and Ukraine had starved. But as an early supporter of collectivisation I felt the disaster had my fingerprints on it.

Tanya's interjection was, as always, a mechanical analogy, 'The oil sump need only be half full for the machine to run, but if the pump fails and the cogs receive no lubricant then breakdown is inevitable. That was the disaster of the famine. There was enough grain to go around. Shortages would have occurred but with efficient and careful management there was enough for everyone. The famine was Moscow's doing, not ours... or yours, Pasha.'

In the early 1930s I had not been senior enough to play a major role. But I did fill the shoes of men above me who had protested to the Moscow bureaucrats over the management of grain supplies during the famine period and who had then been dismissed for their trouble. I prospered by their misfortune. Looking back, it was a cool lesson on how *not* to deal with an all-powerful political leviathan.

As was usual, our conversation continued long into the night. I, ever the pragmatist, simply wanted to sail our ship steadily through the stormy waters of Soviet governance. But Tanya and Pyotr were Kuban Cossacks and for them pragmatism was alien. There was right, and *not* right.

The Kuban Cossack Host are a proud people, fighters and farmers, who were exiled from the Dnieper (now Ukraine) in the eighteenth century. Despite this they fought for Catherine the Great against the Turks, and in return, she rewarded them with eternal use of the fertile Kuban land on the steppe. This reward caused the foundation of the city in 1794 – then called Yekaterinodar meaning 'Catherine's gift'.

In the civil war that erupted after the 1917 Revolution, the fiercely independent Kuban people supported the White Army against the Bolsheviks. Their goal: a separate Kuban republic. The terrifying Kuban Cossack Cavalry Regiment, with their skull-and-crossbones insignia, was the crack troop of the Whites. But whilst the Kuban Cossacks were skilled fighters, ultimately they were outnumbered by the northern Bolsheviks. In April 1918 the Red Army captured Yekaterinodar and renamed the city Krasnodar – meaning (with irony) 'gift of the Reds'. Adoption of the new Soviet name for the city was an order from the north but the Kuban Cossacks remained proud of their heritage and continued their silent animosity towards the new Soviet Muscovites.

The famine years coincided with Tanya beginning work at the food production factory. She had seen the starving peasants scratching around in the dirt of the factory floor for fallen grains from the conveyor. Earlier, during her university years, she had been asked to join the Komsomol. It had been an honour to be considered but though others had jumped at the chance, she had decided against. Tanya understood that whilst party membership conferred privilege it also brought with it an occasional requirement to undertake certain tasks, sometimes distasteful tasks, to assist with the building of the Soviet state. Communist Party membership was rather like a pact with the devil; sometimes your end of the bargain was unpalatable.

But by placing my personal distaste of the system to one side I found that a pragmatic approach was key to not only survival but to advancement as well. As the senior personnel at the Agricultural Institute disappeared during the purges, so my own position within the hierarchy gradually improved and promotion provided a separate route to extra privileges. When food was most short, just before harvest, most of the people of the city survived on *shrot*[31] and a watery cottage cheese, whereas we were allocated extra rations.

In a supposedly egalitarian society I would, just occasionally, feel guilty that we always had bread on our table and a little butter, and sometimes meat as well, when others went without. It is true that both Tanya and I worked hard and achieved much for the Soviet regime but we did seem to do well, at least in relation to others. By the Soviet standards of the late 1930s you might even say we prospered.

---

31   *Shrot* is a high-protein gruel made of leftover sunflower kernels after the oil has been removed.

4

PASHA ZAYKY

Krasnodar, October 1942

Family Zayky
Flat 6, 18 Novokuznechaya,
Krasnodar
Free Russia
Wednesday September 9th 1942

My Dear Tanya, Pasha and Sofia,

It has been so long since I have written; you must have thought the very worst of me. My delay has been because we have been active and also because I honestly believed that no letter of mine would ever reach you. Yesterday, Colonel Kononov told me that Krasnodar is now under German control, and the best news of all, that the Germans have established in the Kuban a separate state which can govern itself. This is wonderful, to be free of Moscow's oppression at last. I am so happy to be able to write these lines.

But I must bring you my own news to explain my silence for more than a year. When the Germans attacked the Soviet Union in late June last year it took us all by surprise. We had thought the political and economic unions which had been signed between the Soviets and Germans would hold fast, or at least delay war for another year or so.

You remember that when we were growing up, Cossacks were banned from the Red Army as they feared insurrection, but that ban was lifted back in the mid-1930s so that, when the invasion happened, it took just a week before the youngest and strongest of the railway workers from Krasnodar were drafted into the Red Army – that included me, of course. Our goodbyes were so rushed; I had no idea what would become of me. The news from the front seemed desperate.

My appointed regiment was the 436 Rifles. We had just a few days' training and were then sent straight to join the men fighting in western Ukraine. Within twenty-four hours of my arrival I realised that our position was hopeless. The Germans had far greater firepower; what use were our rifles against their tanks? Each day saw more and more casualties on our side. Eventually, by August, with the number of men in our regiment just a fraction of what it had been, we were in full retreat. It doesn't take long to break the spirit of an army, and a lack of preparedness, a lack of useful weapons, and most important a lack of leadership from the top, meant that we were well and truly broken.

It was around then that we began thinking there might be another way. The 436 Rifles were comprised of Cossacks both from the Kuban and the Don.[32] Good, strong fighting men all, but we realised that, in retreat, we were heading in the right direction but for the wrong reason! For us Cossacks, why

32 The Don River runs north of the Kuban and was another area of Cossack settlement in the eighteenth century.

were we fighting a so-called 'Patriotic War' for the Soviets? Our patriotism is to our Cossack homelands. For me, patriotism is to our Kuban land. Why were we laying down our lives for the Soviets who had left us starving in the famines of the 1930s? We ought to be joining the German advance not the Soviet retreat.

Our numbers were so limited and our morale so low that when our commander, Major Kononov, walked among us we were unafraid to let him know our feelings. We assumed that, as a long-term professional soldier who had been with the Red Army since the 1920s, he could not possibly have been a Cossack and would probably shoot us on the spot – but we just didn't care anymore. Certainly, the Red Army political officers who seemed never to leave his side wanted us dead for what we said. They spoke of treason and said we should be shot, but Kononov reassured them that we were just tired soldiers, shouting off our mouths.

But a few days later, Kononov grouped everyone together and said the most amazing thing! He said that he was a Don Cossack, that his father had been shot by the Bolsheviks in 1918, and that he had lied about his age and place of birth to allow entry to the Red Army in the 1920s. He knew how we felt, and he felt the same! To the amazement of the political officers he then said that he had been communicating with Count Von Schenkendorf (the German General who had been chasing us), and had agreed to join the German side. He said that he had told Schenkendorf that he thought a number of the men under his command would join him in switching sides, provided that we would be permitted to establish a Russian Liberation Army which set out to overthrow that murderer, Stalin.

Colonel Kononov, though he was just a major then, or Ivan the Great (as we call him!) said that if anybody wanted to stay with the Reds then nothing would happen to them but he hoped that we would all follow him. The political officers were speechless and were quickly disarmed by us! Of course, we would all follow him. Two days later, without a shot being fired, we calmly marched back to the German lines where we were welcomed with vodka and beer and sausage. What a feast.

After that, we marched north to Mogilev in Belarus to the Red Army prisoner of war camp in German territory. There were about 5,000 men there and I must say they were the most dreadful sight. Most had been captured in the early days of the invasion and had tasted no food since. They were dying around us. Kononov has assured us that he has total autonomy over us but we do have a Wehrmacht[33] liaison officer called Rittenburg. I think Rittenburg was embarrassed at the state of our erstwhile compatriots and he spoke very sharply to the camp commandant, although I don't understand German. Later we were told that as the Soviets hadn't signed the Geneva Convention, Germany felt no compunction to adhere to its terms when holding Red prisoners. I suppose this is right, but they were an awful sight.

Anyway, Kononov spoke to all 5,000 of the prisoners. He told them our aim and invited them to volunteer for service in our liberation army. And do you know, 4,000 of them stepped forward – we were amazed. We simply couldn't take them all, we didn't have the officers to organise things on that scale. So Kononov picked a group of us men to interview the volunteers and, in the end, we found 500 good true men to join us – 400 of them Cossacks.

The other men we left behind were despondent, of course, but Kononov told them he would be back soon enough. Although, as

---

33 Wehrmacht is the overarching name of all the German armed forces.

I write, it's been a year and to my knowledge they are still there – or possibly the winter would have seen them off.

A splendid day was 19ᵗʰ September 1941 when the Don Cossack Regiment of the Wehrmacht was formally founded. Count von Schenkendorf read us the directive from the German War Office. I wish we were named as a Kuban Cossack Regiment rather than Don but I think that will come as we grow. By September we were 2,000 strong with eighty officers. Ivan the Great was our Ataman[34] and we were proud to be under his command.

But although we now had right, and God, on our side to battle the Bolshevik curse, the fighting was hard. The offensive of last year ended with the winter. I must say that the Soviets just kept coming and fighting as hard as they could. The Germans were unprepared for the level of resistance and as the days grew colder their summer uniforms became of no use, whilst the oils and diesel fuel in their trucks and tanks stopped working. They had nobody who understood how to maintain diesel engines – Tanya, you should have been there! Only we Cossacks were ready for the Russian winter. So, we held up on the Ukrainian/Russian border, forced to wait. Our delay gave the Reds six months to regroup.

In January and February, we fought partisans in Smolensk and Mogilev and our Ivan was promoted to Lieutenant-Colonel. But it wasn't until the spring this year that matters took a turn for the better because now the Germans started pushing to the south as well as the east. Someone said that the oil fields of Baku are their goal and I suppose that makes sense. An army doesn't march on its stomach any longer, instead its tank tracks

---

34 Ataman is the official title of the supreme military commander of a
    Cossack army.

rumble on oil! The excellent news for me was that between the advancing German front line and Baku lay Krasnodar so I knew that you would be free soon enough.

I had hoped that our Cossack Regiment would be part of the liberating force, but I gather that we are to be sent elsewhere, although I don't know where exactly yet.

So, that brings me up to date. I so hope to hear all your news but as I expect we will be moving around I think it unlikely that any letters will reach me. A tumultuous year. Something I never expected to see; but we are free from the tyranny of the Soviets at last! I am sure there will be hard times ahead but we are going to be a free society. A Kuban land once again. Please fare well my sister and brother. Kiss beautiful Sofia for me, and know that I love you all more than words can ever describe.

Pyotr

I PUT DOWN PYOTR'S LETTER HAVING READ IT FOR A third time. When the Germans had invaded the Ukraine in June 1941 they had taken the Soviets by surprise. The scale of the battle unleashed was unprecedented; the biggest movement of men and machines at war that the world had ever seen. For me invasion brought with it mixed feelings: despite the oppression of the Soviet regime, we had done well. A good flat, good rations, excellent jobs for us both, and Sofia well provided for. She was five and a half now, a quiet, thoughtful child, already reading well, and good at basic arithmetic. Her progress had amazed the staff at the kindergarten. The invasion could wreck all of this.

Tanya held a different view. The Cossack blood running in her heart meant she would justify any attack on the Soviets. There was a chance that Krasnodar would become a German satellite with the tyranny of Communism ended. She would take that chance over all the privileges which had fallen to us through the current regime.

The Germans rolled forwards quickly during the summer and autumn of 1941 but then slowed as the winter took hold. They captured Rostov, about 150 miles to our north, but the Russians swiftly retook the city. During November, German tanks came within 15 miles of Moscow, but then at the beginning of December, Soviet troops, much better equipped for winter fighting, pushed the Nazis back.

For a while it seemed like a stalemate, but then in the spring of 1942 the Germans moved forwards again, this time splitting their forces so that one army went east towards Stalingrad, and the other headed south to the Caucasus. Of course, oil was the booty they were after. Rostov fell once again in late July and then Krasnodar fell on 6th August. On that first day, I was terrified to see hordes of those grey German tin helmets marching through our streets. Perhaps oddly, the tin helmets reminded me of bowler hats and in that way seemed both sinister and strangely comedic at the same time. Up to then, we had only seen them in *Pravda*[35] and on newsreels when they had been attached to dead Germans hanging out of the turrets of smoking tanks. Now they were on the heads of stern Aryan men marching together in rank, eyes front, like automatons wearing funny bowler hats.

There was little resistance in Krasnodar itself, and in fact some Cossacks came out to wave them in. Their infantry was followed by armoured cars and motorbikes

---

35 The main Soviet newspaper.

with sidecars all bearing a German cross. Given the absence of our Russian church from Soviet life some in the street said that the black cross on the vehicles was the mark of Christ. Perhaps this was the return of Christianity to a region where Communist oppressors had kept God at bay for a quarter of a century. The German soldiers wore insignia and belt buckles saying '*Gott mit uns*'[36]. And for many Christians who had suffered persecution under the Soviets, and now watched the arrival of the Nazis, it was reasonable to think they might be right.

There were no tanks though. I was surprised, as we had all heard of the immense Nazi armoured power. Only later did I find out that splitting their advance between the east and the south had caused chronic fuel shortages; so the gas-guzzling tanks had been left behind. The signs of a faltering advance were there from the start.

After the war the standard Soviet propaganda was that the people had resisted the German invasion at every step of the way, but this was not what I observed in Krasnodar. The years of oppression of the Cossack people meant that the anti-Bolshevik sentiment was such that they viewed the Nazi forces as their enemy's enemy; and thus their friend.

For a few days after the fall of the city the Agricultural Institute was closed, and Tanya stayed away from the food-processing plant, but life got back to normal quickly. Of course, there were German soldiers everywhere and that was disconcerting, but provided you got out of their way they offered no trouble. I had an advantage over most people in

---

36 'God with us'.

the city in that I spoke German, at least, to a degree. Many of the founding fathers of botanical science were German, and wrote their textbooks and papers in German. The archaic language contained in those scientific writings was, in reality, not so very different to the modern Deutsche language both spoken and written and so as a student of botany it had been a prerequisite to undertake German language lessons. This alone made navigating our way through the myriad of new regulations slightly less daunting. Another advantage turned out to be our family name – Zayky – which had a more German sound to it than most of the local Cossack names.

By 1942 I had been appointed a professor at the Agricultural Institute, in charge of the grains and grasses department. A great honour for me although, of course, I was aware that many other excellent senior academics had disappeared during the late 1930s. One Saturday afternoon in early September I was working at the Institute preparing for lectures the following week. A German dispatch rider was shown into my study and handed me a brief letter, in German, requesting that I attend City Hall the following morning to see Major Reinhardt, the German commandant in charge of the local Nazi administration.

I was worried; had I done something wrong, said something to somebody out of place? But if that was the case then why would Reinhardt want me? He was the top man – surely an underling would chastise me for a misdemeanour, and in any event I had no idea what I might have done. That Saturday evening Tanya and I discussed matters and went through all our recent movements and conversations but without conclusion. A sleepless night and a chilly Sunday morning.

Having left Tanya and Sofia at the flat I duly arrived at City Hall fifteen minutes early for the 11am appointment. I was sent to the first floor where an orderly pointed me to a wooden pew to wait. Precisely on the hour, I was shown into Major Reinhardt's study. Reinhardt was resplendent in his brushed grey uniform, his cap on his desk. A tall clean-shaven man in his early forties, his sandy hair seemed curiously unkempt for someone otherwise so smart. His eyes were tired, but there was a legacy of a sparkle. His jaw was large, his teeth crooked and yellowed by cigarette smoke, but his mouth fell naturally to a smile. Visually, at least, there seemed to be some warmth.

There was another there, introduced as Oberführer Bierkamp, who wore a black uniform.[37] Dark eyes behind owl-like glasses. He was a similar age to Reinhardt. He did not rise or shake hands and continued to wear his cap over a high forehead and flapping ears. He said nothing.

'Herr Zayky,' said Reinhardt standing, learning forwards and firmly shaking my hand. 'Please do sit down, you will join us for coffee, I hope? Thank you for coming, I do hope that this meeting time is not too inconvenient for you on your family day. Please forgive me. You will appreciate that demands on my time are such that I have to try to fit in appointments where I can, and so I do appreciate you taking the trouble to join me now.'

He spoke in German and I responded, 'It is my honour, Herr Major, although I confess to being uncertain as to why

---

37 Bierkamp's black uniform was that of the Einsatzgruppen (deployment groups), which were Nazi SS paramilitary death squads. They operated in territories occupied by the German forces and almost all the people they killed were civilians.

you want to see me. The Agricultural Institute is of course run by the director, I am merely a department head. How can I be of assistance?'

'Your German is good, Zayky! And this is what we had heard. Tell me – your name – it is not from around here. I know of a good family by that name in Weissenburg in Bayern, do you have some German ancestry by chance?'

I explained that I had been born in Saratov. My parents had both been Russian but that I had not known my paternal grandparents. I explained that I had made an effort to learn German in my youth to further my studies.

'Well the name Zayky certainly sounds German to me and you don't possess Slavic or Cossack facial features. I find your spoken German is good compared to most of your countrymen. I wonder if it is a language which came naturally to you given a possible Aryan ancestry?'

Frankly, I rather doubted his assertion, but it didn't seem politic to say so, and so I nodded in general acquiescence.

'You see, Zayky, we have made a list of all the important people in the area. Those who have special skills which could prove useful. As such, I hope that you might be willing to help us... you see the problem is that all across Europe people need bread. Although we have arrived here to rid you of Communist oppression, the ravages of our advance have destroyed the crops. Both here and in my own home city of Munich food is short and we need to do everything we can to alleviate that.'

To that I nodded in agreement much more readily.

'Your research and the implementation methods that you have developed here in the Caucasus can be put to excellent use throughout Europe. We want you to share your knowledge, to teach others. It is true that we want the Third Reich[38] to live for a thousand years, but at its heart must be highly productive farms, yielding excellent harvests for all our people. So, our aim is to establish a self-governing district here in Krasnodar as the centre of the Kuban Cossacks. Of course, ultimately, you will answer to Berlin just as you did in the past to Moscow but you can be sure that our leadership will be a much lighter touch than you have experienced from your former Communist masters. The important thing here is that crops grown in the Kuban will stay in the Kuban and feed the Kuban. What we want is for you to share your knowledge and know-how with all the peoples of Europe, so that through that knowledge they can learn better how to feed themselves.'

What a speech! Of course, I agreed, although in the circumstances I was hardly likely to say no. But Reinhardt had flattered me and my work in a way that I simply could not resist. Now I spoke in a flood. I was delighted and told him so. I mentioned Tanya, and he said that he had already heard of the work she was doing at the food-processing factory – her skill as an engineer. This was just more intelligence that must be shared. The Communists had wanted this intelligence just for themselves, but now the Germans wanted it for the benefit of mankind. How could I possibly decline?

I left the study with my mind buzzing with possibilities. Reinhardt had explained that throughout the Reich

---

38   Reich: Empire or Kingdom. Charlemagne's Holy Roman
     Empire was known as the 'First Reich' and Otto von Bismarck's
     Hohenzollern Dynasty the 'Second Reich'. The 'Third Reich' was
     construed as the start of a thousand-year reign of Christ on Earth.

various groups of experts were being created to facilitate the dissemination of research. The work to further the understanding of the botanical science of arable crops was one of the most important. Letters and papers from me would be copied at City Hall and then sent throughout Europe to unseen Western colleagues who would add their own papers and thoughts – all would be shared. Whilst I would retain my position at the Institute, I was invited to return to City Hall daily, given desk space, and allocated secretarial assistance. There was even a modest stipend denominated in German Marks. A key stipulation was that they wanted to be sure that neither Tanya nor I had ever been Communists, at heart, and certainly never party members – and this I was happy to confirm. This was the only point during the conversation when Bierkamp, the black-uniformed officer, seemed engaged. On hearing that we had never been Communists he simply made a pencil note on his pad, and then continued his impassive stare.

That Sunday afternoon, Tanya, Sofia and I took the tram to our allotment on the outskirts of the city. It was always a happy time for the three of us and even better as the chilly morning had turned into a gloriously sunny late summer's afternoon. The allotment was just a third of a *sotok*, but plenty for us.[39]

---

39 It was the Tsar who first began the practice of granting plots for urban dwellers to use at weekends, getting them out of city centres and allowing them to grow their own food. The word *dacha* was derived from *davat* (to give) in the seventeenth century. Land area in Russia is often measured in *sotoks*, where one *sotok* is a hundred square metres. Many were granted six *sotoks*, which was considered large enough for a weekend cottage and vegetable garden, but not enough to live permanently – so avoiding the chance of workers permanently quitting industrial life.

The gardens were very sociable places and outside of the city centre we were away from the smoke, soot and fumes. Sharing planting ideas with our neighbours and swapping produce was all part of the allotment experience. Our simple tools were kept in a tiny hut and that afternoon we were digging out potatoes, wrapping each one in newspaper to store for the winter, and harvesting the last of our cucumbers ready for pickling. Sofia normally spent the time working alongside me asking questions about the earthworms, spiders and wriggling insects she found rather than the vegetables. Just occasionally she would lever her trowel out of the ground and shower us with red Kuban soil, prompting fits of giggles.

Despite the warm sun, the allotments were not busy that afternoon. Our neighbours were not there which meant we were easily able to speak about my interview with Reinhardt. Tanya had been delighted to learn what had been said.

'Pasha, you were stupid to ever doubt the German intentions in the Kuban. Here we are just one month into the occupation and life still works. The sun still comes up in the morning and goes down at night as normal. We go to work, my factory is still processing grain, Sofia's kindergarten continues to operate well. Our flat remains our home. And, in case, you hadn't noticed, it seems to me that food in the shops doesn't sell out quite so quickly as it did one month ago.'

I had to agree. She was quite correct.

'And now you have the opportunity of your life. We must thank God the Communists have been pushed aside.'

And so, during the following month, I attended City Hall on a daily basis. Sure enough the academic grouping began to function and yield results. I started to receive papers from all across mainland Europe: Germany, France, Czechoslovakia – all in German of course and my own work had also been translated into that language. I had no problem with that, it seemed appropriate given the existence of the ancient botanical texts for this new library of research to be set out in German. At home we began to be able to get more food and some extra clothes, as well as wood for the stove. From August through September and into October, our life, already good under the Soviets, improved further during the German occupation.

Occasionally I would see Reinhardt, sometimes for a short update, and sometimes just for coffee as he asked my more general advice on the pronunciation of Russian words – he was attempting, fairly unsuccessfully, to learn the language. I was perfectly happy to help and my own German improved steadily.

I did, nevertheless, perceive a slight change in the attitude of some of my colleagues at the Institute. I wouldn't say they became frosty – we academics have never been very sociable in any event – but there was a slight hesitance in the way they spoke to me. It was almost as though they spoke with more respect. At the time, I thought perhaps they might have felt envy, but with hindsight I think it might have been fear.

Tanya noted a similar change at her factory. She had always been considered aloof, a trait which has remained with her throughout her life, but now the chat and laughter which might have been going on in a room or factory hall was generally silenced when she entered. I'm sure that neither of us said, or did, anything to warrant these changes.

In any event we knew that the work we were doing (and in particular what I was doing) was for the benefit of mankind in the widest sense but specifically for the benefit of a Kuban District within a new Fatherland which would help everyone in the end. I suppose that fundamentally what we were doing was for the sake of Sofia's future.

All the Communist Party members vanished. Some, like the former square-cut assistant director at the Institute, were fighting with the Red Army, no doubt taking the role of a political officer deemed essential in each Soviet squadron of men. But others in their late forties and fifties who had not been drafted had remained in the city at the start of the invasion to ensure that the Great Patriotic War would continue to be fought in the factories; they now simply disappeared.[40]

Also, the Jewish contingent in the city were sent to internment camps out of the city centre. This was a surprise at the time. The Soviet propaganda had taught us about the Nazi's anti-Bolshevik sentiment, but nothing about anti-Semitism. The Jewish people were taken away in vans by officers in the black uniforms. The vans, which had been brought in specifically for the job, were high-sided, enclosed, without windows. Occasionally you would see one parked in a side street with people of all ages being crammed inside. It did seem inhuman, but I assumed they were being sent off to a camp where they could all be together. There had been so many ethnic mass movements under the old Soviet

---

40 The Great Patriotic War (Вели́кая Оте́чественная война́) is a term used in Russia and some other former republics of the Soviet Union to describe the conflict between the Soviet Union and Nazi Germany from June 1941 to May 1945.

regime that the use of vans to shift a group of people of a single ethnicity didn't seem unusual.

From my city hall office window up on the second floor I could see the motor depot housing those high-sided vans; the black-uniformed troops lining up before departure, receiving their instructions; then the vans firing up and sweeping out of the yard in convoy. The vans never returned when I was in the office but they were always back, parked in neat rows, the following morning. Only after the war did I learn the true horror. What should I have known at the time? What could I have done? Stalin had also been a proponent of ethnic cleansing and what had I done about that? But Stalin's regime was one under which we existed, we tolerated, in which we operated pragmatically. The new Nazi regime was one which we supported enthusiastically. Quite a difference.[41]

So, in early October 1942, as I put down Pyotr's letter, I reflected that communications from those fighting at the front were much slower to arrive than the academic papers, at the cutting edge of botanical science, which were currently flying round Europe. We hadn't heard from him since he had been drafted into the Red Army and we were both so relieved to learn he was still alive. Alive, and at least as of a month ago, apparently flourishing. There was the anxiety of knowing where he was going next. Surely, for the Germans,

---

41 Estimates vary of how many Jews were killed by the Nazis in Krasnodar in 1942, but it might have been 7,000. Walther Bierkamp (1901–45) was commander of Einsatzgruppe D, an SS paramilitary death squad. The vans gassed their occupants who were then left in roadside ditches which became mass graves. Local villagers round Krasnodar called the death vans 'the killer of souls'.

their Cossack regiment was an asset which would have been best used to help invade the Kuban? Having not made use of them to capture their homeland I had a worry they might be deemed as less valuable troops in other theatres of operation. Cannon fodder, perhaps.

At the allotment in October it was growing colder. We were planting hardy winter peas and broad beans for an early crop the following spring. The Sunday afternoon sky was slate grey and we would only have a short time before we started to lose light.

'I'm so proud of Pyotr.' Tanya spoke in billows of steam rising from her nose and mouth. 'What a fight he has had, and what luck to have been posted with a Cossack commander.'

'Our brother is a true hero of the Kuban people, for sure. But I fear the fight is continuing for longer than should be the case,' I responded. 'I hear from Reinhardt that Stalingrad is still holding out and has not fallen to the Germans as expected. And that does worry me.'

Tanya remained stooped, planting the seeds into the cold earth, but looked across to me.

'Pasha, but why? Everything here is working so well.'

'Because it's October, and remember that last winter the Germans were pushed back. If the Germans fall back from Stalingrad, then perhaps Rostov might also be lost and that would be a disaster. If the Germans are pushed back into the Ukraine, then there is nothing to stop the Soviets coming back down from the north. I'm just worried that suddenly we could find ourselves cut off.'

There were no tanks and few aeroplanes. Had the Germans made it to the Baku oil fields then the Krasnodar railhead would have been an important staging post for the oil heading west, but that hadn't happened. There were lots of German troops in our city, but not enough for me to feel we were safe.

'For us, now, after the last couple of months, the return of the Soviets would be terrifying.'

To the north, another harsh winter was brewing. I wondered whether we would ever harvest our crop of peas and broad beans.

5

PASHA ZAYKY

Posen, December 1942
to January 1945

I T WAS AROUND JUNE 1944 AND SOFIA MUST HAVE BEEN aged eight, when we went to see *Junge Adler*[42] at the Stadt Park Cinema in Posen. An excellent film; marvellous music; at the end Sofia cried, and even I had a lump in my throat. But as we chatted on the walk home it was clear that, even at her young age, Sofia was able to understand the film's propagandist nature. It was an extremely well-crafted device imploring the young to turn their backs on their ill-educated parents and to follow the lead of National Socialism through the teachings of the Hitlerjungend[43] – to follow the slogan 'Youth must be guided by youth'. Young Aryan prodigies should not be constrained by old-fashioned, misplaced conventional teaching, such as that offered by their parents. Instead, they should forge a new

---

42   *Junge Adler* (*Young Eagle*) was a 1944 Nazi propaganda film aimed at children.

43   The Hitler Youth.

German way of life, based upon racial superiority, to last a millennium.

Sofia and I spent time talking through the nuances of the plot, the scenes and the dialogue, so that she could consider how the words and images had been conveyed specifically to shape the opinions of the film's young viewers. In the end she understood the film in both its guises: that of pure escapism, and then quite separately as a method of control.

I couldn't help but enjoy the film, but in truth, the shameless propaganda irritated me; particularly because, despite the welcome we had received in the Third Reich, it was obvious by 1944 that it was unravelling at the seams. Rather than lasting a thousand years, the duration of Hitler's Reich could now be measured in months.

When the Germans had come to Krasnodar in August 1942 we had thrown our lot in with them – for better or worse – but within just two months I began to fear that 'the better' would be short-lived. By the autumn I was fearful that the German advance would falter and eventually reverse and if they were pushed back then there would be no future for us in Krasnodar, or in fact in Russia at all. It meant that we had to get out of the city and head west before our means of escape closed down. Our survival depended on it.

Through the web of correspondence that I had established between the academics of Europe I asked if there were positions vacant as a professor somewhere – anywhere – west of Krasnodar. Thank God, I was afforded a prompt response; and Professor Heinrich Walter of the newly founded Reichsuniversität Posen wrote to invite me to join him as a professor in the geobotany department.

When Poland was annexed by the Nazis in 1939 the old university of Poznan had closed, but after eighteen months it reopened as a centre of National Socialist learning. It was one of a number of 'Germanised universities' designed to imbue Aryan youth living outside of the 'Fatherland' with National Socialist ideology. The Reichsuniversität in Posen was specifically established to be *the* leadership school of the German East. Its teaching in modern sciences was at the cutting edge of research. However, alongside top academics in botany, chemistry and physics were other individuals working to a strict National Socialist agenda. The key Nazis were Professor Petersen of the Department of Prehistory, and more particularly the Dean himself, Professor Reinhard Wittram.[44]

And so, in late 1942, we found ourselves bound to this bizarre 'heads and tails' educational establishment – where 'heads' was at the forefront of academic learning and 'tails' belonged to Nazi fantasists. With hindsight it was, I suppose, a 'flight' from Russia but actually we were very comfortable in our first-class sleeper train from Krasnodar to Posen via Rostov, Kiev and Warsaw. We had our suitcases whilst some small pieces of furniture and my all-important research papers were packed into crates and loaded into the freight car. All our moving costs were paid for by my new Nazi masters.

We finally arrived in Posen on a Saturday in early December, sad to have left our flat in Krasnodar where we had known good times with Pyotr before the war, but hugely relieved to be free of the Soviet threat. The university

---

44　SS-Hauptsturmführer Wittram was a historian, in 1937 he wrote, 'Where a sense of breed and race has awakened, the re-thinking of our people on racial hereditary values will be understood as a process of recovery.'

billeted us in a large bright flat in Blücherstraße and Sofia was enrolled in school just a few streets away. The flat was clean and dry, the stove was efficient, and once our photographs had been placed carefully on the shelves, Blücherstraße quickly became our new home.

By the time of our arrival in Posen, both Tanya and Sofia had become proficient in German. We had all been taking lessons and Tanya had adopted her strict methodological, mechanistic approach to learning. Coupling diligence with her near photographic memory meant that she was practically fluent, albeit still struggling to disguise her southern Russian accent. Sofia, on the other hand, had simply adopted the language almost as a mother tongue. Our rule to speak nothing but German at home had paid off. Fortunately, like me, language skills came easily and she found she could converse with virtually no Russian accent.

Our linguistic abilities stood us in good stead. We had of course been nervous to be Russians arriving so deep into German territory. We were technically the enemy after all. Immediately, we noticed that most non-German workers had to wear badges denoting their nationality, but this was never something suggested as necessary for us. Indeed, the Germans respected our educational credentials without question and we found ourselves welcomed into their society. The Germans had transported many Volkdeutsch people to Posen at the expense of the native Poles who were now relegated to second-class citizens. The Poles were not allowed in many of the city's restaurants, nor in certain cinemas. Even some tramcars had signs in the windows: 'Polish forbidden'. We wondered who might have lived at Blücherstraße before us and realised that we were beneficiaries of German annexation.

My job at the university got underway immediately. Professor Walter allocated me a good-sized study, complete with a desk and bookshelves. My writing and research into arable farming outputs continued and the academic network of knowledge grew. New ideas were bouncing all across Europe. An interconnected web of learning. It was remarkable.

Tanya went to work at the university's *forschunszentrale* (the research centre) advising on a countrywide farming mechanisation project, a job practically tailor-made for her, and Sofia loved her new school. Her teacher, Fräulein Kisman, quickly recognised her talent for science – especially biology.

What was completely obvious was that shops were open with windows full of goods to buy. Not just food, but clothes and furniture, kitchen goods and toys; just about everything possible. The trams ran strictly to their timetables and there were lots of cars and trucks in the streets. The city people were elegantly dressed, taking great care with their appearance, whilst young people were polite and deferential. If a tram was full, then seats would always be made available to women and the elderly. The local bath house was open from 8am until 8pm every day but only for Germans (not Poles). The water was piping hot and everywhere was maintained to the highest standards of cleanliness.

Importantly, whilst there were always soldiers around in the streets they seemed to be on leave, rather than on duty. It was the police who were in charge of the city and they were respectful of the people going about their daily lives, whilst commanding and obtaining respect in return. Unless they were Polish of course.

On arrival in our new home town we were amazed by how much better our life had become. A Reichsuniversität professor earned a pretty good salary and at the end of November I remember we had over 300 Reichsmarks. That certainly set us up well for the coming Christmas.

In Russia, after the Revolution, Christmas had been banned and the old Orthodox traditions were a distant memory. In 1942 we celebrated a Catholic Christmas with all the city! It was Sofia's first real Christmas and one Saturday afternoon she and I bought a tree and decorations. We carried everything back to Blücherstraße and spent a happy evening arranging the tinsel and hanging the baubles. Sofia was delighted; so happy. What luxury; what a life!

In January, Reichsführer Himmler visited the university on an official trip. I, along with many others, was presented to him in a line-up. I expected merely a handshake, but when Professor Wittram explained my background, Himmler paused. In his publicity shots and movie reels he had always reminded me of a slightly comic elementary schoolteacher with a receding chin. But now as his grey-blue eyes, behind a glittering pince-nez, looked at me I stiffened in apprehension. Colourless, thin lips parted to reveal excellent white teeth as he spoke.

'Professor Zayky, the Reich is pleased you are here. I am pleased. Do keep up your work, it is invaluable to us all. I too trained as an agronomist and understand more than most the difference you will deliver to the Reich. Make sure that you get everything you need. If you require any other resources, anything at all, write to my office and I will see you get them.'

And he moved on to shake the next hand. I felt so honoured; how could I fail to have been?

But February brought sadness when my predictions proved sound and the German army effected a 'tactical retreat' from Krasnodar.[45] Some months later, in late July, the Dean, Professor (or more properly Hauptsturmführer) Wittram called me to his study. He could never have been considered a warm man but greeted me perfectly well. Nevertheless, I could tell immediately that there was a serious issue to be broached. We sat down and he handed me a document in Russian.

'Zayky, I cannot let you keep this. It has been passed to me in my official capacity as Dean specifically so that I can let you know. Occasionally, the Reich is able to obtain documents and information by covert methods… You are doing excellent work here in the Reichsuniversität and I am delighted. I hear nothing but good reports and hope that the fruits of your research might help us all reap a greater harvest this year…'

His voice tailed off as he let me read the words he had placed before me. It was an official Soviet report on the war crimes which had taken place in Krasnodar and the surrounding Kuban area arising from the German occupation between August 1942 to February 1943. Specifically, the report covered the trials which had taken place of those

---

45 In fact, the German 'tactical retreat' from Krasnodar in February 1943 was a rout. There was a bloody battle and much of the city centre was destroyed. Having lost at Stalingrad, and failed to reach the Caucasus oil supplies, the Nazi forces began to fall back quickly with the Soviets in pursuit.

who had collaborated with the occupying forces. On the 18th July eight people, local men who had helped the black-uniformed Einsatzgruppe, had been hanged in the main square in front of thousands of city folk. They had been tried and punishment had been swiftly meted out.[46] There was an appendix, however, which was a comprehensive list of other collaborators; all charged with lesser crimes but who had also been tried and sentenced. The appendix was alphabetical and my eye ran to the very end:

> *Zayky, Pavel*
> *Age: 36*
> *Address: Novokuznechaya, Krasnodar*
> *Occupation: University lecturer*
> *Charge: Treason by virtue of collaboration with the enemy*
> *Tried: In absentia*
> *Verdict: Guilty*
> *Sentence: Six years of hard labour*

I croaked some kind of thanks, and handed back the document. I left Wittram's study shaking. The document looked to be genuine, and I could see that it was to the advantage of the Nazis to make me aware. I was a full part of the German Reich now; there was no going back to Russia. Ever.

I was frightened, but angry too. I had not been a collaborator. Not a traitor. What I had done was for the good of mankind. I was working on increasing food outputs for all. Why couldn't they see that?

---

46   The trials in Krasnodar in July 1943 were the first public war crimes trials of the Second World War. https://www.youtube.com/watch?v=Z1DEjCrYeRY

Given a straight choice between Soviet Russia and Nazi Germany, up to that time, the Nazi regime seemed to be much more stable, more prosperous and an altogether better place to live. Unless of course you were a Jew or a Pole. But the meeting in Wittram's study marked the turning point in our experience with the Third Reich.

It happened incrementally, I suppose, starting with the failure of the 1943 harvest. Well, at least, that's what we were told, although I saw no signs of crop failure. I monitored weather conditions all over occupied Europe. I knew what was being planted, where and when. I didn't think the harvest could have been a failure, but that's what the authorities said. It was the excuse used for reducing the rations. Our Blockleiter was a short, fat and smelly man called Hiltze, who told me quite openly that he was disgusted by Russians and was seemingly delighted when the number of ration coupons was officially reduced. Obviously we were all used to rationing. We had grown up in the USSR where rationing was a way of life. Everybody was always hungry in Russia to some extent.

Now more soldiers began to arrive along with all the attendant military infrastructure. And as more troops were drafted to the city so the pressure on housing increased. Wittram sent me a note to advise that our university lodgings had been requisitioned and we were being relocated by the town council.

We were sad to leave Blücherstraße, especially as our new apartment was a single basement room in Georgenstraße. From the street you walked down a flight of steps and then ducked through a low doorway. At least inside you could stand upright without stooping but the only natural light came through a narrow window to the left side of the door. The space was about five metres by four with a double bed at the end which could be curtained off from the rest of the room. Otherwise there was a couch which doubled as a bed for Sofia, a kitchen table, a sink, and a coal-fired stove. Water ran down the walls and everything was damp.

That Christmas, if you had four meat coupons, you were entitled to a hare, but we only had two. I spoke to the butcher and managed to get him to give us half a hare, but a good large one, which we roasted with potatoes. Very tasty. Delicious in fact. Nevertheless, I couldn't help compare our situation at Christmas 1943 to the year before when we had been decorating our tree – things were changing.

During early 1944 work at the university continued but salaries were reduced. Wittram sent a note explaining that salaries for all foreign workers throughout the Reich were being reduced but that the reductions were being aggregated and would be paid back as a lump sum after the war. The phrase 'after the war' was used frequently now. More food, more coal, more money – all available 'after the war'. Good news! As we had very little of any of these things by early 1944.

Air attacks began from the east. The first time the sirens went off for real I was at the University offices on Glogauerstraße. Rather than making for the University's shelter, I headed back towards Georgenstraße to try to find Sofia. The streets were in turmoil! Everybody was running, teeth clenched. Mothers pulling bouncing prams with one hand whilst dragging crying toddlers with the other. Coaches, cars and lorries thundering through the streets at full pelt, occasionally swerving to miss pedestrians running across the road. I ran too but after ten minutes the streets began to empty and within a further five minutes they became lifeless. The sirens switched off and there was dead silence.

People crowded near shelter doorways. Nobody wanted to sit inside the holes, but were afraid to be too far away. They stood silently, looking skyward, some smoking, others swaying gently perhaps through fear. I carried on walking. No one stopped me and eventually I reached our street where I found Sofia in the shelter at the end of the road reading stories to other children. Later on some bombs did fall but Posen escaped the worst of the raids. At that time, anyway.

But by the middle of 1944, the time when Sofia and I had gone to see *Junge Adler*, it was obvious the end was coming. The newspapers reported a new wonder-weapon, the V2 rocket, which some said would make a difference.

Hiltze came to me in Georgenstraße to demand that I join the Volkssturm home guard but I declined, explaining that I was part of the Russian Liberation Army – he was furious and stomped off complaining bitterly about me to anybody that would listen.

But people had started to dig trenches and wonder-weapons or not, Volkssturm or not, by December everybody spent some of their day with a shovel moving soil on the outskirts of the city. At the university we started work two hours later each morning to allow time for trench-digging. It became the people's obsession, it was a form of camaraderie and determination to halt the advance from the east.

However people began to take advantage of the digging as an excuse to get out of normal work – certainly this was true of university employees. When you stopped to think about it, you knew that the trenches were futile; if the Red Army had pushed forward a thousand miles, then a trench dug by well-meaning town folk was unlikely to slow the speed of their advance. And so, although digging the trenches fostered solidarity and engendered a kind of grim 'gallows humour', by the end of 1944 it had led to the ruination of the routine of normal city life. Posen was chaos.

As the fighting from the east drew closer, the newspapers began to consider the number of Russians already living in the Reich. Some suggested the Russian population in Germany was a gigantic 20 million. That was silly, but 10 million was probable. Prejudice grew. I understood why, but it became much harder to carry on living in the city.

Russian language books in the Posen library were suddenly withdrawn. Most of the books were written by English or French writers and had merely been translated into Russian, with only a very few by Russian authors. That made me angry. It was a stupid act to withdraw the books, an idiotic action, similar to the type of thing we had seen under the Soviets.

Now, things began to move more quickly and on Monday 15th January we got news of the Soviet advance over the Polish eastern border the previous Friday. A sinister feeling. By Wednesday of that week Warsaw had fallen and the air raids on Posen had stepped up but, by now, nobody cared about spending time in the shelters – everyone just wanted to get out.

By Thursday the streets were full of people pulling their sledges, piled high with possessions, towards the railway station. There was shouting all around. Crying and screaming. The station itself was a scene from hell. The people were kept on the street with the platforms guarded by the army; only passengers with advance tickets were allowed access. The roads leading to the station building were a teeming mass of terrified citizens who had all realised, too late, that the Soviet army were about to unleash murder upon the city and that there was no escape.

And for us? The Reichsuniversität academic staff were all evacuated. We were deemed as valuable to the Reich and requiring of redeployment elsewhere. It was a nonsense of course. By then I knew that all the universities in Germany had ceased to function. There was to be no redeployment. But the order to evacuate us in the event of a Soviet ground attack had been given months before, and the Germans always followed orders. That Friday, 19th January 1945, Professor Wittram (he had dropped the official SS-Hauptsturmführer title by then) solemnly shook hands and handed over train tickets and travel documents for me, Tanya and Sofia to take us to Berlin. We huddled inside the armoured car, which drove us to the station platform, Sofia clinging to me. Outside, the baying crowd spat and cursed, beating the side of the car with sticks.

We had a suitcase each and Tanya's included an old cigar box containing our precious photographs as well as our university certificates; but my volumes of research notes and the details of the Europe-wide academic web of learning had been left behind in my study at the Reichsuniversität.

I was devastated. We had thrown in our lot with the Nazis but their regime had failed. Now it seemed that only the broken regime's dogmatic adherence to following orders would provide any chance of escape.

6

PASHA ZAYKY

Salzgitter, April 1945
to March 1946

IT HAD BEEN TANYA WHO HAD SECURED OUR
eventual passage to the west of Germany. For the short
time that we were in Berlin I had been terrified of becoming
trapped. It was obvious that the Soviets were coming from
the east and would be bound to inflict heavy retribution on
the Nazi capital – they would certainly spare us no mercy
and our survival depended on getting out and making our
way west.

But the meeting with Kreisleiter Jerter at the
Ostministerum and then Tanya's interview with Paul Pleiger
had led us to Salzgitter: a brutal place; a prison. At Salzgitter
we were separated and segregated. It was a town of pure
misery. At the *personalabteilung* I dealt with the daily list of
worker deaths and their unwilling replacements so the work
was dull on the one hand and chilling on the other. But of
everything the worst was the shelling – the endless cacophony
of bangs, the shaking ground, the sirens. On and on, by day
and night. It drove me mad. I told Tanya I had had enough,

that I needed to get away, but she told me to pull myself together. We could not afford for me to be weak – not this close to the end. She was quite right of course. There was no room for such weakness in this environment. You just had to hang on. Get as much food as you could gather, ensure Sofia was properly fed, sleep if you were able, and make absolutely certain that you said or did nothing to upset anybody.

We arrived in Salzgitter in January 1945 and endured three full months of unremitting hell in that evil place. And then had come that day in early April; in the marshalling yard, when the bomb had dropped and the '*hasenjagd*' had followed. It had been my awakening to the reality of the *konzentrationslager* inmates; the slave labourers brought to Salzgitter to make steel from otherwise uneconomic low-grade iron ore. I had wondered about the daily lists of deaths. I should have realised sooner. Perhaps I had.

In the days after the shootings in the marshalling yard, during that first week of April, a fug descended. I went to work each day at the *personalabteilung* but now there was no work to do. The entire foundry and factory complex seemed to have run out of people. That week my time was spent doodling botanical images on pieces of scrap paper. Tanya turned up at the railway yard each morning. But steel production had ground to a halt – no problem with the diesel shunters this time – just manpower. Such workers that were left at the foundry, and there were visibly many fewer now, were either insufficient in number to actually make steel or were simply not being given any orders by management. So there were no freight train movements whilst scheduled train services had also ceased. The railway yard was silent. She and the other workmen filled in time.

Normally the works at Salzgitter belched black smoke into an atmosphere filled with the drone of machinery, the hammering of metal and the clank of the railways, but during that first week of April after Easter 1945 there was nothing. Even the anti-aircraft shelling stopped and the formations of planes, like clouds of black insects, flew day and night overhead, their passage to Berlin now completely unhindered.

And the weather was good, warm for the time of year, with little rain, and those guards who remained around the complex and its camps became listless. Almost carefree. The sharp protocols of camp life, particularly the curfews and the restrictions on coming and going from the barracks, so keenly enforced until very recently, were now relaxed. What a blessing; it meant I could walk down to see Tanya and Sofia every evening now and that I was no longer restricted to one Sunday afternoon per week. Thank God for that.

But although the guards, well all of us in fact, gave an impression of being carefree, a kind of nonchalance, just a slight scrape beneath the surface, a fraction, revealed the complete opposite. An acute tension. Nervousness. Trauma. The fear of the unknown. We were like feral cats, lazing in the sun, but unpredictable and with the ability to leap, snap, claw and cut, should somebody step just a millimetre too close.

For all of us in Salzgitter, the guards, the Volkssturm, the German civilians, all the foreigners like us, and the remainder of the KZ-Leute in the concentration camps, it was a waiting game. We all knew that the end was coming very soon.

On Tuesday 10th April only a few people came to work. It was just another dull day of botanical doodles and I left at 5pm. I wandered down to Tanya and Sofia's camp to eat with them in their food hall. After we put Sofia to bed we sat on the bench outside smoking a while, taking in the last of the day's warmth. But then at half past nine the alarm signal sounded for the full five minutes, just a continuous howl without any increase or decrease in tone. It was the warning for soldiers from the air, but I couldn't see any planes. We ran back inside and gathered up Sofia to make our way to the bunker. I could hear bombs, but still no planes. No – it was shelling not bombing, and then I could make out machine-gun fire too.

There were very few people in the bunker. A member of the Volkssturm was at the door and told us that it had been reserved for Germans only, but I responded with such a clear German accent that I think he mistook us for German anyway. Certainly, we were not about to leave with Sofia, and it was not like there was a shortage of room. We sat in the bunker all night. The 10th April had been warm during the daytime but our sweat was cold that night.

Gradually, the bunker filled up with new arrivals sheltering from the battle outside. But at least we got updates on what was happening. Two German reconnaissance planes had been circling low over American forces near the factory, but then American fighter planes had driven them away. At about eleven thirty we heard that the American attack had been repulsed and all became quiet by half past midnight. We thought the Americans had been defeated – and I found myself knotted with a mix of emotions and thoughts; some elation that 'our' German troops had done so well; some surprise that the meagre force remaining around the town could have halted the Americans, and in some part a feeling of devastation and sickness that the waiting game had to continue.

But by 1am on Wednesday 11ᵗʰ April the battle started up once more. The rattle of machine guns was much closer now, and fresh incomers to the bunker reported that a huge number of American tanks had appeared on the roads of the town. With our heads tucked down deep in the bunker we prayed, as the thunder of the gods roared outside.

The shriek of invasion, or should that be liberation, continued for nearly three hours but by 5am all had been silent for a while and we ventured out. Dawn had not yet broken but it was to be another warm day and there was that pink ethereal light you get just before the sun. The smell of woodsmoke combined with a noxious sweet smell from the burning hulk of an American tank in silhouette just by the railway crossing. The odour of acetone combined with the rotting fish smell of burning Bakelite. The tank's turret seemed to have shifted sideways on its body like a broken porcelain pot which had been badly repaired, the long muzzle of its gun was drooped, pointing disconsolately at the ground, one of its caterpillar tracks had sheared and was half left on the road behind it like a trail of blood from a wounded soldier. Somebody said that a boy from the Hitlerjugend had shot it with a Panzerfaust.[47] But I didn't believe it.

---

47 The Panzerfaust (armour fist) is an inexpensive single-shot, recoilless German anti-tank weapon of World War II. It consists of a small disposable pre-loaded launch tube firing a high-explosive anti-tank warhead, intended to be operated by a single soldier. The Panzerfaust was in use from 1943 until the end of the war. https://www.pinterest.co.uk/pin/234398355584166656/

Gradually people appeared from other shelters. Crowds gathered. The Nazi party pins and swastika insignia had now disappeared whilst those in uniform emerged without their jackets. There were certainly lots of tanks and lots of American soldiers but the frontline had passed right through Salzgitter and pushed on eastwards – we could hear the cannonade throughout that day but it grew ever more distant. Despite the huge noise of the guns during the night, we heard just three people had been killed during the battle for Salzgitter, and certainly, apart from the dead tank by the railway, the damage seemed relatively slight. In fact, I later saw that it was the forest outside the town which had been cut down by the shelling of the advancing army. Now, boys and girls stood around chatting to the Americans who gave them chocolate.

I stayed with Tanya and Sofia all that day. Clearly nobody was going to go to work and it was not safe to be separated. The KZ-Leute had been released from the camps as had all the remaining inmates at the Lager 21 penal camp. They were like zombies. Half-dead and slowly wandering around the town, almost lethargically they leant against windows until they shattered and then stole anything and everything they could find. The Germans looked on initially but then decided that they were not about to be outdone. And so they joined in, both looting and attacking anybody who appeared to be carrying anything.

At Tanya's camp a Polack walked past carrying half a bag of rice. A group of Germans appeared, just civilians in their sixties, I would say. They kicked the crap out of him. I can still see him on his side curled in a foetal position cradling his head with his hands as his blood ran along the concrete path. I don't know what became of him but that day many came back bloodied and beaten but carrying packs of working suits or blankets. Everything went within an hour or so. The first ones took all the good stuff, the rest simply took everything that was left, or beat up anybody carrying anything better than they had.

By midday the Americans started to pin up notices: a curfew from 1pm to 3pm each day and they would shoot down anybody who gave any resistance, stole or looted. There was a large supply of the notices; they had been preprinted well in advance. They could have been put up at the start of the day, but the Americans clearly had experience of liberating European towns. The pent-up tension of the populace awaiting the arrival of the liberators – the feral cats all ready to leap – was only to be dissipated by actively allowing the looting and the beating. A real bloodletting was a necessary evil in the eyes of the liberators.

And by the evening, despite the curfew having ended some hours earlier, the streets remained deserted. Just enormous quantities of American mechanised military might heading east. Their vehicles were huge. Tanks, tractors hauling massive cannons, and lorries packed full of men with machine guns jammed the streets. There were some small cars for commanders, most of them equipped with very long antennas sticking up into the sky, or tied down to the front so that they didn't foul telephone lines running across the roads.

When the Wehrmacht had marched into Krasnodar they were as an army almost like a human machine. That was one of the reasons why Tanya was so approving of their arrival. You couldn't say the same about the Americans; they looked like a rabble. But a very large rabble. In fact everything about them was large. Yes, obviously they had big machines, but also as human beings they were simply giants. They were all such athletic, strong fellows; although some were plump, and even fat. They were so much better fed than anybody from Europe that I had seen up to that time. Everyone looked solid, stronger and more impressive than the German army had looked during its offensive on Russia, but not as neat and tidy.

Both the ordinary soldiers as well as the officers wore helmets. It was hard to tell who was in charge as nobody was smartly dressed, everybody was covered in dust and sunburnt. But there was no worn-out or torn clothing; everything was new and top quality.

And they had chocolate and tinned rations, which they gave out to us all. That was wonderful.

The following day, Thursday 12th April, I returned to work. There were Americans inside the factory. They had set up their headquarters there. The doors to my offices were open and the desks and sideboards had been broken. Various items of stationery had been looted, even my botanical drawings! I spent the first part of the day setting upright what office furniture could be salvaged and breaking down the remainder for firewood.

At the camps, national flags started to appear nailed to roofs, homemade from bedsheets and paint – French, Polish, Czech and the Hammer and Sickle as well. People started wearing pins of their flags on their jackets. Nazi brown shirts were no longer worn, and proved to be about the only clothing item that remained in the factory warehouse after the looting.

For the remainder of April, news came of a string of German surrenders, with huge numbers taken as prisoners of war. It was the news as supplied by the Allied forces but nobody disputed its accuracy. Over 800,000 German soldiers had surrendered on the Eastern front, and I was so relieved that we had been able to make it far enough to the west to have been liberated by the Americans, rather than to have come back under Soviet control.

We heard about the 60,000 prisoners freed from the concentration camp at Bergen-Belsen. Of course, that had been where the train, hit by the bomb in the railway yard, had been bound. As news of the Nazi atrocities unfolded Tanya and I did not discuss our own part in them. But I had been the registrar for the KZ-Leute that day at the railway yard whilst Tanya had been the person to marshal their waiting train alongside one that had been packed with high explosives. Were we guilty? No. We just followed orders the same as everybody else in the Nazi regime. We did what we were told to avoid the awful consequences of refusal. But I did realise that we were fortunate not to have been given orders that had led to crimes in the eyes of the law.

Of course we felt some guilt but we were not personally responsible. What we did was simply for survival. I was a botanist and a university professor. It was only the circumstances of the war that had led me to the personnel bureau at the Salzgitter factory. Tanya was an engineer and it was only because of the war that she had ended up working on the railway in Salzgitter arranging the transport of slave labourers. It wasn't our fault. We had to survive for the sake of each other. For the sake of Sofia. We were not responsible for the actions of the Nazis. We had never willingly been part of their regime.

Those weeks in late April 1945 became known as the Zusammenbruch[48] – the fall of the Nazi regime. For the townsfolk of Salzgitter, especially the local shopkeepers, the Nazis had brought the steel foundry and prosperity; furthermore the town had escaped with very little Allied bombing. But now, for the ordinary German people of Salzgitter, the end of the war actually marked the start of their troubles. The released KZ-Leute became a scourge, smashing windows, stealing whatever they could find whilst the Americans simply stood by and let it happen. The warning notices proclaiming that looters would be shot were just ignored. Slightly bizarrely, I felt, they still went back to their camps to live and sleep, but I suppose that there was nowhere else for them. We did hear that many prisoners died after liberation simply because their stomachs, having been deprived of food for so long, could not cope with the high fat content found in the American rations. Some ordinary Germans said that the American and British troops knew what they were doing and deliberately overfed the KZ-Leute in the concentration camps after liberation just to create an opportunity for the film cameras. I didn't believe that. But I could see, when we watched those horrifying newsreels in the movie theatres, that most Germans were as appalled as we had been that day at the railway yard when we had first caught sight of those poor wretches.

On the grapevine I heard that a bottle of vodka could be exchanged for a bicycle at the KZ-Camps (a bicycle which would itself have been stolen property of course). The Ukrainians in my camp had unearthed quite a stash

---

48 Zusammenbruch: collapse (of a political regime).

of booze which they had found buried deep in a mine shaft, originally put there by persons unknown (and clearly now departed) for safe keeping. One bottle had come my way in exchange for translating some papers for one of the Ukrainians. A swap of a bottle for a bicycle seemed like too good a deal to pass up and so, carefully hiding the bottle under my coat, I went to the camp at Drütte. It was located in the centre of the factory complex and the barracks were built into the arches of a road overpass.

I got to the entrance. There were no guards; nobody at the gates. I was free to walk in. But I looked on at the scene laid out in front of me. To the left were dead prisoners piled up on the ground. To the right, a bonfire. Former prisoners sat around on the floor, with their backs against the barrack walls, their heads drooped to one side or another. Were they dead too? As I looked on, occasionally one would move his head or hand in some small way. The fire crackled; there was a banging sound, and somewhere a man was howling – in pain or madness? I could not tell. Rats ran openly around the bodies of the dead. There was, in fact, a bicycle. I could see it against the same wall as the inmates, but I turned and walked home, the bottle of vodka still inside my coat.

*

And then on 8th May it was all over. The Germans signed an unconditional surrender. No more curfews or blackouts. At night you could see lights from windows again – such an unfamiliar sight. Hitler and Goebbels were dead; Himmler was on the run. But what of Vlasov and the Russian Liberation Army? The news reports said that, in the very last days of the war, his forces had turned against the Waffen-SS in Prague and had helped the Czech resistance, but nothing more was said. I never heard of him again.[49]

As soon as the war ended so the American forces started to leave. The forest was full of American GIs with ladies of all nationalities exchanging favours for extra rations. There was much laughter and sometimes tears, although the latter were generally reserved for those German ladies who had garnered a few too many extra rations from the liberators so as to now be ostracised by their fellow countrymen and especially women.

We heard that about three and a half million American soldiers were leaving Europe to carry on the fight in Japan. By the middle of the month they had all gone and Salzgitter was now under the control of a garrison of British soldiers. The British were completely different to the Americans. First, they had little spare food or rations so the woodland frolicking rapidly came to an end; second, they were much more like the German troops, smarter uniforms, the command chain was clear; and third, by comparison with the Americans, there were hardly any of them. They were vastly outnumbered by the local people in the town, but that didn't matter. The British were in charge now and the Germans obeyed those in command. That I knew.

Alongside the British came a new organisation called the

---

49 General Andrey Vlasov's Russian Liberation Army finally fought the advancing Red Army on the river Oder in February 1945 but were pushed back to Prague. In early May 1945, following requests from his officers, Vlasov ordered his troops to change sides and attack SS forces to aid the Czech resistance. Immediately after the war Vlasov was captured by the Soviets and taken to Moscow where he and eleven of his senior officers were hanged on 1st August 1946.

United Nations Relief and Rehabilitation Administration. Because so many foreigners had been sent to labour at the foundry whilst the war had been on, Salzgitter found itself with massive concentrations of almost every nationality. As a result, other foreigners based elsewhere in the former Reich now began to gravitate to the town to meet up with fellow countrymen. More seemed to arrive into the camps each day. The Nazi regime, and the war, had caused the largest displacement of human life that the world had ever seen and much of it now converged in Salzgitter. So the UNRRA was tasked with the job of getting all these people back to where they came from. For us, this was very worrying. We had never gained German citizenship. We remained Soviet citizens. There was no way that I ever wanted Tanya, Sofia and I to be sent 'home'.

The first step was to master English, and happily by now my linguistic ability was such that learning another tongue was not that arduous. During the Nazi period English language books, just like Russian books, had disappeared from the libraries, but there was one author whose works had remained freely available: PG Wodehouse. His words lightened the darkest days towards the end of the war. I seem to recall *Money in the Bank*[50] as my favourite. It was, as Wodehouse would have said, 'a topping hoot'! Under the Americans I had read any English language newspaper I could lay my hands on from cover to cover, and watched lots of Hollywood movies. So between all of this I had the

---

50 *Money in the Bank* is a novel by PG Wodehouse, first published in the USA in January 1942. The book was published in English in Germany in August 1943, whilst UK publication was delayed as Wodehouse was under suspicion of collaboration with the Nazi regime.

basics, it was mainly just vocabulary and certain aspects of grammar that I needed to brush up on.

Generally, during that Zusammenbruch period, chaos reigned. Nobody knew what was going on and I reckoned that gleaning as much information as I could afforded us our best chance of thwarting any plan to ship us east. In such circumstances, the best thing to do was to go direct to the actual organisation which had been set the job of relocating the displaced persons to see what I could learn. And so, in mid-May 1945, I arrived at the door of the Salzgitter office of the UNRRA and asked to see the commanding officer.

After a relatively short delay I was shown into the office of a Major Angus McGrath. He wore a British army uniform but a UNRRA insignia on his jacket sleeve.[51]

He was in his mid-50s and the olive drab of his uniform set off his neat grey moustache, and the black lines under his eyes. The skin on his face was blotched red, and I could see the scarring of old burns on his hands as he scribbled away at the paperwork littering his desk.

I stood to attention. The Major spoke in German. 'Good morning, I'm McGrath, commander of the UNRRA here in Salzgitter… and you are?' His British accent was easily discerned but I felt that he had a reasonable grasp of the language.

Nevertheless, I decided to respond in English. 'I am Paul Zayky, coming to present myself to you, Major. I have, presently, been working within the Personnel section at the foundry, but I wonder whether I can be of assistance to you

---

51 http://www.usmilitariaforum.com/forums/index.php?/
topic/176700-unrra-overseas-cap-patch/

here at the UNRRA.' I had rehearsed my opening – 'Paul' rather than 'Pavel'. It wasn't a lie – it was merely a translation. It didn't work, however, as the Major looked at me keenly.

'What's your nationality, Zayky?'

No point in continuing a lie that would ultimately be found out.

'I'm Russian, sir, but have been living in Germany for some time. I wondered whether you might need help with translation as I do speak a number of languages.'

'I see, which ones, Zayky?'

'Russian, Ukrainian, Georgian, Polish, German, English, some Czech and a little French,' I responded rather proudly, listing them off with my fingers.

'Well, Zayky, you've certainly come to the right place… let's get you started.'

That was it! Interview over, I was put to work immediately at the Ausländerbüro (the foreigners' office) working alongside UNRRA officers translating during interviews, and interpreting foreign paperwork.

All foreigners had to register as *ausländers* and were induced to do so by a promise of better rations. You had to state your address and then stay put as otherwise you wouldn't get the extra provisions. The ration cards for each commodity had three red stripes for the *ausländers* but only two for the Germans nationals. For foreigners to get fifty per cent more food proved a continual source of confrontation – mostly from the Germans towards the French and Poles. Fights often broke out when groups of drunken men approached each other; normally resulting in bloody noses and cracked ribs. There were only a few major pitched battles which British soldiers had to break up using their rifle butts. Crucially, however, simply registering as an *ausländer* didn't ensure your passage back to your homeland as you were able to add a note to your file that you didn't want to leave Germany.

But I could see that it was the registration of the *ausländers* that the UNRRA were keen to have on file. It was a key bureaucratic exercise and once you had been added to the record then it allowed officials from anywhere in Europe or, more importantly for us, the Soviet Union, to peruse the files to see who was who – and where they were located. It seemed to me that despite the bait of the extra rations, registration as an *ausländer* was risky.

And so having discussed it with Tanya we decided to keep ourselves unregistered and cope with the more limited German rations.

More positively, however, by now my language abilities were such that I had started to give private lessons during lunchtimes and after work. There were plenty of British personnel needing to acquire some German vocabulary and I even taught some German nationals a little English. An hour's lesson cost a packet of cigarettes but a series of five would set you back a bottle of vodka. But the currency could vary – some paid by tea, others by tinned milk or canned vegetables. But the system worked well for us and with Tanya still working at the railway engine house we found ourselves beginning to become a little better off. Certainly this offset any disadvantage caused by our non-registration.

I provided the UNRRA with fast, accurate work but in return McGrath proved himself to be a good boss, introducing me to the Salzgitter Bürgermeister (the mayor) whose office controlled the flat rentals in the town. The

Bürgermeister was a pleasant old man, and I appealed to him to be allowed a flat given that Tanya and Sofia were still living apart from me within the camp system. Tanya was still coping with the horrible women in her barracks – although they did seem less of a problem now. Somehow the bombing that day at the railway yard had put a steel reinforcement into both of our coping mechanisms.

The Bürgermeister's office duly came up with an excellent flat for us in the town centre Kaufhaus building, in the attic on the fourth floor. It was a long walk up the stairs but it was a wonderful two-bedroom apartment. Newly built, like most of Salzgitter, it was the highest point in the whole of the town. And there was central heating with electricity as well. We actually had an electric cooking hob – I had never seen anything like it before. Technically our bathroom was shared with the flat on the third floor but the man who lived there only had one leg and always stayed with friends who lived elsewhere in a ground-floor apartment. I never understood why the Bürgermeister would give a third-floor flat to a one-legged man – but maybe he didn't like him.

I managed to steal some old beds from Camp 43, which by this time had been abandoned as the previous French occupants had been sent home. Later on, Tanya found us a cupboard and a table, and took out our photographs from the cigar box and propped them up on our new (to us) furniture – so now it was home. I looked at our family set out on that table and just smiled. The sunlight streaming in to our new attic flat was just as strong as the sunlight in the yellowed picture of Tanya and Pyotr fishing on the Kuban.

By early summer that year most of those who had asked to return to Russia had been granted their wish. During their interviews at the Ausländerbüro some said that they would be welcomed back as returning heroes, others that they had heard they would be delivered to health resorts in reward for their sufferings at the hands of the Nazis. The British army trucks took them the 110 kilometres to the transfer camp in Magdeburg, at the border of the Soviet sector. There they were unloaded and never heard of again.

Sunday 24th July 1945 was Russian Orthodox Trinity. In Camp 49 they set up a Russian Orthodox church. We had never been churchgoers but now we began to attend. There were lots of Cossacks who remained in the camps and, although never an outgoing person, Tanya enjoyed spending time with her fellow countrymen. Our priest was Father Nagovsky; Sergey, a young man, tall, clean-shaven, gawky and angular, who gave the impression of being slightly uncomfortable in his own skin. He had a wonderful voice for incantations but was always awkward in his movements. He needed all the help he could get for guidance on the administration of the needs of his flock, many of whom struggled with alcohol addiction brought on by separation from their families, and he sought advice and help from any other local priests of whatever denomination who were prepared to become involved.

At tea after the Trinity service I was surprised to see Major McGrath who turned out to have been a chaplain in the British Army before leaving to join the UNRRA. He had become one of Sergey's helpful local priests – with a wealth of experience built up from years of service starting from his work in the regular army in the trenches during the first war.

'Major McGrath, this is my wife Tanya and our daughter Sofia.'

McGrath shook hands warmly with Tanya and tousled Sofia's hair. 'Angus, please,' he said. It was a warm long late July evening, and when the last of the churchgoers departed after tea Sergey produced two large jars of *selyodka*.[52] We all walked back into town and up the long winding stairs to our attic. Having settled Sofia down to bed, the four of us, me, Tanya, Sergey Nagovsky and Angus McGrath played cards, ate herring and drank more tea as well as sweet vodka long into the night. We discussed the world; politics, religion, fear, death and redemption. Heavy topics, indeed, over which we debated, we disagreed, but perhaps surprisingly given the subject matter, we laughed. In fact, we laughed together all that evening. It was a great night. We all became firm friends.

The 7th January 1946 was Russian Christmas. Tanya, Sofia and I all went to church at Camp 49. Sergey was getting better! It was a super service. We all took communion and Sofia attended confession after. Later, the children put on a play and read poems in Russian and Ukrainian. Sofia was given a cone of sweets and a red needlework box, although the boys were given a train which made Sofia jealous as she wanted to be like Mama! At the reception after the service Angus made a great speech of thanks to Sergey and interspersed English with some jokes told in Russian – I had been coaching him. Everyone howled with laughter

---

52 Salted herring.

although I think his English accent was funnier than the stories he told.

In late February 1946 I managed to buy a radio. It was an elderly three lamp receiver made by Volksempfanger and cost me 1,800 marks. Some of the cost I paid in cash and the rest I was able to pay in cigarettes, having now built up a stack of packets in exchange for lessons. I recall that one packet of German cigarettes covered 60 marks whilst each packet of English or American cigarettes covered 80–100 marks depending on the brand. I struggled to haul the huge set up the four flights of stairs, but made it eventually, then rigged up the antenna. We got a fabulous reception in our high attic room – such a good sound.

The radio made our understanding of the news much more immediate and rather more accurate than some of the more garbled newspaper stories, or the overly gushing reports of the Pathé or Movietone reels. We listened to the United Nations conference and the meeting of the Security Council with talks by Andrey Vyshinsky.[53] In March, Churchill gave a speech in America entitled 'The Sinews of Peace',[54] which was broadcast live late at night – I had to have the volume turned right down so as not to disturb anybody. Having lived under Soviet tyranny, the chilling

---

53 The Soviet foreign minister.

54 On 5th March 1946 Winston Churchill delivered his famous 'Iron Curtain' speech in Fulton, Missouri. Correctly titled 'The Sinews of Peace', the speech was part of a programme that began at 3.30pm CST. Churchill surprised the world with an attack on the spread of Soviet Communism. He said, 'From Stettin in the Baltic to Trieste in the Adriatic, an iron curtain has descended across the Continent.' The metaphor of an iron curtain, as used at theatres for fire protection, referred to the sealing off of a conquered area.

words Churchill spoke that night rang completely true to me.

We also listened in on Russian broadcasts made in the Soviet sector. In early August one item reported on the forced repatriation of Russian defectors to the German Army, making specific reference to the Wehrmacht's Cossack regiment and the summary punishment delivered.[55] 'No single person from that regiment escaped our vengeance.' It was shocking but not difficult to imagine their fate. And, just like our worker colleagues from the camps who had volunteered to return to Russia in the hope of welcome garlands or recuperation holidays, those troops of the German Cossack regiment were never heard from again. They faced either the firing squad or the noose. They knew it; the Allied soldiers who handed them over to the Russians knew it. And as we sat in our attic flat listening to the details of their forced repatriation, both Tanya and I knew it too. I wept. Tanya didn't weep, she never cried, but she ground her teeth and hardened her brow.

Beloved Pyotr – that skinny boy in shorts, no shoes, grinning as he turned to the camera, with his fishing line dangling in the water, his face caught in the dazzling sun –

---

55   At the Yalta Conference it had been agreed that Western Allies would return Soviet citizens. 'Operation Keelhaul' was the forced repatriation of Russians by British and American forces to the Soviet NKVD. Those returned included former members of the XVth SS Cossack Cavalry Corps. In *Victims of Yalta*, Nikolai Tolstoy describes the scene of Americans returning to an internment camp after delivering a shipment of people: 'The Americans returned visibly shamefaced. Before their departure from the rendezvous in the forest, many had seen rows of bodies already hanging from the branches of nearby trees.'

was dead. Those bastards killed him for being true to his real people: the Kuban Cossacks. But we were still alive; we had to survive for the sake of Sofia. There was to be no return to Russia for us.

7

PASHA ZAYKY
Salzgitter, August 1945

S OFIA'S SCHOOL WITHIN THE CAMP HAD PROVED AN
excellent and remarkably durable institution. As the final
stages of the war had progressed, so Sofia's classmates had
come and gone but her teachers, two elderly German ladies,
had remained constant. As a result, and as she approached
her tenth birthday, her German was now completely natural
with no trace of an accent, her mathematics was quick with
her times tables committed to memory, whilst her knowledge
of science, especially biology, was outstanding. When you
have dreams for your children, you hope they might follow
in your footsteps and when she had been younger I confess
to dreaming that she might be the third generation of the
family to become a botanist. But it dawned on me that her
interests lay in animal, and particularly human, physiology –
bone structures – muscle tissue – nerve systems. Not botany;
in fact, Sofia was a budding physician.

The school had originally been established for the
children of the Volksdeutsche peoples working at the plant;
we had been privileged to allow Sofia to attend – a blessing

of Paul Pleiger, or at least thanks to his secretary, when Tanya had originally secured the job at the railway. By the end of the war nobody regarded themselves as Volksdeutsche any longer. You were either a German citizen or a foreigner, and Sofia's classmates originated from Poland, Ukraine, Hungary and Yugoslavia but there were some other Russians as well.

On Saturday 17th August 1945 at the school, completely out of the blue, a van arrived loaded with a special delivery of parcels. Each was wrapped in brown paper and tied with string in a bow complete with a luggage label bearing a child's name written in a swirling green ink. Such huge excitement! The teachers stopped lessons and called out the names on the packages one by one for each child to come up to collect. Each parcel contained a tin of powdered milk, two tins of corned beef, two tins of fish, a bar of chocolate, a packet of tea, a packet of dried plums, sultanas, a little bag of pepper, a tiny tin of cooking oil, a tin of cheese, a bag of sugar, and a packet of custard cream biscuits. You can just imagine the gasps of pleasure from the children as they unwrapped their wonderful boxes of delicious food. But at the end there were three children without parcels: two little boys and Sofia, and all three burst into tears. The parcels were only for those children whose families had registered as *ausländers*.

That evening Sofia sobbed herself to sleep. She wanted to know why she hadn't got a parcel and, of course, we couldn't explain. The parcels were carefully designed to tease out any families who had ducked registration as *ausländers* to that point, and they proved very effective. The *ausländers* already got more food than German nationals and whilst Tanya and I continued to resist registration (and to be fair now that I was earning extra rations from the language lessons we were no longer short of essentials), the children's parcels proved a heavy inducement to mop up any stragglers.

The issue was that the operation by the Western Allies to send Russians back to the USSR wasn't limited to those who had formally defected – like the XVth Cossack Brigade – it covered everybody, including us. Up to then, by avoiding inclusion as *ausländers* in the UNRRA register, we had avoided official detection but the longer we stayed in Salzgitter so more and more people knew who we were and where we were from.

Angus didn't come to Sergey's service at the Russian church that Sunday, and so I went straight to see him in his office on the Monday morning. I remained angry about the children's parcels – it was a dirty, underhand trick by the authorities.

'Did you know?' I demanded. Angus looked blank and then turned purple as I explained what had happened at the school that Saturday.

'I know the ministry men and some German officials were here with the Red Cross, about ten days ago. But I was told that they were just taking names for a vaccination programme. I swear I didn't know this was going to happen, Pasha. I am so sorry. Poor Sofia.'

I believed him. He was a good man. We drank coffee together.

'You know, Pasha, they are turning up the heat. I will do all I can to protect you, I promise I shall, but I think you are going to have to come up with some kind of alternative. There are lorries of people heading east every day.'

Angus was quite correct. Later that week a Russian jeep came into town. Three men in NKVD uniforms entered the

UNRRA and started going through the registers. I think, but will never know for sure, that those previously loaded onto the trucks to head east were promised extra rations or better treatment if they could identify any other Russians who remained. If I'm right, then on that basis our names must have been mentioned. It is almost stupid to think that the harridans of Tanya's dormitory, Shukova, Averina and Gavrikova, would not have given up our names, simply out of spite, let alone if they were promised extra rations of cigarettes. Then, it would have been a straightforward task for the NKVD to check off names given by repatriatees against those remaining on the *ausländer* list to see who was missing from the official register. The NKVD had no power in the western sector, but they could simply arrange for the British army to do their rounding up for them.

It was the purges all over again. We went to bed each night, windows wide open in the summer heat, listening out for the squeal of brakes from a truck full of soldiers coming to get us. This couldn't go on.

The following Monday, 26th August, Angus stopped by my desk at the agency in the late morning as I was writing up the translation of an interview. He spoke quietly and quickly.

'Pasha, I have received a letter this morning from the German Ausländeramt[56] noting your name, among others, and asking your whereabouts. I will have to tell them, although I plan to explain that you are essential to our work here, and therefore that you should be regarded as a reserved person. And, Sergey came to see me last night. On my advice

---

56   Foreign Office.

he has left the church at the camp and gone into hiding. I don't know where he is now; I can't know.'

I felt sick, but Angus was right, he couldn't lie, and making me a reserved person at least might buy some more time. The day dragged on. I found myself completely unable to concentrate. With my pen in my hand I stared at the notes in front of me, watching the words swim around the page.

At 5pm a trim middle-aged woman wearing a pressed grey flannel suit arrived at the UNRRA offices. Her dark hair was worn in a bun, her face was set. I saw her mutter some words to the officer at the front desk who turned and pointed towards Angus's office, his door ajar. She strode over, knocked on the outside frame and then entered, immediately closing the door after her. I could hear raised voices. I tried, in vain, to continue with my translation.

Presently Angus's door opened and he stepped out.

'Pasha, could you join us please?'

With my heart pounding, I rose and walked to the office, my footsteps seemingly ringing loud against the tiled floor, although I'm sure that, in reality, they were perfectly quiet. Angus was by the door and as I entered he placed his hand behind me against my upper arm and shoulder. A movement so quick and imperceptible that nobody else could have noticed, but it provided just a moment of strong, unspoken, support. And I was grateful for it. Angus spoke.

'Herr Zayky, please allow me to introduce Frau Richter from the Ausländeramt in Braunschweig[57]...'

The woman in the flannel suit was seated as I had entered but now rose, took one step forward and shook

---

57   Braunschweig: the town of Brunswick.

hands with a single firm jerk. 'Thank you, Herr Major.' I could see the crow's feet at the corners of her eyes. Her thin lips were painted a dark red, and above her top lip the rouge had bled upwards into deep-set creases made by heavy drags on a thousand cigarettes. I suspected that she had endured a hard war.

'Herr Zayky, my duty here today is to let you know that the new German government, supported by the Allies, wishes for you and your family to return to your Russian homeland. As such I have papers here formally authorising your extradition and repatriation.'

I shot a glance across to Angus in panic, but he momentarily met my eyes with a look that said 'Hold on, Pasha – stay strong.'

'Major McGrath has explained that he regards you as essential to the work here, and has provided me with a letter to this effect; so I will report back to my superiors. Frankly, I would have thought that we have many other, native German translators who can perfectly well fill any void you may create at the UNRRA when you return to Russia, but this must be sanctioned elsewhere.'

I relaxed just slightly. McGrath's ruse seemed to have worked.

'I expect I shall return later next week,' she continued. The conversation seemed to have concluded, but then she said, 'But Frau Zayky, and your daughter? I wonder if your wife's work at the railway is deemed as essential as yours. I expect they could be returned immediately.'

I saw Angus's jaw drop open, as my own stomach heaved.

After the interview, I put together my things to leave as quickly as I could, but ended up getting to the exit as the same time as Frau Richter. It was a large wood-panelled swing door and as I held it open for her, she marched through and nodded in acknowledgement, keeping her eyes fixed forward. She headed on towards a waiting car. Still holding the door, I looked back into the office. I could see Angus, his office door open once more, on the telephone, frowning and staring down at his desk. I left, there was no time to lose now, and half ran back through the town to our building. My mind was whirling with options and wild, half-formed ideas, but they were all so random and at odds with each other. There was no sense of a cogent plan. Angus had said that our priest, Father Sergey Nagovsky, had run for his life. But how could we do that with Sofia? Hiding with a ten-year-old child was not an option; but then neither was us returning to Russia.

As I hurried along, there was a tap on my shoulder;

'Herr Zayky…'

I turned sharply, was this it? Had Frau Richter obtained her orders to reject Angus's appeal so soon, was this a soldier to arrest me? No, it was an old man with a kindly face.

'Herr Bürgermeister…?' The old man smiled warmly at my recognition. I remained grateful to him and his office for helping us secure our apartment some months before, but in the current circumstances I found it difficult to return his smile.

'I'm pleased to catch you, Zayky. On your way home, I expect. Major McGrath mentioned to me that you have rats in that top-floor attic. That's not healthy for your daughter. Here, take these keys. They are for the flat below you at the Kaufhaus, the one on the third floor. It is let to my cousin but he only has one leg and can't climb the stairs. And so he lives with us, actually he's lived with us since 1919. His flat has always been what the English call a bolt-hole. It might help you to have such a bolt-hole, even just for a few days to avoid the rats.'

Thankfully, both Tanya and Sofia had beaten me back to the attic flat. Tanya listened carefully to the events of the day, questioning me closely on the precise detail of what had been said. And then the three of us descended one flight of stairs to the third-floor flat where somebody had been in before us to make up the beds. The flat was dusty and airless but despite the heat of the evening we decided to keep the windows shut so as not to alert anyone to our presence. Upstairs our possessions had all been left in place; well, all apart from our photographs, which were just too precious to leave. We had taken them from their place on the table to join us in our temporary refuge – the bolt-hole.

During the purges, the NKVD would have come at 3am, but that was most uncivilised, and so, that night, the British arrived at 10pm. Despite the closed windows of the third-floor flat, we heard the squeal of the lorry coming to a halt outside the Kaufhaus, the stomp of boots up the stairs, and then the bang on the door of our attic flat above us. We heard them call out Tanya's and Sofia's names – chilling! Some loud footsteps on the floorboards. And then they left, running back down the stairs right past the door on the third floor, as we three sat together, in darkness, on the edge of Sofia's bed, holding our breath.

At 6am the following morning there was a soft tap on the door to the third-floor flat. We had all been awake for an hour, having slept badly in unfamiliar beds and with the terror of our predicament foremost in our minds.

'Pasha… Tanya… it's Angus,' called the familiar voice from outside the door. Thank goodness! We quickly and quietly opened the door and welcomed him in.

'Forgive the early morning intrusion, but I have brought bread, cheese and some milk,' he said as he placed a small parcel and a covered jug on the table. Although we had missed supper the previous evening I found myself with no appetite that morning, but was pleased to see Tanya and Sofia tuck into Angus's breakfast provisions.

'Did they come?' he asked.

'Yes, and they missed us. Thank God for our relocation to this apartment. Angus, thank you for arranging that with the Bürgermeister.'

Angus frowned. 'Well I'm afraid you're still on a rather sticky wicket. They'll be back, you see. Neither of you can go to work today and Sofia mustn't go to school. I've been thinking about what to do now, and I might have come up with something,' he continued.

Despite being late summer, it was just after 6am and there was a sufficient chill in the air for Angus to have come wearing his overcoat. Now he pulled out some crumpled paperwork from an inside pocket, and a couple of rubber ink stamps along with a tin inkpad from his side pockets – his fingertips gaining some stains of red ink in the process.

'Pasha, they are after you all. They know you exist and have both your address and your respective places of work. I'm afraid you can't outrun them, certainly not with Sofia. Last evening I wrote to an old school chum, Davenport. Haven't seen him for years, but I know he has some job or another in the Colonial Office in Whitehall. Given your abilities as a translator, I thought that if I provided a letter of introduction and recommendation then there could be a possibility that they would give you a job in London. If they took you on then you might all get British citizenship down the line…'

Angus handed me one of the papers from the table – a copy of his letter to his friend. I read it briefly, the usual British pleasantries, and then an introduction to me, a little about my previous work as a botanist, an agrarian specialist, and then going on to extol my value as a translator. It was a good letter.

'Angus, thank you so much also for this. But I don't understand how can we possibly escape the Russians to get to London even to allow us to follow up on this introduction.'

'Well I might have been able to cover that, I think. You see the problem is that you are Soviet citizens and therefore the British are duty-bound to return you to your comrades. However, had you left Russia, within say, the first five years after 1917 then you could make a reasonable case to the authorities that you had never been a Soviet and therefore they had no cause to send you back there.'

Now that was an interesting thought. But flawed, I felt. 'I can see that but, as you've said, they already know who we are.'

'Indeed they do, but I think you might need to pretend to be somebody else for the next few days. Sofia, can you play pretend?'

Sofia, still munching on rye bread, but wide-eyed, nodded. She rather regarded Angus as the *dyedushka*[58] she had never had.

---

58 *Dyedushka*: Grandpa, often shortened to 'Dyeda'.

'Yes!' she said eagerly, her mouth still full of bread. 'I'm very good at playing pretend!'

'Indeed, I'm sure you are. Well I think you're going to have to help Mama and Papa to be good at pretend as well.' He turned to look at me again. 'What we need for you all is something that in some parts of Whitehall[59] they call a "legend". Last night I had Joan at the office type some of these up.'

Now he pushed across the other crumpled papers on the table. They were dog-eared and stained. They had been folded and unfolded many times and, in fact, had slightly torn along the creases. They were forged identity papers, one set for each person, recording their travels across Europe – but these were the travels of a family named Zaitsev rather than Zayky, father Pavel, mother Tanya, and daughter Sofia; the new us.

We remained as Russians – of course – but these papers made Tanya and I seven years older. Now I had been born in 1900 and Tanya in 1903. We had left Russia together in 1921 towards the end of the civil war, to travel to Bulgaria to live in its capital where Sofia, named after that beautiful Balkan city, had been born in 1933 (she had gained a more modest three years in age). In 1937 we had moved on to Czechoslovakia, to Posen in 1943, and finally to Salzgitter in 1944. The very last papers he produced were blank, but perfectly genuine, United Nations documents. Angus got us to sign with our new names, where required, and then he applied the official rubber stamps with heavy red ink,

59 Whitehall is the street in London, close to Parliament, where most government offices are located.

just slightly obscuring the edges of our signatures. Our new 'legends' showed that whilst we remained of Russian extraction and ethnicity, we could not be regarded as Soviet citizens. Angus, the ex-army chaplain and senior UN official, had worked a miracle in subterfuge. Now we were officially '*staatenloser*' – stateless. The load on my heart lightened just a little, I began to see some hope.

'Angus, this is wonderful. I don't know how we can thank you enough, but we still need to get ourselves to London and for that I assume we need travel permits. I don't suppose you also have a supply of those too…?'

'Pasha, I'm sorry, but I do not. You're quite correct, however, you will have to go to the BAOR[60] administration in Lübbecke for your travel permits. And I really think that the only safe thing is for you all to do this today.'

*

We left the flat at 7.30 that Tuesday morning. Angus went down first to make sure there was nobody in the street watching out for us, but everywhere was still quiet save for some early morning workers moving around. He escorted us to the railway station and waited to see us onto the train to Braunschweig where we changed to take a fast train to Minden. From there our journey continued on the pretty little narrow-gauge line that ran over the river Wesser, where steamers tugged barges along the narrow waterway.

On the way we rehearsed our stories. Sofia was fine with her new identity and fully embraced the idea of playing

---

60   BAOR: British Army on the Rhine.

pretend as suggested by Angus. But Tanya was much less happy with keeping up a subterfuge. Tanya is a very blunt person. In modern terms you could describe everything she does and the way she behaves as binary. In Tanya's life there is only 'do' or 'not do', there is no concept of 'try' or some other middle ground. Playing pretend was, for Tanya, simply to lie. And lying was a 'not do'. I realised that if we were to obtain exit permits then I would have to do the talking.

Our little narrow-gauge train finally wound into Lübbecke just after 1pm.

Lübbecke, in East Westphalia, is about 130 kilometres west of Salzgitter. Not to be confused with the Baltic port city of Lübeck to the north, the town of Lübbecke largely escaped damage during the war and was occupied by the British in 1945 without significant resistance. Nearby Bad Oeynhausen became the headquarters of the British forces whilst administration matters for the entire British occupied zone were taken care of in Lübbecke town itself.

On arrival, our first call was, on Angus's recommendation, to the Deutsches Haus Hotel for lunch. It was a pretty guest house in the old town centre. Painted white with a leafy beer garden to the side and rear, its restaurant was panelled in dark carved oak. There were several British servicemen in uniforms lunching already, but no other children, and the staff made a fuss of Sofia, which of course she loved. With my anxiety having caused me to skip both supper and breakfast, I found myself famished. The food was good with large portions and I wolfed down a feast of pea soup followed by sausage whilst Tanya and Sofia, who ate rather more modestly, laughed at my moans of delight as I satiated my hunger.

Holland

Lübeck

Hamburg

Bremen

BRITISH ZONE

Celle

Hanover

Lübbecke   Saltzgitter

Berlin

Soviet
Zone

Dresden

French
Zone

U.S.
Zone

French
Zone

Munich

It was a happy lunch but every so often Tanya and I would catch each other's eye. We were about to play a game with very high stakes. By now it was 3pm and it seemed unreasonable to think that we could make it back to Salzgitter that evening and so after lunch we booked a room at the hotel for an overnight stay.

Having finished lunch and booked a room there were no further excuses to put off our game of chance. My nervousness returned. Angus had briefed us on where to go and what to say: in short, to go to the Passport Control Office located in the old town council building in Kaiserstraße, to make ourselves known and then to request military exit permits. This would be the point where we would have to provide our 'new' official papers, and therefore for us to play 'pretend' – for real. If we messed this up not only would we be arrested, we would be extradited immediately. In addition, it was very likely that Angus would end up out of a job (or worse).

As we left the Deutsches Haus and walked back towards the railway station and to Kaiserstraße, it seemed to me that almost the entire town had become British. The shops all had British signs and sold all sorts of goods, unfamiliar to us at the time, but obviously stalwarts of British life – Marmite and Ovaltine amongst others. Even the non-military cars on the street were British Austins and Rovers. Walking through the town was like being on a classic British movie set; I could have sworn that I saw Celia Johnson and Trevor Howard walking by, arm in arm.[61] It was only the traditional German

---

61   Celia Johnson and Trevor Howard played the lead roles in David
     Lean's 1945 film *Brief Encounter*.

architecture that suggested we were anywhere other than some small market town in a southern county of England.

At the Passport Control Office we made ourselves known and then waited, only a short while, before being called up to a counter to be seen by a Miss Fiquelmont, a slim but rather plain and unsmiling English lady in her late twenties. Following Angus's 'script' I explained that I had been asked to attend an interview at the Colonial Office in Whitehall and that we would like exit permits to allow us all to travel, explaining that it would be very educational for Tanya and Sofia to see London. She examined our papers carefully, taking them person by person, looking down at the words and then staring across the counter at each of us in turn. She looked very solemn and we must have done too. Tanya, in particular, glared at Miss Fiquelmont throughout. There was no point in me trying to catch Tanya's eye and fixing a smile on my face hoping that she would realise that hers looked so dark – this was simply Tanya's usual demeanour in such circumstances. The situation was tense and my heart was in my mouth; I knew full well that our cover stories would not stand to close questioning.

'You're very pretty. Do you have a boyfriend?'

'Sofia!' I exclaimed. But Tanya started to laugh – and thank goodness for that.

Miss Fiquelmont first went pink and opened and closed her mouth several times, before saying, 'Why thank you… thank you… errr…' She looked down again at the papers in front of her. '… Sofia. How lovely!'

According to our 'new' papers Sofia was supposed to be thirteen – would a thirteen-year-old ever have said such a thing? But Sofia had ensnared Miss Fiquelmont's heart with the word 'pretty'; now the English lady recovered from her first blush and her face broke into a wide and toothy smile. She almost skipped around the counter and knelt down to Sofia on the tiled floor.

'Well you're very pretty too, Sofia – do you have a boyfriend? If you tell me… then I will tell you!'

'Yes!' whispered Sofia, 'I'm in love with Hans!'

'Well, I'm in love with Billy, but he is in the army far away, and I miss him dreadfully.'

'Don't worry,' said Sofia, 'I know he can come home soon, and then you can marry.'

Miss Fiquelmont filled out our exit permits in no time, and then asked us to wait just a moment more whilst she took them into a small office at the back of the room, where we could see a spectacled man sitting at a desk. We could see her gesticulating, and yes… laughing. The spectacled man was, presumably, her superior and the forms required his final sign-off. My heart was in my mouth – again.

But she returned, still smiling, handed us the signed permits and offered Sofia a Trebor Extra Strong mint, which was gladly accepted.

As we walked down Kaiserstraße heading back to the Deutsches Haus Hotel, Sofia, still sucking her mint, whispered, 'Papa, I'm not really in love with Hans; he doesn't actually exist. I was just playing pretend.'

'I know darling; you're really very good at it.'

The following morning we headed back to Salzgitter, reversing our train journey from the previous day. But we didn't start out quite so early and the train connections on the return were not quite so well timed, so we didn't end up getting back to the station at Salzgitter until nearly 4pm.

On arrival, Tanya had prearranged with the stationmaster that we could use his telephone. I dialled, asked the operator to connect me to the UNRRA. Angus was on the line in moments. Having heard nothing from us for nearly a day and a half, he was relieved and delighted that the plan had worked, so far at least. We waited at the station and within about half an hour Angus appeared in a large black Humber car which he had borrowed from the UN motor pool. We couldn't risk returning to the Kaufhaus and so Angus had gone back there to pack for us. In the boot of the car were our suitcases, whilst our Volksempfanger radio balanced slightly precariously on the back seat. As Angus opened the boot to reveal our cases so Tanya looked at him, then at the suitcases and frowned.

'Yes, Tanya, don't worry, your photographs are all packed carefully in there,' assured Angus; by now he knew us well enough to be able to read our thoughts.

Having correctly read Tanya's mind he then turned to me quite aware that, having successfully obtained the exit permits in Lübbecke, I was now fretting over how the three of us would afford to buy tickets to travel all the way to London. Our trip to Lübbecke and the overnight stay had left us with relatively little cash. Angus had packed my stash of cigarettes taken in payment for language lessons, but although the currency they offered within the barter economy remained strong, I wasn't sure how far they would take us.

'Pasha, whilst you were in Lübbecke I was thinking that I might buy your radio. I don't have a radio at my flat and yours might be useful.'

Angus received his news reports through the UN and direct from the British. He was an avid reader and had never mentioned any desire to own a radio to me before. I could not believe that he really wanted to buy it from us. But the radio was huge and heavy and taking it with us would have been impossible in any event. It was also our most valuable asset and liquidating it for cash right now was exactly what was required. Of course I agreed.

It was then a haggle over price. But not in the conventional sense. Angus started too high and I argued him down – rather than the other way round. But in the end we settled on three pounds and ten shillings.[62]

We pulled up outside Angus's small flat, which was adjacent to the UNRRA offices in Salzgitter. He lived alone in a spartan single room; there was a sink, an electric stove, a desk, a chair, a wardrobe and a single bed. Almost every other square centimetre of floor space was now taken up with two further military camp beds, borrowed from the British army stores and set up for us for the night ahead.

Going back out to the car, Angus heaved the radio off the back seat and staggered back into the room, carefully placing the set on the table. He paid me the cash we had agreed, muttering about setting up the antenna some other time. But then he went to his battered brown leather briefcase and pulled out a cheque book. The camp beds on the floor left him no room to sit at the table but he leant over, extracted his pen and wrote a cheque payable to 'cash' for five pounds drawn on Hoare's of Fleet Street, which he then held out to me.

---

62 Under the old British pre-decimalisation currency there were 240 pennies to the pound and twelve pennies to a shilling. Thus, there were twenty shillings to a pound, and so ten shillings was half a pound.

'Pasha please take this, as a loan between friends. Please simply repay me whenever you can.'

'Angus...'

'Pasha, please, I have been so isolated here at Salzgitter. As ex-army but now in charge of a new organisation to repatriate swathes of population I have found it difficult to be accepted, or indeed trusted, by anybody. The work has been hard, harrowing actually, and you three have proved true friends. This is what friends do. And anyway, you need this money, so please take it.'

Our supper that evening was a repeat of breakfast from the previous morning – rye bread, cheese and milk, although this time we heated the milk on the stove and added Ovaltine, which Angus said would ensure that we all slept soundly.

Angus himself went to stay at one of the small hotels in town. We would be ready for him to collect us the following morning at 5am.

We gave Sofia Angus's bed to sleep in and she was soon snoring softly. Tanya and I were silent, staring at the yellowed cracked ceiling, touching hands between the camp beds. Despite the best efforts of the Ovaltine neither of us got much sleep that night. We were heading west again. Much farther west now, to a city we felt we knew, at least slightly, from the movies. But would London be as it was depicted in the cinemas? Lübbecke had seemed so quintessentially English, but there had been something make-believe about the town. It had been like a film set; created artificially by the incomers as a rose-coloured, idealised vision of their homeland. We had been playing pretend in Lübbecke and perhaps Lübbecke had been playing pretend with us.

Something told me that the reality of London might be altogether more gritty.

Moreover, our plan, and especially the help and ideas we had had from Angus, had worked amazingly well so far. Sofia's rather brilliant improvisation at the Passport Office had made Miss Fiquelmont's day and, in so doing, had smoothed the provision of our exit papers. But we would have to revert to our true selves when seeing Angus's school friend at Whitehall. We had a copy of Angus's letter of introduction, but could not know how far that would help us.

Kolobok. It was all just like the little round, sweet dough-ball – the namesake of the Russian fairy tale that Sofia had loved me telling her over and over. Kolobok, the dough-ball, comes alive and bounces out of the kitchen. By singing a clever song he escapes being eaten by the rabbit, the wolf, and the bear, but in the end he is outwitted by the cunning fox and poor Kolobok is eaten up. Were we just like the magical little dough-ball, bouncing from place to place, cleverly avoiding capture; but were we now about to be gobbled up?

8

PASHA ZAYKY

London, August 1946

A T 5AM THE FOLLOWING DAY THE BLACK HUMBER'S chuffing exhaust note broke the still morning silence, and heralded Angus's arrival to drive us to Hanover on the first leg of our journey to London. It took only a moment to return our small cases to the boot and then, still bleary-eyed, Sofia and I fell into the back seat. Tanya sat upfront – there was no debate over that. She seemed to have got more sleep than me and was alert and focused, looking for anybody around who might be on the lookout for us. I had not noticed the day before, but Angus was not a natural chauffeur. His application of the accelerator pedal was either fully on or completely off – and the same applied to the brakes. I couldn't help but smile as I noticed Tanya holding on to the edge of her seat and wincing slightly each time he crunched the gears. They just differed over their respect for machinery.

But soon Angus no longer had to change gear as we joined a grand highway where each side had two lanes of tarmacked road. I had seen such roads in the newsreels but never before in reality.[63] At that time of the morning there was nobody else on the road, Angus pushed the gas pedal full to the floor and from the back seat I watched as the needle on the Humber's dashboard hit sixty miles per hour. Despite my heavy eyelids that morning, I was exhilarated at the speed of our exit from Salzgitter; away from the reach of the Soviets. By six twenty we were arriving at the front of Hanover's grand railway station and Angus dropped us by the statue of King Ernst August – depicted as a grand old Hussar monarch riding into battle.[64]

Angus hugged Sofia and gave her a bag of sweets for the long train journey ahead. He shook hands with Tanya and me.

'I'd better get going and get this car back to the motor pool before anybody asks too many questions.'

'Thank you, Angus, for being such a dear friend,' I said, but Angus merely shook his head and waved his arm dismissively. It was an awkward goodbye. We owed him our lives. We all knew that.

There was an irony in our arrival at the feet of Ernst August, the hero king of Hanover, that morning. He was a son of the English King George III but returned to Germany, his historic fatherland, as a young man. He had been a bold soldier and fought alongside the British in France, losing an eye in battle. Later, as a Field Marshall, he commanded the British Royal German Legion – a regiment of German

63 The world's first limited access highway was the Vanderbilt Motor
     Parkway in Long Island, New York, opened in 1911, whilst
     Italy created an 'Autostrada' to connect Milan to Varese in 1926.
     Germany's first 'Autobahn' opened in 1935. Hitler was a major
     advocate and by 1936, 130,000 workers were engaged in road-
     building, with a further 270,000 engaged in the supply chain. By
     1940, German Autobahns covered 3,700 kilometres.
64 https://www.flickr.com/photos/16481425@N06/26313739148

soldiers within the British army which, perhaps in ethos and aspiration, was not unlike Pyotr's XVth Cossack Brigade within the Wehrmacht some 140 years later. British kings had reigned over the kingdom of Hanover since the start of the eighteenth century, but when Ernst's niece Victoria became queen of Great Britain in 1837, Hanoverian law decreed they could not be ruled by a woman. And so Ernst took the crown of Hanover. Initially an autocrat, he later won respect and love by creating a modern constitution, a free press, and separating the judiciary from the administration.

But as Angus and the black Humber drove away leaving us in the station forecourt, I looked around us at the ruins of Hanover. The once-palatial main station was a bombed and burned shell and I wondered what King Ernst would have thought now. German rejection of constitutional government and the return to autocracy during the 1930s had led directly to Ernst's grand city being obliterated. The British, under King George VI, Ernst's great-great-great-nephew, were allies no longer.[65]

So, was the bronze figure of King Ernst in the station square a good or a bad omen? I wasn't sure.

The booking hall was housed in a wooden shed to one side of the wrecked station building and, having carefully scrutinised the exit permits issued by the military authority in Lübbecke, the man inside sold us tickets to board the troop train bound for Hook in Holland which was to leave Hanover just before 7am.

---

65 Between the RAF and the USAF nearly a million bombs fell on
    Hanover during the Second World War killing 6,700 and destroying
    90% of the city centre. In 2017, 50,000 people (about 10% of the
    city's population) were evacuated when just three seventy-year-old
    unexploded WW2 bombs were uncovered during construction work.

The tickets cost us all of our Reichsmarks as well as two pounds of our Sterling. But although third-class accommodation was all we could afford, a few packets of cigarettes from my suitcase secured us a separate compartment, away from the hordes of British soldiers also waiting to join the train, all excited to be returning home, and most still reeling from a heavy final night in the city's bars and bordellos. We were thankful for that.

The train was bound for Hook but via a slow circuitous route via Bielefeld, Hamm and the Ruhr, so we only arrived at the Dutch border at 2pm. A passport check. This was a worry as, whilst we had exit papers, we didn't possess passports and once again, just like at Lübbecke, we had to use our new identities as the Zaitsev family. We got off the train holding our cases and waited in a long queue. We were anxious and went to the very back of the line. What would they want to see? But in fact it all passed off very smoothly; the border guards were Dutch but one of them spoke German. They didn't study our documents for long and soon moved on to the final few stragglers who had joined the queue after us.

Having completed the passport check, our anxiousness subsided and the relief in the knotting of our stomachs made us realise just how famished we were, having got up at 5am and missed breakfast. On the Dutch side of the border was a British NAAFI[66] canteen where we got steaming tea,

66 The Navy, Army and Air Force Institutes (NAAFI) is an organisation created by the British in 1921 to run recreational establishments needed by their armed forces. It runs clubs, bars, shops, supermarkets, launderettes, restaurants, cafés and other facilities on most British military bases as well as canteens on board Navy ships. Commissioned officers are not expected to use NAAFI clubs and bars, except on official business, as this is considered an intrusion into junior ranks' private lives

pies and sausage rolls. Sofia was given her hot sausage roll in a piece of greaseproof paper. She wolfed it down with a huge grin and crumbs everywhere.

Back on the train I noted that, comparatively, the damage here was much less than in Germany. We passed through Arnhem where pieces of aircraft were still hanging in treetops and some farms were using sections of fuselage from crashed gliders as chicken coops. Holland was a country of pretty towns, with neat houses fitted with light-coloured cornices painted white or yellow. Lots of people, and nearly all the children, wore strange, pointy-toed wooden clogs. There were few cars on the road, but I had never seen so many cyclists.

As the train moved further west we travelled across sand dunes and lowlands, with the track criss-crossing many waterways and lakes. I could see that the water here practically rose up through the soil. There were lots of glasshouses, mostly empty; some had been totally smashed but a few had been put back into service already. Flowers were the cash crop in the fields, but we were obviously far too late in the year to see the tulips. As a botanist with a career devoted to creating and maximising crops for food production it seemed wonderful to me that farms could be used to grow flowers purely for decoration. Could the benefit of cut flowers be measured against the benefit of grain or potatoes? I reflected that perhaps it could, and that the emotional benefit of those cut flowers to provide joy and happiness could be just as important as food on the plate. I would have loved to have spent time in Holland to speak to the farmers but it was not to be.

We finally arrived in Hook at about five o'clock that afternoon.

There were two ferry departures, one for ordinary passengers and the other for soldiers on leave. Just as when we obtained our rail tickets in Hanover, our military exit papers led us to be shown onto the troop ship, the Empire Kingsman. Once again there was a NAAFI canteen serving English sausages and potatoes – the troops certainly seemed to get more rations than civilians – and we dined well. After supper, we stood on deck watching the lights along the coast come on as the sun went down. Lights – it was still a joy to see them again after the long years of blackout. Such a powerful and positive impact on your spirit. As we left the flower fields of Holland behind, I reflected that, in these times of austerity, electric lights were, perhaps, the tulips of the night.

We had been allocated a cabin deep inside the dark centre of the ship and at 9pm, as the receding port finally disappeared from sight, we went to find our bunks. It had been a long day which, for me at least, had been preceded by a sleepless night. We were utterly drained. Little by little, Angus's plan seemed to be working. Every step was putting us farther from harm's reach and we were now at least 500 kilometres away from Salzgitter and from the British army squad which had been sent to round us up on the orders of the NKVD. Nevertheless, it was still with mixed feelings that we finally left mainland Europe.

Our cabin was airless, the engines throbbed, and the ferry rocked. The soldiers on board were certainly making a lot of noise. But none of this prevented the three of us from sleeping soundly in our hard bunks all night. When we awoke the throbbing had stopped and the ferry was still – we had reached England.

We docked at Harwich, disembarked quickly, and headed for customs and passport control. The worry over passports loomed once again. Although, to be fair, by now we were becoming far more used to our new identities; our back stories were much better rehearsed than just a day or so before, so that even Tanya could play 'pretend' a little. The border officers looked tired and had obviously been on duty all night. They scrutinised our exit permits but didn't ask any questions or ask to see any passports. We had to turn out our pockets and they confiscated the remainder of our Reichsmarks – although we had precious little German currency left. To be fair, they made a great show of writing us a receipt to allow us to reclaim the money on our return journey – a receipt we fervently hoped never to need. But they clearly wanted to do things properly.

Then they checked our suitcases. We had to place them on tables and then stand in front of them as they were opened and searched. In the very top of mine, completely on show as the case was opened, were my last ten packets of cigarettes; the final remnants of the recompense for the language lessons I had delivered in Salzgitter. The customs officer looked down at them, said nothing, picked out a packet of twenty fags, which he slid into his jacket top pocket, then closed the case and sent the three of us on our way. We were in!

We bought our train tickets and as we left Harwich the bright morning sun glinted on the puddles and pools of the exposed coastal mudflats. The glints of light pierced our carriage window illuminating the dust particles hanging in the air as if they were the chalk in a cloudy glass of water. Our first impression of Great Britain was of sun, dirt and devastation. The train took about two hours and we finally arrived into London's Liverpool Street Station at 11am. It was Friday 30th August 1946.

Angus had suggested the Imperial Hotel on Russell Square as our first destination. He had given me a well-thumbed Geographer's A–Z map atlas of London streets, including a map of the London underground railway network which Tanya had examined in detail given its resemblance to an electric circuit diagram.[67] I decided that the cost of a London black taxi was probably more than we should sensibly afford and that travel by 'Tube' was likely to be much cheaper, and so we descended into the bowels of the earth down the long moving staircases. Sofia played at walking upwards as the staircase travelled downwards so that she actually stayed at the same spot – at least until a ruddy-faced Londoner running down steps past her yelled, 'Oi! Young-un! Gertcha!'

I had no idea of the precise translation, but the meaning was quite clear. Sofia stopped, went a little pink, turned and held the juddering handrail for the remainder of the way down. Tanya was clearly enjoying every moment – moving staircases, tiled labyrinthine passageways, and then electric trains with automatic sliding pneumatic doors were works of wonderment for her. We took the Central line from Liverpool Street to Holborn and then changed to the

---

67 The first diagrammatic representation of London's 'Tube' network was designed by Harry Beck in 1931 to replace geographical maps which had been in use since the early years of the twentieth century. Beck realised that, as the lines were mostly underground, physical locations were largely irrelevant to the traveller who simply wanted to know how to get from one station to another. Only the topology of the route mattered.

Piccadilly line for just one stop to Russell Square, rising back to the surface in a huge elevator. The Underground station was not actually in Russell Square itself but the A–Z map led us around the corner and the Imperial Hotel was easily located on the east side.[68]

We checked in. Thankfully, accommodation didn't seem to be a problem, although the cost was astonishing at one pound per night with a minimum stay of two nights. 'Payment in advance please, sir.' We took a room on the seventh floor and cashed Angus's cheque at the concierge. Having paid for the ferry, the train to London, some food and now the hotel bill, our cash was already running low. There was about two pounds and ten shillings left along with 180 cigarettes. How we were going to live once this meagre supply of money ran dry was unclear.

London was hot and dirty. The war was over but you wouldn't have known it from the demeanour of the population. The movies had suggested that all Londoners were chirpy Cockneys, but in summer 1946 everyone we saw looked thin, pale, and sour-faced. Was this the face of victory?

Our lack of financial resources meant that we needed to get to Whitehall to meet with Angus's 'old school chum' as quickly as possible. I sincerely hoped that this would prove possible that Friday afternoon as otherwise I wasn't at all sure how we would make it through the weekend. We certainly couldn't afford to stay at the Imperial Hotel.

A chat with Mr Carter, the Hotel's concierge, whilst poring over the A–Z map, helped us work out which

68   https://www.lookandlearn.com/history-images/XJ149588/The-Imperial-Hotel-in-Russell-Square?t=2&q=Imperial+hotel&n=5

buses to catch and where to change. Only I could attend Whitehall for interview but our plan was for Tanya and Sofia to see some sights whilst I was busy and then for us all to meet up. By now it was a little after 2pm and Mr Carter suggested that we all go to Westminster Abbey. From there I could get to Whitehall easily, whilst Tanya and Sofia could work their way to Buckingham Palace and then Trafalgar Square, with an eventual rendezvous at the Joe Lyons Corner House tea rooms opposite Charing Cross Railway Station at 6pm.

The bus journeys to Westminster worked well and outside the Abbey I bid goodbye to Tanya and Sofia. Sofia gave me her usual hug but Tanya fixed me with her dark eyes. This was yet another interview where our fate was governed by success or failure. It was, of course, not dissimilar to Tanya's meeting with Paul Pleiger at the air ministry in Berlin when she had secured the job in Salzgitter. Her skills had rescued us then. Could I do the same now?

Happily, the Colonial Office in Whitehall was not too challenging to locate and armed with the copy letter of introduction and recommendation that Angus had written, I was soon asking to see his friend, Sir Arthur Davenport. The porters at the front desk of the building dialled a number and a secretary soon appeared asking my business. I explained my recent arrival and wish to see Sir Arthur but she looked at me askance. It was most unusual for visitors to turn up without a pre-booked appointment, she told me. I apologised, but went on that I didn't know the telephone number and had precious little access to a telephone in any event, but that a letter of introduction had been sent in advance, and that I had a copy of that letter with me.

She continued to observe me with disdain for some moments longer but then took the copy of the letter of introduction and, holding it at one corner between her thumb and forefinger, she disappeared.

There was nowhere to sit and so I stood at the front desk whilst the porters made every effort to ignore me.

Presently the secretary reappeared, handed me back the letter, and instructed me to follow her. She set off at a smart trot, her heels clattering on the tiled floor. I was led up a wide flight of stairs, through numerous swinging doors, and along a straight passage. We turned left down a ledger-lined corridor, and then switched right along another. Occasionally there was a window but we were walking too fast to see what was outside, although we were no longer looking out over the Whitehall thoroughfare. I had completely lost my bearings.

Eventually the march ended and there was a wooden chair outside an office.

'Take a seat please, Mr Zayky.' Then she knocked smartly on the office door, turned and left. In a second she had disappeared. The office door remained closed for a further ten minutes but then I heard footsteps approach it from the other side. The door opened and an older lady's head popped out. She smiled at me – at least she seemed rather more warm than the previous secretary.

'Mr Zayky, Sir Arthur will see you now, please do come through.'

There was a desk with a phone and typewriter; the walls were lined with shelves neatly filled with matching box files. There was no window, and an anglepoise lamp shed a small pool of light on the desktop, although a door, half-glazed with frosted glass, allowed a little natural light to filter into the dim anteroom. The secretary knocked on the glass of the door.

'Come!'

'Sir Arthur, Mr Zayky to see you.'

'Thank you, Joan. Mr Zayky, since getting McGrath's letter I've been wondering when you might reach us. Do come in, take a seat.'

Sir Arthur Davenport was in his late fifties but was nevertheless a handsome, broad-shouldered man, who rather bucked the trend of the other London folk I had encountered that day. His suit was black, clean, and well cut. A gold watch chain appeared from his waistcoat pocket. It was a hot day but he showed not a trace of perspiration. His room was large and Joan the secretary's anteroom had been carved out of a corner. The maze of largely windowless corridors and then the dim anteroom had caused my eyes to compensate for the lack of light. Now the late afternoon sun flooded in through the large picture window behind Davenport. His office clearly faced west and he was silhouetted against the light. I squinted at him, the sunlight making it quite impossible to read his expression.

He spoke in measured tones. He and Angus had been at a school called Harrow. He had Angus's original letter on his desk and he spent sometime recalling amusing stories of their schoolboy high jinks and daring deeds. He had served in the first war, just like Angus, but after that had joined the British civil service where his efforts had been rewarded with a knighthood, which was why he had the title 'Sir' instead of 'Mr'. This meant that you were supposed to call him by his first name rather than his surname – which seemed surprisingly informal to me. He was also something called a Deputy Under-Secretary which apparently made him a relatively high-ranking diplomat, although it seemed odd that, if he was doing well in his career, his role as a secretary was prefixed by both the words 'deputy' and 'under'. But I didn't comment, and laughed heartily at his stories thus generating occasional nods of approval at my appreciation.

Joan reappeared with a tea trolley and a plate of tiny sandwiches – puffy white bread immaculately cut into miniscule squares each containing a mere trace of cucumber.

'Thank you Joan, please leave us. I shall be mother.'

He rose from the desk, and walked round behind me to the trolley.

'Lemon or milk, Zayky? You chaps normally prefer lemon, is that right?' That was right. There was silence as he poured my tea and handed me the most delicate bone china cup and saucer. But then as he poured his own he spoke again.

'Now look here, old man, I regret you might have had a wasted trip.'

The tea cup was at my lips but my mouth went dry. I replaced the cup on the saucer and it chinked a little as my hand shook. I put the cup and saucer on the desk in front of me and clasped my hands together on my lap.

'The thing is that getting you into Britain is not a matter for us here at the Colonial Office. It's a Home Office issue through their "Aliens" section. I gave them a ring on receipt of McGrath's letter, but the message from them is that London is already full of refugees, and taking in three extra immigrants from Russia when your motherland would be only too pleased to have you back is not really on the cards. Do you see?'

He had returned to his chair and eyed my reactions across the desk as he sipped his tea. I continued to sit with my hands now wedged between my knees in some effort to conceal my rising terror. Angus's plan had been brilliant and, up to now, each step along the way had been faultless – but ultimately it had failed. The British were not going to take us in. Everything had come crashing down. We should have just run from Salzgitter and gone into hiding.

I simply couldn't speak. We had no money, and no knowledge of Britain. That we would be handed across to the Soviet authorities in London was now an inevitability. We would begin the journey back to Russia across Europe. I wondered if we would even make it that far before we were shot. Please God, that perhaps somebody might be willing to take Sofia, just a mere trace of a hope that she might be spared the fate of her parents, although I had no idea how this might come about.

My devastation was total.

Sir Arthur said no more. He merely sat back in his chair and continued to gaze across the desk at me whilst I made no effort to meet his eyes, and just stared down at my quivering hands and legs. I am not a brave man. It wasn't my fault, none of this was down to me. I was just a botanist at a university who wanted the best for his daughter.

Eventually, when he could see that my tea, which was still sitting on his desk, must have turned cold, he tapped a small call bell and Joan the secretary promptly reappeared.

'Oh Joan, would you mind escorting Mr Zayky along to see Lord Windover.'

He stood and held out his hand.

'Good to meet you, Zayky. Good luck for the future.'

I took his hand and he shook it, and then my arm fell to my side. He sat down again, picked up his phone and began dialling a number, whilst Joan opened the door.

'Do follow me, please.'

I dutifully followed, asking no questions. I had no idea who I was seeing next or why.

I was escorted through another warren of corridors and eventually deposited by Joan in yet another dim anteroom where the door was signed 'The East and Central African Department'. Once again I took a seat and very shortly a man appeared.

'Are you Mr Zayky?... Viscount Windover, but call me Andrew... So pleased to meet you. Have you had tea already?... May I offer you another cup?... Do come through, Sir Arthur suggested that you and I should have a chat.'

Viscount Windover delivered his staccato sentences in a clipped British accent.

'Do you have time?' he continued. I wondered just how much time I did have.

Unlike Davenport, Viscount Windover apparently had no secretary and his main office was just as dimly lit as his anteroom.

'So I think, as Sir Arthur explained, I'm afraid that you working here at the Colonial Office and becoming a naturalised British citizen is just not on. Jolly frustrating for you, I'm sure, but I wondered if you might just be willing to consider an alternative.'

For the first time I raised my eyes to look at him. Windover was younger than Davenport, maybe only in his late thirties. Lean and angular with deep-set eyes, black hair, a pointed nose and shiny cheeks. He wore a blue naval uniform with stripes on his epaulettes which I later learned made him the rank of Commander. But, uniform or not, he lacked something of Davenport's panache. His smile was fixed and he leaned forward towards me in his seat. He reminded me of a fox terrier dog. He almost panted.

'The thing is that in Major McGrath's letter to Sir Arthur he mentions that at one time you were a leading botanist in Russia working on agrarian output and crop yields – is that correct?' I nodded, tentatively. Where was this going?

'Well, my role here is to administer His Majesty's dominions in East Africa. The British Government is most concerned that, at this time of need and shortages, the colonies do all in their power to raise their agricultural output to increase exports to Britain. At a town called Kitale on the western border of Kenya is an agricultural research station in need of a new director. We need an agrarian specialist for the role but, with so many men still abroad in the forces and so many scientists engaged in other important roles in Britain, we have nobody we can send.

'So, given your circumstances, and your background in botany and especially farinaceous crops, I wondered if you might be willing to consider the job? There would be a decent salary and, I think, a jolly life in Kenya, although not, I'm afraid, a British passport. That would continue to be a Home Office matter. So you would remain officially stateless…' At this, he changed his facial demeanour from that of fixed smile to a regretful look. A happy face to a sad face in one quick movement. But then he restored the fixed smile once more and continued.

'… but you never know what might happen down the line. What do you think, old chap?'

I was wide-eyed, but obviously, I agreed.

'Well if you're game then there is no time to lose. You see we have a seat on the flying boat bound for Lake Naivasha near Nairobi leaving from Poole Harbour at 09:30 tomorrow. If you are taking the job then you need to fill that seat. I will make immediate arrangements.'

'But my wife and daughter, they can join me?' I asked, tensing as I sensed a problem.

'Of course, of course. In fact, as part of the job you're expected to be accompanied by your family.' He craned his neck towards me, nodding as he spoke, and I relaxed again.

'Although, not immediately, old boy. I'm afraid there is just one seat available on the flying boat tomorrow. Your family will be welcome to come out to join you by ship, although with all the troop movements that will take some time to arrange. Our ships are all completely full for the time being. Give it a month or two… well probably three or four months, truth be told.'

Having obtained my agreement, Viscount Windover swiftly made his goodbyes and keenly handed me on to another, more junior, member of staff introduced as 'Smith' – just a 'Mr', having failed, at least as yet, to gain any higher title. Smith provided me with a £20 cash float, a chit to allow me to collect a train ticket from Waterloo Station the following morning and a letter of instruction to BOAC[69] to grant me a seat on the half past nine flying boat service to East Africa. He told me that Tanya should contact him as he could arrange much cheaper London accommodation whilst waiting for their passage to Kenya. The arrangement was that the Colonial Office would cover all of my travel expenses in full. Thereafter they would meet all the costs of Tanya and Sofia's accommodation and eventual travel but these latter costs would need to be repaid from my salary in due course.

In later weeks I was to reflect on my interviews at the Colonial Office that afternoon. Had they been able to use our predicament to serve their own needs? The meetings had clearly been orchestrated in advance. Just how honest was Davenport's account of his conversation with the Home Office resulting in the complete refusal of citizenship? And if there had been a chink of hope, would I have accepted the position in East Africa quite so readily?

Although the comparison was to prove unfair, at that moment, the proposed move to Kenya felt like the impending transportation of a convict to a Siberian gulag. But at least it meant our continued survival.

I was an hour late for the rendezvous at the Lyons Tea House, partly through the delay in dealing with the final paperwork at the Colonial Office with Smith, and partly as I

---

69 British Overseas Airways Corporation (BOAC) was the British state-owned airline created in 1940 by the merger of Imperial Airways and British Airways Ltd. BOAC inherited Imperial Airways' flying boat services to British colonies in Africa and Asia and during WW2 shifted the base of operations for these services from Southampton to Poole in Dorset England. In 1974 BOAC and BEA (British European Airways) merged to form British Airways.

dragged my feet back up Whitehall towards Trafalgar Square and the Strand wondering how to explain all this to Tanya.

They were at a table on the first floor. The building had escaped the bombs and was tastefully decorated with patterned tiles. A pianist was playing 'Ain't She Sweet' in a tinkling high octave. Tanya had a pot of coffee and Sofia was drinking milk from a large conically shaped glass. As I sat down at the table Tanya took one look at my face.

'Oh my God, they're sending us back,' she said.

'No, but they are sending us somewhere…'

I ran through the conversations that had taken place in Whitehall. I was able to outline what had happened very quickly as Tanya sat and looked at me in stunned silence; but then her questions began in a torrent. I told her everything again, several times over, in fact. I didn't have the answers for most of her questions and I tried to guess. That made her angry.

'Pasha, we arrived in London this morning, we speak precious little English. You are leaving us tomorrow, and we have to remain here for months, without any certainty of what will happen?'

Tanya is the most ruthlessly pragmatic person I have ever met and rarely allows emotions to confuse practicalities, but now her anger combined with apprehension. I explained that after I left for Africa they would have to remain at the hotel over the weekend, but then go to see Smith at the Colonial Office on Monday to switch to the cheaper accommodation.

'And you got them to write you a letter to this effect?'

I had not.

'And, this Smith person, you know his first name? His department?'

I hadn't asked.

'And you still have Angus's copy letter?' I flushed, as I had realised on my walk back along Whitehall that I had left my copy of Angus's letter of introduction in Windover's office.

We caught the buses back to Russell Square in silence with Sofia squeezing my hand and Tanya's in turn. 'Mama, and Papa, please don't fight,' she implored.

At seven o'clock the following morning I boarded the train at London's Waterloo Station to take me to Poole Harbour to connect with the nine thirty flying boat to Africa. Tanya and Sofia had accompanied me from Russell Square. Tanya had recovered from her understandable anger the day before and reconciled herself to the inevitability of the situation, but it didn't mean she was happy. I stood at the open door of the carriage looking slightly downwards at Tanya and Sofia standing on the platform, forlorn, holding hands. The guard walked by, up the platform towards the engine; he passed between me and Tanya and Sofia and slammed shut the door. The window was fully opened and so we could still speak but the closing of the door marked the separation between us.

We had been in Britain for less than twenty-four hours and we were now being wrenched apart. Tanya and Sofia had fifteen pounds of the cash handed to me by Smith at the Colonial Office but little grasp of English, no work, and no friends. As the train moved off, Tanya held out her hand and I grasped it, just momentarily, as the moving train pulled our fingers apart. Sofia, crying, ran along the platform.

'Papa, papa, I love you.'

Tanya didn't cry. Tanya never cried. I cried.

9

TANYA ZAYKY

London, September 1946
to March 1947

As the locomotive heaved and strained to get the wheels of the long train rolling so it shot great plumes of smoke and clouds of soot into the air. The soot congealed in the air with the discharged steam of the engine to form smuts, which descended on Sofia like a black rain as she pelted along the platform, trying to keep pace with the accelerating carriages, hand outstretched, calling for her papa. Now as she walked back along the flagstones of the platform towards me I could see her tears had combined with the smuts to cause long grey streaks down her cheeks and stains on the collar of her pinafore.

I spat on my handkerchief and started to rub off the dirt from her face but she pushed my hand away. Momentarily, she looked up at me, fixing me with her dark eyes, but then she buried her head into me, wrapped her arms around me, and sobbed. I placed my arms around her and we held each other on that empty platform as the railway workers walked by. They had seen it all before.

Что нам делать? What are we to do?

At that moment, on that platform, I prayed for us. As a daughter of the 1917 Revolution, whilst I hated the Soviets for the oppression they inflicted on our Kuban land, I had had no time for prayer up to that point in my life. I thought back to our little church at Camp 49 in Salzgitter and Father Sergey, a well-meaning young man but hopelessly out of his depth, with so many displaced persons, malnourishment, alcoholism, and his futile fight against the Allies' desire to return his parishioners to a Russian death sentence. But I had never prayed at the church in Camp 49, despite all the carnage of war, the bombs, the concentration camps, and despite all those deaths at the railway marshalling yard that terrible day. None of those things had made me pray. No, I just went to the church to accompany Pasha so that he could be sociable with the other Russians and Cossacks, and so that Sofia could play with the other children. I just went along for her sake really.

But that Saturday morning, the last day of August 1946, in an unfamiliar and unwelcoming city, with hardly any of the language, with darling Pasha gone, and with Sofia sobbing and clinging to me (and me to her) – I prayed.

And then I had an idea. Why hadn't we thought of it before? If there had been a Russian church in Camp 49, surely there must be a church in London?

The street outside Waterloo Station was full of taxis[70]

---

70 A taximeter records distance when a cab is in motion, or time when the cab is stationary, and adjusts the fare accordingly. It was named after its German inventor, Baron von Thurn und Taxis (although this is debated) and first used in Berlin. Early taximeters were totally mechanical and the 'clock' had to be wound by hand. London's cabs have been licensed since 1696, initially through the City of London and later through Parliament. The fitment of a taximeter was made compulsory in 1907.

parked up in a long row waiting to whisk people off to destinations throughout the city. But at this early hour of a Saturday morning fare-paying passengers seemed to be thin on the ground, and I could see the drivers dozing, smoking, reading the paper or, for those farther back along the line, standing in the road beside their cars chatting, and drinking tea from flasks. Holding hands with Sofia, I went to the first one on the rank.

'Pardon me. Would you take us to the Russian Orthodox church?' I asked, despite my accent stilted and thick. The old man in the driver's seat lowered his paper and looked across at me. His blue flat cap was pulled down over his ears, his face was grey but tinged yellow, and so lined that his cheeks looked like little pulled curtains all bunched together. A cigarette, very nearly burned to nothing, was stuck to the middle of his bottom lip.

'Do what love? Come again?'

'Please can you help us to find the church in London that is for Russian people?' said Sofia with a rather better English accent than I could muster at that time, and I could see that now he understood.

'Ahh right you are, me darlin'. Roosian you say? I know it, I know it… but I just can't place it, but always up for a challenge. Don't worry, ladies, we'll find it… hop in!'

And so, we set off in our little blue taxi cab into the streets of London. It was a strange vehicle as it didn't have a door or a seat on the passenger side of the front just a small loading platform. And, although the driver's cabin had a roof, our seating area at the back was open with a folded hood behind us. Its top speed seemed to be about jogging pace and the engine made almost as much noise as our driver who started chatting the minute we got in although I couldn't understand a word he said. The cab clattered its way through the streets and over the Thames river. Halfway across the bridge our driver waved out of his window (his side of the car had a door strangely) to a cab which seemed to be almost hobbling along in the opposite direction. As they reached each other both cars stopped so that the drivers could speak, causing tailbacks of buses and traffic in both directions and some hooting.

'Ere Stan, d'you know where that Roosian church is?'

'Yeah, that'd be St Philip's down Buckin'm Palace Road, ain't it. Thas where they close the road, dun' they when they 'ave their Easter at funny times.'

'Thanks mate – course they do! There are,' said our driver triumphantly turning around to us. 'Told yus we work it out!'

And it was only once he knew where we were going that he tapped his taximeter to set the fare running.

'Two and six please, darlin',' he said as he dropped us outside a large old English church. 'Good chattin' to ya.' He waved as he drove off still with the same fag, nearly burned away, stuck to his bottom lip.

We looked around. When I had heard that the church was located in Buckingham Palace Road my heart had lifted. We had walked past Buckingham Palace when we had been sightseeing the previous day (the King hadn't been there) but it had looked very grand with the soldiers outside with their tall fur hats. I had assumed that if the Russian church was in the same road then it must be equally as splendid. In Krasnodar, St Catherine's Cathedral was a monumental building, with tall white stucco arch-topped elevations set below towers surmounted by wonderful golden onion domes. Surely London would have something similar especially if Buckingham Palace was its neighbour. But despite the name of the road, the palace was nowhere to be seen, and instead we were staring at a dirty, dull English church, with tarpaulins covering the roof and boarded windows. Its neighbour, much less the King's palace, was a bus depot – albeit a grand one with a white modern frontage.[71] The street was wide and busy but utterly nondescript and lacking in charm. There were a few people in the street that morning but nobody took any notice of us. The hoots, clanks and throbs of trains echoed close by.

Disappointed by the shambolic appearance and lacklustre location, but with no other plan, we ventured down the alleyway to the side of the building to find the main door. It was still only a little past eight o'clock and I half expected the church to be locked but the door opened easily. We entered the gloomy interior of the porch, and paused momentarily before venturing into the narthex.[72] Before us stood grand

---

71 St Philip's Church, 188 Buckingham Palace Road, was built in 1887 for the Church of England who obtained a long lease on land owned by the Duke of Westminster. In 1921 the Church of England closed the Parish of St Philip's and sublet the church building to the Russian Orthodox Church Outside Russia. Victoria Coach Station, built in a distinctive Art Deco style, opened in 1932, next door to the church at 164 Buckingham Palace Road. Sadly, the Russian Church was forced to leave St Philip's in 1955 when the Church of England sold its long lease so that the building could be demolished to make way for an extension to the coach station.

72 The narthex is an architectural element typical of early Christian and Byzantine basilicas and churches consisting of the entrance or lobby area, located at the west end of the nave, opposite the church's main altar. Traditionally the narthex was a part of the church building, but was not considered part of the church proper.

double doors, rather different to the drab and unprepossessing exterior entrance. We pushed against them and the doors swung open to reveal the main body of the church itself. Cool but scented air, a wonderful vaulted ceiling, from which huge lit candelabra hung low illuminating the altar opposite. All around gold leaf twinkled in the candlelight, tapestries hung ornate and unfaded, and the murals of the saints looked down on us from their high position atop the altar steps. The interior of this place of worship utterly belied the exterior; we had entered a holy and sacred place.

Nobody was there, and we sat in a pew and waited, without any understanding of what we were waiting for. But presently a little priest arrived. Such a short man, in a flowing robe and the most luxuriant beard. Instinctively we bowed our heads as if in prayer, although in reality we had been whispering to each other rather than to anybody, or anything, else.

'Good morning, new visitors to our church here. Welcome to you both!' He spoke Russian but with such a familiar accent.

And so it was that we first met Archpriest Father Michael Polsky – our Batioushka – our Little Father.

It took Father Michael just one look to recognise our need for help. The exhaustion and anguish which must have been written on my face, coupled with the grey tear stains on Sofia's pinafore, delivered our message of desperation.

'Come… come. Tea, I think…' He took us to his vestry office and as we sipped strong, sweet, scalding tea we told him our story and listened with rapt attention as he told us his.

He was, quite simply, an extraordinary man. Just like my beloved brother Pyotr, inside Father Michael beat the heart of a Kuban Cossack. A Cossack fighter indeed – but a fighter for hearts and souls rather than for glory. A man of belief, commitment and determination. He had been born in Novotroitskaya only 250 kilometres east of Krasnodar. His mother's side were warriors – his uncle had become a Cossack general – but his father's family were readers and chanters in the church, and this was the fight which inspired Michael.

He was ordained in 1920 at the height of the civil war, in Yekaterinodar – Krasnodar's old name – when the White Army were hopelessly outnumbered by the marauding red Bolsheviks. Realising that the incoming regime wanted to promote the doctrine of Communism to usurp the old religion, Father Michael made his way to Moscow to commit his full support to the Patriarch.[73] He remained alongside His Holiness as a rock and support at the Holy Trinity residence throughout constant threats from the Reds, but in the end they were both arrested and Father Michael spent three years in the Solovki concentration camp in Siberia.[74]

---

73   His Holiness Patriarch Tikhon was the 11th Patriarch of Moscow and all Russia, the primate of the Russian Orthodox Church. He fought against the Soviet regime's desire to promote atheism and also condemned the policy of collective farming which led to the famines. He was deposed in 1923 by the Soviet sponsored 'Living Church' and died in 1925. He was made a saint, first by the Russian Orthodox Church Outside Russia in 1981, and then by the Church in Russia in 1989.

74   Solovki on the Solovetsky Islands of the White Sea, off Northern Siberia, was converted from a monastery to a prison in 1923. Initially, it was openly called a concentration camp and only in the late 1920s was the term 'corrective labour camp' applied. Solzhenitsyn christened it the 'mother of the GULAG'. GULAG, established in 1930, (ГУЛАГ an acronym of Главное управление лагерей, *Glavnoye Upravleniye LAGerej* 'Main Camp Administration') was the government agency to administer the Soviet forced-labour camps under Stalin.

He recalled that over the entrance of Solovki ran the words 'Через труд – Свобода!', or in English: 'Through Labour – Freedom!', curiously prophetic of the Nazi banner *'Arbeit Macht Frei'* (work makes you free) erected above the gates of Auschwitz concentration camp some ten years later.

By 1927 Tikhon had died and Sergius had been appointed the new Patriarch. Shockingly, in an attempt to end persecution by the Reds, he declared the Russian Orthodox Church's absolute loyalty to Stalin and the Soviet Union. Father Michael regarded Sergius's action as a complete betrayal and decided that he had no option but to break communion. His task was now to let the world know of the true situation of the Russian Church and support a new clergy that accepted no compromise with the Bolsheviks.

With the help of guards, who secretly continued to hold their faith, Father Michael made his escape from the Solovetsky Islands by boat to the port of Kem in northern Siberia. From there he began a 4,000 kilometre trek towards Persia. Posing as an itinerant workman and keeping a small toolkit with sacred vessels hidden within, he made his odyssey celebrating secret liturgies for believers as he came across them.

But by now it was 1929 and the period of collectivisation and de-Kulakisation in Russia had truly begun. Travel for illegals without papers was extremely hazardous and an escaped priest, wanted by the GPU,[75] was likely to face summary execution. Father Michael continued his journey

---

75   The GPU (State Political Directorate) was the Russian secret police, created in 1922. It was the forerunner of the NKVD.

carefully, judging whom he could trust to shelter him and provide food and water in exchange for confession and blessings.

Finally, at 11pm on 24th March 1930, the eve of the Annunciation of the Virgin Mary, believers showed Father Michael the secret paths between the Bolshevik border posts that led him from the Soviet Union into Persia. He continued his travels and made his way to Jerusalem where he met Archbishop Anastassy who was later to become the President of the Council of the Russian Orthodox Church Outside of Russia. Father Michael was assigned the parish of Beirut where he remained until 1938 when he was posted to London to take charge of the Russian Church Abroad in Britain.

Sofia and I sat with rapt attention throughout Father Michael's story of his travels. It was an epic tale of faith, wonder and danger. The narrative of our own travels from Russia to London was rather more modest by comparison.

'But I fear that you face grave danger now,' said Father Michael. I looked surprised.

'But why?' I responded. 'We are safe now. Pasha is employed by the government, they can't send us back now.'

'You are likely to remain here in London for many months, and whilst I must praise the British for their stoicism during the long years of war, it has left them intolerant of foreigners. You speak little English and you have explained that your travel documents, such as they are, show you under the name of Zaitsev, whilst your husband has been employed under his real name. I fear that your trip back to the Colonial Office without correct letters or documentation will lead to your arrest and swift deportation. By the time

Monday comes your husband will be working for the British in Africa, he will not even know of your fate. For the British, you are a "loose end"; easily resolved by handing you over to the officials at the Soviet embassy with the added benefit of reinforcing the cordial relations between allies at the same time.'

He was right. Pasha was, in all probability, quite safe now that he was off to work in Africa, but that was not sufficient reason to allow us to rely on the British.

'My children, you must come with me. You must come to live at our Podvorya[76] until you are able to join your husband.'

Father Michael, our Batioushka, took us from St Philip's to a part of the city called Barons Court, and a house at 14 St Dunstan's Road. It was a large building just a short walk from the Underground station. The main front door was approached by a flight of stone steps rising up from the street, but, first looking quickly left and right, Batioushka led us from the pavement down some steep stairs to a separate basement door below the main entrance. He opened up with a small key and led us inside. There was a kitchen, a dining room, a bathroom and a bedroom. It was clean and tidy although the furniture was old and the curtains frayed. The windows looked out to whitewashed walls outside.

'Here; this is where you will stay.'

And so began our six months in London.

Above us in the house, on the ground floor, was a chapel; above that were several small bedrooms and another bathroom, and then on the top floor was Batioushka's

76 Podvorya: home chapel

bedroom and office with slanting walls under the roof. We never returned to the Imperial Hotel in Russell Square as Batioushka arranged for an English-speaking member of the Russian congregation to visit, sign us out and collect our cases. I was relieved to see our belongings again, and of course our photographs carefully extracted from the old cigar box and immediately positioned on the bedside table of our room.

As I look back now at our time at St Dunstan's Road it seems like just a brief moment, but at the time I remember that each day stretched on for an eternity. The house was not a prison, not at all like the camp in Salzgitter with its guards and strict rules, but it did feel as though we had been incarcerated. We had been caught within a sinister city and were being held for our own protection. Batioushka was the most lovely man. He did his utmost to make us feel welcome and introduce us to other members of the Russian church in London. Indeed, he arranged for one of the senior members of the congregation, Countess Kleinmichel, to call at the Podvorya every day to tutor Sofia in the dining room. But in those early days at St Dunstan's Road, with Pasha gone, without any real idea of what the future might hold, it felt as though we were under indefinite house arrest.

I cleaned and cooked. My cleaning was good and thorough but cooking was not my strength although Batioushka never complained, and there was always a crowd around the dining table at supper time. On Sundays, I would accompany Batioushka to St Philip's for the service but otherwise we rarely left the confines of the house, although I would occasionally go shopping to carry Batioushka's basket, although I was always careful to say nothing in either

Russian or my heavily accented English. Food was still on ration and Father Michael had only one ration book, but he was well known among the market traders.

'Oi 'ello 'ere's little Rasputin!' they would yell as he walked through the stalls, his beard parting slightly in the breeze and his robes flowing behind him. He always got some bones or some other bits and pieces that were 'off ration'. The standard fare each evening at St Dunstan's Road was a meaty Kuban borscht, accompanied by intense discussion on the politics of the moment.

Nearly every day I would write to Pasha, often enclosing a short letter from Sofia or a drawing. Well, perhaps my letters were weekly rather than daily – I was never a good writer. Anyway, one of our congregation would post the letters addressed 'care of the Field Research Office, Kitale, Kenya'. On Batioushka's advice I marked the return address as St Philip's Church in Buckingham Palace Road, rather than the Podvorya in Barons Court. For weeks on end, there was no reply.

Then one day in early October, Batioushka returned from St Philip's triumphantly clutching a blue aerogramme on which Pasha's swirly writing was clearly visible. My hands shook with excitement but despite the anticipation I carefully cut open the gummed letter with a kitchen knife so as to avoid tearing or ripping any of the treasured words within. At last I unfolded the thin blue sheet.

Kitale Research Station,
Wednesday 25ᵗʰ September 1946

My darling Tanya and darling Sofia, it was such a wonderful relief to receive your letters here this morning. There were four of them which came all tied together; I can't imagine why they had been delayed but now that doesn't matter at all, I was so delighted. Our separation was so sudden, so hurried, so cruel, that it felt to me like I had lost you both. I have been bereft. Thank goodness for Father Michael; it seems that our prayers have been answered and you have found safe shelter in London. I am so thankful for that.

Kenya is wonderful but very different to anywhere else that we have lived, the climate has been good so far but is now getting hotter by the day. I spent the first weeks after my arrival in the capital Nairobi, but have now been transferred to Kitale in the west of the country where we have been allocated a single-storey house which the British call a bungalow. It is built of brick but in size and design it is more like a wooden dacha. Tanya it will be the most wonderful home for us and I cannot wait until we can all be together here.

The soil quality in the west of the country is better than the land around Nairobi but the farmers are simply unaware of modern techniques. I really think I can make a difference. It is fabulous to be a botanist once more.

I keep writing to officials at Government House trying to get them to arrange for your passage but it has been difficult for them to respond as we have not known where you were. My letters to you, care of the Colonial Office in London, have been returned which made me very concerned indeed for your safety. So now, at least, I can begin to make arrangements in earnest, although I don't know how long it will all take, so please be patient for a while longer.

My darlings I can't wait until we see each other again. Keep safe; keep well; and know that I love you both with all my heart,

Forever, Pasha, Papa

I thanked God. We had re-established contact. A link. We knew each other was alive and now there was hope. Hope didn't make the days pass any faster, but at least now most days we received a letter. I had little to say in my letters back; it was not safe to speak of the Podvorya so I just said that I cooked and cleaned. We continued to hide away, frightened to speak to anybody outside the immediate circle of Russian parishioners who came to visit St Dunstan's Road in case anybody should report us to the authorities who then might attempt to deport us. But, in his letters, Pasha was his usual self; each day we received reports of successful cropping interventions, stories about local farmers, the native tribesmen, the weather, the bungalow. Everything, in fact, apart from all what I wanted to hear about, which was when we would get our boat tickets. It was so lovely to hear from him, and there was hope, but it was frustrating.

Summer faded to autumn and then to winter and that winter in London was cold and damp. Actually, I think that every winter in London is cold and damp. I hate it. In the Kuban our winters were cold and dry. Proper freezing temperatures – you knew that you had to wrap up properly when venturing out. But in London the temperature varies so widely – freezing one day and yet mild the next – but always damp; newspapers become soggy, the clothes you put on are never fully dry, and you suffer from a cold and a hacking cough for months on end.

And everything was dark grey. London in 1946 was a grey city but the lack of colour was made much worse during the smogs of the winter months when the famous London fog blended with the soot belched out from the power stations to create a noxious blanket. An unhealthy green tinge was added to London's dark greys. Sometimes I would put a damp towel at the bottom of the basement door to stop the cloud seeping into the house. When you picked the towel back up, after the smog had cleared, there would be a thick black line of soot from where it had blocked the gap under the door.

Later on, during the 1950s, the smogs would get much worse and eventually something would be done to put a stop to them, but that winter of 1946 the smogs which enveloped London served to reinforce the sense of imprisonment that we felt.

The morning of Friday 13th December brought the usual heavy smog. The damp towel was placed under the door and you couldn't see the other side of the street through the ground-floor chapel window. Countess Kleinmichel arrived just after 9am to start her usual lesson with Sofia but that morning's smog matched our mood. It was like a black dirty shroud around us. Sofia had none of her usual zest for learning that day, and whilst I was continuing my cleaning it was without my usual vigour. Eventually, after an hour with Sofia staring at the ceiling or gazing out at the smog, the Countess realised that her usual teaching methods were hopeless.

'That's it!' she cried. 'No more stuck inside, we must go out! Batioushka! Batioushka! Where are you?'

After a brief pause, Father Michael appeared, demanding to know the problem.

'We need to go out, Father Michael. Being stuck in this house is driving us all crazy today. We need to get out of this fog and go somewhere quite different.'

'Well, I can't go too far today, I must attend St Philip's later on,' the little priest protested.

'No, it will be fine, we will all go together. Come along, coats on, scarf around your face Sofia!'

You couldn't argue with the Countess, but we had no idea of her plan.

She led us the short walk around the corner to the underground station, where she bought tickets, and we caught a train to take us the few stops to Kew. Kew Gardens – Pasha had mentioned it in the past as the largest collection of plants in the world but obviously his own stay in London had been far too brief to allow him to visit. We walked up from the Underground station following the signs to the 'Victoria Gate'. We crossed a main road – particularly hazardous in the smog – to a small ticket booth where the Countess bought us all tickets at sixpence each.

'Closing early today cos of the smog,' declared the man in the booth.

'Jolly good, well I'm sure we will still have plenty of time,' responded the Countess, as she marched off up the pathway with me and Sofia behind her and Batioushka at the rear holding his beard with his black cassock fluttering beneath his winter coat. I glanced back and caught sight of the ticket man slightly leaning out of his booth watching us disappear into the grey-green mist. Visibility along the path was only a few metres and we stayed close together. I was a little confused as I couldn't understand what we would be able to see in the gardens in deepest winter when they were shrouded in the smog. But then as we walked Sofia grew wide-eyed.

'Look, Mama, look! A palace!'

Quite simply the largest greenhouse I had ever seen had suddenly appeared. It was at least 100 metres long with curved ends and a huge curvilinear turret of wrought iron and glass. Coming into view so suddenly its huge appearance was nothing less than awe-inspiring. The whole area around the greenhouse was smog-free, it was as though we had walked out of a dense forest into a sunlit glade. Of course, the heat escaping from the greenhouse was dissipating the smog – that had been the Countess's idea.

'The Palm House!' she declared. 'Come along!'

We entered through heavily sprung iron and glass doors set into a central arched portico and were immediately struck by the intense heat inside. Quickly, we unbuttoned our coats. The air was hot and moist, it filled your nostrils and warmed your chest, quite unlike the cloying, choking smog in the streets outside. Pasha would have loved to have been with us, and I mentally started to note the various Latin plant names I could see. The whole interior was a mass of fronds of palms and ferns. Gigantic wide succulent leaves – so many shades of green, and flowers too – in winter! Of course we had greenhouses in Krasnodar and I had seen plenty of greenhouses as we had journeyed through Holland on our way to London, but nothing like this. The most magnificent greenhouse containing simply magical plants.

'Jeremy! Watch where you are going!' called a voice, just as a little boy turned a corner whilst running at full pelt towards us. The warning was moments too late and he crashed into Batioushka who staggered backwards laughing – whilst the boy fell back on his bottom and stared up at our little priest, all resplendent in his black *zostikon*,[77] his luxuriant beard and his tall *kalimavkion*[78] now slightly skewed to a jaunty angle. The boy looked terrified, but Sofia helped him to his feet.

'Hello,' she said. 'Where are you going?'

With his eyes still firmly fixed on Batioushka and continuing to wear an expression of fright albeit now mixed with wonder, he pointed towards a tall wrought-iron spiral staircase emerging from the green jungle beyond.

'Can I come too?' said Sofia. The boy looked at her; his cheeks were rosy, his face like that of a cherub. His collar was half up in the air and half tucked under his sweater. He was thin and his white legs stuck out like pins beneath his short trousers. His clothes were clean and looked fairly new but were all much too large.

He nodded in response to Sofia's request, and the look of terror evaporated as he smiled.

'Yes, but come on!' and off they both ran. He made it to the spiral stairs first but Sofia was clicking at his heels as they ran to the top with their soles clanking on the metal treads. I could hear their squealed gabbling but they were already out of sight by the time Jeremy's mother turned the corner.

'I'm sorry,' she said, 'I must apologise for Jeremy. It's been such a long time since we have been out and about, and it was a long journey here, so he is letting off steam.' Her voice was loud and clear, not raised, but almost sonorous.

---

77 A *zostikon* is a Russian Orthodox priest's cassock.

78 A *kalimavkion* is a Russian Orthodox priest's head wear, rather like a tall black top hat but without the brim.

I wondered whether I should speak. Was this dangerous? Sofia had run off and I hadn't had time to even think about that. Batioushka had composed himself after his collision and had walked on with the Countess talking and pointing at the various plants.

The boy's mother was tall, taller than me, wearing a long beige fitted coat with a tight waistline belt and double buttons up the front. The collar and the cuffs were a dark fur, her gloves were a white lamb's leather. Her hat was at an angle with a large feather protruding from one side.

'Not at all,' I said, 'he has just made friends with my daughter and they have set off to explore the upstairs gallery.'

'Oh that's good. He doesn't usually speak to anybody his own age, spends all his time with grown-ups… well, just me, actually.'

I wondered how long it had been since Sofia had had an opportunity to play with anybody her own age. Probably not since the camp in Salzgitter – she had had the most unusual upbringing and schooling.

'Greta; Greta Chevalier, pleased to meet you.' She held out her gloved hand and smiled warmly. Gleaming mahogany-red curls, blue eyes and a smile that revealed beautiful white teeth, so unlike my own. She held her back straight and her head high, and when she spoke her voice rang out so that others would pause to look round to see who was speaking.

We shook hands and, as our children played, walked slowly round the Palm House. Occasionally Batioushka and the Countess would look back at me to check on my safety but they seemed satisfied and despite my usual reticence with people, as well as the dangers of our life in London, it was so refreshing to speak to somebody different. And Greta Chevalier was so completely different… from anybody else I had ever met.

Born a few years before me she had followed her father onto the stage and became an actress, singer and dancer during the 1920s. From what she said she must have been successful as she had managed to buy a house in Chelsea in London by the mid-1930s. She had fallen in love with a man who had asked for her autograph one night at the stage door and they had married in 1935. Their son, Jeremy, had followed in 1936 and so was exactly the same age as Sofia. After Jeremy was born Greta stopped working and began to rely on her husband for income. He was a motor mechanic but never successful. Greta had bought him a garage premises so that he could run his own business but it transpired that hard work was something of an alien concept and he spent time waiting at other stage doors for other, younger, actresses and dancers. Time spent at home in Chelsea was usually marred by drinking binges which often ended in violence. In the end Greta threw him out.

'I can't think why I'm telling you all this,' she explained. 'But my marriage ended just as the war started. We rented a house in Surrey to be safely out of London, but I'm a London girl and hated it in the country. I haven't really spoken to a soul for years.'

There was a sense of tragedy about Greta. A beautiful woman, clever and talented, she was smart enough to understand that the music halls had been eclipsed by the movies and that her career had ended. Thankfully she had enough money put by; she clearly adored her son but in truth, realised that otherwise her life was barren.

I thought about Pasha and my frustration at his overly colourful letters describing Kenya and his agricultural work. How Greta would have loved to have had somebody to write to her with such enthusiasm. To have somebody thinking of her. To have somebody to talk to – even if currently separated by thousands of kilometres. I felt guilty.

The Countess and Batioushka came back and found us, and I introduced Greta. As we had been told, the gardens were closing early but we had seen everything the Palm House had to offer and the children were clearly exhausted but happy. We went back outside, and the smog had lifted. Now it was freezing but sunny, and the day had become bright and blue. We slowly walked back out to the main road in our little group.

'We are just here,' said Greta pointing to her left. I followed her finger and saw a light green car. It was a rather tall and grand motor and, out of more than mere curiosity, I wandered over to have a closer look.

'Other than Jeremy, Peabody is the only decent thing to come out of my marriage!' said Greta. 'As a motor mechanic, he told me that the best car was a Rolls-Royce and I have never regretted a moment of ownership.'

Of course I knew about Rolls-Royce – their engineering prowess was world-renowned as second to none – even in Russia. Their aero engines had probably helped the Allies to win the war. Close up I could see the car's green paint was faded and flaking but some patches still gleamed brightly in the afternoon light. The silver winged lady – the mascot on the car's bonnet – reminded me of Greta herself; slim and beautiful but with just a hint of melancholy. So many other cars parked in the street or puttering along the road wore liveries of black, grey or brown, whilst this gaily coloured light green motor was a triumph of both style and engineering. Peabody was certainly an apt moniker for the car.

The Rolls was loaded with possessions, a stack of suitcases in the back was piled against the glass division between the passenger compartment and the chauffeur's seat. A large trunk had been attached, rather precariously I felt, to a rack at the back of the car. Greta and Jeremy had finally had enough of Surrey and had given up their rented cottage to return to their townhouse in Tite Street, Chelsea. The idea was that Jeremy would now go to school in London, whilst Greta hoped for something which, one day, might approach a social life.

The car had lain dormant throughout the war, its petrol tank quite dry, and they had saved up petrol ration coupons for months to allow them to fill up for the journey back to London. Having finally set off, they had made it as far as Kew only to be halted by the smog, which made driving conditions simply too dangerous to continue. They had parked up to visit the Botanical Gardens as a distraction to fill the time.

But as I looked on at the Rolls I could see something was wrong. The car drooped on one side and it wasn't the camber of the road that was the problem. I walked around to the driver's side.

'A flat tyre, I'm afraid,' I said.

'Oh no – what a disaster! I will go back in and see if they have a telephone so that I can phone a garage.'

'No no, we can easily fit the spare and get you on your way.'

And so, with Batioushka and the Countess looking on agog, I hitched up my skirt and knelt in the road, found all the tools needed from under the bonnet and in the compartment beneath the driver's seat, unscrewed the wheel hub, jacked up the car, swapped the flat for the spare wheel, and retightened the nut. Now the car sat proudly awaiting the next leg of its journey.

Greta was delighted and clapped her hands. 'Tanya you are so clever!' her words ringing in the street. 'However did you know to do all that? Goodness! Well, you'll not be taking the Tube back to Barons Court. A lift home is the least I can do. Come on everyone!'

A Rolls-Royce is a very large car but even so, when loaded with four adults, two children and all the belongings of a London stage actress and her son, the interior space was somewhat cramped. But we did all fit, just about. I sat next to Greta, with the Countess squeezed in alongside me on the front bench, whilst Batioushka, Sofia and Jeremy settled into the luxurious rear seat even though their legroom was rather restricted by all the piled-up cases. Batioushka had a lovely time waving to all the passers-by who mostly waved back at him.

Whilst Greta was impressed by my ability to change a tyre, I was equally impressed to note her superb driving skills. Having suffered Angus's high-speed jerky motion in the Humber in Germany, coupled with his grinding gear changes, Greta and Peabody the green Rolls-Royce made slow, but smooth and steady, progress. The gear lever switched through the ratios silently, as she double declutched with precision, obstacles were anticipated well in advance so that her braking was considered, and her hand signals were positive and accurate so that other road users knew what to expect.

Greta clearly respected the engineering qualities of the car and she won my respect in return.

Having dropped us off at St Dunstan's Road an arrangement was made for Greta and Jeremy to call for tea the following week. Our friendship blossomed rather like the succulent plants in the greenhouse on the day we met. It turned out that Greta's old social circle had evaporated away during the war and she was just as friendless in London as she had been in Surrey. We travelled to Chelsea to join them for their Christmas lunch just a couple of weeks later, and they joined us for our Orthodox Christmas supper a few weeks after that. Having Peabody parked up outside the house in St Dunstan's Road caused one or two neighbours' curtains to twitch.

Sofia and Jeremy played so well together. There was never a murmur of dissent between them. More than brother and sister, the lack of an age gap almost made them like twins. Greta and I were so different, in so many ways, but our mutual need for companionship, coupled with respect for our distinct qualities, made us great girlfriends. And I had never had, nor needed, a girlfriend before. It really had only ever been Pyotr and then Pasha, but Greta, tall, glamorous, loud, direct and strong, made those dark London days more tolerable.

And Pasha's letters kept on coming, a fresh aerogramme arriving nearly every day. Earlier on, during our time in London, I might have been cross and frustrated at his daily babblings, but Greta approved, and I realised just how lucky we were to have him.

January 1947 was cold. The coldest any Londoner had ever known with maximum daily temperatures rarely above freezing and minimum readings falling to −20 degrees centigrade, although I was happier because the extreme cold weather removed the smog and even the dampness to an extent. But as the cold continued into February the stockpiles of coal froze solid at the mines and the fires at the power stations burned low, without the usual fuel supplies. Power cuts became normal and food rations which had remained in place since the war were cut further. Now even potatoes were rationed. Even without smog the sky, during that February, was a constant grey. The sun did not shine for twenty-two out of the twenty-eight days that month and with no sunlight by day and no electric light by night the mood in London grew as dark as the weather. Nobody smiled and at St Dunstan's Road the bowls of meaty borscht had given way to clear consommé.

But the post kept coming and to my absolute relief, in early February, Pasha reported that the authorities had finally promised to make space for us on a ship to Africa. Thank God.

By the middle of the month, when the BBC was reporting that farmers were using pneumatic drills to attempt to harvest root vegetables from frozen fields, Pasha confirmed by letter our booking on the SS Winchester Castle. We were scheduled to depart Southampton for Mombasa, Kenya, on Monday 3rd March 1947. My heart leapt!

On the Saturday evening before our departure Batioushka and the Russian parishioners organised a party for us at the Podvorya. It seemed that every Russian in London was there. Everybody had brought something notwithstanding the severe shortages they all faced. Greta and Jeremy came too and we sang and danced to the piano and fiddle. I hadn't danced since I had been at the technical university in Krasnodar – I was never very good – but with the table and chairs pushed aside we reeled and whirled and laughed. Batioushka turned out to be very light on his feet! Greta sang some of her old music hall songs, which Ivan the pianist loved, although I wasn't certain that the Countess fully approved!

Our time in London had been dark and forbidding. We had been confined to the house in St Dunstan's Road, only leaving to visit St Philip's on Sundays and occasionally to carry Batioushka's shopping basket. But, despite the best efforts of the weather, London had finally brightened – things seemed better now; well at least they did for us now that we were leaving.

Eventually Monday morning came. Our cases were packed once again; our photographs carefully put away. I had never seen Sofia so excited. Greta and Jeremy arrived in Peabody to drive us through the frosted roads to Waterloo to take the train to Southampton. Batioushka travelled with us. Once again, Waterloo Station was witness to a sad farewell, and once again it was those who were left behind who shed the most tears.

Batioushka kissed Sofia and me.

'Thank you for your kindness, my Batioushka.'

'And thank you for your love, dearest Tanya. I was never certain of your faith, but your love was undoubted and that is the greatest gift.' He drew a pressed white handkerchief from the pocket of his *zostikon* and dabbed his eyes.

Sofia and Jeremy solemnly shook hands.

'Will you write?' he asked. 'I will write to you every day.' They wouldn't of course, but they knew that they were the best of friends.

But Greta was in floods of tears as we hugged. It was her theatrical nature I suppose. I didn't cry, I never do, but I held my lips tight and swallowed back quite hard. When we settled back into our seats, as the train finally moved out of the station, I blew my nose – another London cold perhaps.

At Southampton, the railway platform was directly on the dock and I collected our tickets from the Union Castle Line office as directed by Pasha in his letters. I think for me it was the moment that I had the tickets in my hand that I knew this was real. The tickets had cost £63, a simply incomprehensibly huge sum of money at that time; accompanying them were the essential papers allowing us to leave Britain and gain entry to Kenya – even without passports.

Everywhere there were people, mainly soldiers, and it seemed there was not an inch of spare room anywhere on the boat. Our cabin was on C deck. It was tiny and had no heating but it was ours alone, not shared – thank goodness. At 1pm preparations began for casting off; three tugs approached, two to pull and one to push the boat through 180 degrees, to turn it to face the ocean. And then, at dead slow, we made our way past the liner the "Queen Mary" and out towards open waters. The dockside cranes all had their jibs pointing to the sky. Sofia said that it looked as though they had turned their back on us in a huff. The largest flock of seagulls I had ever seen cried and swooped all around. We looked at each other. We were en route to Africa. We were free.

10

PASHA ZAYKY
Nairobi and Kitale, Kenya, 1946

YOU NEED TO STAND BY THE FULLY OPEN WINDOW of the carriage door to properly be able to say goodbye to somebody and I waved and waved to Sofia as she pelted along the platform that morning in late August 1946 vainly trying to keep up with the accelerating train. As the platform finally came to an end and the train made its way onwards, clattering over the maze of points at the throat of the station, I leaned out as far as I could and looked back at her forlorn figure rapidly diminishing in size as the distance between us grew. But you daren't lean out of a train window for too long and so I gave her one final wave, and then made my way back to my seat in the carriage compartment. As I walked down the corridor the rocking of the train caused my tears to splash onto my freshly polished shoes. When I sat down I wiped the black leather clean with my handkerchief in case the salt should stain.

I had cried when we had left homes and cities before but I had never felt such a rush of mixed emotions as I did that day. London was certainly not our home. We had no home.

Home is certainty. Home is where we place the photographs from our old and battered cigar box. Our only certainty was each other, which I was tearing apart, and we only had single copies of our photographs, which obviously Tanya had kept with her. If there ever had been other prints of those pictures, then they had been lost years before.

There was nothing that I could do. The role in Kenya offered us a complete break from the past, from Europe, from the Soviets. It was a stroke of luck that I had been in the right place at the right time (it had still not occurred to me then that on receipt of Angus's letter the Whitehall officials had conspired to create a situation which effectively forced me to accept the job in Africa). But with the role came this terrible – and yet surely only temporary – wrench that drove me apart from Tanya and Sofia. It created a most agonising pain in my chest. Heartache is just like indigestion of the most severe kind. I sat back in my seat breathing heavily through my mouth and fidgeting. My fellow travellers ostentatiously turned the pages of their broadsheet newspapers and I was faintly aware of a slight click of their tongues or a tut: emotion – so beloved of Eastern Europeans – is frowned upon by the British.

And yet mixed in with the pain of our separation was elation, anticipation, excitement, coupled with just a little anxiety. Elation that I was going to be a botanist once more. I love what I do, and to have a chance to be a botanist in Africa is more than any Soviet-trained scientist could ever dream of. Africa is the cradle of man's development. I was going back to where it all began. My anticipation and excitement were immense. Of course, I knew full well that I was a good botanist. I had proved my worth when I had run the web of agrarian scientists throughout the Third Reich. Our combined research had led to significant gains then and I was determined to repeat this now. But to harbour self-doubt is a simple human trait which exists in all of us to some extent, and so anxiousness coexisted with all the other emotions railing inside me during that train journey from London to Poole.

When we reached Poole the train terminated at the dockside. Officials in dark blue suits checked my papers and exchanged the written authority I had obtained from Smith at Whitehall the previous day for a cardboard ticket for the nine thirty flying boat service to Africa. I looked through the windows of the dockside office out to the waters beyond and could see the largest and most amazing aircraft that I had ever laid eyes upon. Compared to even the biggest wartime bombers or gliders that I had seen, either in the air or crashed on the ground, the craft at anchor in the harbour was simply massive. It was, I was told proudly by the BOAC man at the desk who handed me my ticket and watched me admiring the craft, an Empire flying boat with a wingspan of 35 metres and a length of 27 metres. It had four engines and a float hanging from each wing but beneath its hooked nose the bottom of the fuselage rose up out of the water so that the windows of the pilot's cabin sat like eyes above the neck of a huge grey turtle. At the front just below the pilot's windows and above an arrow-shaped flashing – the mark of the BOAC – was the name 'Cleopatra'. I wished that Tanya was with me. How she would marvel at this monstrous machine, which was clearly the pinnacle of aeronautical engineering.[79]

---

79 https://commons.wikimedia.org/wiki/File:BOAC_
    Short_S.33_%27C%27_Class_Empire_Flying_Boat_"Cleopatra"_
    circles_Durban.jpg

A motor launch took me and my fellow passengers out to the vessel, lightly rocking on the waves in the morning sun. I was seated most luxuriously and some short time later the engines were switched on. The anchor had obviously been raised and the flying boat began to make its way to the start of its take-off run. At the appointed moment the speed of the engines increased and the drone of the motors was replaced by a thunderous roar. Flying boat Cleopatra shook and I was pushed backwards into my seat by a great unseen force. Somewhere drinking glasses were rattling and chinking but I was only subliminally aware as the entire plane and all its passengers gave their full concentration to the take-off. It was almost that we willed the plane into the air – after all how could such a machine possibly fly? But it did. And, quite suddenly, the view of the dockside from my window shrank in size. It was as though the ground, and everything around it, had fallen from a cliff whilst we had remained quite still. Only my stomach told me that this was not so.

My journey to Africa was uneventful. That is not to say that the journey was anything less than utterly wonderful, it is just that, as part of this story, I don't feel the need to recount the flight in full detail, glorious though such details would be. Suffice to say that even now, as I write, I look back with some degree of guilt at the sheer luxury of the accommodation coupled with the immense speed of my progress at a time when almost everything else in the world was dowdy, slow or broken. Having not eaten well since I had been at the Reichsuniversität in Posen, I dined like a king on the flying boat, on roasted meats, fresh vegetables, salads, and sweet puddings, superbly prepared and washed down with fine wines. From Poole we flew to Marseilles, to Augusta in Sicily and then onwards to Alexandria in Egypt, landing at dusk. I was billeted in the Cecil Hotel.

In the morning of the second day I ate bacon and eggs for breakfast before being urged back on to the flying boat to take off from a mile-long stretch of the Mediterranean to start our flight down the African continent. Following the highway of the Nile, we stopped at Cairo and, straight after take-off, flew over the top of the pyramids and the Sphinx. Pausing at Luxor, and Wadi Halfa (at the southern border of Egypt with the Sudan) we finally stopped for a second night at Khartoum's Empire Hotel.

On the third day we landed at Malakal in the south of Sudan, then Port Bell in Kampala, Uganda, on the northern shore of Lake Victoria, before heading to a place called Kisumu on the eastern shore of the lake. At last we were flying over Kenya and headed south-east to Lake Naivasha where we landed just before 5pm. There I said goodbye to Cleopatra with all its luxury and attentive crew. It would continue its southbound journey through Africa for two further days via Mombasa, Dar-es-Salaam and Mozambique to finally arrive at Durban in South Africa on the fifth day after leaving Poole.

On arrival at Naivasha I was directed to a bus wearing a livery of faded blue and cream. The driver, a grinning black man in a white suit with a white peaked cap, welcomed me on board. However, despite the driver's clean and pressed uniform, it seemed that my luxurious progress had ended. The bus's hard wooden seats coupled with its ancient creaking suspension along the uneven roads made for an uncomfortable two-hour journey to Nairobi where I arrived shortly after nightfall.

The thing that struck me most during that first bus journey – my first real impression of Africa and Kenya outside of the sanctuary of the flying boat – were the people. By which I mean the indigenous population. There was so much life. So animated and so colourful, both by their facial expressiveness and through the movement of their limbs (which seemed so much longer then European arms and legs) but also in the colours that they wore. It does seem strange to remark on this now, but for me at that time, these colourful, noisy, laughing people were such a far cry from the inhabitants of an austere, depressed, smashed Europe that they were a sight of pure wonder. I spent all my time staring at the people from the windows of the bus as they walked along the side of the road.

The men walked ahead of their wives, tall and proud in coloured robes which draped down from one side of their neck and hung like flower petals against their sleek bodies. Their womenfolk shuffled along behind them, burdened by enormous, brightly coloured loads strapped to their backs and suspended from leather straps around their foreheads. The British notion of chivalry seemed not to apply in this reach of their empire. Young women seemed in many cases not to wear clothing on the top half of their bodies and some carried water containers, with great poise, balanced on their heads whilst a baby was strapped to their back within a makeshift cradleboard. Both men and women wore their hair short and cropped or even completely shaved.

As we arrived into Nairobi I began to see Asian faces too. They seemed to be mainly shopkeepers, scurrying around rather bedraggled shops and stores made from corrugated tin. Shorter in stature than the African natives, they wore smarter long robes in white or cream and, on their heads, either turbans or small white caps which looked rather like those worn by naval sailors. There were no Asian women to be seen, however.

The British were also very evident although far fewer in number. Whilst some of the men wore civilian cream-coloured double-breasted suits, most seemed to be in a uniform of short-sleeved shirts, knee-length shorts, long socks and black shoes. On their heads they wore either cream-coloured pith helmets or slouch hats where one side of the brim drooped downwards whilst the other was pinned against the side of the crown. British women, on the other hand, all seemed to wear long floral summer dresses beneath wide-brimmed sun hats.

And there was the smell too. That was the other most notable thing that no book I had ever read had mentioned. Smell was everywhere, for the most part it was a scented woodsmoke, a hot spicy aroma, but then as we entered the city a profusion of other smells entered through the open windows of the bus from farm animals and exhaust fumes, to sewage and body odours. You might consider these smells to be noxious or unpleasant, but that wasn't the case as combined with the woodsmoke they created a wonderful cocktail of aromas that infused my body. Somehow those smells underlined the vigour and the vibrancy of this new place. The abundance of smells matched the clamour of the city perfectly and stays with me today. As I write this – I can smell Africa!

Following instructions to alight at the Norfolk Hotel I was approached by a British man in the obligatory cream suit.

'Zayky, I presume?' He held out his hand, and as I shook

it, 'Hopkins Scotlab; I'm pleased to meet you.'

For a few moments I thought the man had the strangest name, but before I had actually called him Mr Scotlab I realised that his surname was Hopkins and that the Scott Agricultural Laboratory was the name of the main government research centre, as mentioned briefly by Smith at my briefing at Whitehall some days before!

'Not much luggage, I see. Good stuff. Let me walk you to reception.'

It was dark now but the Norfolk Hotel was well lit with electric bulbs and I could see it was a curious-looking building – seemingly an unhappy merger of numerous architectural styles. To one side a long colonial colonnade, with a church bell tower on top, to the other a modern attempt at a half-timbered medieval hall. In between the two an entrance portico sat beneath a roof which might have been fixed atop a chateau. It was all most incongruous but I forgave it once we stepped inside and I met the cooled lightly blown air from the numerous electric ceiling fans.[80]

I was checked in and Hopkins assured me that everything was 'on account'. He asked that I meet him by reception at nine thirty the following morning to drive me to the Scott Laboratory for my initial briefing.

That Monday evening Nairobi's Norfolk Hotel seemed so very different from the Imperial Hotel of Russell Square in London where we had all checked in, on Angus's recommendation, the previous Friday morning. Both traded on a faded glory but whilst the London hotel was staffed with sour-faced receptionists and porters, smelled

---

80   https://www.pinterest.co.uk/pin/32651166032854231/

musty and damp, and, like almost everything else in European cities, was covered in a layer of soot, the Norfolk was buzzing, the aroma of the scented woodsmoke was strong, and everybody smiled. I felt a flood of relief at my own situation followed by an equivalent wave of despair in knowing full well that Tanya and Sofia were fending for themselves in an unwelcoming, hard-nosed city. London was a world away from me then.

But, despite my concerns for my wife and daughter, I ate a good supper and slept soundly. The following morning I bathed, shaved and breakfasted in my room before donning my freshly pressed suit and laundered shirt in readiness for my meeting. I knew Hopkins would be on time and he drove me the four miles to the west of the city centre where the buildings of the Scott Laboratory sat amid developed agricultural land.

At the Laboratory Hopkins introduced me to Dr Bumpus, the head of the facility.

'Good to meet you, Zayky, we are all looking forward to having you on board. Let's chat as we walk the fields...'

The Laboratory had been established when an old first war sanatorium had closed down in 1922. Initially there had been ten acres of land but this had grown to seventy-three acres before the second war, all carefully planted under research conditions. About a third was devoted to coffee investigations with the remainder taken up with cereals, legumes and grasses. There were three key functions: to solve agricultural issues peculiar to Kenya and its farming needs; to provide technical advice and expertise; and to train the natives in Western agricultural methodology.

'Although we need to train most of the whites before

we can even start on the blacks,' remarked Bumpus wryly. 'Zayky, let me start with something of a history lesson.

'Of course Mombasa, down on the coast, had been known to the Europeans for centuries. During the last century[81] the Sultan of Zanzibar extended his rule over the East African mainland tied in, as it was, with both the ivory and slave trades. The local tribes resented his incursions but, frankly, could do little to resist.

'Back at home, British public opinion was fuelled by reports from David Livingstone and other explorers of the day, who harped on about the evils of the East African slaving. And so, in the end, it was British pressure which forced the Sultan to banish slavery back in '73.[82]

'Obviously, the British told the Sultan what to do; albeit policing the ban on slavery was difficult, to say the least. But then, in the mid '80s, the Germans quietly set to work on local tribal chiefs in the land to the south to get them to agree to the Kaiser being their overlord rather than the Sultan. The chiefs' assumption was that a power in faraway Europe would exercise less control than one based just further along the coast – quite wrong of course.

'But through those German efforts a new colony to the south – German East Africa, or Tanganyika – which was created around 1880 – became part of the Boche empire, and that made the British sit up!

'The Sultan was pressurised into handing over control of the land that was left and by the end of the century the British East African Protectorate covered the land north of a

---

81 The nineteenth century.

82 '73: 1873

line between the island of Pemba and Lake Victoria, and ran up as far as the Nile watershed.

'Of course, the land had been farmed in tiny plots, by hand, for thousands of years by the country's various tribes, over forty-odd of them at the last count, about two and a half million natives here in total. The Kikuyu are probably the most dominant – about one in eight – mainly based around Nairobi, the Highlands and the Rift Valley. The central highlands combined a benign climate with decent quality land, excellent for a variety of cash crops – notably tea, coffee and tobacco – and the railway up from the coast was completed in the early part of this century. Economically, it made sense for the British settlers to have the most productive land and so the Kikuyu population were moved to reserves. The "White Highlands" then became lands of plenty.

'But then during the first war the Germans fought an extremely effective guerrilla campaign throughout East Africa. Many of the settlers were called up to fight and farming resources were depleted.

'In 1920 the East Africa Protectorate was renamed Kenya in honour of its highest mountain. After the Great War there came a new type of settler to the newly formed Kenya. The British had set up a scheme to encourage ex-servicemen to come to Africa to take up farming: "Land Fit for Heroes", they called it. But most of the heroes were former city-dwellers who had been sold a dream with absolutely no experience of pioneering or farming. Yes, there were a few good years during the '20s when crops grew despite the new farmers rather than because of any expertise. In fact, the Kikuyus were welcomed back as squatters to work small plots for themselves, in return for working the majority of the land on behalf of the settlers.

'As time went along, so lack of rotation caused the soil to became exhausted, incorrect irrigation leached out the nutrients, and crop disease ran riot. It all came to a head just as the Great Depression of the '30s caused the value of Kenya's cash crops to collapse on the worldwide commodity market. People were ruined. And as the depression ended so the world moved into yet another war.'

Bumpus paused and bent down to study an ear of maize.

'How many white settlers are there?' I asked.

'Oh about 10,000 in all, I suppose,' he answered. 'There are about 30,000 Indians just in the cities – they were originally imported at the end of the last century to build the railway, two and a half million blacks and then 10,000 of us British… err, well, Europeans.' He stuttered slightly, looking up at me. I was reminded that I was Russian. Not black, nor Indian, but not British either. It was to become a familiar feeling.

'The thing is, Zayky, that now, following this second war, much more food is needed, and we have the science and technology to ensure we can deliver bumper crops year after year. Small unproductive plots of farming land need to be consolidated to make much larger, more economically viable blocks. Output must be increased, both to feed the local residents and to provide food, back home, for Britain. The Kikuyu squatters will need to be moved back to the reservations to allow for our modern intensive-farming methods. They won't like that one bit, but it's for their own good, as well as for ours.

'Obviously, eugenically[83], the blacks aren't up to the levels of us whites, but they're not entirely stupid, and once they can see modern farming technology in action, then its infinite superiority over their primitive practices should become quite clear.'

I spent a full day at the Scott Laboratories, examining the plants in the fields, looking at soil samples and asking the various scientists about their work and aims. I was presented with numerous reports, whilst Dr Bumpus and several other fellows spent some time quizzing me on my own background and knowledge. I felt that I managed to satisfy them as to my intellectual credentials notwithstanding that the journals that had published my botanical work to that date were either Russian or German. At the end of the day Hopkins returned me to the Norfolk – exhausted but exhilarated.

The following day I was to make my way to my new base, the Agricultural Research Station at Kitale, a town in the west of the country, at the very edge of the White Highlands, close to the border with Uganda. Building on the work of the Scott Laboratories my role was to advise

---

83 Eugenics, meaning 'well born', was the term coined in 1883 by British scholar Sir Francis Galton, cousin of Charles Darwin. Based on his study of upper-class Britain, Galton believed that an elite position in society was due to a good genetic make-up and thus the human race could direct its future by selective breeding. His views caught on and during the first half of the twentieth century many countries introduced sterilisation programmes targeting the mentally ill, alcoholics and criminals. It is thought that around 65,000 Americans were sterilised during this time period, without their consent, including many African American women. After WW2, when Nazi Germany's use of eugenic principles to attempt to justify atrocities became apparent, eugenics lost all credibility.

the local farmers on implementation of the latest farming methodology. The goal was to drive up agricultural output. What was being asked of me now was very little different from the imperatives of Soviet collectivisation in the Caucasus before the war, or the Third Reich's demand for standardisation and collective best practice during the war years. I was excited and daunted.

In the morning, I breakfasted early and made my way to Nairobi Station to catch the 9am train headed north-west.

Nairobi was a railway town; it had been founded in the nineteenth century to be the central hub of the railway network as it was predominately flat land. In fact, originally the land had been a swamp. In many ways Nairobi railway station was, in 1946, just like a station in any major city. It heaved with humanity all urgently focused on the journey ahead and catching the correct train, but these were the same people I had seen from the bus, and so there was a difference to the peoples of Nairobi Station not evident at Waterloo. Smiling, babbling, bartering and haggling. There was colour and noise and the smells of course. Body odours in profusion now mixed with hot steam oils and coal sulphur. Soldiers, both British and the native *askaris*,[84] white settler gentlemen and ladies but lots of native travellers with children and baggage. The station concourse bustled with porters plying for trade either with trolleys or just a willingness to carry the largest loads on their backs in exchange for a few pennies. All sorts of tradesmen seemed to sell every type of foodstuff, as well as blankets, buckets, and even sandals which, on quick inspection, appeared to be made from old car tyres.

---

84   *Askari*: a native soldier serving the British.

The 9am departure was clearly the main train of the day. This was to be a long journey and seeing the clamour for seats from all comers I was very happy to be holding a first-class ticket. The first-class car was right at the front, just behind the engine. The train was long and I made my way through the hubbub bumping various passengers and porters with my case and bags. Having finally arrived at the first-class car and deposited my bags in my allocated compartment, I thought I might step outside once more to take a look at the locomotive before setting off. The engine, named 'Karamoja' on the side of the driver's cabin, was huge and most unusual, having two sets of driving wheels, articulated, with the steam boiler set between them.[85] I stared up from the low platform at the two turbaned Indians making ready to set off and one of them glanced back down at me and gave me a toothy grin. Once again, on my travels, I wished that Tanya was with me to witness this sight.

The train set off; initially I couldn't see out of my window as natives were clinging on to the sides of the carriage and I could hear them clambering around on the roof. But in fact most jumped (or fell) off relatively soon after leaving

85 The Ugandan Railway was, despite its name, almost totally situated within Kenya to provide the white-settler farmers access to the Highlands. Steep inclines necessitated a narrow gauge of 1 metre allowing much sharper curves so the line could weave its way up and down the hills. The immense weight and length of the trains resulted in a need for locomotives which were hugely powerful but could nevertheless negotiate the tight curves. The Kenya Ugandan Railway EC3 class were 4-8-4+4-8-4 Garratt-type articulated steam locomotives to 1,000mm gauge and built by Beyer, Peacock & Co. in Manchester, England in 1939. 'Karamoja' is preserved at the Nairobi Railway Museum.
http://www.trains-worldexpresses.com/700/704-03m.JPG

the station and the vista opened up. The journey was indeed long although the scenery was spectacular. We headed upcountry back towards Naivasha where we skirted round the eastern edge of the lake. Mount Kenya, which up to then had been shrouded in cloud, now revealed itself in its full glory and magnificence, the peak capped by snow. But the train slowed up as we hit the steep inclines and I could hear Karamoja ahead of me slaving and straining to haul the long procession of carriages around the sharp bends. It took me several hours to read the collection of reports I had brought with me from the Scott Laboratories, but the train ploughed on and on for hours more.

The scenery remained awe-inspiring but I just wanted to arrive. Eventually we pulled into the town of Eldoret at 9.15pm, a little over twelve hours after leaving Nairobi – a distance of just over 300 kilometres as the crow flies but much longer by the meandering train line. At Eldoret the train separated. The rear section was picked up by a fresh engine to head west towards Kampala in Uganda, whilst Karamoja was due to rest and refuel for a few hours before heading off again on the branch line to Kitale, seventy kilometres farther to the north. I stretched my legs a little on the station platform for half an hour before returning to my compartment which had, by then, been converted into a bunk for the night. We started out again just after 4am, but I didn't hear us get underway and I was eventually awoken at 6.45am by the steward's gentle knocking on my door to alert me that we were due at Kitale in under thirty minutes.

As I finally stepped down from the train, still bleary-eyed and slightly shaky, a tall native man approached me and held out his hand.

'*Bwana*, it is good to meet you. My name is Mohammed, I am working at the research station and I have come to take you to your bungalow.'

He was, I thought, in his early thirties, wearing a dark green shirt, dark trousers, and with a large machete (or *panga* as it is known locally) hanging from his side. A friendly smile, a firm handshake, it was a welcome greeting.

He took my cases and led me to a slate-grey Austin motor car parked in the road outside the station yard. We set off rapidly creating a cloud of dust behind and kangarooing slightly as Mohammed changed gear with something of a crunch. He would have to do better than that once Tanya arrived, I thought, smiling to myself.

We drove out of the town and arrived at the research station about two miles south of the town. As we approached I could see the various agricultural plots, and the crops – maize, coffee, tea, plantain, and pyrethrum.[86] My heart slightly quickened.

'There is the laboratory, *Bwana*,' said Mohammed, pointing to a small brick building. 'And here is your bungalow.'

My heart jumped. I had been uncertain what a bungalow would be like in reality but this was just like a Russian *dacha*, a beautiful *dacha*, exquisite, and clean. Built of brick with a corrugated iron roof, verandahs, large picture windows all bordered by a picket fence outside. I jumped out of the car and, leaving Mohammed chuckling behind me, ran inside. The building was arranged in a T-shape. Along the head of

---

86 Pyrethrum: a natural insecticide made from the dried flower heads of *Chrysanthemum cinerariifolium*.

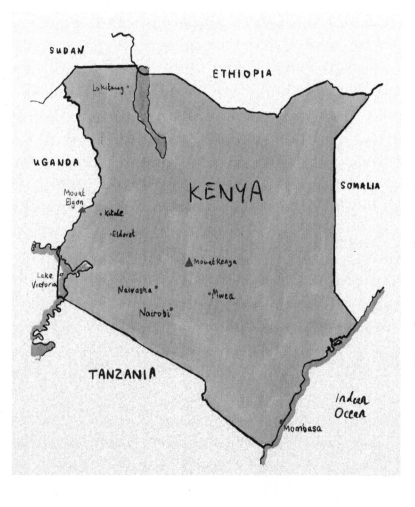

SUDAN

ETHIOPIA

Lokitaung

UGANDA

Mount
Elgon

Kitale

Eldoret

KENYA

SOMALIA

Mount Kenya

Lake
Victoria

Naivasha

Mwea

Nairobi

TANZANIA

Indian
Ocean

Mombasa

the T were the four main rooms, two bedrooms, a dining room and a sitting room, and then the trunk of the T comprised a kitchen, bathroom, WC, laundry, and another smaller bedroom.

There was lots of furniture too; admittedly most of it was old, but everything was in perfectly good repair. A good dining table and chairs, an iron double bed in the main bedroom, easy chairs in the sitting room as well as a writing desk. The sitting room and main bedrooms both opened out to the verandahs by large double doors to reveal the finest view of Mount Elgon, its peak dominating the vista.

Mohammed left me to settle in, promising to return later to show me round the research station and introduce me to the other workers once they had arrived as it was still before 8am in the morning. In the drawer of the writing desk I found fountain pens, ink, and blank aerogramme paper. I settled down to write to Tanya and Sofia, addressing my letter to them care of the Colonial Office in Whitehall.

There is so much more to say about the research station, Mohammed and the other staff, about Kitale Town and its local people and farmers, but I cannot continue this account until I can explain how Tanya, Sofia and I were finally reunited.

Those first weeks at Kitale were full of wonder for me in terms of my work. Each day brought new discoveries and expanded my thoughts on exactly what was feasible in this amazing agricultural land. But my nights were sleepless. I had no news of my wife and child.

The British prided themselves on the Royal Mail and their pride was completely justified. Kitale was to the extreme west of Kenya and Nairobi was several days from London even by the fastest air route, but despite the distance I knew that the postal system worked with extreme efficiency. And so when my first letters to Tanya and Sofia addressed care of the Colonial Office went unanswered and were eventually returned 'not known' I was sick with worry, with no idea what might have taken place.

It was not until the very end of September that a bundle of letters from Tanya arrived, giving me her news, and their address in London 'care of St Philip's church in the Buckingham Palace Road'. Smart, of course, smart and cautious, but her letters were always brief and to the point. Never any 'colour' in those letters from London – I always wanted more – but that's Tanya, and me too, I suppose!

I was so relieved and immediately set to work writing to Dr Bumpus at the Scott Laboratories and to Government House in Nairobi requesting that a cabin be allocated on a ship to get Tanya and Sofia across to Kenya. I wrote daily and stressed that I could not fully engage in my work until we were reunited. Nevertheless, they said it would take months – family members were a second priority to troops and supplies – but I was finally able to write to Tanya in early February 1947, when the newspapers reported on the coldest winter that England had ever known, with the news that a passage to Kenya for the two of them had been agreed.

If it had been a long train journey from Nairobi to Kitale then it was even longer from Kitale all the way down to Mombasa on the coast. Made all the more tedious because I couldn't wait to get there to meet Tanya and Sofia arriving off the ship. I knew they had embarked on their voyage on Monday 3rd March and, in fact, had received a couple of letters from them posted on board the ship. Without passports, Tanya and Sofia could not disembark during the seventeen-day crossing but letters handed into the purser's office during the voyage were then posted from the various ports en route and so had reached me. The letters didn't say but I guessed that poor Tanya and Sofia would have been going crazy to be stuck on board for so long.

I was determined to be there when their ship finally docked at Mombasa on that Wednesday morning, 19th March 1947.

I watched it come into port. I waved and waved, and maybe I saw them waving back, I wasn't sure. But I waited impatiently on the other side of the immigration desk, shielded off from the main reception area by a wooden partition. Everybody else came through. Hundreds of people milling around. But no sign of Tanya or Sofia. I waited and waited. The crowds had started to dissipate. Was there a problem? Why were they so long? Was there somebody I could ask?

And then they were there! Sofia ran at me at full pelt – it was as though she was still running to keep up with the train leaving Waterloo Station all those months previously. She ran right into me and I staggered backwards, as she flung her arms around me and clung on – she had grown! And then Tanya set down her case and, with Sofia still clinging to my front, came around to my side. Slowly and deliberately she wrapped me and Sofia in her arms and held on to us all as we kissed. Tanya was not like me. She was not known for emotion, but she kissed me again and again, nuzzling into my neck as I choked back my tears.

'I love you, my Pasha,' she whispered. We were a family again!

11

PASHA ZAYKY
Kitale, Kenya, 1947

Pip Faulkner had turned out to be a true friend when I was without Tanya and Sofia during those months that saw out 1946 and began 1947. We were both feeling a huge sense of loss, and although mine would be resolved, his could never be; nevertheless, we were a source of mutual comfort. He was an old man then, about seventy I would think, whilst I was turning forty. So, we were a generation apart, but there was something about Pip, and maybe something about me, that drew us together in friendship. He was a tall man, six feet perhaps and, despite advancing years, he strode everywhere with his back upright – no sense of a stoop – quite unlike me actually. You got the sense that he was enormously strong. When he spoke he made use of his physical demeanour, a huge open smile, and a roar of laughter.

He was very nearly the first person I met after my arrival in Kitale. His farm was just a short walk away from the research station; the next plot along the Eldoret road leading south. When we stood on his verandah looking out over the fields he would place his arm around my shoulders. I had a sense of well-being and solidarity. I needed that so badly in those early months in Africa with my wife and child thousands of miles away.

What was it about Pip? You were immediately struck by his warmth although when the conversation became more intense and you dug down, just a little, you could sense that his natural bonhomie was tinged with melancholy. The answer dawned on me one day. He was just like Pyotr, my lost brother-in-law… my lost brother. He was an older version of that skinny grinning lad with the fishing rod, barefoot by the Kuban river, in the overexposed photograph.

I decided not to share my thought of the similarity between Pip and Pyotr with Tanya but I was excited to introduce them to each other. I thought they would get on – and I was correct. Pip had spent the afternoon with us at the bungalow. The evening had come. Sofia had been put to bed, exhausted after a day of activity exploring all sorts of wildlife around the research station with the ever-attentive Mohammed following her and making sure she came to no harm. Our cook, Boniface, had prepared supper (it had taken me time to get used to native servants, and it took Tanya longer) and now the three of us sat drinking coffee on the verandah.

During the preceding months I had learned snippets of Pip's story but now it seemed the time to ask him to recount it all, in detail, for Tanya's benefit, but for me as well really.

I was christened Philip at birth, but found that, as a toddler, I couldn't pronounce the 'f' of Philip and so was renamed 'Pip' from the age of two onwards. Although in the army I was known as 'Squeaky' (squeaky pips… the army conjures a nickname for everybody!).

My father had inherited a drapers' shop in a southern suburb of London, called Bromley. It was a decent business and though nominally managed by Dad it was actually run by Mum and later by me, once my army stint had ended. Dad's passion was always for property and by the end of the 1890s, with careful management coupled with one or two lucky investments, he owned a decent-sized portfolio of houses and business premises in South London. We were never rich but we were certainly comfortable.

Bromley was a dull town and, aged eighteen in 1893, I joined the army desperate for travel and some greater experience of life. I certainly got that. I found I was a good soldier and well suited to life in the army, I spent some time in India, and rose up to the rank of sergeant. Later on, I was posted to South Africa.

In early 1898 I came home on leave and was back in Bromley. I stepped out with Ena. She was three years younger than me and we had known each other all our lives – her family kept a china shop just a few doors down from us in the High Street. Childhood sweethearts, I suppose. I returned to my regiment in Africa but almost immediately received a letter from Ena and, as a result, requested special leave to return to England for us to be married.

Our service was at St Peter and St Paul, Bromley, and afterwards everyone came back to the shop at Atlas House in the High Street[87] for tea and cake, but there was no honeymoon for us. Tensions were running high in South Africa at that time and

---

87   Atlas House, 46 High Street, Bromley, Kent, was the birthplace of the author H.G. Wells, where his parents ran a crockery shop. A Primark store occupies the site today.

I went straight back out there. I got a telegram in the October to say that Roy had been born.

A year after that the Boer War began.[88] *It was the bloodiest and costliest conflict since the war against the French eighty years before. As a trained infantryman serving in South Africa, the Boers had my respect, although they had little respect for anybody else. They are a hard race who had struggled for, and won, survival in Africa for about six generations by then. Great farmers; they knew the land intimately and were superb horsemen. Fiercely nationalistic – they hated the British. What we know now is that the Germans had quietly set about arming the Afrikaners with the latest weapons and as a result British command massively underestimated the Boers' effectiveness in the field.*

Like I say, it was bloody. The Boers threw everything at us and, in the end, engaged in hit-and-run guerrilla tactics. In turn the British retaliated with a 'scorched earth' policy – we burned their homesteads, destroyed their crops, and slaughtered their livestock – anything to prevent supplies getting through to them. Kitchener said that we had to 'uproot a whole nation' and so we put 120,000 of their women and children in

---

88 The Second Boer War usually known simply as the Boer War
    began in October 1899 and ended in May 1902. The Boers were
    the Afrikaans-speaking white South Africans descended from the
    Dutch East India Company's settlers at the Cape of Good Hope
    in the seventeenth century. Following defeat at the Cape in the
    first Boer War the Boers had trekked north during the 1830s
    to establish the Orange Free State and the Transvaal Republic
    both subsequently recognised by the British. However, the late
    1880s gold rush made the Transvaal the richest country in Africa.
    Ostensibly fought to facilitate (British) migrant workers' rights
    in the Transvaal the Second Boer War was really fought over the
    control of the gold fields.

tented villages surrounded by barbed wire. Now we know that 'concentration camps' are terrifying and fill us with revulsion but back then it was just a term we used. The 'concentrating' of that race of people in one place to stop them sending provisions to the guerrilla fighters. But one in four of the inmates in the camps died of malnutrition or disease.

Technically, and through sheer force of numbers, we won that war, but the loss of life, the cost, the loss of face, and most of all, the hatred we engendered, made for no more than a pyrrhic victory.

I was done fighting by then, my service period had come to an end and I left the army and returned to England in early 1903 when Roy was four. Fighting in Africa meant I had missed all his years as a baby but I was determined to make up for that on my return. And they were good years. Ena and I were happy, living in one of Father's small houses in nearby Catford. I spent my days helping in the shop or dealing with tenants or the builders refurbishing of one of Father's houses. Any spare time I could find I spent with Roy, making models, playing soccer, or just reading and walking.

Later on we used to spend hours trying – mostly unsuccessfully – to repair our motorcycle, a 1911 'FN Four'.[89] We would lay out the various oily engine parts on the kitchen table, examine each component carefully, and wonder how everything fitted together. Ena would then return – scold us for making such

---

89   The FN Four was made in Belgium by Fabrique Nationale from
      1905 until 1923. It was the world's first production inline-4
      motorcycle. It was also, at one point, the world's fastest production
      motorcycle with a top speed of 40 miles per hour.
      https://upload.wikimedia.org/wikipedia/commons/3/3b/FN_363_
      cc_viercilinder_1905.jpg

a mess — and we would hastily push everything into an old wooden soap powder box normally losing some essential spring or split pin in the process.

When the first war came with its impassioned call for volunteers I was thankfully just too old, at thirty-nine, to be considered. The maximum fighting age was thirty-eight, but as the casualties mounted so the need for manpower grew more urgent. Compulsory conscription for married men was introduced in May 1916, at which point the maximum age was raised to forty-one.[90] There was no way a draper would be considered an essential occupation and so my draft letter duly arrived, my old rank was reinstated, and I reported for duty once more. I was sent to the Somme and somehow I managed to survive that hell unscathed.

Six months after my call-up Roy, my son and my best friend, turned eighteen. A bright boy, he had attended the Bromley Grammar School where he gained a scholarship for free higher education. Two years before, at my suggestion, he had joined the local group of Navy Cadets.[91] I figured that being affiliated with the Navy meant that when the time came for his call-up he would join the 'senior service' rather than the Army. I wanted to do everything possible for him to avoid the trenches in France. Sure enough he was drafted into the Navy, but his

---

90 The maximum fighting age rose to 50 by the end of World War One.

91 Sea Cadets date back to 1856 when sailors returning from the Crimean War formed Naval Lads' Brigades to help orphans, created by the conflict, who ended up on the back streets of sea ports. In 1899, The Cadets received Royal recognition when Queen Victoria presented the Windsor unit with £10 for uniforms – an event now known as the birthday of the Sea Cadets – celebrated on 25th June. In 1919 the Admiralty officially recognised the 34 brigades and changed the name to the Navy League Sea Cadet Corps.

excellent service with the cadets combined with his grammar school education meant that he joined the Royal Naval Air Service rather than being sent to sea. Ena and I were distraught – the idea of joining the Navy had been to avoid Roy becoming cannon fodder on the battlefields – the thought of him flying was much more terrifying.[92]

But Roy didn't become a statistic of war. He trained as a pilot – although they didn't give you much training back then – and flew Sopwith Pups[93] and later Camels from Britain's aircraft carrier HMS Furious. He told us after it was all over that he had taken part in the first ever raid launched from an aircraft carrier.[94]

Ena and I were proud of our son, but so relieved when the war ended and both Roy and I could all return home to Bromley once more. Despite his obvious ability as a flyer Roy had only achieved the relatively lowly rank of sub-lieutenant

---

92 In World War One the life expectancy for an Allied pilot was just eleven days.

93 The Sopwith Pup was a single-seater biplane fighter entering service in 1916. Officially called the Sopwith Scout, the 'Pup' nickname arose because pilots considered it to be the 'pup' of Sopwith's various aircraft. The nickname caught on and set a precedent so that most of the firm's later planes acquired animal names (Camel, Dolphin, Snipe etc.). Sopwith was said to have created a 'flying zoo' during the First World War.

94 The first raid from an aircraft carrier was made in July 1918 when seven Sopwith Camels, launched from the converted battlecruiser HMS Furious, attacked the German airbase at Tønder destroying two zeppelin airships.
https://upload.wikimedia.org/wikipedia/commons/thumb/3/38/
Dunning_Landing-on_Furious_In_Pup.jpg/769px-Dunning_
Landing-on_Furious_In_Pup.jpg
(in the picture notice the deckhands grabbing hold of the tail to prevent the plane falling off the end of the ship's runway into the sea).

and, following my advice, decided not to extend his career in the Navy once the hostilities ended.

Early in the January of 1919 Ena got caught in freezing rain whilst walking the four miles home from our Bromley shop back to Catford. For some reason, there had been no buses that winter's evening. She had never benefited from robust health and now the flu took hold. She retired to bed and passed quite quickly.[95]

Later in the year Roy married Emily. A likeable, giggly girl from Catford. She made Roy happy and that was a good thing as both of us were suffering in the wake of Ena's death. But as 1920 came around Roy and I started to chat about the future.

Bromley remained as dull in 1920 for Roy and Emily as it had been for me twenty-five years earlier. Ena was dead and my parents had passed away during the war years. Running the shop was tedious – I had never warmed to the idea of being a draper and Roy was certainly not keen. The property portfolio, built up by my father, was now run and managed by professional real-estate agents so that we merely collected an income. There had to be something more.

It had been Roy who came up with the idea of Kenya, or British East Africa as it was still called then. I wrote to the Colonial Office and we were offered 1,000 acres of farmland here in Kitale at £5 per acre. If we took up the offer then Roy,

---

95 The flu pandemic from January 1918 to December 1920 was unusually deadly. In order to maintain morale, wartime censors had minimised reports of illness and mortality in Britain and the USA but reported the epidemic's impact in neutral Spain, creating a false impression of Spain as especially hard hit and giving rise to the nickname 'Spanish Flu'. It killed 50 to 100 million – three to five percent of the world's population – making it one of the deadliest natural disasters in human history.

Emily and I would each be allocated a passage to Africa for £1 per head.

Britain was dowdy and dirty and with Ena gone there was nothing to stay for. My time in South Africa had been bloody but I had never doubted either the beauty or the potential of land there – and Kenya was a land of peace. Our minds were made up.

The shop in Bromley quickly found new owners and the real-estate agents set about selling up some of the property investments. I gave the money to Roy and Emily as there was no point in me owning anything in the new country.

It took a year to organise everything but we had such high hopes. A new and exciting goal.

Excitement can be a cruel mistress though. You make things so big in your mind. You know instinctively that you shouldn't but, as you end your life in one place, you hate everything about it. Once you have made the decision to leave you mentally divorce yourself from your old life – and by the same token your new life becomes wonderful in your dreams. The vivid coloured prints of Africa in children's picture books stay in your mind's eye; the thought of smiling natives; plentiful tasty food; and most of all a warm dry climate, made our hearts yearn for the next stage to begin.

But we were disappointed on arrival. Today Kitale is a thriving town – the club, the bank, the shops, the farming traffic coming and going. In 1921 however it was just a few earth and grass huts. The land seemed barren and dry and the natives who had been displaced so that we could buy their land seemed (not unnaturally) sour. Those picture book images that we had held in our mind had led us to expect something quite different. At least I had been in Africa with the Army and Roy had spent time travelling in the Navy, but for Emily who had only ever left London previously for odd day trips to the seaside it was a huge shock. She was very homesick at the start. Things did improve but it took time. Emily remained unhappy and, with hindsight, blamed Roy and me for the decision to move to Africa – and she was probably right to do so.

The agricultural station was there then and Pennant, the old director, was a helpful chap. As far as I could tell, he didn't seem to have much more idea about farming than we did, but he did, at least, introduce us to the few other locals in the town; and helped us learn some Swahili. The natives slowly came around; they became less sullen and began to work for us. Two bungalows were built, one for Roy and Emily, and one for me. In time, barns and pens were erected as well. But the farming was always tough. We had no idea what we were doing. Each year brought new challenges – drought – locusts – crop disease. A shopkeeper and a pilot from South London have no ingrained sense as to how to manage land – it just wasn't in our blood and, in the end, we had 400 acres made over to pyrethrum with the rest as grazing. Thank goodness that I still had some of the property investments left at home as we only barely eked out a living in Africa.

The 1920s gave way to the 1930s and things only got worse. The value of crops plummeted during the worldwide depression, and the income from my few remaining let properties back in South London fell too, as tenants defaulted or appealed for rent reductions. I wouldn't say we were starving, we were far from that in Kenya, but it was a hard living in the 1930s.

It was in 1937 that Roy had the idea for buying the plane. Whenever he took a trip back to Nairobi by train he always made time to call in at the aerodrome where Wilson Airways had its base.[96] *Roy loved to chat to the pilots and began to take a few flying jobs and charters for the airline. He was a brilliant flyer. Passengers were always reassured when Roy was in charge. Quite often I would accompany him on the trips to Nairobi and get to go up in the planes too. Sometimes we were even able to set down at the airstrip in Kitale.*

Roy came to me one day.

'Dad, I've been chatting to the boys at the Aerodrome. There's a Gypsy Moth for sale down there and I wonder if it might be worth us making the investment to buy it.'

'Go on,' I said, 'I'm listening…'

'It's Knight of the Mist. It was Mrs Wilson's first plane delivered to her and Tom Campbell-Black back in '29. It did good service but crashed at Nairobi after a poorly performed stall turn two years ago. It was badly damaged and it just sat in a hangar but recently they've put it back together, lots of new parts from de Havilland's, as well as a brand-new uprated engine, and now it's fully operational again.'

---

96   Florence Wilson, scion of a wealthy shipowning family, came to Kenya with her husband after WW1 where they became successful farmers. After her husband's death in 1928 she returned to England, briefly on business, flying on a plane owned by John Carberry, a wealthy Irish playboy (10th Baron Carbery). Wilson fell for the pilot, Tom Campbell-Black (a WW1 aviator) and they had an affair. This resulted in her beginning an airline in Kenya in 1929. She injected £50,000 – a colossal sum then. Campbell-Black became manager and chief pilot. By 1936 the airline's base was at an aerodrome to the west of Nairobi. At the outbreak of WW2 the government confiscated her aircraft and drafted her pilots into the Kenya Auxiliary Air Unit. Wilson Airways was dissolved in 1940. Nairobi West Aerodrome was renamed Wilson Airport in honour of Florrie Wilson in 1958 – she died in Karen, a suburb of Nairobi, in 1968.
https://airandspace.si.edu/collection-objects/wilson-airways-modern-business-demands-air-travel

I nodded.

'But they have decided that the Moth is a bit too old and a bit small for them. Mrs Wilson had wanted it fully restored because it was her first plane, but in reality it's not what they fly these days.'

'And you think we should buy it?'

'Dad it's £500... I know that's a lot... but talking to the chaps I reckon we can earn a shilling a mile. I've done some numbers and I think we could get £60 a month. What do you think?'

Of course we bought it! But with one condition... 'You've got to teach me to fly, son!'

We had a deal. I wrote to the real-estate agent in London who was handling the fag end of Dad's properties and got him to auction off what was left. A bad time to sell and we didn't get much, but it was enough to buy the plane, a stock of spares, and have some money put by for fuel. It seemed a complicated process to register the Knight of the Mist and as it was paid for from my account at Barclays Bank we bought the plane in my name rather than in Roy's – it was just easier.

We cut a runway on the farm and built a hangar. Roy started flying; running farmers backwards and forwards to Nairobi, couriering small packages and farm machine parts here and there, although the components had to be pretty small as the Knight of the Mist couldn't take much in the way of payload.[97]

He didn't seek to undercut Wilson's, and they did indeed run much bigger planes – although occasionally Florrie Wilson would be in the clubhouse at the Nairobi Aerodrome and give him a stare.

---

97   Knight Of The Mist pictured in Zanzibar, April 1930.
     https://campsmoke.files.wordpress.com/2009/08/tom_campbell_
     black_in_zanzibar.jpg
     Tom Campbell-Black is in the centre of this picture.

'I hope you're well, Mrs Wilson.'

'Make sure you look after my aeroplane, young Mr Faulkner!' she would declare.

'I promise I shall, Mrs Wilson.'

But Roy had been right. Once he was flying more or less full-time our income picked up. And yes, he taught me to fly! I got my pilot's licence. Our life in Kenya was on the up – quite literally!

When the war came both Roy and Knight of the Mist escaped the call-up to the Kenya Auxiliary Air Unit. Roy's papers stated he was a farmer rather than a pilot, and farming was a reserved occupation, plus I think the plane's previous crash meant that it was 'off the books' in some way. It had been an insurance write-off at the time, although it was now probably better than it had been when new. Nevertheless, Roy flew many courier missions for the Kenya Auxies and still got paid a shilling a mile.

The engine needed an overhaul every hundred hours or so. There were full facilities down at the Nairobi Aerodrome and we were always careful to keep enough money aside for the maintenance schedules. That said, we did do some work ourselves, and in the end had a decent workshop within our hangar on the farm; although I always recalled our old FN Four motorbike in pieces on the kitchen table at Catford and shuddered slightly at the thought. We were flyers – not engineers!

All this time spent flying meant that we totally neglected the farm. In truth, it had never been our passion nor had it ever really succeeded. The natives carried on. Now they worked the land for themselves and gave us a share; in return, we brought them in seed from Nairobi or Mombasa.

But once he was flying almost every day Roy also neglected Emily. They had never been blessed with children and she had

continued to struggle with life in Kenya – particularly with some
of the more unpleasant wildlife such as the siafu.[98] *She sought*
solace by attending the club in Kitale Town regularly, daily in
fact. And she had a wide circle of people there. When she came
back from the club, often dropped back by one of her friends, she
would normally go straight to bed. Roy and I would usually leave
at sunrise, and Emily would only wake much later in the day.

One evening in late September 1945, after a day's flying,
Roy had gone to the club in Kitale Town to find Emily. From
what I understand, when he got there, Emily wasn't ready to
come home and words were said. Roy left and began to walk
home back towards the farm when he was knocked down by a
car. The car didn't stop but Roy was found by another passing
driver who took him to the hospital in town. He died from his
injuries three days later…

No parent expects to outlive his children and when you
lose a child, quite suddenly, violently, it is as though you have
become afflicted with a permanent disablement. I think, well
I hope that, in time, you can learn to live with it, but I don't
think that you can ever recover.

---

98 *Dorylus*, also known as *siafu* ants (from Swahili), are army ants
found in Central and East Africa. The soldier class among the
workers is larger, with powerful shearing jaws. Seasonally, when
food supplies become short, they form marching columns of up
to 50,000,000 ants. They are considered a menace, although easily
avoided; a column can only travel about twenty metres per hour,
but sometimes does travel through a house. The bite is painful,
each soldier leaving two puncture wounds. Removal is difficult as
their jaws are extremely strong. In East Africa, the Maasai, when
suffering from a gash, will use soldier ants to stitch the wound by
getting them to bite on both sides of the cut and then break off the
body. This use of the ants as makeshift surgical staples creates a seal
that can hold for days at a time, and the procedure can be repeated,
if necessary, allowing natural healing to commence.

But there were practical issues too. With Roy gone, the flying income ended but the farm continued to struggle to make any kind of meaningful return on which we could live. However, Emily at forty-four was still a very good-looking woman and following Roy's death was also an heiress of 1,000 acres. As a result, her potential suitors were not slow in coming forward. She chose Bill Pietersen, a Boer about ten years her senior and who had been in Kenya for decades.

Although Kitale had been tiny when we had first arrived in the 1920s it had grown steadily, and the population had been bolstered by the arrival of a large community of Afrikaners. In the years after the Boer War thousands had trekked north or come up by sea to find a new life in East Africa. Many of them had come to nearby Eldoret, and from there it was a relatively short journey further to Kitale. Like I said, when I had been in southern Africa back at the turn of the century, the Boers were good farmers, and in western Kenya they proved far more proficient in working the fields than the British landowners.

Pietersen and his then wife had left the Orange Free State in 1911. A few years later he had found himself in Kitale and built a reputation as a good farming tenant. His first wife gave him two sons but then went off with an Australian to New South Wales. Bill brought up the boys on his own; no easy undertaking for a working farmer I would think. From what I understand the boys were tearaways back in the day, but they've grown into strapping twenty-year-olds and fine labourers.

Bill and Emily married in November, just over a year since Roy passed away. I don't blame her, it was a completely pragmatic decision, and I can't say that she and Roy had enjoyed a happy marriage since coming out here.

As for me, I still have my bungalow on the farm, and I have a perfectly passable relationship with Bill. He spends a bit too much time and cash at the card tables in the bars in town for my liking, but he is certainly a brilliant farmer. He and his boys have transformed things on the land. It does irk me though that the money to buy the farm came from my dad's investments, but now my presence is only just about tolerated rather than welcomed. Perhaps I feel a bit like those natives that we displaced when we first arrived.

Pip had stopped speaking and we all sat in silence for a while.

'What about the plane – the Gipsy Moth?' asked Tanya. Her tone, combining with her Russian accent, framed the question more as a demand than a polite request. I sighed inwardly. I knew she would be interested in the aeroplane, but at the end of such a story surely this wasn't the moment to raise it. But Pip was not one for wallowing in emotion and was relieved to move the conversation on. Maybe Tanya's natural instincts were right and she understood him better than me, even after such a short time. Quite unconsciously, across the generations and across the continents, she treated him as she would her brother whilst he, in turn, responded in the matter-of-fact way of a sibling, where love is a simple given.

'Well it's still in its hangar, where Roy put it after its flight that day. Let me take you to see it in the morning.'

12

TANYA ZAYKY
Kitale, Kenya 1950

Back in England, when staying with Batioushka at St Dunstan's Road, I had never heard of the Happy Valley set.[99] I think it was Bill Pietersen who I first heard mention it one day when he was sneering about the British. I gathered that 'Happy Valley' were words mentioned with a raised eyebrow, or by men, to each other, with knowing winks. I was in the dark. But once Pip had explained it to me, I found that I couldn't look at the pretty British wives meandering about the stores in Kitale Town in the same way. They slightly sickened me.

Pasha tells me that, too often when I speak, I can be blunt and abrupt, unconcerned about any prevailing social niceties. As a result, all through my life, I've garnered black looks from those around me. Now I had arrived in Kenya, it seemed as though I didn't even have to open my mouth.

---

99   The so-called Happy Valley set was a group of hedonistic aristocrats who settled in Wanjohi Valley, Kenya, near the Aberdare mountains, during the 1920s. The group became infamous for decadent lifestyles, drug use and sexual promiscuity.

Maybe just the look on my face gave away my thoughts about those English ladies, with their gaily coloured frocks, painted faces and shrill laughter displaying fawning adoration of any male company which came their way.

Despite our own hatred of the Soviets, when we had lived in Nazi Germany some had considered that, as Russians, we were the enemy. They were normally people in the lower orders, just like Hiltze the horrible Blockleiter in Posen for instance. Immediately after the fall of the Nazis the British and Americans had wanted to repatriate us to Russia. At the time they had been allies, but by early 1946 Winston Churchill had coined the term 'the Iron Curtain' and in 1949 the Soviets had tested their own atomic bomb – the Cold War had truly begun. Thank God that in Kenya the Cold War, and its attendant nuclear threat, seemed very far away, but once again our country of origin and, in my case at least, a thick accent, cast us as the enemy.

Not that anybody would dream of saying anything. They were British after all. They would be polite to your face and stab you in the back the moment you turned away. But whereas they spent all their spare time in the settler clubs – either the Kitale Club local to us, or the 'Muthaiga' in the capital for the aristocrats, the 'Nairobi' for the Government officers, or the 'Railway Club' for the lower classes (although obviously no Boers or blacks) – we were not made to feel quite as welcome. The British ladies would enjoy horse riding in the morning and perhaps pistol practice in the afternoon – often with a dashing officer beside them to hold their shaking hand steady as they took the shot. They took tea at 4pm and then gin at 6pm, but only because, by then, their handbag flasks, consumed as they sat in toilet cubicles, would have run dry.

So as a Russian, and moreover, a woman, they were prejudiced against me, more so than they were against Pasha – a man, but also a master at winning esteem. But I was prejudiced against them too, those vacuous, gin-soaked strumpets. Although, when I look back on it, perhaps they were thoroughly bored and desperate for attention, just like me.

And I had been so bored during those early months in 1947. For me, Kitale had nothing to offer. Of course, I spent my time teaching Sofia, although by then, following her hours of study under the direction of the Countess back at St Dunstan's Road, her English was better than mine in any case. So, we concentrated on our shared love of the sciences, although with Sofia it was always biology rather than physics which excited her the most. She borrowed books on human anatomy from the library and then spent time quizzing the doctors at the Kitale hospital on various matters relating to physiology. I was worried that they would tire of her but they never seemed to. I spent my days just reading whilst Mohammed and Boniface cleaned and cooked, utterly rejecting any attempt by me to help. I would long for supper time when Pasha and Sofia would both be home to tell me what they had done that day, for it appeared to me that unless I was to ride or shoot or take tea as a good dutiful wife should – or indeed to conduct extramarital liaisons as many of the less dutiful wives did – there was nothing else to do.

A couple of times I was called upon to fix ailing motor vehicles, or tractors. Once whilst visiting Pip, Emily Pietersen asked me to take a look at their car, which had failed to start. The cure was perfectly obvious: simply a wire disconnected from the coil. I reattached the offending lead and the car fired up immediately. Emily was delighted as it meant she could go off to the Kitale Club, although Bill Pietersen glowered at me, turned his back, and walked away as his wife drove off towards town. But fixing motor vehicles was man's work and, in fact, in Kenya most of the mechanics were natives or Asians. The whites, and certainly not white women, didn't get their hands oily.

In the September after our arrival Sofia was enrolled as a boarder at the High School in Nairobi. This was a wrench for all of us. After everything we had been through, our trek across Europe, followed by the enforced separation from Pasha, to have Sofia spend school term times in Nairobi whilst we remained in Kitale was awful. But clearly her education had to take priority. The girls' High School in Nairobi had been founded in the late 1920s but had, only recently, moved to a new site in a north-western suburb of Nairobi called Kileleshwa and was now fully equipped with brand-new classrooms, halls and dormitories. Sofia didn't want to leave us but, all the same, she was really excited at the thought of going to a proper school – her education to that point had been fragmented to say the least.

We travelled down to Nairobi together on the train – a special one laid on for the returning pupils. Sofia's belongings were packed into two of our small suitcases and didn't take up too much space in the racks above our heads. Some of the other girls had enormous amounts of luggage, and at Nairobi the porters' trolleys were stacked high with trunks and cases with lacrosse and hockey sticks balanced on top. There was a queue for taxis but eventually we got to the front and on arrival at the school attended assembly for all the girls and parents with a welcome speech from Miss Stott, the school's rather fearsome headmistress. Then there was lunch in the canteen. But after lunch we had to say goodbye. Pasha shed a tear but Sofia was stoic, hugged us both, and then simply turned and got on with her unpacking, in her dormitory, with all the other new girls. We caught the overnight train back to Kitale, both sad, with little conversation.

My lack of outward emotion at our separation from Sofia should not be mistaken for some lack of feeling on my part. I was bereft. We both were; but Pasha had his work to fall back upon, whereas without Sofia my days became even more empty. There had to be something else.

One evening that September Pip joined us for supper. I was miserable, and was making both Pasha and Pip suffer as a result.

'Look,' said Pip, 'I'm pretty bored too, you know. Apart from you two I have nobody to talk to and nothing to do with my life anymore.'

I turned my head to one side to face him, and allowed my mouth to twist, momentarily, into a condescending smile. Pasha sighed loudly. But it was Pip who interjected.

'Why not let's take a look at the aeroplane – the Knight of the Mist?'

'I've seen the aeroplane. You showed it to me.'

'I know you've seen it but why don't we fly it?'

I stopped eating, and placed my knife and fork carefully on my plate; again I tilted my head towards him, but now with no hint of condescension as he continued.

'Okay, this might well be a mad idea but it's been forming gradually over these last few weeks. The Gipsy Moth was perfectly airworthy when Roy put it away in the hangar almost exactly two years ago, and it's sat there ever since. I'm sure that it will need some work to overhaul, it having lain dormant for so many months, but we have all the manuals, and we have a workshop, and Tanya – you're an engineer.

'We could work on it together and then see if we can get a certificate of airworthiness. If we can get that, and then get the runway spruced up... I do have a pilot licence, you know... at least I did have; it's lapsed now – but I think that I would only need a medical to get it renewed and, despite my advancing years, I reckon that Dr Bourke in town will clear me for duty. Well, we could take her up... what do you think?'

Pip's son, Roy, had held a 'B' licence allowing him to carry fare-paying passengers and operate commercially. But Pip had also successfully passed his flying test, entitling him to an 'A' licence, meaning that he could fly on a private (non-commercial) basis.

Now Pasha cut in: 'Pip, are you sure? The plane might need major work after all this time... and you haven't flown for a couple of years now...'

I shot Pasha a glance which told him everything he needed to know to end this particular line of challenge. He had his work in Kenya, Sofia was safely at school; this was something for me – and for Pip.

We began work on the Gipsy Moth the very next day. I had spent the night going through everything systematically in my mind. In short, I was thrilled with Pip's idea – as excited to get to grips with Knight of the Mist as Sofia had been to get to school in Nairobi, but this was a job not to be taken lightly. Pasha was obviously nervous and, to be fair, with some justification. I had no experience of aircraft maintenance and by his own admission, Pip was an ex-soldier rather than an engineer. But if Pip had felt that just a quick brush down of the plane might be all that was required then I had other ideas. I only do something if I do it thoroughly and in the correct sequence. This was certainly not a task to be rushed.

The Knight's hangar was, in reality, just a thatched shed, and so each day, our first task was to pull the plane out into the sunlight and swing his wings into position. One feature of the Gipsy Moth was that its wings pivoted where they joined the body to fold right back against the fuselage,[100] not dissimilar to its insect namesake.[101] Roy, having served on aircraft carriers where space had been at a premium, had really admired this aspect of the design and being able to accommodate the Knight in a relatively narrow shed had made construction of the hangar much more straightforward. Nevertheless, space was still tight inside; you could, just about, work on the engine with the wings folded back, but you certainly couldn't attend to anything else.

Originally, from the factory, the Knight's livery had been yellow and black, but on restoration, down at the aerodrome in 1937, he had been repainted in a bright blue with the registration VP-KAC added in white letters. I rather approved, although during Roy's use the blue had become faded. But once the two of us had pulled him out of the hangar each day and locked the wings in place, even in his

---

100 Fuselage: the main body of an aircraft.

101 Geoffrey de Havilland, an avid lepidopterist (a branch of entomology concerning the scientific study of moths), specifically designed the wings to fold like a moth so the plane was nicknamed 'Moth' on the drawing board.

dusty and faded state, the Knight looked truly magnificent stretched out to the full nine-metre span.

Over the following weeks I read the manuals and the service sheets from cover to cover; I reorganised the workshop and cleaned all the tools; inspected every part of the fuselage and wings; and tested and retested the linkages. We checked the engine's compression and I rebuilt the top-end with new rings, gaskets and seals, all sent up from Nairobi. I renewed the magnetos and the electrical wiring, some of which had been eaten away by rodents during the time the aeroplane had lain dormant.

It took over a month before I was willing to fire up the engine – at that stage I just wanted to listen to the pistons in their cylinders. Unlike Pasha and Sofia I struggle to get to grips with new languages but I can hear machinery. I let it speak to me and I understand exactly what is going on. When the Knight had been rebuilt for Mrs Wilson in Nairobi, de Havilland's had sent a brand-new engine from England, a Gipsy Major motor, as fitted to their latest Tiger Moth planes. It was a beautiful piece of engineering. I listened – it spoke to me – I adjusted, notch by notch – quarter turn by quarter turn. It took days. Pip worked beside me doing precisely as bid – nothing more, nothing less. If I was a surgeon then Pip was the perfect operating assistant but above all the engine was a model patient.

You have to be careful where you place your feet and hands when getting inside biplanes to avoid causing damage, and now I carefully applied new Irish linen to the wings and body to re-cover old repair sections and then painted three fresh coats of bright blue dope all over. Now the Knight truly sparkled in the sun outside his hangar. He was ready!

At the start of November, I wrote to Nairobi's west aerodrome to make arrangements for an inspector to come to Kitale to provide a certificate of airworthiness. By return mail a date was proposed and on Monday 10th November Flight Sergeant Tim Broughton flew into Kitale. Mohammed picked him up at the airstrip and drove him out to the hangar on the Pietersen Farm.

He spent an hour with the Knight checking, testing, asking me what had been done, inspecting the past service records, and finally starting the engine, before pronouncing the plane airworthy and fit for flight. Delighted, albeit not surprised, Pip and I took Sergeant Broughton back to the bungalow where Boniface had prepared us lunch.

'So, Mrs Zayky, when will you begin your own flying lessons?' Broughton asked.

It was obviously a question which had occurred to me during the preceding weeks while we had been working on the plane, but now that we had the certificate of airworthiness the possibility of me piloting the Knight took centre stage.

'Can I get lessons here in Kitale?'

'Well, Jock Matheson is a qualified instructor and he flies up to the Kitale airstrip at least once a week. I'm sure that he can easily come down to the farm here and tutor you in your Moth – he's a good man. And I don't think you'll find a better plane to learn in than the one you have right here. Let me have a word with him when I get back later today, and then he can come down to see you the next time he's up.

'And of course, when you're ready you can come down to Nairobi and I can put you through the pilot test. It will be good to have another woman on the books in Kenya; we find it makes the chaps behave themselves in the clubhouse!'

Pip gave one of his bellowing laughs at that.

'Tanya, once you're up and flying nothing is going to stop you in this country!'

'Pip, the Knight is your aeroplane; would you mind me flying him?'

'Well I might own it legally but with the love you've injected into him over these last weeks, I think we can agree that you are now the true owner of the Knight of the Mist.'

Later that afternoon, with Sergeant Broughton safely on his way back to Nairobi, Pip and I inspected the Knight one further time. Fully fuelled, she was ready for us. Pip clambered up into the rear cockpit...

'Contact!' he yelled as he engaged the magnetos.

With my palm on the mahogany propeller, and my fingers held proud, I swung the blade. The engine fired first on one cylinder, then two, and then all four. It was like a slumbering yet obedient hound answering the early morning command of his master, rising to its feet somewhat unsteadily at first, but within seconds ready for work. With the engine in fine song, I pulled away the chocks from the wheels and climbed up to the front cockpit as Pip carefully increased the throttle and we began to inch forward. The farm's airstrip, originally created under Roy's direction, had been newly re-cut for us. Pip and I had walked the full length of the runway just an hour before to ensure it was sound, and now we taxied to its start, where the windsock reported that the wind was towards us. I looked up to the mirror above my head so I could see Pip behind me. He raised his hand – thumb up. I nodded and grinned. Thumbs up! More throttle – more speed – that wonderful engine – this wonderful aeroplane – our 'Knight' lifted Pip and me into the air and we were away!

The weeks of preparation, my painstaking efforts to understand every nuance of our flying machine, the attention to detail in the disassembly and then reassembly of every part, the evenings spent squinting at the manuals and their diagrams, the building excitement; and yet nothing prepared me for the ecstasy I felt at that moment of take-off. It was quite the most exquisite feeling of rapture, thrill, just a tinge of fear, and… something more, yes… motherhood! It was the oddest combination of senses, but utterly exhilarating.

We flew north, over the town and to the plains beyond. I looked down to see bands of animals running this way and that, looking everywhere but upwards, in a desperate attempt to escape the sound of the Knight above them. A herd of impala and zebra, the front-runners leaping in their own flight, highlighted brightly by the afternoon sun, and then shaded momentarily by the wings of our Moth as we flew past.

On that first flight Pip let me take the controls. Obviously, I knew the theory and precisely how the controls worked but feeling the Knight respond in the air to such light touches to the stick and to the rudder, feeling his sensitivity once airborne, was sublime. I already knew the language of the engine but now the Knight himself was dancing – although on that first flight I realised that I had much to learn to interpret his every move and need.

We flew for an hour before Pip approached for landing. The only real problem of the Moth's design was the restricted view offered straight ahead, making landing slightly challenging. So, with the wings tipped left, and the rudder pushing our nose to the right, we turned sideways just slightly to allow a better view of the approaching runway. Lower and lower – the airstrip came up to meet us – Pip moved the rudder back to the centre and at the last moment eased off the power. The Knight's nose swung back straight ahead and our wheels and tail all touched the grass together. A perfect three-point landing, exactly as described in the textbooks. We came to a stop almost, as the English would say, 'on a sixpence', the Knight having used up hardly any of the runway.

We taxied to the hangar and switched off. I jumped down and gave the outside a thorough inspection – all good. The following day I would check the engine, clean the plugs and top up the oil, but my senses told that none of this would yield any issues of note. Together we unlocked the wings, folded them back and then carefully pulled the Knight by its tail back into the cool of its dock. I looked round at Pip, grabbed him, and hugged him. What a wonderful man! I had only known him for a few months but it felt to me as though we had been together for all our lives. I loved my Pasha, but even after such a short time found I had another type of love for Pip.

'Well, I hope you've had fun flying around the skies in my aeroplane,' came a voice. A figure was silhouetted in the entrance of the hangar. The late afternoon light outside made it impossible to identify the owner of the voice by sight, but the hard edge of his accent was unmistakably that of Bill Pietersen.

'Hello, Bill,' said Pip. 'Did you see us?'

'I expect most of Kenya saw you – you're not easy to miss in that thing. But what I want to know is how much you're going to pay me. I might not be able to fly but that plane is, by rights, mine and my Emily's, and I reckon you need to pay up for your joyride.'

'Now hang on Bill, the plane is mine…' responded Pip. Whilst I am never good at reading other people's emotions it was not difficult, now, to sense the tension and rising anger in both men. Pip was first to carry on.

'Through Emily you've got this farm, even though it was me that paid for it when we first came out here. And I don't begrudge you it. Good luck to you! But this plane… well, I bought it, funded all its servicing, put the fuel in it; and I've got the paperwork to prove it. It's mine, Bill, not Emily's, and certainly not yours.'

But now Pietersen was shouting back at full belt. 'You can try to wriggle, Faulkner, but you've abandoned it these years, left it in my shed right here, on my farm. So, like I say, by rights, it's mine now!' and he stormed off.

Pip didn't join us for supper that evening. The day had been exhausting and he had gone back to his own bungalow to get an early night. I remained jubilant, telling Pasha about every moment of our day, from the inspection of the plane in the morning, Sergeant Broughton's recommendation for lessons, to the full details of that first flight. And Pasha too had seen us, from the farm where he had been working that afternoon, over to the north of Kitale Town. But it was inescapable that Bill Pietersen's interjection, as we had shut up the hangar, had taken some of the edge off the triumph of our day.

'You'd better leave it with me,' said Pasha. 'I'll speak to him.'

Pasha is so good with people. The following day he tracked down Bill in one of the fields and they made a deal. Bill conceded that the Knight belonged to Pip, but agreed terms on the rent of the hangar together with take-off and landing fees. He just wanted to make some more cash; a little extra to allow him to play for ever higher stakes at the gaming tables whilst his wife drank herself to a stupor in the club. By contrast, we found that we spent very little money in Kenya. With our housing costs all covered, Sofia's school fees were affordable, and we didn't need or wish to spend our spare time buying drinks in the club, or gambling in the bars. It meant that Pasha's monthly salary was mostly saved in the bank. We could easily cover the fairly modest sums demanded by Bill Pietersen as well as the cost of my flying lessons.

December and January in Kenya are dry and hot – great months to learn how to fly. Most days I would fly with Pip but even Pip confessed that having been taught only by Roy there were plenty of things he didn't know. Jock Matheson was a trained instructor and good tutor. He came up once a week with the cargo plane from Nairobi, arriving early in the morning and flying back late in the afternoon. It gave him most of the day to spend with me. Most of the time we were up in the air but some of it we spent drinking tea and talking.

'Ye must use your eyes to fly, Tanya,' he said, eyeing me steadily, his words rolling from his mouth in an unusual lilting brogue which Pip said came from a city called Glasgow in Scotland. 'Ye dinnae need any of the other instruments up there in the Moth. Most of what they'll be telling you'll be like hangin' y' bum oot the windae in any case! It'd be just like believing everything you read in the newspapers! Garbage!'

I struggled slightly to follow every word he said but I caught the gist. 'So, y'must use your eyes to see how far the ground is below ye and to see how level your wing tips are against the horizon. The only dial to trust with y' life is the compass. It's only with that one where your own judgement will never be more accurate than its needle.'

I had Roy's old maps: 1:2,000,000 where an inch represented over 30 miles. But, in reality, these were of limited use. Nothing like the maps we know today. There were the roads, railways and rivers of course but if you drew your finger very far either side of these arteries then the legend simply read: 'unsurveyed'.

'Ye set your course to follow the roads and rivers, Tanya; then ye set your compass. We are high above sea level here in Kenya; the air is thin, and at these altitudes, in your Moth, you'll get about two hours in the air. That's about 150 mile' before y'll be needing to land to refuel.'

But there is only so much to be learned by drinking tea. It was in the air, as we swung low over the foothills of Mount Elgon, that I learned how I could be a master of the Knight. I had learned the simple mechanics of flying from books but now I needed to glean the intuition and instinct in the heart of every good pilot. I needed to understand the nuances of flight, not just of my craft but of all that is going on around; often quite unseen.

One day, which I recall very well, we were flying across the foothills; the altimeter read 8,000 feet above sea level but the ground was probably around 600 feet below us and I needed to climb to get over the ridge ahead. Quite suddenly, however, I found the Knight to be afflicted with a strange lethargy. As the hills slowly drew closer, with their green slopes emerging from the hazy shroud in which they usually existed, I could see the altimeter falling slightly. I opened the throttle and drew back the stick but the Knight failed to respond. The engine sounded as perfect as ever, but it was as though he was exhausted, with nothing extra to give me. I carried on ahead, and the trees on the hillside began to separate and stand out individually. We were still losing height. More stick, more throttle.

I was calm. Jock remained calm too; there was no sense of alarm from the mild-mannered Scot sitting ahead of me. In fact, he almost seemed to be daydreaming, his head cocked to one side, staring at the struts and ties between the wings. But it was now obvious that we were also losing speed and heading straight for the hills. The Moth was behaving rather like its insect namesake aiming for the candle flame. I could feel the weight of the wings dragging on the controls, bearing us down. I heaved and pulled but just could not lift us.

When you begin to see the branches of individual trees, with their leaves twitching in the wind, then you know that you are too low.

It was then that Jock took command. He banked sharply, dusting the trees with a plume of blue exhaust smoke. He pushed down the Knight's nose and swung us deep into a valley whilst our shadow rode the hill ahead. We lost altitude until we almost reached the valley floor and then, slowly, in spirals we climbed all the way back up, until we were high above the foothills once more.

'That'll be a downdraft you had right there, Tanya!' he said, grinning at me when we got back.

'As y' get close to a ridge, so it is that the wind from the glen, over the other side, tips over the top and forces down on ye. Ye can try to fight it, but whit's fur ye'll no go past ye and you cannae never beat it. It's very common around the highlands here in Kenya so you'll need to be canny and know how to deal with it.'

It was a good lesson, and a well-needed one, just at a point when I was growing slightly overconfident. When you fly, never do anything without knowing precisely what might happen were you to do something else.

I secured my 'A' pilot's licence in early January 1948. Pip and I had flown down to Nairobi, setting off at sunrise when the air was still, and refuelling en route. We had landed at 10am, and for the rest of that morning, Flight Sergeant Broughton put me through my paces, both in the air and in the classroom allowing himself half a smile as he wrote out my pass certificate in the aerodrome office. I walked into the clubhouse at lunchtime, waved the certificate, and everyone applauded… and demanded a drink. Jock was delighted.

'So Tanya, I wud'nee usually be asking a lassie such as yerself for a dram, but I think that, on this occasion, you owe me!'

'I think I do, Jock!'

'And me… And me too,' came voices from all around the bar. It was an expensive afternoon, but worth every penny. Pip flew us back home, landing at the airstrip at 6.50pm, just as darkness fell. No twilight in Kenya!

Obtaining my pilot licence in early January meant that an early flight with a purpose was to return Sofia to school after the Christmas holidays. She had completed her first term at the High School with a crop of good reports from her teachers, although she had struggled to fit in easily with her classmates.

Very nearly twelve years old and having travelled the breadth of war-torn Europe, Sofia had lived through much more than any of the dainty daughters of the white English settlers of Kenya. Moreover, having spent all her years almost exclusively in the company of adults, she found little in common with her peers. For their part, her schoolmates regarded that Russian girl, with her furrowed brow and dark piercing eyes, who spoke so abruptly, and who was quite possibly an enemy spy, with an ambivalent mix of disinterest and downright hostility. As a result, Sofia had found that she was happiest spending most of her free time in the school's kitchens chatting in Gikuyu to the cook and his staff, or walking the grounds with one of the team of gardeners. Gikuyu is the language of the Kikuyu and Sofia, already fluent in Russian, Ukrainian, German and English, now learned the sing-song dialect of the native people with ease and pleasure.

Pip and I had flown over the High School en route to my pilot test. On our way back that day Pip had circled low to work out exactly where best to put the plane down at the school.

On the morning of the first day of term, Pip and Pasha saw us off. Pasha was nervous at seeing both his girls climb aboard the Knight to fly off on the journey south, but Pip reassured him that all would be well. And our journey to Nairobi School was completely uneventful, other than my pleasure at seeing Sofia, sitting ahead of me in the front cockpit, pointing down at elephants and giraffe and waving wildly to herdsmen on the plains – who to her delight waved wildly back!

We landed by the hockey fields, and almost immediately a small group of girls surrounded us. Air travel was, by then, fairly common in Kenya but it was not the usual mode for girls returning to school after holidays. I got down and began to inspect the Knight in the way that a groom might examine the muscles of a thoroughbred horse post a resounding victory; Sofia got down and began extracting her bags from the locker in the side of the plane. A native came up. She greeted him warmly and they babbled away to each other, happily, in Gikuyu.

'Mama, this is Joshua, one of the groundsmen here.'

The man smiled widely and bowed slightly. 'Good morning, ma'am,' he said, 'we are so pleased to have Miss Sofey back.' He took Sofia's bags, despite her protests that she was perfectly able to carry them.

I smiled back at him, but just as I was about to speak another voice was heard.

'Now, what on earth is all this commotion?' The small crowd, and Joshua, vanished immediately. Slightly surprising, given there seemed to be no cover between the aircraft and the school buildings, which were all some way away. But now there was just me, and Sofia, and a short, fearsome-looking rotund lady with white hair and protruding eyeballs, wearing a black flowing academic gown. I recognised her immediately – it was Miss Stott, the headmistress.

'Ah, Sofia, welcome back; you had a good Christmas I trust, but will you introduce me?'

'Miss Stott, this is my mother, Tanya.'

'Miss Stott, we have met, it's good to see you again...' The look on Miss Stott's face was enough to realise I was in trouble. I realised immediately that I should have asked if it was possible to land at the school in advance.

I am still rather embarrassed to recount the dressing-down I received, but suffice to say that it was made clear to me that landing a plane on a school playing field without first requesting permission was 'poor form'. I'm not used to being told off, but this short lady held such gravitas, and delivered her words in such a way that I squirmed with embarrassment. The elation I had felt just moments before, on landing, with Sofia's nonchalant unpacking of her bags, whilst her schoolmates gathered round, had completely disappeared.

But Miss Stott could see that her words had struck home.

'Well, look,' she continued, 'I do see that Sofia lives a very long way away, and so I feel sure that a letter to Miss Vasey, the school secretary, requesting permission in the future would be met with a favourable response.' I looked up, and she smiled at me.

'And it is a very fine plane. Was that one of Mrs Wilson's?'

'It was, Miss Stott, her very first actually.'

Miss Stott looked impressed and began walking round the Knight.

'Now, Sofia,' she called over her shoulder, 'say goodbye to your mother and run along.' Sofia dutifully kissed me and then did as she was bid.

'Mrs Zayky, might you have time for a coffee before you need to return north?'

I explained that, in fact, my plan was to take off and fly on to the aerodrome, where the Knight was booked in for a routine inspection along with new plugs and filters. I would have lunch in the clubhouse and then fly back to Kitale in the afternoon. So yes, I had time.

'Well, Mrs Zayky, to make amends, perhaps you could do me a favour…'

Miss Stott was redoubtable. She could, perhaps, be best described as a cannonball of a woman. As we walked the corridors of the school, both pupils and staff alike moved aside to let her pass. She exuded energy and made conversation littered with sharp little truths which made you smile at the time and then reflect on their meaning in the much longer run. Her passion was her school. It was her machine and it ran with precision; she had my full admiration for that. She had been the architect of the plan to move to the new site some years before. She had campaigned tirelessly for the funds to create the new building and now she was working on the authorities for a library and a chapel. She was also, it turned out, a keen amateur photographer.

In her study, after we had finished coffee, she went to a cupboard and extracted her camera. 'A Leica 3,' she said proudly. 'Of course, I should have a British one, like an Ensign, rather than this German device, but do you know, the Germans are really rather good at making things.' I did know!

As soon as I realised her passion for photography I knew how I could help. We spent the remainder of that morning in the air, flying over the school. The girls looked up from the fields, as Miss Stott leaned, rather precariously for my liking, from the cockpit snapping away on the Leica and whooping with delight. We lunched at the aerodrome clubhouse, where the other pilots looked slightly askance at my guest with her black gown and bulging eyes, then flew back to the school. I was clearly forgiven for my errant behaviour and Miss Stott said she would ensure the strip would be kept mown and rolled for me for the future!

The trip to the High School that morning was one of my first flights in Kenya but as our years there rolled by, so my flying became much more essential – not just to cover Sofia's commute to and from school, but also to allow Pasha a far greater freedom of movement than he, or indeed his employers, had thought possible.

During the late 1940s and into the '50s, the British invested significantly in Kenyan agriculture. They wanted greater output, both for the domestic market but also for export. Some of the food was sent to Britain but the greater amount was sold on world commodity markets to raise cash to help Britain pay the interest on the enormous debts it had run up during the war.[102] The employment of Pasha and his role within Kenya was part of the British drive for greater productivity from its Empire. Just occasionally, and very quietly, Pasha would remind me that it had been the same for the Nazis and their quest for greater output when he had been at the centre of the network of agricultural specialists during the war.

Now we were airborne it meant that Pasha was no longer tied to Kitale. It's fair to say that Pasha was no natural air traveller – a nervous passenger for sure – but once I had persuaded him into the front cockpit, the benefit was obvious. Movement by road and rail in Kenya was excruciatingly slow, and so allowing me to be his pilot meant he could attend briefings at the Scott Laboratories,

---

102 In 1945 the US loaned Britain $4.33bn, then in 1946 Canada loaned Britain US$1.19bn. Both loans were charged interest at 2% – so £27.5m per annum. To put this sum in context in 1945 the entire Kenyan Government Budget was £6.8m of which only £500,000 was devoted to agriculture. In 1946 the Kenyan agriculture budget was raised to £3m in an attempt to increase productivity. The war loans to the US and Canada were finally repaid in 2006.

and later at Government House, and then fly straight out to disseminate the information to the farms. He could give hands-on practical explanations of the latest best practice rather than simply sending out memos which few, if any, read.

With the research station at Kitale as our base, we travelled the country. Pasha visited farms all over, speaking to the landowners, the herdsmen, and the local seed suppliers. He lectured in the town halls and gradually his fame spread. There was no doubt that when it came to expertise in agriculture, and especially with regard to the farinaceous crops, such as maize, Pasha's knowledge was unsurpassed in Kenya and, probably throughout the entire African continent.

Word got back to Nairobi that farming information and assistance had taken on a new urgency within Kenya – exactly what the officials at the ministry wanted. Gradually the extension of Pasha's work, covering the land by air, grew from a benefit to an outright necessity. It was then that the Department of Agriculture began to fund expenses for the air travel. A shilling a mile, which meant we could pay Bill Pietersen's rent and landing fees and still turn a profit – and that made Pip give a belly laugh!

13

PASHA ZAYKY

Kitale, Kenya, July 1953

Kenya High School, Nairobi,
Saturday 31ˢᵗ January 1953

Dear Mama and Papa,

I hope you are well. The window over my bed in my new dorm has a nice view of Ol Donyo Sabuk, and you can see Mount Kenya in the distance. We had our typhoid jabs yesterday. Angela went first, fainted, and broke the needle, so matron had to get a new one for the rest of us. She was very cross.

It was horrible to hear about the murder of the Ruck family last weekend. Angela said the Mau Maus chopped them up; even the little boy as he was sleeping in his bed. We have a new Mau Mau drill now: if the bell sounds for ten seconds then we must all get under our desks and curl up. We are not allowed to raise our heads to see what's going on. Miss Stott told us that our lessons will carry on under our desks.

Lots of the native staff have gone now, including most of the cooks. They just disappeared without saying goodbye. As a result, some of the teachers have to spend time in the kitchens. Joshua is still here and has been very nice (Mama you met him once, do you remember?), but I'm not allowed to spend time alone with him any more, even though we have been friends for six years. We still see each other in the corridor between lessons for quick chats but as the saying goes не болтай, *you know what I mean.*

I am looking forward to seeing you both soon,

Love Sofia

S OFIA, NEARLY SEVENTEEN, WAS DOING AMAZINGLY well at the school with top marks in both languages and the sciences. Working hard towards attaining her advanced level General Certificates of Education, she remained inspired by the medics at the Kitale hospital and hoped that one day, despite her lack of British citizenship, it might be possible to travel to England to train as a doctor.

Why did I keep that particular letter from her, from January 1953? Once read, Tanya threw letters like that away. We only retained official letters relating to my job or matters regarding the Knight of the Mist. You only need your mind to store memories – not keepsakes. For some reason that I still don't understand, for us, the only exception to this rule was our small collection of photographs. Occasionally, Tanya would steal past that picture of her and Pyotr fishing on the Kuban and lightly brush his face with her fingertips. She thought I didn't see.

So there must have been something about that letter that made me fold it back into its envelope and file it away in the leaves of a book on the study of Kenyan grasslands, only to discover it again many years later. Perhaps I recognised, and treasured, the mixture of childhood innocence, in its last flush, coupled with the first inklings of the knowing awareness of adulthood.

In the letter she said не болтай – or literally 'don't chat'.[103] She knew that Tanya said it when I was chatting with Kenyan farmers for too long when she wanted to get back into the air to fly us home before nightfall. It was a familiar phrase to us because of its use as wartime propaganda in Russia. It had been their effort to try to ensure that enemy spies didn't get information. The British used the phrase 'Careless Talk Costs Lives' whilst the Americans said 'Loose Lips Sink Ships.' However, rather than using the phrase as a plea to simply stop talking (as Tanya would to scold me), I realised that Sofia was using it in its correct context. The full translation of the propaganda phrase was: 'Don't chat the enemy is listening.' And we knew that she had to be careful what she said as all girls' letters home were read before the envelopes were sealed.

In the six years that we had been in Kenya, things had changed. The propaganda phrase 'Don't chat!' assumed relevance once more as the country moved from peace to a war footing – a war of terror waged by guerrilla fighters.

I remembered my first impressions of the country as I sat on the bus from Lake Naivasha to Nairobi in 1946 – the noise, the colours, the smells. Kenya was a land of plenty and all its people of varied colours and backgrounds seemed happy and content. But even in 1946 nationalist organisations, most notably the Kenya African Union,

---

103 https://www.pinterest.co.uk/pin/535787686898896329/
  'Don't chat – the enemy is listening!'

were campaigning for the end of British colonial rule and freedom for the native population. Ostensibly the KAU promoted peaceful campaigning but as the last six years had elapsed so a darker, violent, protest group emerged – the Land Freedom Army, or the Mau Mau. The first mention of that name had been made in 1948 but nobody really knew where it originated; some suggested it was a corruption of the Kikuyu 'muma' meaning oath. Partly political, partly religious, its members lived in the forests and committed appalling atrocities on white settlers but mainly upon other natives, especially those Kikuyu who had refused to take oaths of allegiance or who were Christian. During the early 1950s, the frequency of attacks increased and the level of fear and terror among the settler population ratcheted up accordingly.

By October 1952, killings – black on white, white on black, black on black, and the maiming of livestock – had grown to epidemic proportions and Kenya's new governor, Sir Evelyn Baring, declared a state of emergency calling in the British army.

It seemed to me, and to all the other Europeans living in Kenya during those years, that all this trouble emanated from just one man who, in fact, had left London to return to his native Kenya just a few days after me, back in 1946, although he had travelled by ship rather than air. His name: Johnstone Kenyatta, although he had shortened his first name to Jomo.

Kenyatta had been a force in native Kenyan politics before the war but had spent sixteen years in Britain from 1931 during which time he had studied at the London School of Economics and also visited the Soviet Union. On his return to Kenya in 1946 he received a hero's welcome from the native community and was immediately seen as leader of the nationalist movement. That his return coincided with the emergence of Mau Mau violence could not be ignored. He was the ringleader – everyone said so. As soon as the state of emergency was declared in 1952, so Kenyatta was arrested. The settlers breathed a sigh of relief – surely now the Mau Mau violence would end. But it didn't. It grew much worse.

Kenyatta's trial in December 1952 took place in Kapenguria, thirty miles to the north of us in Kitale. Reached only by dirt track, Kapenguria was a most desolate place, deliberately chosen well away from the Kikuyu heartland of Nairobi as the remotest possible location to avoid trouble. The local school was converted to a courthouse, and all accommodation was requisitioned by the judge, the prosecution and the courtroom clerks. Kenyatta was housed in a makeshift compound with his guards in tents. His defence team had nowhere to stay in Kapenguria and, as a result, were forced to lodge in Kitale. They made the journey to court each day by Land Rover – along the unmade track – there and back.

Thankfully, and correctly, the judge had found Kenyatta guilty of leading the Mau Mau movement and sentenced him to seven years' hard labour. This was, apparently, the maximum allowed by the court but the judge regarded it as inadequate and recommended that on completion of the term Kenyatta should continue to be 'restricted'. The sentence would be completed in the desert close to the Sudanese border; a place called Lokitaung.

Although the centre of the trial had been close to us, and the barristers had been staying in Kitale Town, the circus of Kenyatta's trial had passed me by. Of course I had picked up snippets from the press but I took little interest in these goings-on. I was concentrating on the improvements to agricultural efficiency and by late 1952 spent much of my time inspecting the farms producing the all-important food exports, and reporting my findings to the Kenyan Agricultural Ministry in Nairobi. I even attended occasional meetings at Government House including with Governor Baring. Tanya was busy flying me round the country and although much of my time was spent consulting in the White Highlands – where the Mau Mau attacks were most frequent – we had not felt any personal impact.

I had huge sympathy for those poor farmers whose cattle had been maimed by the terrorists. The raiders came out of the forests at night, crept up to the grazing stock, hacked at the hamstrings with their *pangas* and left the cattle crying in agony until the farmer found them the following day and used his rifle to put them out of their misery. The theft or wanton destruction of produce – such as burning down the grain stores – made me angry. Tanya found it all shocking and was pleased that the British army were doing all they could to end the trouble. The local police or Special Branch offered a reward of five shillings for each terrorist confirmed killed, and the white settlers yelled out: 'The only good Kuke[104] is a dead Kuke.'[105]

---

104 'Kuke': short for Kikuyu.

105 During World War 2, and in the early years after, a common phrase in both Britain and the USA was 'The only good German is a dead German'. Here the Kenyan settlers adapted the well-known phrase to fit the fact that most of the so-called Mau Mau terrorists were of the Kikuyu tribe.

Wednesday 15th July 1953 was market day in Kitale. Sofia had come home from school for the start of the summer holidays and was excited to go to town and visit her friends at the hospital. So market day was a good excuse for us all to go in. Our idea had been to go early but actually I had been called off to check on the progress of a pyrethrum plantation close by whilst Tanya had spent most of the morning stripping and rebuilding the Knight's carburettor, and so much to poor Sofia's frustration we had delayed setting off until after lunch. Mohammed waited outside the bungalow in the Austin and as usual I was the last one out of the bungalow. Tanya was in the front and I climbed in the back with Sofia.

Having dropped Sofia at the hospital we carried on farther into the main street and market.

'I shall park here, *Bwana*,' said Mohammed, pulling us in to the side of the road at the start of the main street. 'I shall turn around and be ready for the off when you come back to me.'

There was always noise and colour on market day, but by this time in the early afternoon the stallholders were usually packing away. That day, however, the marketplace seemed busier than ever. There seemed to be more of everything. Many more people around, native salesmen selling trinkets, and lots of shouting. Police, too, and I noticed a couple of dark official-looking Wolseley cars parked further along the street. Tanya made straight for the ironmongers to collect various items for her workshop ordered the previous week, whilst I wandered through the market stalls inspecting the residual local produce on offer even though, by this time in the day, it was all rather wilted.

As I walked I was conscious of the crowd becoming slightly more dense. White settlers, both Europeans and Boers, were milling around but weren't interested in the stallholders' wares. Many were holding beer jugs and I could see through the windows of the various bars I passed that they were crammed full. Perhaps there was some sporting event I wasn't aware of. Both the English and the Afrikaners loved cricket, or perhaps it was a rugby match, although I thought it wasn't the season for that sport. Either way the crowd was there for something other than the market and had spent some considerable time in the town's pubs and drinking establishments. Even though the remaining market stalls stretched on ahead, I decided that I had seen enough for one day. The crowds were impeding my way and I didn't like their mood. I turned and began to weave my slow way back.

'He's gone free – the black bastard!' It was a yell, I didn't see the speaker, but as one the crowd tightened and surged the opposite way to me. I was trying to make progress back towards the car but now I was against the tide of the mob and found myself being washed back up the street. Shoulders were either side of mine. I'm tall but skinny, whilst these were all big fellows. I wasn't strong enough. Suddenly I was scared.

'What's going on?' I yelled.

The man in front of me, his breath stinking from the pub and tobacco, hissed in response.

'It's Kenyatta! He's as guilty as hell and his do-gooding barrister from England, who knows nothing, has got him off scot-free, on appeal.'

'Well we're not having it,' said another in a thick Afrikaans accent, 'this is our fucking country, we made it what it is. We're not having some kaffir-loving English bastard advocate tell us what to do with our criminals.'

'Let's string them both up, Kenyatta and his shit of a lawyer, they've both got blood on their hands and should pay the price.'

At this the mob roared approval and I was, quite literally, drawn off my feet and carried down the street. I realised that the mob were heading towards the local courthouse and I was being swept along with them.

Of course, I should have remembered reading that the Kenyatta appeal would be heard in Kitale, the authorities having realised, this time around, that Kapenguria to our north was simply too inhospitable for a sound legal process to take place. I had thought nothing of it at the time. News like that was merely background noise to Tanya and me – we did our best to stay away from comment and conversation surrounding politics.

'*Bwana*! *Bwana*, take my hand!' It was Mohammed, tall and upright, immediately ahead of me. As I was being propelled backwards he was reaching out a long arm past the men directly in front of me. If my feet had been on the ground I probably couldn't have reached him, but elevated as I was, my reach was increased and I tilted forward and grabbed his hand with both of mine.

Mohammed was thin but he was tall, tough, wiry and determined. He pulled me past the men bearing down on me and I felt the side of my face graze as I was yanked past a suited shoulder blade. The skin on my cheek was pulled so far back I thought my eye would come out but somehow

Mohammed pulled me towards him through the mob and then managed to twist behind me – pushing me onwards, against a surging tide of men, back towards our car.

'Black shit!'

'Get back to the forests.'

'Get out of our town.'

I heard the sound of phlegm being expelled accompanied by the thwacking sounds of fists hitting home and realised that Mohammed was being spat at and punched behind me. I said nothing, but allowed the man behind me to push me out of danger. And finally we were free of the melee. The car was there and Tanya was already in the front seat, terrified. Mohammed opened the rear door for me. I could see blood from both his lips and nose although he expressed no discomfort at all.

'Miss Sofey, *Bwana!*' He jumped in the driver's seat, started the car and we headed back to the hospital. Tanya and I leapt out and ran inside the small building calling for Sofia.

Dr Bourke appeared immediately.

'Mr and Mrs Zayky, Sofia isn't here, she left about a quarter of an hour ago to walk back into town to find you both… is everything okay?'

'Oh my God,' cried Tanya, 'she is walking back right towards the mob – we must have driven right past her.'

We ran back out to Mohammed.

'Turn the car around, Mohammed! Turn round – Sofia's back there!'

Why hadn't we seen her as we had driven back down to the hospital? Perhaps she had gone into a shop or just been hidden from view as there were still plenty of people all around. We drove back towards the noise, peering from the windows left and right, looking for Sofia. Suddenly Mohammed jammed on the brakes and both Tanya and I were flung forward. Why had we stopped?

Ahead of us the crowd was parting – jumping aside. It was just like a folded page of paper being torn at the seam. The cause was the two Wolseley cars, which were now in motion. They had had no room to turn around and were simply reversing out of the mob at speed, one behind the other, their gearboxes screaming in protest. I could see the driver of the car heading straight for us. He was turned around, one hand behind him on the steering wheel, the other holding the back of his seat. White knuckles; set jaw; cold eyes. We were stationary and now we pressed ourselves back in our seats waiting the impact of the crash.

But it didn't come, at the last second the cars swerved past us and continued in reverse along the road. As they sped past I just noticed large mounds covered in blankets in the back seats. I could see the dents in the doors from the kicks of the mob and the cracks in the glass from hammer-blows.

Mohammed crunched our Austin back into gear and lurched forward but now the crowd was running back towards us, streaming past our car and charging after the departing Wolseleys. Suddenly we saw Sofia, standing beside the road crying. We were still moving as Tanya opened the front door, grabbed her and pulled her in alongside her on the front bench.

'Mohammed – carry on ahead – don't try to turn round in this.' Mohammed did as bid and pushed onwards.

'Sofia, climb into the back alongside Papa!' Sofia, still sobbing, did as she was told, but the crowd were not interested in our car and continued surging past. I saw glints of steel. During the time of the Mau Mau rebellion most men carried a gun and now many had their weapons drawn. Kenyatta had obviously been in the back of that Wolseley and they meant to kill him.

Mohammed jammed on the brakes once again. A police officer had jumped in front of our car, seemingly quite unconcerned for personal safety. He opened the front door and climbed in. Alongside Tanya. We were speechless.

'Go left here, please,' he commanded; we turned left off the main street and then following his pointed finger left again. 'Pull over here, please.'

A man came up to the window. I looked hard and recognised him as the local District Commissioner. The area governor of the Kitale region. He was quite a young man to hold such a senior position, tall and good-looking – square-cut. I had met him at a few farming meetings although we had only ever exchanged odd words. I had rather gleaned the impression that his interests didn't extend to farming productivity. Tanya wound down her window.

'Mr and Mrs Zayky, good afternoon. I'm so sorry about the furore here; I'm afraid we have an unusual situation. The crowd do seem restless and so when Mr Kenyatta and his barrister came out of the courthouse we moved them to the hotel and then placed our officers under blankets in the cars, as decoys, to draw the crowd away.

'We noticed your car in town a little earlier on. Would you mind acting as a taxi for us? Could you take Mr Kenyatta and his barrister Mr Pritt back to the Research Station for us? I'm afraid the atmosphere out there is a little too hot for them to go anywhere else.'

I realised that we were at the back door of the town hotel. As the District Commissioner turned away from the car so the hotel door opened and two figures emerged. A policeman opened the back door of the Austin and the two got in. Sofia and I both swung our legs onto the rear seat squab and the incomers knelt down in the footwells. I could see one was black the other white, but no words were spoken and the policeman carefully arranged the blankets to cover them completely. The officer looked at me and Sofia.

'Pop your legs back down and rest on them please, sir… miss, if you would, please.'

Gingerly we did as we were told.

'Now, please slowly make your way back to the Research Station. Try to avoid eye contact with any of the crowd out there, just look forward. Drive steadily and don't stop.'

Mohammed began turning the car but stopped as the District Commissioner came up to the window once more.

'Very much obliged, Mr Zayky, Mrs Zayky – I shall be in touch…'

We did indeed drive steadily back out of Kitale all looking straight ahead, our necks fixed taut – expressionless. The crowds were still wandering in the road, swaying and staggering. Swagger sticks and guns were still held by their sides, but from the corners of our eyes we could see they were returning to the bars and pubs for further refreshment. Mohammed's nose was still dripping blood and his lip was swollen, but he carefully wove the car in between the pedestrians blocking our path; who were seemingly oblivious to our presence on the road and certainly completely unaware of our hidden cargo.

On our return to the agricultural station the two black Wolseley cars were parked up outside the laboratory. Even though we had left the main street of the town and its drunken rabble behind us, we had kept our extra two passengers hidden below the blankets, our feet resting on their upturned backs throughout the ten-minute journey.

Now we stopped and the two blanketed mounds in the back of the Austin shifted and groaned. Sofia opened the door on her side, reached down, pulled back the blanket and took the hand of a large black man. I recognised him instantly from the images I had seen in the East African Standard – it was Kenyatta.

He was tall and broad-shouldered, but certainly thinner than I recalled from the pictures I had seen previously. He wore an open-collared shirt and a safari-style jacket with light trousers. His beard was grey but even from the other side of the car I could see that his eyes were bright and piercing.

'Please,' he said to Sofia, 'may I have a glass of water?'

As Sofia hurried off to do as she was bid I looked to help the man struggling out from my side of the car. In his mid-sixties, short and a little stout, he placed a trilby hat on his balding head and straightened his horn-rimmed spectacles to look up at me.

'Pritt, Denis Pritt – thank you...' I shook his outstretched hand; his other hand held a crumpled briefcase which had obviously been held tightly to his chest during the trip on the floor of the Austin.

As Sofia returned holding the glass of water so I was conscious of figures alighting from the Wolseley cars and coming towards us. A tall man in a dark suit spoke:

'Johnstone Kenyatta; under the Emergency Powers (Defence) Act of 1939 as invoked by the Governor of the Crown Colony of Kenya, I am detaining you as an individual deemed dangerous to the state. You will come with me please.'

Kenyatta slugged back the water and returned the glass to Sofia. He shrugged his shoulders and looked across to Pritt, who was clearly bewildered.

'You can't do that… he's a free man. He's just been freed by the court in Kitale. This is a travesty.'

But the man who spoke and his colleagues now said nothing and simply ignored Pritt's protests. Two men stood either side of Kenyatta, each took an arm and frogmarched him back to one of the dark Wolseleys. The rear door was opened and Kenyatta was pushed inside. The man who had arrested Kenyatta turned and spoke again.

'Thank you for your co-operation, Mr Zayky; good day to you.'

And in a moment the cars started up and pulled back out onto the main road. They moved off at speed and were quickly out of sight.

Pritt looked up at me once more. He was swaying slightly, not unlike some of the more inebriated rioters on the streets just minutes earlier.

'I think I might need something a little stronger than a glass of water if you were able…' he stuttered.

We all went back to the bungalow where Mohammed served us lemon tea – with Pritt's laced with a large shot of vodka. As we drank our tea, so we heard a car draw up outside the bungalow. Some words were spoken and then Mohammed appeared with a letter for Tanya. She tore open the note.

'It's from the District Commissioner. Mr Pritt, I am to fly you to Nairobi at first light tomorrow – the government will cover the expenses. Apparently, your belongings from the hotel in town have been packed and your case has been dropped here.'

I got up and checked. Sure enough, Pritt's brown suitcase had been placed alongside his briefcase beside the bungalow's front door.

I returned to my chair and for a while we sat silently, none of us sure what to make of the events which had unfolded. Tanya is perfectly happy to sit in silence. She only says what needs saying; but silence is not my natural state and presently I began to make conversation with this stout little man sitting in our drawing room taking tea and vodka. As I refilled his teacup from the bottle, his shaking hands began to steady. Whether it was a reaction to the stress of the day's events or to the vodka, although I suspected he was no stranger to the latter, Pritt began to tell his tale. As a lawyer defending workers' employment rights he went on to become a member of the British parliament for the Labour Party in the 1930s.

'It was then that I first visited Moscow. Comrade Stalin showed how to run a truly collectivist state – where the people are happy and equal. He showed great leadership by cleansing the Russian Communist Party of wayward members who did not fully embrace the Marxist–Leninist doctrine.'

I noticed Tanya stiffen, but neither of us said anything. Pritt clearly had no idea that we were Russian émigrés – either that, or he didn't care.

'At the start of the Cold War I protested against the

creation of NATO;[106] a treaty of warmongers.[107] But the establishment conspired to poison the people against me and I lost my Parliamentary seat. So I restarted my legal career to defend the oppressed.

'That's why I am working for Jomo's release; of every case I have taken on, this presents the most blatant injustice. He was convicted of managing the Mau Mau whereas quite the reverse is true; he was the man trying to calm the young radical hotheads. Jomo Kenyatta is not only a man of peace, but is one of the most remarkable leaders and thinkers I have ever encountered.

'The British rigged Kenyatta's conviction and we showed that at the original trial the procedure was flawed. We succeeded! The judges today ruled the original trial as void. Jomo should be a free man now – but the bastards have taken him again.'[108]

---

106 NATO: The North Atlantic Treaty Organisation is a military alliance created in 1949 between the USA, Canada and the Western European states. The first NATO Secretary, Lord Ismay, stated its aim was 'to keep the Russians out, the Americans in, and the Germans down'. All members agreed that an armed attack against any one of them would be considered an attack against them all.

107 In the early 1930s Denis Pritt successfully defended Ho Chi Minh, repelling a French request for his extradition from Hong Kong. In 1954 he was awarded the International Stalin Peace Prize and in 1957 became an honorary citizen of Leipzig in communist East Germany. East Germany also awarded him the Gold *Stern der Völkerfreundschaft* (Star of People's Friendship) in October 1965. He died at his home in Hampshire, England, in 1972. Denis Pritt Road in Nairobi is named after him.

108 The ruling made at Kitale on 15th July 1953 voiding Kenyatta's original trial was reversed in Nairobi in August 1953. Pritt continued to appeal, first to the Supreme Court in Kenya and then to the Privy Council in London. However, in July 1954 the Privy Council rejected Kenyatta's final appeal without citing any reason. No further grounds for appeal were permitted.

Early the following morning, Mohammed drove Tanya, Pritt and me out to the runway on the Pietersen Farm; we would normally walk the short journey, but had to be careful to ensure that Bill Pietersen didn't lay eyes on Pritt. I helped make the Knight ready and then watched Tanya take off with Pritt on their journey back to Nairobi. As the plane gradually drew out of sight so a black Wolseley car arrived at the hangar. A native *askari* driver jumped out from the front and opened the door for the District Commissioner.

'Ah, I seem to have missed being able to say cheerio to Mr Pritt, but I'm glad that he is safely on his way back home. I can telegram Nairobi to tell them to expect him. They can then ensure that his flight out of the country is all arranged.'

Despite his words, the District Commissioner did not look at all disappointed at having missed the opportunity to say goodbye.

'Thank you, Mr Zayky, did everything pass smoothly? No unpleasantness, I hope.'

The District Commissioner paused before saying the word 'unpleasantness'.

'No, no unpleasantness…' I said.

'Jolly good, I must say that Her Majesty's Government is really most grateful to you and your wife for your actions yesterday, and then flying him back for us today – these things don't go unnoticed old chap… Good day, Mr Zayky.'

I wished him a good day also, as he climbed back into the rear seat of the Wolseley. The car was clean and polished but still displaying a cracked windscreen and the dents inflicted upon it by the mob the previous day.

I let Mohammed drive back to the research station without me as I wandered back on foot contemplating the events of the last forty-eight hours. Kenyatta, I had seen only fleetingly, but even in those moments he struck me as a towering figure, with sharp piercing eyes and able to take in a situation in moments. Not unlike Tanya in some ways.

Pritt, on the other hand, was a strange, egotistical little man, clearly brilliant, but somehow fatally wounded by life. However, he had painted a very different picture of Kenya and its troubles. Pritt's insight was quite unlike the view reported by the papers and from the mouths of the white settlers. Of course, his views on Communism and the wonders of the Soviet state were at such odds with my own that my instant reaction was to simply dismiss his statements surrounding Kenyatta and the Mau Mau as the deranged ramblings of a rather drunken man. But to ignore his claims entirely seemed wrong. He had backed up his statements with facts, for example the bribing of the judge and the witness, and unless these were barefaced lies (which I doubted) then much of what he said had to carry weight.

In both the USSR and then in the Third Reich, we had found ourselves working within nation states propounding good wholesome aims and espousing fine principles only to then govern their people in a brutish and soulless manner. The governance of those states had proved to be utterly amoral. Was this true of the British also?

Obviously in Russia and Nazi Germany we had had to work within those regimes simply to survive. We had never tried to improve our own outcomes by taking advantage of the totalitarian regimes in which we had found ourselves; or as the British say 'feather our nest'. We simply did what we had to do for the sake of ourselves and Sofia. Until then we had stayed out of politics in Kenya, but as of the previous day, by getting Kenyatta and Pritt away from the mob we had, unwittingly, become involved. The British seemed grateful and perhaps we could leverage their gratitude. That wouldn't be taking advantage. Food for thought.

As I dawdled, however, it was the District Commissioner whom I found myself contemplating. He had reminded me of somebody, but I couldn't quite place my finger on who it was. He was a tall man, and I supposed quite handsome to some eyes. Clearly a man who put the imperial administration at the heart of his life. I knew enough about the British to know that if you attended the correct school, and either you, or more likely your father, greased the correct wheels, then a career within diplomatic service was opened to you providing rank, privilege and ultimately honour within the British system. The District Commissioner was clearly a man very much immersed in this system, still quite young, possibly only forty and already a DC (albeit in a Kenyan backwater). He was probably somewhere in the middle of his career and looking to go all the way.

And then I remembered whom it was he reminded me of. The assistant director of the university back in Krasnodar – the tall, handsome, square-cut Communist party favourite, who had called on me, in my lecture theatre, to denounce colleagues. Two decades on, and in a different continent, under an entirely different regime, the young District Commissioner might have been his twin.

14

PASHA ZAYKY

Nairobi, Kenya, November 1953

D ESPITE KENYATTA'S CONTINUED DETENTION IN
the desert, the Mau Mau insurgency grew ever
more violent during the tail end of 1953. A terrorist war
that the British were losing. Mau Mau hit-and-run tactics,
knowledge of the land, of settler farms and particularly of
the forests – for their camps and hiding places – trumped
conventional British army warfare. Whilst the Mau Mau
carefully planned sporadic attacks and employed their
pangas alongside homemade rifles (which used household
bolts as firing pins) to devastating effect, the British used
Royal Air Force Vampire Jets to carpet-bomb suspect areas
of forest with little impact other than acres of broken trees.
The Mau Mau had the upper hand.

Up until then, in Kenya, I had concentrated my efforts
on increasing the efficiency and productivity of the European
or white-settler-run farms. My agricultural training in the
Caucasus – the breadbasket of the USSR – allowed me
an edge in understanding the issues and potential of the
Kenyan land. And so, despite my base remaining in Kitale to

the west, my experience led to me touring the entire country and especially the most productive White Highlands north of Nairobi. Most of the large farms had airstrips close by and in any case Tanya could, more or less, put the Knight of the Mist down anywhere.

The farmers seemed to like me, perhaps because I didn't have the bombastic nature of so many of the establishment figures within the colonial administration. Whatever it was, I seemed to be able to effect some changes and, notwithstanding the unfolding terrorist emergency, Kenyan agricultural output began to rise.

However, in the final months of 1953 the Department of Agriculture in Nairobi issued new orders. From then on, when visiting the white-settler farms, I was also asked to examine local native smallholdings. Now I also had to report on the agricultural viability and efficiency of the native plots.

My response was simple – native farming in Kenya was a disaster! In the late 1940s the then governor, Sir Philip Mitchell, had proposed a communal approach to native farming. Native co-operative groups were established, generally comprised of Kikuyu workers, who were allocated second-rate land, usually 'on the contour' – literally the side of a hill – with a view to creating cultivation through irrigation and fertilisation. However, the European/white-settler farmers demanded that the native farms should not compete against them and so the co-operatives were banned from producing cash crops such as coffee and tea.

The result was total failure. Land on the side of a hill can never be transformed to successful agricultural use no matter how good the irrigation or fertilisation. In the absence of coffee and tea crops then maize might just have fed a few small families but never generated enough cash to facilitate any kind of household social development. Worst of all the Kikuyu farmers simply didn't want to farm collectively. Mitchell, it seemed to me, had envisaged the native farmers as harmonious, non-competitive socialists when, in fact, the complete opposite was true. By the early 1950s the contour farms had more or less ground to a standstill.

Kikuyu had farmed the fertile White Highlands between the wars. They had worked for the white settlers but had been able to run their own small plots as squatters alongside. After the second war, the new agricultural methods, which in many cases had been introduced by me, had resulted in the relocation of the squatters away from the prime arable land to the new collective farms with poor output and prospects. It is no small wonder that, in many cases, the erstwhile Kikuyu squatter farmers took one look at their new circumstances, and simply vanished into the forests to become Mau Mau terrorists. I completed my written reports to the administration on the state of the native farms. Their situation was hopeless and I said so.

It was sometime in November 1953 when I was summoned to a meeting at Government House, Nairobi, to outline my findings on the state of native farming in Kenya. I had by then attended many meetings in the capital, some at the Ministry of Agriculture, some at the government-run Scott Laboratories on the outskirts of the city and indeed some, rather more official, engagements at Government House. Tanya had flown me into the city early that morning, landing at the High School. We had been greeted by an excited Miss Stott who had been promised a flying safari to photograph elephants for a talk and slide show she was planning for the girls. Tanya was glad to oblige.

I had a car and driver waiting for me at the school to take me on to Government House.

The meeting had begun at 10am behind closed doors. I waited in the corridor outside and eventually after an hour was called in. The day was bright, but despite two sets of large French doors leading out to the gardens of the colonial mansion, the meeting room was darkened. The shutters to the French doors were all but closed, with just a crack between them allowing two narrow bands of daylight to pierce the gloom and to silhouette the clouds of cigarette smoke which had accumulated in the previous hour. The room was rather bare; just a few portraits hung on the walls, indistinct in the poor light, and a long table ran from the entrance towards the garden windows. The table could have sat twenty but in fact there were just seven men present along with a female secretary sitting in a chair to the right of the entrance doors with a notepad on her knee. Despite the smoke and gloom I could recognise Roger Swynnerton, the new head of Kenyan agriculture, at the head of the table. He was obviously the chairman of this meeting, although not the most senior man in the room as to his left was the Governor, Sir Evelyn Baring.

It was indicated that I should sit at the foot of the table and thus some distance from the attendees. Swynnerton began:

'Zayky, good morning. Thank you for joining us; our apologies for having kept you waiting. But let's get down to it. We have asked you over the previous couple of months to comment on the state of native farming in Kenya and your reports have been thoroughly negative. There's an emergency going on in this country, don't you know; we need everyone to work together to overcome the Mau Mau and it seems to us that what you're saying is letting the side down.'

I hadn't been prepared for this. How stupid! If my background in the Soviet Union should have taught me anything it was never to rail hard against the dictates of the regime. It was never politically acceptable to damn policies of the state outright, no matter how incoherent or short-sighted. This had been so obvious in 1930s Stalinist Russia, so why on earth should I have thought that it was any different in 1950s British Colonial Africa? British bureaucrats were more urbane than their Russian counterparts, but direct confrontation remained equally unacceptable. Swynnerton and the other faces around the table glowered at me. I had done wrong.

I immediately became contrite. I was sorry. As a Russian, it was possible that my use of English as a second language had led me to phrase my reports poorly. That got some nods round the table. My actual views may have been miscommunicated. More nods. Would they like me to reconsider my reports in the light of my possible use of incorrect phraseology due to linguistic issues and resubmit them? Yes – they would. Nods and even some smiles through the gloom. I escaped the smoke-filled, and now choking, gloom of the room but was asked to remain at the mansion in case the committee had further questions. Disaster averted? Was I – to use the British phrase – 'out of the woods'? I hoped so.

It was dismal, though, that I had had to use my Russian citizenship as an excuse to dig myself out of the hole. Being a Russian in the West during the 1950s was not easy. The threat of internment as the enemy was a constant worry, even in East Africa. Albeit that threat had receded slightly by 1953 as China had taken over from Russia as the lead Cold War aggressor given the military stalemate at the end of the Korean conflict and during the Soviet political vacuum post Stalin's death.[109] Nevertheless, in our daily lives, I tried to avoid any mention of our Russian heritage, so that whilst my experience of agriculture in the Caucasus was a huge influence on my work I usually didn't refer to it in my reports. I aimed to model myself as an English university professor, stooped, bespectacled, with only the merest trace of accent in my speech. Now I had fallen back on my Russian roots to explain my political faux pas and it felt like a retrograde step – something which might come back to haunt me.

I went into the gardens, explaining to the *askari*[110] outside the room where to find me should I be called back. I was disconsolate and wandered through the grounds studying the plants and flowers in the manicured borders. I was slightly surprised by some of the specimens – quite strange to see them in a formal garden setting. I crouched down to study one rather more closely.

'I shouldn't touch that one.' The voice came from behind me. I looked round and up to see Sir Evelyn Baring standing behind me. I rose.

'Good afternoon, sir, thank you – no I shan't touch that

---

109 Stalin died in March 1953, and almost immediately the Soviet Union adopted a less hostile relationship towards the West. There was no obvious successor as Party Secretary and it took three years before Khruschev emerged as the new leader of the USSR.

110 *Askari*: native soldier.

one: *Gloriosa superba* – the flame lily. [111] Quite beautiful, but nearly every part of it is poisonous – in West Africa it's used by some tribes as the poison tip for their arrows. I must say I'm a little surprised to find it here in your garden.'

'Well, it has many medicinal uses too you know. The alkaloid it produces is colchicine, which is very good to relieve gout if you're a sufferer…'

I did know about its medicinal uses.

'Yes, but in moderation only, sir, as too much can cause severe diarrhoea – keep your dogs away – but it's a very effective snake repellent too, I believe.'

'You know your plants, Zayky – I think you are as good as they say. Come walk with me. Do you know, when Molly and I came here last year it was to be the swansong of my diplomatic career. Now we have lost India, Kenya is the jewel of the British Empire. I've governed Rhodesia and South Africa and both of those countries offered their fair share of worry and indeed bloodshed – I did well and as a result, as a reward and honour, Kenya would be my final posting. All anybody had told us before we came was that this was a land of plenty, occupied by happy settlers and happy natives. When Mitchell retired no mention of uprising had come through in any official reports, none of the Mau Mau stories had emerged. Mitchell kept them all quiet in case they should jeopardise his anticipated knighthood. We believed that governorship of Kenya would consist of ceremonial duties, laying the foundation stones of new municipal buildings in Nairobi, and shaking hands with smiling natives.

---

111 *Gloriosa superba* – the flame lily.
http://powo.science.kew.org/taxon/urn:lsid:ipni.org:names:535953-1

'Zayky, my passion is wild plants and I thought that East Africa would offer me the most fabulous opportunity of plant-hunting. An easy final five-year tour followed by a long retirement. Instead, I am seen as the Governor who has allowed the Empire's most bountiful asset to descend into civil war. Reports from all areas depict the entire country in disarray, with all the information flowing back up the diplomatic line to the Government in London.'

'Sir, I am so sorry that my reports caused you increased upset, it was just my lack of understanding of the language...'

'Zayky, that's rot! We both know that your understanding and use of English is perfectly good, rather better than most of my British staff, actually. You can wriggle from your hot seat in the meeting, claiming language issues, but I have to wriggle over the veracity of your reports. We both know that you are completely correct: native farming is a disaster. The problem is what to do about it!'

Baring spoke in that clipped, almost staccato, way that I had come to recognise as a trademark of the upper-class English schooling and army system. He was a tall man, angular, thin. His nose, the most prominent feature of his face, was long and pointed not dissimilar to a right-angled triangle. However, to adopt the true look of a member of the British upper class, to accompany his clipped accent, Baring had to hold himself as a patrician, and in this he failed. His complexion was pallid, his eyes were heavy and darkened. A patrician walked in strides whereas Baring shuffled. A patrician's face fell naturally to a look of arrogance whereas Baring's demeanour was one of diffidence bordering on timidity.

As we walked through the vast gardens of the colonial Government mansion, Baring would stop occasionally and bend down to examine a plant or flower, or he would pause in his speech as he contemplated a particular vista or border. Our shared love of botany created a comradeship between us. I felt empathy for Baring. I also knew now that it was no longer necessary to try to hide my Russian roots.

'It seems to me,' I said 'that what is needed are Stolypin reforms…'

Baring paused again but now to look at me rather than his plants. 'I'm afraid, Zayky, that you will need to enlighten me.'

At the start of the twentieth century Russia experienced a problem of rural overpopulation – every year saw an excess of fifteen more births than deaths per thousand peasants. In 1905 the impact of starvation culminated in a peasant revolt. The Tsar's prime minister, Pyotr Stolypin, realised that serfs liberated in the nineteenth century still lacked any financial security. Farming in Russia at the start of the twentieth century was just like the English open fields system of the Middle Ages.[112]

Stolypin believed that tying the peasants to their own private landholdings would produce profit-minded and politically conservative farmers. He introduced the unconditional right of individual landownership, capitalist-

---

112 In medieval England little land was owned outright. Instead the Lord of the Manor had rights granted to him by the King. The Lord controlled two or three large fields divided into many narrow strips of land. The strips were farmed by individual peasants who lived in a nucleated village adjacent to the Lord's manor house. The Lord levied rents and also required the peasantry to work his personal lands. This was the feudal system. In the seventeenth century new agricultural methods in England saw the enclosure of land into farmsteads. The open-field system ended.

oriented modern farmsteads, as well as affordable lines of credit for peasants to allow them to invest in their land.

But regime change in Russia meant that Stolypin's plan ended badly. The newly independent farmers who emerged as a result of the reforms did very well, but inevitably their success created jealousy; they became known as the Kulaks (literally 'fist', or by extension 'tight-fisted'). After the 1917 Soviet Revolution, Lenin declared the Kulaks as 'bloodsuckers' and their farms were renationalised.

The similarity between the agricultural situation in Russia at the start of the century and the plight of Kenyan native farmers by mid-century was inescapable. Stolypin had shown the way forward in Russia by his creation of a class of agricultural 'Kulak' landowners. In Kenya it was time to do the same thing.

As we walked through the gardens of the colonial mansion, I put it to Baring that the communal farming arrangements should be unravelled, with removal of restrictions on coffee and tea crops. Most important of all, however, was land reform to grant native farmers property rights over fertile land.

Baring stopped walking and turned to me.

'It's a bold plan you're proposing, Zayky, but it has merit. I will need to convince Whitehall, but they are desperate for a solution as none of the conventional methods of subduing these bastards is working.'

Baring paused.

'Of course this can't be a plan made in your name – you are Russian after all – Whitehall would certainly not buy that; and it can't be my scheme as... well, frankly, Zayky, there is too much risk attached. No, we shall get you to write it and Swynnerton can put his name to it.'

'I don't think Mr Swynnerton is too keen on me,' I ventured.

'Oh nonsense, don't be moved by the tomfoolery this morning. That was all merely a game of words to be minuted by the secretary, typed up, and then sent off to London with the diplomatic reports to keep the mandarins of Whitehall sanguine.' Baring paused before continuing.

'No, our meeting today was to create an illusion of action where there is none. Swynnerton is just as flummoxed as me – as we all are. We need a bold solution, Zayky. Come inside and join me for lunch, we shall get Swynnerton too. We need to put some flesh on these bones.'

And so it was, over lunch that day at Government House, that the 'Swynnerton Plan' was created. Lunch, and then through the afternoon and into the night. Tanya sent word for me to come to the High School to fly back to Kitale, but Baring ordered a car to bring her back to the residence so that we could spend the night. I saw her only briefly that evening.

'What is going on, Pasha? Are we in trouble? It is as though we are arrested although they have shown me to a very nice room.'

'Not at all, my darling,' I spoke reassuringly although all that day my heart was in my mouth, and I was only half sure that my words of reassurance were valid. Swynnerton's name may have been attached to the plan but I could be quite certain that were it to fail then it would rapidly become known as my idea all along.

My proposition was simple – win over the hearts and minds of the Kikuyu by the creation of a rich, landowning class to generate employment and disseminate wealth. Mau

Mau freedom fighters hiding in the forests would not be around when the land deeds were handed out to Kikuyu loyalists. The new landowners would provide employment to others; good cash crops could be sown, harvested and sold allowing a range of other consumer goods to be bought. If it worked then the forest-dwelling Mau Mau would become marginalised and out of touch with the farmers and villagers as they grew more prosperous. In turn, the villagers and farmers were likely to feel better disposed towards the colonial power. Kikuyu sympathy for the terrorists would evaporate, and without widespread support the insurgents would gradually emerge from the forests, lay down their weapons, and go back to farming.

As that day in November 1953 turned into the next, and then as the remaining weeks of the year passed by, so the plan was formalised and approved by London. Tanya and I now had more or less permanent quarters at Government House. I met with Roger Swynnerton daily often with Sir Evelyn Baring in attendance. Initially, there was some settler resistance particularly when the ban on natives growing cash crops was lifted. In reality, however, the white settlers knew perfectly well that native farmers were never going to create significant competition on world crop markets. The sense of what we were trying to achieve was clear.

But in the short term the terrorism got worse. Fear gripped the entire nation although, in reality, the violence was concentrated in the fertile Rift Valley and in Nairobi – a city which in Baring's opinion was now experiencing a complete breakdown of law and order. The Mau Mau were said to be murdering Kikuyu loyalists, Kikuyu government officers, and anybody suspected of informing on them to the authorities. Armed robbery, witness intimidation, protection racketeering, and the boycotting of European products were all part and parcel of the Mau Mau network of terror and fear.

According to the administration's figures there were 60,000 male natives living in Nairobi and three-quarters of them were of the Kikuyu tribe. But by the start of 1954 the rumour mill had it that the Mau Mau were no longer recruiting Kikuyu alone. In the tight quarters of the Nairobi slums members of other tribes were said to be taking up their cause. The rebellion was growing.

15

TANYA ZAYKY

Nairobi, Kenya, April 1954

IT WAS A SATURDAY MORNING TOWARDS THE END OF April 1954. Pasha had another meeting that morning at Government House. Poor Pasha had thought that becoming an agricultural officer in Kenya would allow him to practise his beloved botany, but he no longer spent time in the fields, or the laboratory, or speaking to the farmers working the land. Now it was a carousel of stuffy meetings with pompous officials agreeing policy and generating paperwork. Over the last six months he had swapped botany for bureaucracy. Today's meeting was apparently some 'hush hush' gathering…

'Hush hush? What is that?' I asked.

'A secret briefing, apparently,' he replied. 'The Governor has asked us all to come in this morning – no agenda – no advance papers… but just all of us there.'

'All of us…' That didn't include me – instead, Pasha was referring to the leaders of the administration in Kenya. Bizarrely, he recognised that, by some strange quirk, he had become part of that group.

As usual, I had landed the Knight of the Mist at the High School early that morning and the government car had been waiting to whisk Pasha off to Government House. Sofia had appeared in her school uniform, which now she was in her last year of school was looking slightly too small. There were, apparently, no lessons for her that Saturday, and shortly after Miss Stott came over to wish me a good morning. I had opened the engine cowling and was studying the carburettor.

'Something amiss with the engine, Mrs Zayky?' asked Miss Stott.

'I think there might be a slight blockage in the carburettor, possibly some contaminated fuel, but it was certainly stuttering towards the end of our flight in. I don't think I want to leave it – I might take it in to Choudry's just to wash it through with paraffin and adjust it carefully on the bench.'

'Well, I'm afraid I can be of no help to you with that… other than perhaps to offer to get Joshua to run you to the garage in our car.'

The workshops at Nairobi aerodrome had all the equipment I needed to clean and recalibrate the carburettor but the airfield was to the south of the city, whereas the school in Kileleshwa was in the north-west. Having flown in to the High School many times I had built up a good relationship at Choudry's garage in the centre of the town – rather closer than driving all the way to the airfield. Sunny Choudry had begun his car repair shop in Nairobi before the war. He built up a stock of old auto components which he cleaned, painted and recycled for sale, he had a couple of big car ramps, and a small lot of used motors outside. Sunny himself was now well into his sixties but he had trained a good team of mechanics including his son Rashid. Importantly for me, he had a decent engineering shop including a lathe and a milling machine – and trusted me to use them as I wished, charging only a small rental fee in return. It helped that the High School had long used Choudry's to maintain their cars, and even their lawnmowers, and so were good customers. On my arrival Sunny would smile and wobble his head from side to side.

'Ahh, Mrs Zayky, how lovely to see you. You are very welcome at Choudry's garage today. And how is Miss Stott, please? I hope she is very well.'

That Saturday morning the Knight's carburettor was swiftly removed and Joshua dutifully brought the car round. Miss Stott delighted Sofia by granting permission for her to accompany me on the journey into the city centre, and although I sat up front next to Joshua, she babbled happily to him from the backseat, in a mixture of English and local Gikuyu dialect. It was still early in the day and with little traffic on the road we made swift progress to Choudry's, parking up outside, just in front of the used cars for sale.

We entered through the large, and high, concertina folding doors into the maintenance area where several old motors were in the air on ramps in various stages of repair, whilst a crash-damaged truck sat to one side and was undergoing some fierce metal management at the end of a hammer. Sunny appeared immediately to greet us, and was his usual self, ushering me through the maintenance bays and into the machine shop beyond, where I soon had the carburettor stripped down on the bench. Outside, the day had grown grey and a misty drizzle of rain had started to descend but it hadn't stopped Sofia and Joshua, both disinterested in the activities at Choudry's, wandering off to peer through the windows of shops nearby.

The hammering, clattering, chatting and laughter coming from the maintenance bays was pretty noisy, but I had the machine shop to myself and I shut out the sounds to concentrate on my task. The smell of freshly oiled metal was the only company I needed. As I cleaned away the tar residue which had obviously caused the problem with the carburettor, I reflected on Sofia's progress. Now she was eighteen, and a tall girl, but plain. Some may say that, as a mother, it is not right for me to say such a thing about my daughter but I am always objective, and honest, and it was the case. After all, I am plain as well. But certainly, she had my eyes, my intensity, my attention to detail. I didn't think that she had inherited Pasha's ability to win people over to his way of thinking but she was certainly a match for his intellect. School work was not a challenge; she simply soaked up knowledge, and all she could talk about was the prospect of becoming a doctor.

Despite Pasha's hope, she had never made friends her own age at the High School, only with her teachers and indeed with the native staff. In her letters home during her junior years we heard all about adventures with the cooks in the kitchens or about her drinking sweet chai and learning Gikuyu from the groundsmen. But as the Mau Mau emergency had worsened so the native staff at the school had melted away until only Joshua was left, and he must have been told to keep his distance. More recently, Sofia's letters lacked the colour and excitement of those from her earlier years.

Pasha recognised that, reading between the lines of her letters, as the native staff had left the school so Sofia had become friendless and lonely. That was why she had been so animated in the car that day, chatting to Joshua who, alone with us in the car, was only too happy to have the freedom to chat back.

As I carried on with my cleaning, my mind wandered to what Pyotr would make of Sofia's progress. She had been just a toddler when he had last seen her before going off to war and to his eventual death. He had doted on her then – he would be so proud of her now! I could picture him laughing – his big belly laugh. My mind wandered back to the day we fished together on the Kuban as children. That picture; our photograph. And then again, remembering him laughing at our table in the old flat in Krasnodar. And when he stopped laughing I could see him wrapping his bear-like arms around his tiny niece, but so tenderly. No laughter then, only joy. Pyotr the Cossack, brash and loud, full of vigour and life but being so careful not to damage something so precious.

Sofia's dream was to study medicine in London, specifically at Queen Mary College. She had already applied and Dr Bourke from the hospital in Kitale had provided the reference. I had seen a copy of his letter and confess to having glowed with pride. In a typically understated British way he expressed his huge admiration for her knowledge, her ability to learn, enthusiasm, and her desire to explore beyond the obvious in any given medical situation. The College had responded quickly to offer her a place subject to her passing her advanced certificates of education. Their letter of acceptance had confirmed her living accommodation, a small grant to cover living expenses and even an offer to cover half the cost of her passage to England. Passing her advanced level certificates was unlikely to present a problem for Sofia. No; the obstacle to her dream was a continued lack of passport – without that she couldn't leave Kenya and certainly couldn't enter Britain. This was now the significant problem that had to be resolved – for her sake.

I had continued my cleaning and fettling whilst pondering Sofia's fortunes. The now gleaming carburettor had been carefully adjusted, and was ready to be reattached to the Knight. Carefully, I wrapped the component in brown paper so as not to leave finger marks. But as I did so I became aware that the noise that I had shut out from my head previously – the din from the maintenance bays – had changed in tone.

The hammering had stopped and so had the laughter. There was shouting but it sounded like it was coming from the street. Also, I realised I could hear a loudspeaker; a British voice but high-pitched and nasal, the words indistinct. Clutching the wrapped carburettor, I walked from the machine shop back into the maintenance bays. Sure enough, the earlier clamour and activity had ended and the men were crowded together around the concertina folding doors to the outside looking out into the street beyond the used car lot. They were silent. Sunny was in the middle, his son Rashid to his side. The men's backs blocked my view and I walked up to them; Sunny moved aside slightly to let me see, his face set grim.

Through the drizzle in the middle of the street was a green open-backed British Army Land Rover with a loudspeaker horn fixed to the corner of the windscreen. The driver was speaking into a microphone, '... collect no more than one bag... leave the rest of your belongings at home... exit into the street peacefully...'

In the back of the Land Rover a machine gun had been mounted on a swivel turret and a British soldier slouched against it. The gun stock was under his shoulder, his right arm dangled to his side, with his left draped over the breech. His casual stance indicated that nobody was in imminent danger of being shot but he and the gun were there, nevertheless. Along the other side of the street, beyond the Land Rover, a line of troops were using their rifle butts to bang against the doors of the houses and shops. After bashing on the door the soldier outside would wait for just a few seconds. Either the door would be opened immediately by the occupiers and the soldier would rush inside or, if it remained closed for just a moment too long, it would receive a kick from the soldier's boot which proved no match for any door or frame.

Once inside a house, shouting could be heard; banging; the sound of upturned tables and chairs, smashed glass and crockery, and then within a few seconds one or more native men would appear. Kikuyu. Some partly clothed, some carrying a suitcase, others empty-handed – all with their heads held down. All ran along the street pushed onwards by the soldiers' rifle butts. As I leaned forward to follow their line of travel I could see a Bedford truck, parked farther down the road. As they arrived at the tailgate so those already inside leaned out to help the newcomers climb up. A group of soldiers stood ready, their rifles held at their hips.

The soldiers made a lot of noise – shouting – boots stomping. The loudspeaker on the Land Rover blared. There was the commotion and wreckage of crashing in through the doors and smashing inside people's homes but, as far as I could tell, the men being rounded up were silent. No resistance. Nothing said.

And then soldiers appeared in Choudry's car lot. 'Kikuyu! Head down! No, leave that! Here! Now! To the truck! Move!'

And in a moment Choudry's mechanics were running to the truck. Any tools which they had been holding had been dropped to the floor. The soldiers pushed past Sunny, Rashid and me and on into the maintenance bay. One ran through to the machine shop door, looked inside, saw there was nothing. Clearly there were no more Kikuyu in hiding, that was the clear purpose of this inspection. Then, as fast as they had come, they all ran back out and along to the next premises. Nothing at Choudry's had been damaged but he had just lost most of his staff.

But by now, the driver in the Land Rover had stopped talking into the microphone. The noise began to subside. Somebody blew a whistle. The Land Rover moved off and drove up the road to the truck which then led off with the Land Rover behind. The squad of troops followed on foot, whilst the soldier on the machine gun in the back of the Land Rover swung his weapon to the left and right looking for any trouble. There was none.

Sofia walked disconsolately back to Choudry's car lot. The drizzle had soaked her school uniform. Her long black hair was matted to her face but I could see she was fine.

'Mama, they took Joshua,' was all she said.

16

PASHA ZAYKY

Nairobi, Kenya, April 1954

BARING SPOKE FIRST. HE STOOD TO ADDRESS US.
'Gentlemen, thank you all for coming this morning. What you are about to hear does not go beyond this room, although as you will learn, some of the decisions taken over the last few days are being put into action as we speak. Their impact will be far-reaching.

'I need not tell you all of the scale of the issue that we face. Kenya is under attack from within. A most insidious and evil poison has entered this otherwise beautiful land. Kenyatta is under lock and key in the desert but still his Mau Mau pursue their deadly vendetta against our rule of law and order. During the past fifteen months there have been more than 100 deaths – acts of murder and manslaughter – of which not more than a handful have been successfully prosecuted.

'What we are experiencing here, in Kenya, is a civil war within the Kikuyu tribe. There are those, loyal to Britain, who appreciate the security and wealth we provide under the umbrella of our Empire; and there are those who for reasons of self-interest, greed and a quest for power, wish to oppose them.

'It is down to us few, around this table, to use our ministries of state to restore order in Kenya. To allow those who work for the common good to prosper and to ensure the subjugation of all those who oppose order, good sense, and the rule of British law.

'Last year Mr Swynnerton, assisted by Mr Zayky, formulated a plan to raise up the status of the loyal Kikuyu natives in this country. To provide them with ownership of fertile land; to allow them access to cash crops; employ their fellows; and, provided they work hard, to grow rich. This plan still has some way to go until full implementation, but I am sure that it can win over the hearts of the natives.

'However, gentlemen, Mr Swynnerton's plan alone is, I'm afraid, insufficient. It is certainly a bold endeavour, creating far greater reform than has been experienced in any part of Africa to date. And it is a carrot for our native donkey. But every donkey needs a stick as well as a carrot.

'To date we have sent in police and troops to try to root out insurgents and we have asked the Royal Air Force to conduct bombing campaigns on suspect areas of forest. Frankly it has been to little avail. Today, gentlemen, we begin something bolder; a bigger stick to beat our native donkey. A stick which is as ferocious as Mr Swynnerton's agrarian reform is benign. General Sir George Erskine[113] has

113 General Sir George Erskine GCB KBE DSO (1899–1965) commanded the 7th Armoured Division during World War II. A close personal friend of Winston Churchill, in 1953 Erskine took full command of British forces in East Africa to manage the response to the Mau Mau uprising. In retirement he was Aide-de-Camp to the Queen 1955 to 1965 and Lieutenant Governor and Commander-in-Chief of Jersey 1958 to 1963.

been with us now for almost year, having been sent here by the Prime Minister. Sir George, if you please…'

'Thank you, Governor. Gentleman, in consultation and agreement with the Governor, I have today ordered the commencement of Operation Anvil. From 8am this morning squads of British troops, native *askaris*, and the entire Nairobi police force, have been sent into the city of Nairobi to round up and detain all male Kikuyu residents and itinerants. In addition, members of any other tribes considered to be Mau Mau sympathisers will be brought in. The planning for this operation has taken several months and has been conducted in complete secrecy so as not to prompt suspects to go into hiding.

'Some 4,000 soldiers and policemen have been deployed in this task today. The entire operation will take approximately two weeks but for all practical purposes most Kikuyu men will be detained over this weekend. I estimate that some 50,000 will be in custody by tomorrow evening.'

'But where on earth will you put them?!' I gasped. Erskine lowered his eyeglasses and looked down the table at me.

'Mr…?' he looked at the attendee list on his meeting papers. 'Ah yes, the Russian fellow… Zayky.'

Now it was Carruthers Johnson who spoke. Johnson was effectively Baring's second in charge in Kenya. He was nicknamed 'Monkey' on account of his face, which looked for all the world like that of an ape. Perhaps it was overcompensation from a lifetime of teasing but where Baring suffered from a weak constitution and a lack of self-confidence, Johnson was toweringly strong in both body and mind. From the higher echelons of the British upper class, the undoubted power behind Baring's throne, Johnson was Machiavellian, ruthless, and frighteningly polite. In many ways he reminded me of Himmler.

'Sir George, if I may… Mr Zayky has raised a pertinent issue. This weekend most of the detainees will be held, at varying times, at the city centre bus station. However, from there they will be sent by truck to a tented compound we have established at Langata, south of the city. There we will begin screening. A simple process to separate those Kikuyu suspected of Mau Mau sympathies from those who are clearly innocent of such thought. The latter group, which I expect to be the majority, will be sent to the Kikuyu reserve. The former will be sent forward to other camps for further screening.'

I interjected again: 'Mr Johnson, I am grateful for your clarification. But if over half of the 50,000 detained in Nairobi this weekend are sent to the existing Kikuyu reserves, that will result in severe overcrowding. The land area in the reserves is not sufficient to support an influx of that size. In addition, many Kikuyu have never been outside of Nairobi; the reserves will be entirely alien to them. Are there plans to expand the size of the reserves?'

'Indeed, Mr Zayky, it is likely to be quite busy in the short term and I am sure that many people will be very happy to be reunited with long lost kith and kin. But I think that in the medium term the existing reserves will prove perfectly adequate to house everybody especially if, using your excellent methods, they can improve the quality of their agricultural output.' Johnson paused and smiled.

'I should think that you will be very happy, Zayky, as the Mau Mau sympathisers who are not returned to the reserves will be put to work on significant land improvement schemes, which will be to your very own design.'

Baring stood again.

'Thank you, Johnson; Erskine. Excellent work today, and we shall look forward to an altogether quieter and more law-abiding city from Monday. Gentlemen, I think that brings us to a good point to break for coffee...'

Operation Anvil began on Saturday 24th April 1954. It was a complete success and marked a turning point in the defeat of the Mau Mau insurgency in Kenya. Up to then I had given the administration the benefit of doubt. Denis Pritt had suggested the administration rigged Kenyatta's trial but Pritt himself had been flawed and, as a Communist sympathiser, detestable – and so I had let it pass. My own suggestion of land reform was bound to create winners and losers and I could already see that the winners, under my plan, would be those loyalist Kikuyu who supported the British. But the original suggestion had been mine – and so I let it pass.

However, from late April 1954 the British colonial administration in Kenya was engaged in a systematic cleansing of the ethnic Kikuyu tribe from society. There could be no confusion; this was just like the Jewish pogrom undertaken by the Nazis; it was just like the purges of officials and academics under the Soviets. Back in Krasnodar, in Posen, and in Salzgitter, we had let all that pass. And I was certain we would let the round-up of Kikuyu in Nairobi pass as well – all that had changed was that I was no longer giving the administration any benefit of doubt. The NKVD, the Gestapo, the British soldiers – they were all the same. Did it matter? I wasn't part of it. I was just a botanist trying to improve the food supply.

During the formulation of what became known as the Swynnerton Plan I was asked to consider what else could be produced from the land. Tea and coffee were the main Kenyan cash crops; the infrastructure to process them was in place, whilst world markets were ready, willing and able to buy as much as could be produced. It was hard to think of anything else which could be sown on good arable land to generate as much hard currency. The issue here was to look at lesser-quality land and think laterally.

In rural areas the farmers' main food was *ugali*, a porridge made from ground maize. But maize was grown on land which might be better used for tea and coffee. What was needed was to use lesser-quality land to produce alternative food for the natives so that more fertile soil could switch over to higher-value cash crops.

Having spent hours poring over topographical maps I was able to make use of Tanya's flying skills and Miss Stott's passion for photography to create a portfolio of aerial pictures. Mwea, sixty miles north-east of Nairobi, was an arid plain of impervious clay used as a common land for grazing. The Thiba river ran through the centre and rarely ran dry.

In Asia the staple food was rice rather than maize but in Africa rice had only ever worked to the west of the continent in areas of high rainfall. Now it dawned on me that the clay soil of the Mwea plain leant itself to the establishment of an irrigation scheme fed by the Thiba; a network of canals and trenches to transform the Mwea plain into rice-growing paddy fields. This might just work – and the output of rice would feed the farmers so that the maize crop could be supplanted by coffee and tea.

A fine idea in theory, but digging canals and trenches through the clay soil by hand would be a gargantuan task. It would take years and the cost would be so enormous that the payback from increased agricultural output would take decades. In short, it didn't make economic sense.

But Monkey Johnson jumped on the plan.

'Mr Zayky, this is inspired!'

'I'm sorry, Mr Johnson but it's not viable. The cost of constructing the irrigation system is too huge.'

'Zayky – you refine the plan – work out the detail of the blueprints. But allow me to take care of the costs.'

The Kikuyu were rounded up and entered what became known as the pipeline. First they were sent to the Langata reception camp and later on further reception centres created at Manyani and Mackinnon Road. There was an introductory interview and then a classification of each man into streams labelled white, grey, and black. If you were white, it meant you were not suspected of Mau Mau involvement and were sent off to the reserves; grey meant that you had Mau Mau tendencies but could be rehabilitated; whilst black meant you were hardcore Mau Mau and not for turning. Supposedly the greys were sent to work camps close to the reserves and the blacks were sent to long-term detention camps.

In theory the pipeline system of screening, identification, and then reform and rehabilitation of insurgents was tough but fair. In practice it transformed Kenya into a hell on earth. The reserves were hugely overcrowded – vast tented villages. Initially just campsites but when the villagers became suspected of supplying food to the Mau Mau fighters, still hiding out in the forests, so they were turned into prisons. First they were surrounded by ditches filled with sharpened bamboo stakes or cactus needles, but later on they were fenced with barbed wire and watchtowers were set up with armed guards put in place.[114] The villages of the reserves became concentration camps. The residents existed in overcrowded and filthy conditions. Food was short and outbreaks of typhus were commonplace.

And yet the occupants of the villages were fortunate compared to those in detention. There were five camps established at Mwea for blacks and greys in the Mau Mau pipeline system. It was from these camps that Monkey Johnson created the manpower to turn my idea for the irrigation system into a reality. The cost was not financial, but it was certainly huge.

Politicians such as Baring and the British Colonial Secretary from London, Alan Lennox-Boyd, made 'stage-managed' visits to Mwea, much as Stalin and the Moscow elite had made visits to the countryside during the period of collectivisation in the Soviet Union. They saw nothing untoward. On the other hand, as architect of the scheme, I was a regular visitor and no attempt was ever made to shield me from the wretched brutality of 1950s British colonial rule.

The authorities used coerced labour to dig the canals; these were the 'blacks' or the hardcore Mau Mau prisoners. Then the 'greys', those who might have been rehabilitated, were used to work the paddy fields and farm the rice.

---

114 https://pro.magnumphotos.com/image/PAR295881.html

Coerced labour was simply slave labour by another name. At the Hermann Göring factory in Salzgitter concentration camp, labour had been used to make steel from very low-grade ore, an otherwise uneconomic proposition. At Mwea the Mau Mau sympathisers worked with hand tools to build an irrigation scheme which otherwise would have been completely unaffordable.

I had identified a total area for development covering about 26,000 acres or forty square miles, and by late 1954 some sixty-five acres had been planted to rice with many thousands of acres further in preparation.

The man in charge at Mwea and responsible for turning my plan into reality was Terence Gavaghan.

17

TANYA ZAYKY
Gathigiriri, Kenya, June 1954

'*KAZI NA UHURU*' RAN THE SIGN IN SWAHILI ABOVE the gates of the camp. It was crudely made. A white wooden board with black painted letters. Unlike Pasha and Sofia my Swahili was never good but even I could easily translate those words into English: 'Labour and Freedom'. Years later the phrase would be reversed and used as a slogan of Kenyan independence: '*Uhuru na Kazi!*' But the sequence of the two words – labour and freedom – was critical. The British sign above the camp gates put the word labour before freedom and, in so doing, made its intention clear.

I thought back to my evenings at the Podvorya in St Dunstan's Road in London. Those clumsy, badly cooked suppers that I prepared for my Batioushka, Father Michael, the Countess Kleinmichel, and the other parishioners of the Russian Church Abroad who gathered at the house. It all seemed so far away now but I could remember the long conversations over coffee vividly; the political debates, the church teachings, and the stories of times past. Tales of triumph, as well as the stories of oppression.

As a young priest, persecuted by the Communists, Father Michael had been interned in the Soviet Gulag of Solovki… what had he told us of the sign above the gates there? Yes! I could recall: 'Через труд – Свобода!' ('Through Labour – Freedom!'). That was the slogan above the entrance to the Gulag. Now, nearly three decades later, in another continent, ran the words '*Kazi na uhuru*'. Same context, same meaning, same sequence, same barbed wire; different regime.

Back in 1946 we had been so completely appalled by Batioushka's reminiscence of the sign at Solovki because, by then, everybody knew of the banner over the gates of the Auschwitz concentration camp: 'Arbeit Macht Frei' ('Work makes you free'). The 'freedom' offered by the Nazis was certain death in the gas chambers but it was, at least, a freedom of sorts from the terrible daily ordeal borne by the inmates of the most infamous of the concentration camps. What was chilling was that the Nazis almost certainly didn't know the Soviets had already used the phrase 'Through Labour – Freedom!' when they coined 'Arbeit Macht Frei'. In 1954 the British knew about the Nazi phrase but seemingly had failed to spot the connection when putting up a sign over their camp gates. The irony was that three quite separate regimes willing to intern non-conformers and minority ethnic groups had, completely independently, come up with the same words as legitimatisation.

I turned and looked back at the Knight which I had taxied to the end of the runway at Gathigiriri, one of the five Mwea camps, to be ready for the return trip. Pasha had been met from the plane by the British engineers and had already disappeared, gone off to inspect the construction of the irrigation system. He would be an hour or so, leaving me the time to find fuel.

As I turned back towards the camp, a man was standing in front of me.

'Do you approve? The sign, I mean. Had it put there just a day or so ago. Same words as they use over at Ngenya;[115] we need to motivate these Kukes if they're going to build your husband's canals anytime soon, you know.'

I said nothing and he continued.

'I'm sorry, I do apologise, I haven't introduced myself; Gavaghan, Terence Gavaghan... and I have assumed that you must be Mrs Zayky... am I right?'

We shook hands. Pasha had mentioned this man to me but not in any detail. Gavaghan had no hat or cap but was tall, over six feet, with a solid, powerful physique and dark cropped hair. His shirt was smart and pressed and his khaki shorts were knee-length. Blue eyes and a crooked nose. He exuded strength and masculinity. I could not fail to see that he was incredibly good-looking; he seemed to glance at me in a pitying way – but perhaps I imagined that?

In Salzgitter the KZ-Lager's gates had been made of wrought iron. Here, at Gathigiriri, the gates were of a flimsy wooden construction, nailed together, but lined with a criss-cross of barbed wire with coils of thorny wire along their top edges. They were hung from sagging posts and the sentries had to pick up the ends and drag them open as we approached. As we walked together through the entrance

---

115 Ngenya, another Mau Mau internment camp in Kiambu District, north of Nairobi, used the sign 'Labour and Freedom'. Its use at the Gathigiriri camp in Mwea, or the use of some similar sign, is assumed but unconfirmed.

the sentries stood to attention. Overhead a guard in a watchtower surveyed the camp by training his rifle left and right – much like the soldier at the machine gun in the back of the Land Rover that day in Nairobi back in late April.

On the inside of the barbed wire perimeter fence to my left and right were a series of white painted wooden huts with corrugated iron roofs. In front of me was a parade ground and behind it a number of open-backed army trucks parked up in rows. But beyond the parade ground and the stationary trucks were rows and rows of tents. The terrain was flat and the rows of white triangular canvas tents stretched on to the horizon. Twelve together in a line and then a walkway, then another twelve and on and on. Watchtowers rose up like storks probably between every twelve dozen tents, each tower contained a guard and his gun, distinct as a tiny black silhouette. There must have been thousands of tents and I guessed that each one housed four men. Nevertheless, the camp seemed largely deserted. Obviously most of the men were off digging canals, but there were a few stragglers standing close to their tents in ragged clothes, or nearer to me, carrying provisions towards an unseen cookhouse, or sweeping near the parade ground, which seemed utterly pointless given the ground was just brown dirt. In all cases there were guards nearby watching them, guns held ready.

There was also the overwhelming stench of human faeces. That foul, yet sweet, odour was all around. Just as you thought you had grown used to it so another waft of airstream would hit you and make you swallow back on the bile rising inside.

As we walked, heading towards the parade ground, suddenly I heard a scream. It came from inside one of the huts. Piercing, agonised and blood-curdling. Another scream. Everyone heard. Some looked over to the white huts, others simply carried on without any noticeable reaction.

A sharp crack. It was the sound of a whip. I had stopped dead and found myself looking towards the white hut to my right. The sounds had come from there, but there was nothing to see. The door was closed. Voices, yes – both English and native – but the screaming had ended.

As I stood listening for another scream so the warm silence of mid-morning was replaced with a new sound. A low drone; a single monotone. A plane circling above? It grew slightly louder and was much more immediate in the air around us than could have been the case if it were an aeroplane overhead. It rang in my ears. It was, if anything, more disturbing than the screams. It was a human sound, a moan. But not made by one man alone, instead it was a chorus. I had no idea how many men were left in the camp that morning but it seemed that they were all singing a single long, low note.

Ahead, towards the parade ground, I watched as a man holding a broom, one of the pointless sweepers, was pushed to the ground, face first, by two native *askari* guards. In a moment, one had knelt so that his knee was hard on the man's back, trapping him down, whilst the other remained on his feet and stamped the heel of his boot against the back of the man's skull. Even at a distance I could see the man's nose and mouth pressed hard against the earth, his arms spread out to either side, one of his hands with palm down, the other still holding the broom, which also lay flat alongside him on the dirt.

Gavaghan was, throughout all of this, utterly unperturbed.

'Yes, here at Gathigiriri we take in the hardest of the insurgents. The able-bodied work by day, but later on we ask them to confess and recant their Mau Mau doctrines. You know, they take un-Christian blood oaths to fight the British, with sometimes animal or even human sacrifice. The Mau Mau are a seething bestial mass and we need to rid society of them. They are however somewhat stubborn.'

He smiled.

'So I'm afraid that sometimes the confessions are quite an effort to extract. It can take a few days of continuous work.'

Gavaghan looked across to the closed white hut before continuing.

'Occasionally you do get unexpected noises during the confession process, and recently the other Kukes have started this strange collective vocal howl or drone as a form of protest. Quite inappropriate, of course, and so we have to take immediate action. We find that getting the howlers to eat a mouthful of dirt seems to put a stop to it... Anyway, this way to the fuel dump, Mrs Zayky, follow me... It's very good to finally meet you, I have met your husband previously of course... What a difference he has made here. Just a few of us seem to have achieved great work. Many thousands of native Kenyans will have much cause to thank us when our work here is done...'

Gavaghan chatted on. I said nothing.[116]

---

116 Terence Gavaghan (1922–2011) was a Kenya District Officer given special powers by Carruthers 'Monkey' Johnson to do whatever was necessary to 'break' Mau Mau detainees during the Kenyan Emergency Period. The Kikuyu detainees nicknamed him *Karuga Ndua* – Big Troublemaker.

At the fuel dump two jerry cans were filled and a limping prisoner was commanded to carry them back to the Knight – a guard remained with him, gun at the ready. Now we were the other side of the parked trucks towards the campsite. Gavaghan, still talking, walked by my side as we rounded past the parked-up trucks and the parade ground came back into view. I could see the gates had now been shut but beyond them, in the distance, we watched a growing plume of dust. We stopped walking and watched. An army truck, bouncing along the dirt road leading to the camp, came into view.

Once more the gates were dragged open and the truck entered, lurching to a halt in front of the parade ground. Immediately, guards who had been resting unseen in various shady locations around the buildings came into view and began to gather round the rear of the truck. There were suddenly perhaps twenty of them, and all were chattering with one another rather excitedly, I felt. A man stepped down from the truck's passenger seat and walked swiftly across the parade ground to where we were standing.

'Mr Gavaghan.'

'Ah, Mr Cowan, a new load for us today.'

'Indeed so, sir.'

'Mrs Zayky, may I introduce Mr Cowan, chief prison officer here at Gathigiriri.' I shook hands with Cowan, a man almost the exact opposite of Gavaghan: short, crumpled and ugly.[117]

'Cowan has implemented a procedure for us here. Something called the dilution technique and it is proving extremely successful… Carry on, Cowan.'

---

117 John Cowan was the staff officer in charge of works camps for
    Embu district including the Mwea camps.

Gavaghan turned to me.

'What we need, you see, is a systematic approach to breaking these people. They come here thinking they can outwit us, ignore us, work slowly; but we need to show them beyond all doubt that their resistance is futile and that they need to obey – and yes – to confess. Right from the start we need a quick and efficient repudiation of their Mau Mau sympathies and then we can get them working for the common good.'

As I watched, the twenty or so prisoners – thin and ragged – were let down from the back of the truck. Once each man had climbed down from the lorry he instinctively held his hands above his head – even though there was no order for him to do so. The guards, who had now grown silent, stood to one side and waited until the last man was out of the truck.

And then they set about them.

I had never seen anything like this. The guards used sticks and rifle butts, fists and boots – and their nails and teeth as well. Each had identified a man from the truck and beat that man until he was on the ground, bleeding and cowering or unconscious.[118] The entire process must have taken just a few minutes but for me, as a spectator, it lasted an eternity.

I was dumbfounded and horrified but spellbound as well. And Gavaghan knew I would be. It was as if he had laid on this whole show just for me. When it was over he turned

---

118 The 'dilution technique' – the implementation of systematic and relentless brute force to break detainees, was introduced by Cowan and promoted by Gavaghan. It was first used at Gathigiriri but soon extended to other camps. Baring halted the method following a death in 1957 but it was quickly reinstated as nothing else was found to be as effective. In official papers it was known as 'Operation Progress'.

towards me. Now he said nothing but looked down at me, narrowed his eyes, pursed his lips, and nodded. As we walked past, I could not help but cast my eyes down to look at the bleeding, crying, men. That the beating had led many of them to soil their clothing just added to the stench of Gathigiriri. One, barely conscious, looked directly back up at me, for just an instant. Our eyes made contact but then he looked away. And I readjusted my vision straight ahead, and walked faster onwards, through the gates, back out towards the Knight.

I climbed up on the wing, was handed up the two jerry cans one after another and poured their contents into the fuel tank. I got down and shook hands once more with Gavaghan who tuned on his heel and left.

I watched him walk away, back through the gates of Gathigiriri, which were closed after him. I walked round to the far side of the Knight to look back out towards the Mwea plain – I put the camp and its stench behind me. I pulled a cigarette from a battered packet of Players which had been in my pocket for goodness knows how long. I hardly ever smoked. The cigarette was bent from where it had been crushed by me in its packet at one time or another. As I held it in my lips and tried to raise the match to the tip, I missed, and realised how badly I was shaking. I threw the fag away, unlit, in disgust.

The idea of growing rice on the Mwea plain by creating an irrigation system had been great.[119] But it was just one

119 Rice growing in Mwea was begun in 1954 on 65 acres. By 1960 the land under irrigation had grown to nearly 2,500 acres. In 2017 the total area under irrigation was 26,000 acres managed by over 7,000 households/farmers. The main crop is basmati rice but tomatoes, French beans and maize are also grown. Rice is now Kenya's third staple food after maize and wheat.

of Pasha's suggestions to Baring. He had thought it would be unaffordable but it had been incorporated into the Swynnerton Plan in any event because Monkey Johnson said he would work out how to manage the cost. Pasha could never have known that the realisation of his idea was going to cause such pain and suffering – that the true cost went way beyond any financial commitment. Pasha and I were not part of this system. None of this was our fault. Whether it was Krasnodar, Salzgitter or Kenya, we seemed to get caught up in other people's atrocities. We were never involved, we just did what we did to keep each other safe – to keep Sofia safe.

But those beaten, crying men were haunting me. Spectres. The blood running from their hairline, their tear-streaked faces, their darkly stained trousers. The bloodshot eyes of that man who had looked up at me. Only for an instant. But an instant is enough for recognition. The spectre and my recognition of his pain. My sorrow. His cognisance of my presence even in his beaten stupor. Was there more? I continued to gaze out to the plain of Mwea. I was shaking less now. But I knew. Joshua was the ghost I had seen.[120]

---

120 See appendix on the Mau Mau insurgency.

18

TANYA ZAYKY
Kitale, Kenya, May 1955

THE KNIGHT BANKED LEFT SHARPLY AND I HELD onto the side of the cockpit, grimacing ever so slightly, as Molly Baring whooped with delight from the seat behind me.

The Barings were on tour upcountry. They had travelled by rail along the line to Eldoret, stopping off there for inspection and had then journeyed on to Kitale to meet 'the great and the good' for presentations and cocktail parties. Sir Evelyn had confided to Pasha that such tours were a necessary, but utterly detestable, part of the governorship duties. Having Pasha as a known friendly face was a huge relief to him, even if we Zaykys were not considered part of the Kitale set. They had a shorthand for it– 'Are they PLU?' would be the question: 'People Like Us'. Pasha's innate charm normally got him through any social interactions but I, with my thick accent and blunt demeanour... well, I was never PLU as far as the smart British women were concerned. It seemed to me that to be PLU you had to wear the correct style of pretty dresses, drink the correct type of gin cocktails and sleep with other people's husbands. None of those things appealed to me. Pasha also never made it to PLU but he was, perhaps, part of 'the great and the good'. At least in the eyes of the white farmers who actually cared about increasing their agricultural output, and most importantly in the eyes of Kenya's Governor.

To be fair, dear Pip Faulkner never fitted in either. He was eighty now and over the last few years had shrunk in height as older people so often do. Previously tall and upright he now stooped, walked with the aid of a stick, and wheezed a little as he spoke. His laugh was no longer loud, raucous and from the belly, but despite the advance of years, he remained our truest friend in Kenya. Pip was British through and through; he, Roy and Emily had been early settlers in Kitale, but they had also failed to pass the entry criteria to join the colonial set. The British were always polite, certainly to their own countrymen, but Pip and Roy had never fitted in – they had failed as farmers and after Roy had taken to the air as a commercial pilot they had become mere 'trade'. Once Roy had died Emily had taken up with Bill Pietersen – a Boer. Any thought that she could fit into the smart colonial society set had evaporated after that. Emily certainly drank the gin cocktails but apparently she didn't sleep with the right husbands.

Of course I had laid eyes on Molly Baring at Government House when I had been with Pasha, and the Kenyan newspapers often made some mention of her when at her husband's side during official functions, but we had never spoken.

'Sir Evelyn says that his wife is very much looking forward to meeting you,' Pasha had told me when the news of the

Governor's trip to Kitale had come out. I must have looked slightly blank. 'Apparently Jock Matheson flew them down to Mombasa recently. During the flight their forthcoming trip to Kitale was mentioned and Jock sang your praises as a superbly intuitive pilot and wonderful engineer.' At this I glowed – dear Jock. These days I rarely ventured down to the Nairobi aerodrome, preferring to fly into the High School and attend to any workshop issues at Choudry's in town, but from time to time Jock would fly into Kitale and come down to our bungalow for tea or supper, or a bed for the night. Occasionally there would be some minor ailment with his plane and he would ask for my opinion – usually just listening to the engine would be enough for me to help with a diagnosis.

On arrival he would usually exclaim, 'Och, Tanya, how ye dein? It's been dunky's since I last saw ye!' or something similarly unintelligible. I had about as much chance of understanding Jock as he would have understood me if I had responded in Russian. But language isn't required to comprehend the warmth of a heart.

*

When the train pulled into Kitale Station on the morning of the Governor's visit both Pasha and I had been asked to ensure we were in the line-up of people assembled on the platform for presentation. The young District Commissioner who had overseen our rescue of Jomo Kenyatta and Denis Pritt on that day in Kitale Town just under two years before had, as Pasha had rightly predicted, been rapidly promoted on to higher things within the colonial diplomatic service.

Godwin, the new DC, was a much older man, genial but ineffectual, serving out his final years prior to retirement. During the troubles of the Emergency Period in Kenya, Kitale to the extreme west remained a peaceful place. There were no Kikuyu around for the authorities to worry about, and Godwin was a safe pair of hands to run a backwater when younger, more energetic staff were needed in the centre to work at containing the insurgents.

For an instant my mind pictured Gavaghan that day at Gathigiriri – 'Operation Progress' was certainly a game for younger men. But it was true that, although a state of emergency continued in Kenya, by April 1955, one year after the round-up of Kikuyu in Nairobi and their detention in the camps and enclosed villages, day-to-day violence had ended. Well, at least violence on the streets had ended; violence in the camps was a different matter – as I well knew.

As the Governor's train rounded the curve and came into sight so Godwin finished marshalling our straggling receiving line into a priority order – and yes – we were positioned right at the end! 'Karamoja', the enormous articulated Garrett locomotive, pulled into the platform, but instead of the usual long and heavy procession of coaches and baggage vans as you would normally see pulling into Kitale, this train had just two cars – it seemed such a waste of motive power to me. Perhaps this was meant to be an indication of colonial might, but having Karamoja pull just two coaches when it could easily shift twenty or more seemed a case of stupidity rather than a demonstration of British supremacy. I always hated inefficiency, especially where machinery was concerned.

Karamoja drew to a standstill; the Kitale brass band struck up 'Land of Hope and Glory' and Godwin moved forward to help Sir Evelyn and his wife down the steps of the carriages onto the platform. As I saw Sir Evelyn I gasped slightly and stifled a smile as, in his dress uniform, he put me in mind of grand old King Ernst August – the statue of that old Hussar on his horse riding into battle outside Hanover Station which we had seen, and admired, nearly ten years before when Angus had dropped us off in Hanover to begin our journey from mainland Europe to London and eventually on to Kenya. I well remembered our fear at the thought of being caught and repatriated to Soviet Russia. A fear that was like a sickness. How things had changed for us since then.

But Sir Evelyn was certainly the Hussar although without a horse of course. Whilst the statue of King Ernst had depicted him with the feathers on his helmet standing upright and proud, Sir Evelyn's ostrich plumes flopped downwards. His epaulettes were long and tasselled, and he wore a red sash along with several large medals that looked like overly ornate ladies' brooches. Frankly, he looked bizarre, but everybody stood to attention and so did I.[121]

Gradually the Barings moved along the receiving line. With each new person Godwin would introduce them first by position or rank and then by name – the Barings would smile and shake hands. Sir Evelyn would offer a few words of conversation here and there; but Lady Baring, dressed in a bright yellow floral, slim-waisted dress with white high-heeled shoes, white gloves, a wide-brimmed hat and a tiny

---

121 https://harvardmagazine.com/2005/03/10-downing-streets-gulag.html

handbag which hung from her arm, remained smiling but silent. Always one step behind her husband.

Eventually they arrived at the end of the line – to us.

'The head of the Agricultural Research Station in Kitale, Professor Pavel Zayky, and Mrs Zayky,' announced Godwin, but Sir Evelyn knew that already.

'Ah, Zayky, so glad you're here. I'm very much looking forward to seeing the field work you've been doing. A busy day today of course and this evening we have cocktails and then a dinner in the hotel, but perhaps tomorrow we can tour some of the farms hereabouts and I can see the research station. That will be in order, Godwin, I hope?'

Godwin looked slightly taken aback. The Governor's suggestion obviously cut across other, carefully made, plans for the visit.

'Well of course, sir, I'm sure that can be arranged, although there is the meeting with the district judges tomorrow morning and I know they have pressing matters to discuss…'

'Hmmm, yes well, I suppose we need to keep the judiciary happy, but how about lunch at the Research Station tomorrow before we have to leave in the afternoon? Yes, I think lunch, assuming that's in order with you, Zayky…?'

Pasha nodded eagerly. 'Very much so, sir, we shall look forward to entertaining you then.'

Lady Baring had shaken hands with us both during this exchange but now, for the first time since leaving the train, she spoke, addressing her husband but looking at me.

'Evelyn, I don't think the judges tomorrow will need to see me, and if we are joining Mr and Mrs Zayky for lunch then perhaps I could travel to them a little earlier. I gather that Mrs Zayky is quite the aeronaut!'

The Governor nodded approvingly. 'I'm sure that's fine darling… Godwin… all right with you?'

Godwin bowed slightly both in deference and to signify agreement whilst all his facial features registered disapproval.

But Lady Baring looked delighted. 'Splendid! That's settled then, shall we say that I will see you at eleven for coffee and then Evelyn can join us all for lunch at one?' We smiled and said nothing; her question had been rhetorical. 'Perfect!' she said.

And they were gone. Whisked away by Godwin into the waiting black Wolseley car and off for the first engagement of their visit. The receiving line relaxed visibly and straggled once more as it broke up into smaller chattering groups. The engine driver got down from Karamoja, and one by one the members of the brass band gave up playing their tune, put down their instruments, and lit up cigarettes.

Nobody seemed to want to chat to us, so we went back to our Austin, where Mohammed was waiting, and left.

The following morning at 11am prompt the black Wolseley arrived at our bungalow to deliver Lady Baring. As the car drew up so the driver jumped out and opened the door. Pasha ran down the wooden steps of the bungalow and held out his hand in greeting and to help her from the car. I remained standing on our verandah.

'Hulloo!' cried Lady Baring, making no attempt to move from the back seat, and looking straight past Pasha up towards me. 'Look, I know we said coffee but honestly I don't think I need any… shall we go off straightaway to see your plane – I'm so excited!'

I furrowed my brow slightly but followed her beckoning and climbed into the back of the Wolseley alongside her. As

I directed her driver on towards the hangar at the Pietersen Farm, Lady Baring wound down her window and yelled to Pasha.

'See you and Evelyn in a couple of hours. We shall try not to be too too late!'

As we sped off along the dirt track I turned around in my seat to see Pasha disappearing back into the bungalow. I couldn't see his face, but his shoulders were shaking with laughter.

In the back of the car Lady Baring held out her hand.

'Molly,' she said simply.

'Tanya,' I replied.

'Look,' she said, 'I'm sorry but these upcountry inspections are simply frightful, and when I knew that there was going to be another woman pilot, well, I had to get away!'

'You're a pilot too?' Why on earth had I not known that?!

'Yes, trained when Evelyn was made Governor of Southern Rhodesia – I had my own Moth too – wonderful thing… what's yours?'

By now the hangar was in sight.

'Let me show you…'

To say that Molly Baring approved of the Knight would be an understatement. We pulled him out of the hangar and swung his wings into position. Molly just kept walking round, cooing and respectfully laying the palm of her hand on his fuselage. I felt like a proud mother.

She gestured inside the hangar. 'Do you have a spare flying suit in there that might fit me?' I did, of course. I was pleased to note that whilst she wore another dress – blue today – the pretty high-heeled shoes worn when she had got down from the train had been replaced, today, with flat pumps.

Whilst she was changing, Pip appeared and when Molly emerged I introduced them. They chatted amiably for a while but then Molly said, 'Now look here, Mr Faulkner, I am thoroughly enjoying our talk but I haven't got changed into this flying suit for nothing. Tanya, can Mr Faulkner not join us for lunch?'

Molly had a way of inviting you by making the request to somebody else. Of course, Pip could join us for lunch.

'Well then, I see no time like the present to get the Knight up in the air. Mr Faulkner, will you please excuse us? Tanya, I do hope you will allow me to take the controls...'

I was just slightly nervous in allowing Molly to take the rear cockpit. I usually sat to the rear (the Knight's dual controls meant you could sit either front or back but sitting at the rear provided better visibility especially during take-off and landing), but I could see how much it meant to her. She explained that, in 1944, after two years as Governor of Southern Rhodesia, Evelyn had been promoted to become High Commissioner for South Africa. This was a significant role and one where his personal safety and security, and that of his wife, were taken most seriously. At that point Molly's flying career ended.

'They just wouldn't let me do it anymore... said that women didn't have the physical or mental strength to deal with the rigours of piloting and that anyway it wasn't fitting for a governor's wife to fly. What rot! But I was just slightly too naïve back then to argue with them and Evelyn didn't want me to rock the boat – or waggle the joystick, I suppose! So, whilst nobody's looking, I thought I'd sneak away and see if we could zoom off!'

And she was a good pilot. Intuitive and, despite her effervescence, careful. Not as good as Jock Matheson, and in all honesty not as good as me, but much better than some of the fly-boys I had seen making clumsy manoeuvres above the Nairobi aerodrome. But she did make a noise! Usually you can't hear much in an open-seat aeroplane when wearing a flying helmet, but Molly hooted and screamed with delight as the Knight calmly obeyed her commands at the controls. Most of the time I was grinning, but I confess that some of the more dramatic pitches made me grimace just slightly.

We were in the air for about ninety minutes, buzzing over Kitale Town, and travelling on into the beautiful foothills of Mount Elgon where I remained mindful of the perils of the downdraft which had caught me out that day with Jock. But happily we encountered no unusual air currents, just savannah, elephants, buffalo, and fabulous forest.

I took over the controls to fly us back to the landing strip on the Pietersen Farm but communicating by hand signals via the rear-view mirror Molly begged to be allowed to make the landing. Deep breath. The Knight is a most forgiving aeroplane and the touchdown was bumpy but, given her lack of recent practice, I could hardly fault Molly.

We taxied to the hangar, switched off and climbed down one after another. Molly was utterly triumphant. She stood before me laughing and clapping and then, quite suddenly, without warning, lurched forward and hugged me. A proper, warm hug!

'Thank you Tanya, the Knight is amazing, the most super craft. Thank you for trusting me to fly him and to land him. My God, I feel alive!'

And I did too. That had been fun. Not simply flying around the country taking Pasha to inspect various farms and agricultural workings, but instead just a pure joyride! The pair of us were like schoolgirls grinning and giggling as we released the Knight's wings to swing them back against the fuselage and then pulled him back into the hangar. Molly changed back out of her flying suit. Whilst flying she had kept her dress on underneath and had pulled up the skirt to get into the trouser legs. As a result the skirt was now rather crumpled. Well, I certainly wouldn't judge her!

We were, by now, very late for lunch – we were always going to be – but Molly said, 'I really want a cigarette.' She pulled out a packet, put two in her mouth, lit them both, and passed one to me. We sat on the bench outside the hangar and smoked.

'So, what's your story, Tanya? What on earth brought you and Pasha to Kenya?'

I told her. We only had time for one cigarette and Molly drew deeply on hers, so I had to make the story short, but it was time enough. Nevertheless, there was much I missed out, some for the sake of brevity, and some because it was history that should not be remembered. But in the end, I supposed that the reason we had spent our life running and had ended up in Kenya was for the sake of Sofia. We just wanted the best for her really.

Molly was wide-eyed at my tale. 'We have three children, all at school in England, and I miss them terribly. As the wife of a Viceroy, motherhood is the most painful sacrifice…'

She dragged on her fag before carrying on. 'And Sofia? Where is she now?'

'Well, having finished at the High School she volunteers at the hospital in Kitale reporting each day to Doctor Bourke – I am so proud. It would be fabulous if she could train to be a doctor one day. She has a place at Queen Mary's…'

'But you've said she's nineteen so why doesn't she go?'

I looked at Molly and explained that we remained stateless at best, or Soviet citizens at worst, and that without passports we could never leave Kenya. Molly looked down and said nothing as she rubbed her fag butt into the ground with the sole of her flat shoe.

'Well, I think we must speak to Evelyn about that,' she said finally.

On the short ride back to the bungalow we carried on smiling and chatting but something of a cloud had entered my mind. I knew that Sofia would be joining us for lunch, Mohammed would have gone up to the hospital to collect her. On the face of it this was a good thing as I certainly wanted to introduce her to the Barings. But I knew that Sofia felt angry over the way the British had dealt with the Mau Mau. She was fiercely of the view that the repression of the Kikuyu had been mean, harsh and indiscriminate. She had seen the cruelty that had been meted out by the colonial administration on the streets. She had not forgotten how Joshua had been dragged away that day in Nairobi, a year before – taken off at gunpoint, with his hands raised high in the air. Joshua had been one of her few friends in Kenya and she had not seen him since that day.

And I had never let on about Gathigiriri. Not to Pasha and certainly not to Sofia – it would only have made matters worse. Sofia just didn't appreciate that life can never be free from conflict no matter how hard you try. Pasha had tried to explain it to her.

'Sofia, wherever you go, whatever country you live in, there is always a public enemy. The enemy are hated. Why? Well, it varies, but generally it's because of race, nationalism, politics, or religion; or some combination of those reasons which are broadcast to the public. A public who are then asked to unite in a firm stand against the enemy. In reality, the enemy as a whole may not have done too much evil; possibly only a few might have been guilty of some, or all, of the charges made. But the view taken will be that it is the enemy, in its entirety, which has done wrong. Conversely, the regime which levels the charges will be seen as blameless, as having been hurt. Its people need to show solidarity, strength and resolve to correct the wrongdoing which has been inflicted upon it.

'The fear of the public enemy and the moral quest for justice helps keep the good folk of the regime from protesting and rebelling against life's many other inequities. And so having a public enemy helps keep the peace. When this happens where you live, and like I say, it always does… well, you can protest that it's unfair – but to what end? Even if you show you're right, nobody will thank you and another public enemy will emerge down the line. So, the best thing is just to live quietly within your chosen regime and make the best out of it. Just make sure to keep your wits about you to recognise if the next public enemy is likely to include you. If it does – then move on swiftly, always remembering that a few white lies often help smooth the way when old friends become enemies and old enemies become friends.'

But to all this she had just responded, 'So the only good Kuke is a dead Kuke?'

Pasha had sighed.

My daughter was single-minded and headstrong. Qualities to which I could relate, but which Pasha felt were traits which should never be allowed to outweigh common sense, pragmatism, and social dexterity.

For Sofia to upset the Barings over lunch would not be helpful. And anyway, I liked Molly.

As we arrived back at the Bungalow from the hangar so did Mohammed in the Austin with Sofia sitting next to him. We were about an hour late and so were they. Sofia must have kept Mohammed waiting at the hospital – I wondered if she might have done that deliberately – not a good sign.

But introductions between Molly and Sofia were quickly made and Molly, perhaps still riding high after her flight, chattered away to Sofia seemingly paying no attention to Sofia's taciturn demeanour.

We went inside where Pip was waiting for us. 'Lunch is ready whenever you like, madam,' said Boniface. I was a little embarrassed, we hardly ever had guests, and certainly not the Governor and his wife. I knew that Boniface would have made a special effort. Lunch would have been ready on time, an hour before.

But Pasha and Sir Evelyn were not in the house either. Peering out, I could see them in the distance walking, chatting and inspecting the crops, grasses, and wild flowers growing in the fields of the research station. Pasha would have been in his element.

'Mohammed, please go and tell Professor Zayky and Sir Evelyn that lunch is ready.'

Boniface brought us cold lemonade and we stood, sipping at our drinks, waiting for Pasha and Evelyn to arrive. Thank goodness for Pip, who kept the conversation ambling along whilst Sofia and I said little.

Eventually, having apologised to each other, and to Boniface, for our lateness, we all sat down to a lunch of soup followed by rather dried-up pork and vegetables with an apple pie as dessert. It wasn't the finest food but once again my mind flicked back to the thoughts I had had the previous day on the platform at Kitale Station as we had waited in line for Sir Evelyn and Molly. The raw fear we had felt that morning at Hanover Station, when we had been dropped off by Angus at the foot of King Ernst's statue, was in sharp contrast to how we felt now, entertaining the Governor of Kenya and his wife in our bungalow, to a lunch prepared and served by our staff. 'Live quietly, make the best, but keep your wits about you' was a mantra which had served us well.

'So, Evelyn, young Sofia here has a problem,' said Molly over her apple pie.

'I see, dear, and what is that?'

'Well, it seems that although she has lived as a fine British citizen for nearly ten years, has been properly educated, passed all her exams, and gone to work at the local hospital, she doesn't have a passport. Without that, it is nigh-on impossible for her to take up her place at Queen Mary's in London. Now Evelyn, what we need are more doctors, and dare I say, more FEMALE doctors, wouldn't you agree?'

Evelyn knew very well that to agree with his wife was his pathway to happiness.

'I see. Yes, that won't do at all. Well, from here we go to Kitale Station to catch our train back to Nairobi. Why don't we all go together and then I can send a telegram to my private secretary at Government House to arrange a day and time for Sofia to attend to receive a passport. If we can get a response before we leave, then perhaps we can get everything arranged and in the diaries today. How would that be?'

We rose from the dining table and Boniface served coffee in the sitting room. Sofia was taciturn no longer. The change which had come about her following Molly's request of Evelyn was transformational. My usually plain child was now blushing and radiant.

As we stood holding our coffee cups Pasha showed Evelyn some specimen seed heads which he had carefully placed into a glass case.

Molly feigned a look of boredom. 'I think the rest of us are not as interested in seeds as you two,' she said as she looked around the room. 'And so who are these people?' she asked, walking over to the mantlepiece where a curled-up, yellowed photograph sat atop a battered wooden cigar case.

'That's Mama and my uncle Pyotr when they were young,' said Sofia, now eager to correct her earlier reticence. 'They were fishing on the Kuban river near Krasnodar in the south of Russia. Mama, Papa and I walked out of the Soviet Union when the Germans left. All we had were those family photographs in that old cigar box. I can't remember uncle Pyotr very well, but he was a war hero, killed fighting the Nazis...'

I said nothing. Public enemies do change.

19

MISHA CHESHIRE
Kenya, 1963

MAMA FINALLY LEFT KENYA IN LATE 1955 TO TAKE UP her place at Queen Mary's in London to train as a doctor. She had attended the short ceremony at Government House in Nairobi where the Governor had presented her with a dark blue British passport, her name – Miss Sofia Zayky — inscribed in copperplate writing in a cutaway section at the bottom of the front cover. I've still got it, that old passport. It's in a battered wooden cigar box along with various other ancient and dog-eared papers. At the ceremony in Government House, Baba said how Dyeda had wept with joy.[122] Baba would always let her eyes rise to the ceiling and purse her lips in resignation whenever she told me a story where Dyeda had cried. She said that he cried at almost anything, whilst she never did. As a small child in short trousers, if I fell over, grazed my knee and howled she would exclaim, 'Misha don't be like silly Dyeda, you are a Kuban Cossack, not a crybaby!'

---

122 'Baba' short for *Babushka*: Grandmother in Russian. 'Dyeda' short for *Dyedushka*: Grandfather.

But it's funny that every time during my childhood, when she sat me down, and carefully explained the old family photos one by one – who was who and when and why, and on and on, even though she had told me it all a hundred times before – her voice would crack and her words would choke. Just a little.

'I never cry,' she would say to me in Russian, as she rubbed her eyes and stared at the pictures in their gilt frames; pictures of me in school uniform, my mama and papa on their wedding day, and that other picture of a little boy and girl by the river – fishing. For some reason that one had never been put in a frame.

Baba might never have cried but that didn't make her hard-hearted. I know, and always knew, that I was blessed with her utterly undoubted love. She cared for me with single-minded passion and devotion. A love which never wavered almost as if it were programmed into her. Like she was a machine where every permutation or operation had been encoded into a silicon chip to be performed without fault.

And she told me everything; how they had railed against the Communists, their eventual flight from Russia, poor Uncle Pyotr – a hero – and how, in the end, they had been welcomed by the British to transform farming in Kenya. Every story, every scene and conversation, had been stored away in her computerlike mind and over the course of years was faithfully reported back to me. I took in every word. It was as though I had been there too.

So Dyeda had cried when Mama received her passport but I expect that, despite anything Baba might have said, they would have both been weeping as the SS Rhodesia Castle gave two final blasts on the horn and moved slowly away from the quay at Mombasa bound for Southampton. My mama, Sofia, their only child, up on deck waving frantically, so excited to be finally given the chance to fulfil her dream. They watched as the ship sailed on towards the horizon until it finally vanished from sight. Then they just held each other and shook, not with fear or even sadness but because of some altogether stranger cocktail of emotions. The satisfaction of her obvious delight, the relief of her escape from Soviet citizenship, their pride in her achievement, stirred together with the heartbreak of separation and the memory of how unwelcoming London had been just a decade earlier. Their wonderful daughter had gone to begin a new life, which had been simply unimaginable a few years before.

But Dyeda Pasha's work in Kenya was not yet complete, and so whilst my grandparents gained their own British passports the following year, Pasha pleaded with his wife to allow him to continue his work on the farms, and the implementation of the Swynnerton Plan. In any event they should, he reasoned, give Sofia the space she needed to grow and mature. His thinking was quite correct of course but the chronic pain of separation remained like a knife embedded in flesh, although it did mean that as Pasha carried on his work Tanya was able to take her husband all around the country and so continue her passion for flying and for her aeroplane, the Knight.

Pip Faulkner passed away in 1959 at the grand age of 84. At his funeral Pasha and Tanya mourned the loss of a true friend, more like a brother, but only a handful of others turned out. Bill Pietersen was out of town on urgent business whilst Pip's former daughter-in-law Emily, by then aged 59, had descended into a permanent alcoholic haze. However, despite Pip's passing and past antagonisms, the arrangement to use the Knight, store it, and take off and land from the farm's runway still worked well enough; although Bill, always in need of more cash to pay mortgages taken to cover his gambling debts, took the opportunity to charge a rent for use of the plane as well. But flying remained a source of joy for Tanya and she ensured the Knight remained in tip-top order.

Throughout the 1950s African nationalist organisations had gained strength, most notably in Algeria where the failure of French colonialism had left 170,000 dead. US President Kennedy, fighting the Cold War, believed that African nationalist movements created a hotbed for Communist sympathisers. Given the global situation it was therefore imperative for the European countries controlling the African continent to effect an ordered withdrawal, leaving behind newly created nation states which remained friendly to the West.

In 1960, whilst in South Africa, the British prime minister, Harold Macmillan, said: 'The wind of change is blowing through this continent. Whether we like it or not, this growth of national consciousness is a political fact.' And during that year some eighty-five million African natives achieved independence from their French, Belgian and British colonial masters as seventeen countries threw off the colonial yoke. 1960 became known as 'the year of Africa' and at a conference at Lancaster House in London, the British Government decreed that Kenya would eventually become a parliamentary democracy based on a universal franchise. The country's white settlers were appalled.

In May 1960 the Kenyan African National Union or 'KANU', a name clearly designed to emulate Kenyatta's old KAU party, was formed. It represented an alliance between the Kikuyu and the Luo, the two largest Kenyan tribes. Traditionally they had been at each other's throats but now they were drawn by the scent of independence and a desire for 'African Socialism'. KANU immediately made Jomo Kenyatta their leader, ignoring the fact that the British continued to hold him in detention in the desert.

The Barings had retired to Britain in 1959 and another career diplomat, Sir Patrick Renison, had taken over as Governor. Now, Renison hastily reminded the people that Kenyatta, the 'African leader to darkness and death', had been convicted of managing the evil Mau Mau.[123]

In February 1961 the first free Kenyan election took place. Over one million voted and KANU, which had campaigned on a pledge not to take their seats unless Kenyatta was set free, won a 68% share of the vote against the opposition KADU party, which had been financially (although covertly) backed by the British. KANU's clear victory forced the British hand and the seventy-year-old Kenyatta was released in April.[124]

In November, a month after the birth of a son named Uhuru (Swahili for freedom), Kenyatta was interviewed by the BBC. For three quarters of an hour he spoke calmly and eloquently, he wore a dark-coloured Western suit but

---

123 Governor Renison failed to mention that in 1958, some four years after Kenyatta's final appeal was rejected, the prosecution's star witness at the original trial, Rawson Macharia, confessed to perjury.

124 https://www.nation.co.ke/news/Jomo-Kenyatta-troubled-years-in-London-/1056-2491722-fn26h1/index.html

sported his trademark *kofia* hat. It was the first indication to the world that he had been misjudged.

On 1st June 1963, Jomo Kenyatta became the first prime minister of a self-governing Kenya. From prisoner to prime minister, his reinvention in just over two years had been astounding.[125]

*

'*Bwana* Zayky! *Bwana* Zayky! Telephone, please,' came Mohammed's voice across the fields.

Pasha, on his knees examining the octopus-like tendrils of maize root stock, looked up and frowned slightly: he had told Mohammed not to say *bwana*. *Bwana* or 'master' was no longer appropriate language in post-independence Kenya. Pasha rose to his feet and allowed himself a shrug – perhaps *bwana* should never have been considered 'appropriate'.

The cool season in Kenya lasts from July to October when the long rains from May to June give way to drier months at a relatively constant 17 to 18 degrees centigrade, but August is often a little wetter and it was raining hard as he trudged back to the research station's laboratory.

He went inside the brick building where Mohammed was standing at the desk holding the receiver up in the air and waving it towards him.

'*Bwana!*'

'Mohammed, thank you, but please stop calling me *bwana*.'

---

125 Later on, in December 1964, Kenya would become a republic and Kenyatta would be its first president.

'I'm so sorry, Professor, but I needed you to come soon.'

Pasha took the receiver, which squelched as he placed it against his ear soaked from the rain.

'Hello?' he said distractedly as he removed his rain-spattered glasses and wiped his eyes dry with the back of his hand.

'Professor Zayky?' It was a woman's voice; a native woman.

'Yes indeed, good afternoon.'

'This is Mama Ngina, do you know me?' Pasha stopped wiping his eyes and shot a look across to Mohammed who was standing to attention in the corner of the room his eyes wide and fixed on the telephone receiver. As he caught Pasha's glance he nodded vigorously and further stiffened his stance.

Pasha composed himself. Mama Ngina was Prime Minister Kenyatta's wife, his fourth wife to be exact. Thirty years of age in 1963, and daughter of a Kikuyu chief, she had been a gift to Kenyatta from his home province of Ngenda in 1951. His first wife, Grace Wahu, lived quietly away from the limelight whilst his second, Edna, had attended the independence celebrations but then returned to England with her son.[126] Kenyatta's third wife had died in childbirth (although their daughter had survived), and so Ngina was the new prime minister's most visible partner. Eventually

_____

126 Kenyatta studied at the London School of Economics before WW2 and remained in England during the war when he became a farm worker (agricultural work was a 'reserved occupation' so avoiding army conscription). At home in Kenya he had married in 1920 where he had two children, but in England he married again, a white lady, and they had a son in 1943.

when the country became a republic Ngina would become first lady, but from the moment of independence she was at her husband's side and bore him three children (with a fourth born in 1965). As a visible symbol of motherhood and independence from the old colonial regime, Ngina was seen as the mother of the nation and became known as Mama Ngina Kenyatta.[127]

'Good afternoon, Mrs Kenyatta. Please forgive the long delay in coming to the telephone, but I was out in the fields here at the research station. How may I help you?'

'Well, Professor Zayky, it is very nice to hear you; my husband tells me that you were good to him one day in Kitale some years ago. And I know that you have an excellent reputation for advising our farmers and growers. I was speaking to my husband yesterday and he suggested that you and Mrs Zayky should join us for tea at home in Ichaweri over the weekend. Are you free this coming Saturday afternoon?'

*

On Saturday morning, as usual on any trip to Nairobi, they landed at the High School; and as usual Miss Stott emerged to greet them.

'Tanya, Pasha, how lovely to see you – come, come!' she smiled, her eyes bulging as normal as she led them across the playing fields back to her study. On entering the building, Tanya noted that the children and staff still stopped and

127 https://biznakenya.com/wp-content/uploads/2014/10/uhuru8.jpg
Jomo and Ngina Kenyatta with their son Uhuru in the 1960s. Uhuru Kenyatta went on to become Kenya's fourth president in 2013.

stood back for her, just as they had years ago when Sofia had been at the school and when Tanya had received her dressing-down from the headmistress for flying in, and landing, unannounced. The power of Miss Stott's personality was as massive as ever but Tanya noted that her body lacked some of her old strength. Now she no longer swept through the building like a cannonball, and instead paused to catch her breath. As she paused so everybody else in the corridor also stopped and remained quite still as if they were playing a game of musical statues.

As Miss Stott leant against the whitewashed wall, wheezing slightly, she gestured towards a small native girl.

'Ann Mithamo, very well done on reading your prayer aloud in assembly yesterday, a clear, loud voice, jolly good,' she said breathlessly and, looking back towards Tanya, nodded approvingly her aim to convey the impression that she had stopped to deliver words of encouragement to her pupil rather than because she needed a rest. But whatever the reason for her pausing in the corridor, Ann Mithamo was delighted to receive such high praise and smiled broadly.

'Thank you, Miss Stott.'

Native African and Asian girls had been admitted to the High School since 1961 – just another aspect of Macmillan's 'Wind of Change'.

Over coffee in her study Miss Stott showed off her latest photos, including the aerial shots taken during her last flying session with Tanya in the Knight. Pasha made approving noises as the headmistress explained each shot, but Tanya was silent. She sensed the old lady had something more to say. Eventually, Miss Stott replaced the photograph album on the shelf and looked back at her guests.

'You know, I have had such a wonderful time here, with my girls. I'm so proud of this school coming through the war, coming through the emergency, and now a new beginning in an independent country. It all heralds great change. Change which, I think, I may be too old to deliver. I think it's time for me to step back and so I have let the governors know that I shall be retiring this year.'

Pasha gave a look to indicate concern and pleasure at the same time.

'Well that will be a huge loss for the school, but will give you a very well-earned rest,' he said.

Tanya, in her usual way, was rather less diplomatic. 'Will I still be able to land on the school fields?'

'Dear Tanya, I fear that you may not. Now you no longer have a child at the school, it might be more challenging for Miss Leevers, the new head, to grant permission. I think our old arrangement might need rethinking, I'm afraid. It's all part of the changes really...' Miss Stott looked down at her empty coffee cup examining how the coffee grounds had dried and hardened onto the base. 'Now tell me... what news of Sofia?'

*

A black government Wolseley car collected them from the High School and took them the short drive to State House, where they would stay overnight. The incoming administration had quickly renamed Government House as State House when it became the official residence of the prime minister. Externally, little had changed, save for the country's new flag flying above the grand main portico. Inside, however, whilst the old colonial furniture remained, the pictures and portraits had gone, replaced with photographs and paintings of Prime Minister Kenyatta, as well as tribal wall hangings and rugs. Pasha and Tanya had stayed there often in times past when attending meetings and as a stopping-off point on trips around the country; but less so in the last few years after Sir Evelyn Baring had left and during the run-up to independence. Governor Renison had had matters more pressing than agricultural output to consider.

The staff remained unchanged, however, and all remembered Pasha fondly. A light lunch was served in their room, and the butler asked them to be out at the front of the building to be collected at 2.30pm.

Despite it being his official residence it was well known that Jomo Kenyatta disliked State House. He said it was haunted and he would not sleep there. Given the extent of vitriol which the British had launched against him from the building, it was hardly surprising that he had no wish to spend more time than was necessary with ghosts of the past. Instead he preferred to commute daily from his real home in Ichaweri, a small village in Gatundu Kiambu County, about an hour's drive north of Nairobi, and it was to here that Pasha and Tanya had been invited for tea.

At 2.30pm they waited under the portico and gasped as the prime minister's personal Rolls-Royce limousine appeared and, with the only noise audible being the crack of its tyres on the gravel of the drive, the car drew to a halt. The driver, in full chauffeur's uniform with peaked cap, left his seat and opened the rear door for them. Tanya had not been in a Rolls-Royce since she had travelled in Greta's Peabody, in London in 1946. Peabody had exuded a faded glory of a glamorous past but was, in honesty, a little dented and tired. The prime minister's Rolls-Royce, on the other hand, was anything but tired. It was, quite simply, the most luxurious car on the planet. [128] They gladly entered the sumptuous and air-conditioned cool of the huge rear compartment and settled back for the drive to Ichaweri. Excited at their invitation for tea with the prime minister and his wife, they were perhaps only a little apprehensive as to whether some hidden agenda lay behind their bidding to attend.

It took just a little more than an hour before, in the outskirts of Ichaweri, the Rolls-Royce pulled up at a set of large metal gates. For a second Tanya was reminded of the gates of Gathigiriri camp but the thought quickly went from her mind. There was a sentry box in the road, outside the gates, and a soldier with a machine gun stepped forward, looked in at the driver who then wound down the electric window to the car's rear compartment. The guard stared at them through the open window.

Nodding, the guard turned and barked a command to a person unseen; the gates swung open and the Rolls-Royce proceeded through. The drive from the gate to the residence took only a moment and they arrived at the steps of a small white bungalow, not much different in size to their own bungalow at the research station, although obviously newer and more modern in construction. As the driver stepped out and opened the door for them they could see that the Rolls-Royce looked incongruous outside such a modest little house.

---

128 https://owaahh.com/wp-content/uploads/2017/10/Jomo-Kenyatta-Rolls.jpg
Prime Minister Jomo Kenyatta, with his brand-new Rolls-Royce Phantom V limousine in 1963

And then the prime minister and Mama Ngina arrived to greet them.

'Ah-ha! Professor… Mrs Zayky, thank you for coming to our home. I hope you enjoyed the drive here…' chuckled the great man gesturing, with his walking stick, towards his enormous car.

Tea was served on the verandah, and a butler appeared in white gloves with a teapot and delicate bone china, green and white cups and saucers, all rattling and chinking on a tray which he set down on the table. 'Thank you, Njinu,' grunted Kenyatta as the butler poured his tea. There were small cucumber sandwiches and slices of cake. It was all quite exquisite.

For some while they made polite but perfectly happy small talk as the Kenyattas chatted about the house and garden, about their children; they smiled and asked about Sofia. Obviously Pasha spoke more than Tanya but she worked hard to smile back and to say the odd thing.

'Do you know, Professor, Mrs Zayky, I am a blessed man? Blessed with a loving family and a loving nation, but blessed too because my life has been saved on more than one occasion.' He paused; Pasha realised this was an oration and the time for conversation had ended.

'The British almost certainly saved my life when they arrested me. Governor Baring accused me of managing the Mau Mau when exactly the opposite was true. I have always emphasised the need for peaceful reform. I wanted an end to the violence. If I had not been arrested and taken away then there was a real chance that the young radicals, the Mau Mau themselves, would have had me shot. It is a bizarre thing that the British were not, in fact, my prison warders, but rather they were my bodyguard.

'Of course, they certainly did all they could to end my influence here in Kenya. They took me to the desert, they rigged my trial, they demolished this house. They even carted away the bricks, and gave away my land to somebody else!

'But then my life was saved again, one day in Kitale, when you and your family ferried me to safety. I had just been set free from prison, on a legal technicality, it was all most improbable, and the crowd out in the street were furious. Had it not been for you, I and my long-suffering lawyer, Mr Pritt, would have been strung up. That mob would have seen us hanged that day. You took a great risk by putting us in the back of your car. And I shall always be thankful to you for it.

'Of course, later on, when the British realised my release was inevitable, they evicted the man they had installed on this land and rebuilt my home with new bricks. And a very good job they made too. The British always build things well, I think, built to last, just like my Rolls-Royce. You're not British though, I think?'

Having been asked a specific question Pasha was keen to clarify the position.

'Oh no, Mr Kenyatta, we are indeed British and very proud to be. We were born in Russia but came to Kenya many years ago and became British citizens.'

'I see, I see, yes,' said the old man. 'I too spent time in Russia; I was most interested but, in the end, unconvinced by their regime.[129] I can understand why you wanted to leave there. But I want to think about that man who was

---

129 Kenyatta visited the Soviet Union in the 1930s.

335

evicted by the British so that I could move back here to this house. Obviously I am pleased he left, it is to my advantage, however, I expect that the man I displaced is upset. I think there are similar claims on land all around Kenya now. Some of the plots are small, like this one, but some are huge. For every plot of land I think there is somebody enjoying its use and somebody else who is displeased. I have to do what is fair for my people and for the good of this country. I know that much of the best land in Kenya is farmed by a minority group of white settlers who obtained it at little or no cost at the expense of the local people. Should these white settlers now be evicted with their lands redistributed in the name of African Socialism? In the name of fairness?'

This could have been a rhetorical question but Kenyatta didn't phrase it as such and paused to allow Pasha to respond. There was silence for a moment then, 'I think, sir, that might be counterproductive.' The old man grunted for him to continue.

'Kenya is unlike many other African countries, such as South Africa, Rhodesia, or Ghana, in that it has little mineral wealth. There are no mines, no diamonds, no gold. Instead, Kenya offers good land and an easy climate for crops to grow. Your crops are your gold. For years now I have helped farmers, yes, the white settlers, to improve their agricultural output and until now that has been to the benefit of the British colonial machine. The taxation raised from the sale of the crops, the coffee and tea, on the world commodity markets has earned money for Britain. That tax income will, from now on, belong to Kenya. You can invest it. To evict the white farmers will disrupt the workings of those farms for a long time. You would cut off your only real income stream.'

Kenyatta nodded.

'It doesn't seem fair that the whites could have treated my tribe so harshly, treated me harshly, and all the other natives of Kenya, and yet can now continue to reap the profit of the land. But yours is the practical solution, and I believe you are right. I must ensure that Kenya is solvent. We must have the money available to create a strong and sustainable nation.'

He paused again before continuing.

'But what of the Mau Mau, the fighters returning from the forests? They come back to their old farms and villages but find that all the land has been given to the members of their tribe who were loyal to the British. They lost the war but won the freedom and yet the very people they fought against have got rich at their expense. This, I think, was the so-called Swynnerton Plan, but I am told it should, more truthfully, have been called the Professor Zayky Plan, isn't that correct?'

Was this a compliment? Possibly not; in any event Pasha decided not to explain his role in the formulation of the plan, but rather he said, 'Well, sir, the same issues largely apply to the Kikuyu lands just as they do to the settler estates. You need to feed the people. The fighters returning from the forests are not skilled farmers, their arrival back in the villages simply means more mouths to feed, although it does provide a bigger workforce. Of course, I can understand it creates division and inequality, but those are political issues which I would think can be overcome. Food shortages are much harder to resolve. When we were in the Soviet Union we saw how a relentless and ideological desire for complete equality rendered the exact opposite: a few privileged people got reasonable rations but the majority starved.'

Pasha failed to point out that the Zaykys had been one of the privileged few, but it was an unnecessary detail; Kenyatta had understood his point. This time the silence was much longer before he spoke.

'Again, Professor Zayky, I think you must be correct. Famine in this country would be unthinkable. But the calls for vengeance will not go away and I will have to calm the people. I will have to do what the British failed to do that day in Kitale when the crowd became murderous. I will have to stop them stringing up those who have been loyal to the old regime and justify, as best I can, the reason that nobody will be punished for all the beatings, the rapes, the thefts. Nobody will answer for all the deaths. I must ask them to forgive and forget the past.[130]

'But, Professor Zayky, I think this must be the final piece of advice that we accept from you here in Kenya. You have made such a difference to our fortunes as a nation, and as I said earlier, you saved my life. I hope that in return this country has provided you and your family with some riches and lustre to enable you, with our thanks, to move on. Your work, in Kenya, is done.'

Kenyatta stood. Tea was over. Pasha, Tanya and Mama Ngina all stood too. The two couples shook hands.

'Goodbye, Professor, Mrs Zayky.'

---

130 On 20th October 1963, Kenya celebrated its first 'Kenyatta Day'. Jomo Kenyatta said: 'Let this be the day on which all of us commit ourselves to erase from our minds all the hatreds and the difficulties of those years which now belong to history. Let us agree that we shall never refer to the past. Let us instead unite, in all our utterances and activities, in concern for the reconstruction of our country and the vitality of Kenya's future.' In 2010 Kenyatta Day in Kenya was renamed 'Heroes Day'.

Njinu the butler ushered them back out to the front of the house. The Rolls-Royce had disappeared and been replaced with a black Wolseley, the driver in slacks and an open-necked shirt stepped out and opened the rear door.

20

MISHA CHESHIRE
London, 1955 to 1962

MAMA HAD BEEN NINETEEN WHEN SHE MOVED TO London to take up her place studying medicine at Queen Mary College in 1955. The medical school was situated just off the Mile End Road, about six miles east of Buckingham Palace. The war had ended ten years before and whilst the job of reconstruction was underway in the heart of London, the east of the city remained a wasteland of bomb sites and boarded-up buildings. Before she had left Kenya, Mama had been told that she had been allocated accommodation at the school's hall of residence, 4 St Helen's Terrace, London E1. Pasha and Tanya thought this sounded a fine address. However, the reality was rather different and the halls were a vermin-infested slum. Not that Mama was ever bothered by vermin – she had lived in Africa and was well used to wildlife of all sizes. But the streets were populated with vermin of another kind. The young street urchins kicking footballs were never any trouble but in the 1950s, the broken East End was home to a gang culture engaged in drinking, gambling, prostitution, smuggling and protection racketeering – this was the real vermin.

East London's post-war gangsters are sometimes depicted as glamorous, albeit hardened, villains displaying a chivalrous 'honour among thieves' culture; almost as though they were latter-day Robin Hoods. For many outside the area it was impossible to believe that the East End, which had withstood all the bombs of the war and never allowed the Germans to beat their morale, could so soon after the end of the conflict descend into such a pit of lawlessness and depravity. But it did. The medical school was an oasis of learning and excellence but the boundary of the oasis didn't extend beyond the walls of the college itself.

Of course Baba and Dyeda wrote every week to tell Mama their news; well, Dyeda wrote and Baba would also sign the letter. Out of duty, Mama wrote back but rather like Baba, the art of correspondence did not come naturally. Sofia was not a person to make a fuss about her circumstances, indeed she remained so excited to be studying medicine at last, but she did comment occasionally on the drunkenness, the beatings, and the 'working girls' who were no more than slaves. In Kenya, Pasha and Tanya worried about their child as parents do the world over. Sofia was headstrong. In their letters they would implore her to take care but the tone of her replies always betrayed a wearied frustration over their concern.

'Yes, yes… I do take care… I wish you would stop worrying.'

But what more could they do from Kenya?

*

'Sofia!… Sofia Zayky!'

Not a sharp rap, the knocking was more like a trio of dead thuds against the door of Sofia's room. It was a Sunday afternoon in early December 1955. The day was cold but not raining, although the clouds had a yellow pallor and the sounds of the street outside lacked resonance – the timbre was of deadened wood. And so it was with the knocking.

Sofia was sitting on her bed reading, attempting to supplement the poor light from her window by a dim, faintly flickering electric bulb hanging from a single pendant in the middle of the ceiling; there was no attempt at a lampshade. The room was rather less than three metres square, enough for a single bed and a small chest of drawers with a wash bowl and mirror on top. Sofia's single suitcase stood to one side. There was no carpet on the floor, not even a rug, and the gaps between the floorboards allowed easy passage for the rodents and the insects. There was no heating and Sofia wore her warmest winter dress and woollen tights with a blanket wrapped around her.

Having lain awake most of the night because of the din from the drunks disgorging from the pub next door at the end of the lock-in at 3am, as well as from the itching of bedbug sores around the tops of her calves, she had found herself drifting off to sleep as she tried to make sense of the medical journal on her lap.

'Sofia Zayky…!' The knocking woke her up. A woman's voice; loud. Sofia made a face as she put her book to one side and got off the bed.

'Hello?' she said through the closed door. A woman, yes, but there might be a man with her. Too dangerous just to open the door to a stranger.

'Sofia, it's Greta, may I come in?' The knocking lacked resonance but the voice did not. It was loud, clear and sonorous.

Greta? Greta! As Sofia drew back the bolt at the top of the door her heart leapt. Greta Chevalier, Jeremy's mother! The nice, rather grand lady and her son who they had befriended back in 1947 when Sofia and Tanya had stayed with Father Michael at the Podvorya in Barons Court. Both she and Jeremy had been eleven then. It was a lifetime ago. What on earth was Greta doing at her door this Sunday afternoon?

She opened the door and before her stood Greta, tall, slim and elegant. Her full-length fur coat a deep mahogany-red, matching the colour of her gleaming hair. Beautiful; she hadn't altered a jot: white skin, high cheekbones, red lipstick and wearing the same expression on her face – exactly as Sofia remembered her. But eight years on and Sofia now understood the expression: it was a look of melancholy.

Greta took in the scene before her – the thin, bedraggled child, the unmade bed, the blanket thrown to one side, the filthy room.

'Oh Sofia, darling! Come here!' She threw open her arms and Sofia lurched forward and flung herself around her. They clung on to each other as they both sobbed.

'It's so good to see you Greta – I'm sorry I haven't written. How is Jeremy?' she choked out through the tears with feelings of guilt rising inside, knowing that she should have made contact to say hello to her old friend. There was just too much of her mother in her and she had been too wrapped up in the excitement, and terror, of her first term at the college.

'You silly child, there is no need for apologies. Your mother wrote to me and said that she was worried about your living conditions – and I see that she was right. You're coming home with me. Come to live with me and Jeremy at Tite Street, we have a spare room, and a bath, and heating.'

'Oh no, Greta, I have to live here for college. They gave me this room. I need to study.'

'Darling, they have given you nothing in this slum. You will come home with me, and you will stay with us for however long you like. Tite Street is just a short walk from Sloane Square and so you can catch the tube to Mile End each day. But I will have you warm, fed and clean. And Jeremy would so love to see you again. You will come, won't you?'

Sofia was headstrong – determined, single-minded. But she was also intelligent, sensible, freezing cold, dirty, and just a little frightened. If ever there was a time for good common sense to prevail over any bloody-minded desire for independence then this was it. She looked up to Greta and nodded.

'Good, now pack up your things and let's get out of this awful place.'

They headed down the stairs, Sofia's suitcase bumping against the wall. A few of her housemates opened their doors a chink as she went past but nobody said anything, or called out a goodbye. Sofia had made no effort to make friends and the housemates knew that the departing girl's room would be taken by another soon enough. She had been aloof, that Russian girl. Plain looks and never bothered to speak. They wouldn't miss her.

Through the front door and out into the street. Peabody! The green Rolls-Royce was waiting outside, parked against the kerb. It was, perhaps, a slightly darker shade than Sofia had remembered, although maybe that was just the effect of the wintry yellow late-afternoon light.

Greta opened the rear door so that Sofia could put her case inside. As she did so they became conscious of a man walking up the outside steps from the building's basement.

As Greta helped Sofia push her case into the back of the car, the man positioned himself right beside them, leaning against the front door. He was fifty, short and thin, almost emaciated. His hair was dyed-black and shiny. His face hung from his forehead as a ladder of deep creases of yellowed skin prickled with white stubble. From the side of his mouth his cigarette was half gone and the smoke rose up to his right eye, which was half closed in response.

'Now, now, now, what do we 'ave 'ere? Two pretty ladies, I'm sure, but where's your fella, love?' He looked at Greta. 'Inside is 'e? Or ain't there one? You both 'ere on your jacks? Now that's silly, ladies, a dangerous part of town this is.'

Greta glared back at the man but he was unperturbed.

'And yous with this loverly car, too. Now I think it's a bit dangerous you driving, especially as it's getting dark. I think you ladies shud go off to the Underground station and go home and let me drive this fine car back for you. Just give me your address and I'll deliver it.'

So it was clear that the man wanted the car.

'Move out the way and we shall be off,' said Greta, loudly, clearly.

'No, I don't think so,' he replied. 'You don't turn up to my manor in your fancy car and not pay the price, lady. I ain't never seen you around these parts before and don't never expect to see you again. And you can take off that fine coat and put that in the back as well.'

The menace was unmistakable. Sofia caught the stink of tobacco, beer and old vomit from his dirty suit jacket.

'You need to understand that I'm in charge round here, see. I kicked off those kids you'd paid to watch the car; but it wouldn't start up when I tried – reckon you've done something to it. So lady, start it up now so I can be on my way and you can be on yours.'

Sofia looked on, horrified and terrified. But Greta stood her ground.

'I said move out of the way!'

'Now I don't usually strike women but you're making me angry, lady, and perhaps you need a lesson on how to behave. Maybe I need to show you the back of my hand!' He threw away his fag, now down to the butt, and began flexing the fingers of his right hand.

'You lay one hand on me, Jack Cahill, and I will see that your mother knows all about it!' retorted Greta, her words echoing around the otherwise deserted street. Her voice, just as sonorous, but now suddenly laced with an East-End accent, which had not been apparent before. And the man, or Jack as he obviously was, quite literally jumped backwards and stared at Greta aghast. Suddenly their difference in height was evident. Greta was taller, she was stiff-backed and her fists were clenched. Looking for all the world like a lean Doberman guard dog, hackles raised, straining at the leash and ready to strike down an intruder, she stood and sneered. Her lip curled into a look of half condescension and half mockery.

He gazed back.

'Yeah… I know you… Greta Harris, thas you innit?'

'Yeah, thas me, Jack Cahill. And I know you, too, and your mother, and everyone else round 'ere. Cos this IS my manor. Now fuck off, you wanker!'

And, without a further word being said, he turned and simply walked away, sauntering down the street seemingly without a care in the world.

Once Cahill had turned a corner and was out of sight they climbed aboard and Greta flicked the battery switch hidden under the seat – the deterrent which had, so successfully, thwarted his attempt to steal the car. Peabody started instantly, moved away from the kerb and proceeded down the road. Sofia noticed various curtains twitching as they drove past the shabby houses; evidently there had been an unseen audience during the altercation in the street. Greta kept her head faced firmly ahead and her jaw set, but her chin trembled and just occasionally she flicked up her hand to wipe away any trace of moisture from the corner of her eyes. Gradually as they moved out of the East End she relaxed.

'I was born just one road along from there. Jewish parents, of course. Started singing and dancing in the local pubs as a young girl and managed to make the move into the music halls. As I made a bit of money, instead of drinking or gambling it like most of them, I salted it away, and eventually I was able to move west. I changed my name, changed the way I spoke, changed the clothes I wore; started to mix with different people. I climbed my way out of the East End; few others ever did.'

She paused.

'Please don't ever tell Jeremy that I swore.'

Sofia never did.

*

Life in Tite Street, Chelsea was altogether more agreeable than trying to survive in the Mile End Road. It would be wrong to say that Greta was rich – she certainly wasn't that – but she had saved enough money during her successful years to allow them to live a modest life of somewhat faded glamour. Jeremy was so happy that Sofia had come to live with them and they picked up their relationship as de facto twin siblings from exactly the point where they had left off some eight years earlier.

Jeremy was, by then, at acting school – The Royal Academy of Dramatic Art in Gower Street[131] – and the house in Tite Street became an early evening stopping-off point for all sorts of aspiring young actors for tea and sandwiches before heading up to clubs in the King's Road.

When Sofia came in from her day at medical college it would not be unusual to find the likes of Tony Hopkins running through lines with Jeremy in Greta's front room.[132]

Jeremy was a good actor too, but had a tendency to put himself down and lacked the supreme confidence of some of his peers. Sofia was his support. She attended every

---

131 The Royal Academy of Dramatic Art (RADA) was founded in 1904 by Sir Herbert Beerbohm Tree, an actor manager, at His Majesty's Theatre in the Haymarket. In 1905, RADA moved to 52 Gower Street. George Bernard Shaw donated his royalties from his play *Pygmalion* to RADA, and gave lectures to students at the school.

132 Sir Anthony 'Tony' Hopkins CBE born December 1937 is a film, stage, and television actor. He graduated from the Royal Welsh College of Music & Drama in 1957. He trained at RADA where he was spotted by Laurence Olivier who invited him to join the Royal National Theatre.

performance, helped him practise his lines – she gave him strength. As his loving sister she provided objective non-confrontational encouragement which he could rely upon. Greta did too, of course, but your sibling will always be more honest than your parent. Greta knew that and was glad to have Sofia there.

But whilst Jeremy would even introduce Sofia as his sister there was no doubt that the two were unrelated. By the late 1950s Sofia was in her early twenties, the point in any life at which nature bestows the most beauty, but nevertheless to any observer she was plain. Dark-haired, fairly tall, thin, not at her ease with most people, fiercely intelligent, but with the most piercing eyes which burned like coals. On the other hand Jeremy was devastatingly handsome. Possibly a fraction shorter than Sofia, he was blond, blue-eyed, slim rather than thin, urbane and fashionable.

A five-minute walk away up on the King's Road was Jeremy's favourite club, the Pheasantry, an old, crumbling ruin of a building which two centuries earlier had been the home of a famous bird breeder, hence its rather strange name.[133] Now it housed an assortment of bedraggled apartments and studios above the ground with a basement

---

133 The Pheasantry, 152 King's Road, Chelsea, gets its name from the business of Samuel Baker who developed new breeds of oriental pheasant. The current building was erected in the 1850s and over a century later, when almost derelict, it was home to a number of bohemian cultural icons of 1960s London. Today, the extensively renovated building houses a branch of a pizza restaurant chain. The basement remains a cabaret and music club. https://rbkclocalstudies.wordpress.com/2013/06/27/the-princess-at-the-pheasantry/
The Pheasantry in 1974, after its 1960s cultural peak but prior to major restoration.

which was a venue for the new rhythm-and-blues music scene. Sofia was never really interested in music but Jeremy would drag her along, as well as Tony Hopkins and various other hopeful thespians, to listen to the blues and watch new young talent stepping up to play – people like Jimmy Page, Charlie Watts, Jack Bruce and later a seventeen-year-old Eric Clapton who played with his first band, The Roosters, and lived upstairs in one of the rooms.[134] But at a certain point in the evening, normally sometime past midnight, the live music would end and the disc jockeys would take over. Jeremy would walk Sofia back to Tite Street.

'Good night darling,' he would say, kissing her lightly on the cheek.

'Good night to you,' she would respond, '… and be careful Jeremy – please.'

'I promise I shall.'

And then he would walk back up to the Pheasantry. By the time he returned to the club the scene would have changed and young men, fuelled by booze and pills, would dance frenetically through to first light. Sometimes things got rough and occasionally, when Jeremy finally emerged in Tite Street for some tea the following afternoon, he might have bruises, or his shirt or trousers would be torn. Sofia and Greta worried about him.

By 1960, Sofia had gained her medical degree and had become a junior houseman at St George's Hospital located at Hyde Park Corner in West London, which was more or

---

134 Jimmy Page went on to play guitar in Led Zeppelin, Charlie Watts plays drums in the Rolling Stones, Jack Bruce was a bass player most notable for the band Cream. Eric Clapton played guitar in various bands and has enjoyed a long solo career.

less walking distance from Tite Street – or a bus ride if it was wet.[135] As a student she had been out on a few dates but romance had never blossomed. In truth the only boy she loved was Jeremy, as a sister loves her brother, and she knew very well that his romantic interests lay elsewhere.

Sofia's mate would need to be her intellectual equal as well as somebody who could easily allow for, and compensate, her own social awkwardness. It was in 1962 that she came across just such a man, Jim Cheshire, who would be my father.

Jim, a surgeon at St George's, was twenty years older than my mother and, in fact, her tutor. Like her, he had been an only child but my grandparents on his side had died years before.

As a boy, he had won a scholarship to the British public school Charterhouse in Surrey[136] where he was normally at the top of his class. On finishing school in 1934 he studied at Magdalene College, Cambridge, and then at St Thomas' Hospital in London, qualifying in 1941. With the country at war, he joined the Royal Army Medical Corps and quickly became a surgical specialist with the rank of Captain serving with the partisan forces in both Italy and Yugoslavia. Gradually

---

135 St George's Hospital was established at Lanesborough House, Hyde Park Corner, London in 1733. It was rebuilt in the early nineteenth century, but moved to its current location in Tooting South London in the 1970s.

136 'Public schools' in Britain are sometimes confused with free state schools but, in fact, are quite the opposite. Wealthy parents generally have to pay significant fees to allow their children to attend. Often, these schools carefully select the pupils they admit and apply entrance tests. Scholarships are grants to cover the school fees of the most able students who attain the highest pass marks in the entrance examinations.

his skills in post-injury trauma surgery began to be noticed and he rose up the ladder of seniority. After 1945 he remained in the army serving as a surgical adviser to the Greek government during the Greek Civil War,[137] when the former Communist allies who had fought the Axis forces suddenly became the enemy. He was finally demobilised in 1949 just at the point the newly formed, free at the point of use National Health Service was getting into its stride, and Jim secured a post as a surgeon in the orthopaedics department at St George's.

During the war, whilst in the field of battle, Jim had noticed that some of the captured Germans had previously been treated for severe leg fractures by the use of metal rods or nails inserted into bones. [138] He could see immediately that this alleviated the need for rigid external plaster or traction. Jim brought the new idea of mending bones with metal rods and pins to St George's and transformed patient recovery times in the process.

Most surgeons at St George's were insufferable. They behaved like operatic prima donnas during surgery,

---

137 The Greek Civil War (1946 to 1949) was fought by the Greek government army (backed by the UK and USA) against the military branch of the Greek Communist Party which included many personnel who had fought as partisans against the German and Italian forces between 1939–1945. The Communists were defeated and the conflict is considered as the first proxy war of the Cold War.

138 Orthopaedics is the branch of surgery concerned with conditions involving the musculoskeletal system, trauma, spine diseases, sports injuries. The use of intramedullary rods to treat fractures of the femur and tibia was pioneered by Gerhard Küntscher of Germany. This made a noticeable difference to the speed of recovery of injured German soldiers during World War II and led to more widespread adoption of intramedullary fixation of fractures in the rest of the world.

treating their operations as theatrical performances whilst bullying their surrounding support staff. But Jim was different and the junior housemen queued up to work in his theatre where his genial, twinkling presence was a source of delight.

Jim delighted in a love of music and had raised more than a few eyebrows by insisting that a gramophone should be installed in his operating theatre to satisfy his need for Mozart during operations. In fact, he had worked out its usefulness to calm both patients and staff during his time in the army, especially during traumatic operations when only rudimentary anaesthesia had been available. Sometimes at the end of surgery, when his students were allowed to close up, the record might get changed. Something more modern – upbeat – some rhythm and blues perhaps. Jim adored his work and by the early 1960s had reached a level of acclaim and adoration by the other medics to raise his status to something akin to a rock and roll star. Now he found he liked the soundtrack to go with it.

Chatting after one such operation where Bo Diddley's 'Road Runner'[139] had been spinning on the turntable whilst Sofia had been stitching up, Jim said that he had particularly enjoyed the track. Sofia mentioned that she had seen a band at the Pheasantry play the song just a week earlier.

'May I come down one evening too?' he said.

---

139 Ellas McDaniel (1928–2008), known as Bo Diddley, was an American singer, guitarist, songwriter and music producer who played a key role in the transition from the blues to rock and roll. His use of African rhythms and a signature beat is a cornerstone of rock, pop and hip-hop music. He influenced many artists, including Elvis Presley, The Beatles, The Rolling Stones, and The Clash.

Now my Mama was well aware that Papa was, by then, in his late forties and yet had never married. Jim was mature, highly educated, sober and yet possessed with a great sense of fun; he wasn't terribly good-looking but was fairly tall with nice eyes. Sofia assumed that Jim was a confirmed bachelor who might prove a good friend for my uncle Jeremy. Almost certainly a better long-term friend than some of the boys Jeremy would normally meet at the Pheasantry in the small hours.

And so the arrangements were made and a few days later Jim came round to Tite Street. Greta had prepared a light supper and Jim, smart in a freshly pressed dark blue suit, brought a bottle of wine and some Black Magic chocolates. Jim, Sofia and Jeremy headed up to the club just after nine o'clock and Sofia positioned the three of them in a favourite booth with Jim sitting between her and her brother.

The drinks flowed and Jim was keen to pay. The band played and the sound was good, and got even better as they drank a little more.

'Would you like to dance Sofia?' he said.

'Err… wouldn't you like to ask Jeremy to dance?' she replied. 'It's fine, nobody minds in here, you know.'

He laughed.

'I don't think Jeremy is interested in me, nor me in him.' And he turned to look across at Jeremy who had left the booth and was now holding court with two other, painfully fashionable, young men who were obviously transfixed by his blue eyes.

'And I would prefer to be allowed to dance with you…'

Neither Mama nor Papa were good dancers. But dancing is a bit like tennis; a game which is great to play with somebody at the same skill level as you. However dancing has the edge on racquet sports as, nearly always, it is a precursor to love.

Neither Greta nor Jeremy were remotely surprised to find that Jim became a regular visitor to Tite Street, often staying over, on the couch, I think. Never one to mix easily with her peers, Sofia found in Jim a soulmate, whilst Jim found the strikingly intelligent erstwhile daughter of Soviet Russia, with bewitching eyes, constantly questioning and thoroughly compelling. It was, in fact, a perfect parallel to Dyeda Pasha's love for Baba Tanya.

21

MISHA CHESHIRE
London, mid-1960s

DYEDA PASHA AND BABA TANYA RETURNED TO London as true, passport-holding British citizens in autumn 1963. They knew better than to refuse the direct order from Jomo Kenyatta to leave Kenya; and in any event, he had been correct: it was time for them to move on.

In truth, Pasha might have been more concerned had he not secured a job offer in London already. On retirement as Kenya's governor, Sir Evelyn Baring had been elevated within the British nobility and made a lord. Now as the newly styled Lord Howick[140] he became deputy chairman of the Colonial Development Corporation,[141]a British

---

140 In Britain, newly created lords or 'peers' select a title which reflects a place with which they are associated. In Baring's case his wife Molly had inherited Howick Hall, which had been in her family for 600 years. Evelyn adopted her ancestral home as his title.

141 The Colonial Development Corporation was established in 1948 to assist British colonies in the development of agriculture. Following the independence of many colonies, it was renamed the Commonwealth Development Corporation in 1963 and was permitted to invest outside the Commonwealth in 1969. As part of the Commonwealth Development Corporation Act 1999, the CDC was converted from a statutory corporation to a public limited company renamed CDC Group plc, with all shares owned by the UK Government.

government organisation established after the second war to provide aid and loans to the Empire and former British colonies to improve their economic welfare and outcomes. Normally this was achieved by granting them the necessary finance to increase their agricultural output. Baring's experience made him perfect for the job but it was ironic that when Jomo Kenyatta sought cash from the British for his newly independent Kenya, it was former governor (and jailer) Baring who was the ultimate decision-maker.

Sir George Taylor had become director of the Royal Botanic Gardens at Kew in 1956. A formidable Scot, Sir George threw himself into the task of transforming Kew into a relevant government resource, searching for the most talented botanists, and successfully lobbying for additional funding. Kew was one of the more important agencies providing advice to the Colonial Development Corporation, and Sir George and Evelyn sat on several committees together. It was thus Evelyn's suggestion that Sir George should create a new role around the study of East African crops at Kew on a decent salary. Following Kenya's independence it was obvious to Evelyn that Pasha's skills could be put to better use in London and that the new role at Kew would be perfect. They needed their best botanists back in Britain. It only occurred to Pasha, years later, that the order for them to leave Kenya might have resulted from a request from Evelyn to Kenyatta, who complied on the promise of additional loan funding from the Colonial Development Corporation.

Dyeda and Baba left Africa on the Rhodesia Castle sailing from Mombasa in late September 1963. The Kenyan Department of Agriculture even paid for the voyage. For a Russian botanist, who never thought he would be able to leave his home country, the ability to have conducted so much research and built such a reputation in East Africa had proved transformational.

They had, of course, endured the Emergency Period in Kenya. The Mau Mau insurgency must have been terrifying, but thankfully they were based mainly in the more peaceful west of the country and, anyway, British justice prevailed in the end. In fact, coping with the Mau Mau was just one aspect of their journey to become British citizens. They had carefully negotiated their way through the most brutal and bloodthirsty period of genocide that the world had ever known – the middle twentieth century. Oppressed by Stalin's ruthless regime in Russia, they had cleverly avoided the clutches of Nazi Germany and had been carefully selected by Britain to provide expertise in its most valuable colonial asset, and then endured the terror of native nationalism. Through all this my grandparents and mother had skilfully trodden a winding path to avoid the atrocities and the totalitarianism so that finally, and rightfully, they had been granted British citizenship.

One advantage of the colonial life in Kenya was that living had been cheap. Their bungalow at the research station had come with the job, as did their staff. The money spent on food and clothes was little and (unlike many other white settlers) their consumption of alcohol was tiny. For the most part they had even been able to claim back the cost of avgas,[142] maintenance and rent for the Knight. So, in reality, other than the modest school fees for Sofia when

---

142 Avgas: the aviation fuel used in spark-ignited internal-combustion engines to propel aircraft.

she had been at the High School, the vast majority of Pasha's salary had been saved.

Now they reaped the reward and had enough money in the bank to buy a ground-floor two-bedroomed flat in a new, purpose-built block in Kew, within walking distance of the Botanic Gardens and Underground station. Their flat in Krasnodar had been on the first floor with high ceilings; in Kitale their bungalow had been much larger; whereas in Kew, their flat was small – tiny even – but it was heated, dry, vermin- and insect-free. Most of all, however, it belonged to them, as British citizens. Baba was so proud to take the old photos out of the old battered cigar box and carefully place them on her new living room mantlepiece.

Dyeda's role at the Botanic Gardens had, quite literally, been made for him and he spent his days working in the laboratories or travelling to London to sit on committees in Whitehall, held in rooms not far away from the offices of Sir Arthur Davenport and Sir Andrew Windover, the British government mandarins who had singled him out for service in Kenya some fifteen years earlier. His work in Africa proved the perfect preparation to allow him to advise on agriculture in the post-colonial world. And, just occasionally, Evelyn Baring would drop in at Kew for tea and discussion on flora.

As Dyeda went off to the Botanic Gardens each morning so Baba caught the bus to the Russian Hostel in Earls Court where she volunteered to help organise and clean. Well before she returned to London from Africa, her Batioushka, Father Polsky, had moved on to head the Russian Church in Exile in New York where, most sadly, he passed away in 1960. But the Countess Kleinmichel, Sofia's tutor from the Podvorya in Barons Court, was still a leading force in the

Church and would occasionally come to Earls Court to drink tea with honey with Baba, and talk about the old days.

It was to Baba's perpetual sadness that she never flew again. Sometimes, when her bus was stuck in London's dense traffic, she would rub away the condensation on the steamed-up window by her seat on the top deck, and look out through the little porthole up to the grey sky above, and curse at the fact that 'her' aeroplane, the Knight, was gathering dust back in its hangar on the Pietersen Farm.

But if mornings were spent doing good works for the church, afternoons were usually spent in Tite Street with Greta. Sometimes Tanya would tinker with Peabody in the motor house to correct some minor ailment, or fix a sticking door in the house, or mend a wobbling shelf in one of the wardrobes – there was normally some small job to do. Then it would be a good opportunity to stay on for supper with Sofia and Jeremy. Jim would usually appear too; and if Pasha knew there was a party then he would make his way up from Kew, although sometimes he would get stuck at a long meeting or have an official dinner.

'So where is Pasha this evening, Tanya? I'm sorry he is not with us all.' Greta had been over the moon when Tanya had returned to London. Having Sofia stay with them had been wonderful and had made a world of difference to Jeremy's happiness, but she was even more overjoyed when her friend had come back too. But, of course, she had never met Pasha – he had already been in Kenya by the time Tanya and Sofia were at the Podvorya in 1947 – and in truth, whilst possibly out of character, she had been a little nervous to meet him. That had proved silly of course; in the event, she loved Pasha – everyone did.

Greta and Tanya were in the kitchen preparing a supper of spaghetti Bolognese – dried pasta, minced up chuck beef, some tomato paste, Smedley's tinned peas and carrots, and grated cheddar cheese for the top. Neither lady was a good cook, but it didn't matter.

'Oh, he's with Angus this evening...'

They brought the food through to the table and Jim jumped up and started to help ladle out the portions. Jeremy was pacing up and down reciting lines, which Sofia was checking from a typed and stapled script. Occasionally she would add the odd word which Jeremy had forgotten prompting an additional 'Oh bugger!' from the actor. The family had long since stopped admonishing such language.

'Come on, you two, to the table please, you can give Mr Osborne[143] a rest now!' commanded Greta, and they duly obeyed. 'So who is Angus?' she said, turning back to Tanya, 'I have heard you mention him from time to time, but how does he fit with your story?'

Tanya, unlike Pasha, was never a natural raconteur but she was still Russian and thus recognised the power of a good story told over supper. 'Well, when we walked out of the Soviet Union with the retreating German army, we had just the clothes on our back and our few treasured photographs in that old cigar box. We headed as far west as we could and Angus McGrath was the British major in charge of the

---

143 John Osborne (1929–1994) was an English playwright and actor, known for his excoriating prose and intense critical stance towards established social and political norms. Osborne was one of the first writers to address Britain's purpose in the post-imperial age. The success of his 1956 play *Look Back in Anger* transformed English theatre.

prisoner of war camp where we found ourselves when all the fighting was over.'

'The British wanted to send us back to Russia though, didn't they, Mama?' said Sofia.

'That was all part of Churchill's deal with Stalin at Yalta,'[144] interjected Jim.

'Yes, but very few of the good British soldiers actually wanted to follow those orders as soon as they realised that Stalin was a murderer and that everyone they sent back was shot on the spot.' Tanya paused, staring into space, remembering. 'So many good men had died fighting the evil Nazis, just like lovely brave Pyotr, my brother, that for even more to die at the hands of their own countrymen, after the war, was pure wickedness.'

The pasta on her fork grew cold.

'The thing was that Papa became very useful to the British; why? Well, because he spoke so many languages; when they were dealing with so many different nationalities, they appreciated the need for a good translator. So it was Angus who made sure that we were looked after. He protected us from being sent back and in the end got us introduced to a couple of his old friends in London who arranged for us to go to Kenya. Do you remember much of it all, Sofia?'

'No, not really, I remember a time when we had to pretend to be another family or something like that.'

---

144 The conference near Yalta in Crimea held in February 1945, was the second wartime meeting of the 'Big Three' – US President Franklin D. Roosevelt, British Prime Minister Winston Churchill and Soviet Premier Joseph Stalin – to discuss Europe's post-war reorganisation. One agreement was that the western Allies would return all Soviet citizens who found themselves in western zones to the Soviet Union, irrespective of their wishes.

'Ah yes, that was all play-acting. Yes, all good fun. Jeremy, you would have been good at that! But Angus is a fine man, a part-time priest actually. He went on to work for the United Nations in Switzerland sorting out refugee problems around the world. It was his work that led to the office of the High Commissioner for Refugees winning the Nobel Peace Prize.[145] He retired after that.

'Anyway, he is a member of something called the Reform Club,[146] and that's where they are this evening, for some celebration dinner I believe. I laughed at your papa this morning, Sofia. He was trying on his new dinner suit and black bow tie – he looked like one of the little bobbing penguins at London Zoo!'

They laughed; the weight of the conversation surrounding their journey west and the deaths of so many Russians at the hands of the Soviets was duly checked by the thought of Pasha as a penguin.

'Well, I have some news to tell you all,' said Sofia. 'I'm going to become a GP in a practice in Richmond, just a stop along the Tube line from you in Kew, Mama.'[147]

---

145 United Nations High Commissioner for Refugees (UNHCR), created in 1950 with headquarters in Geneva, was a successor organisation to the UNRRA, and International Refugee Organisation. Its superb humanitarian work led to the UNHCR winning two Nobel Peace Prizes, in 1954 and again in 1981.

146 The Reform Club is a private members club in central London. As with all London's original gentlemen's clubs, it comprised an all-male membership for decades, but was the first to change its rules to include the admission of women on equal terms in 1981. Since its founding, the Reform Club has been the traditional home for those committed to progressive political ideas.

147 GP: General Practitioner, is the first point of contact between a patient and the British National Health Service.

'A GP, Sofia?' questioned Jeremy. 'Doesn't that mean that you will have to see and talk to ill people all day long? Chatting to strangers isn't your strongest suit, dear sister.'

'Well you may have a point, but with my training over, Jim and I don't want to carry on working together in the hospital; and the NHS is in desperate need of GPs.'

Jim stepped in to defend Sofia and provide a little extra justification. 'The thing is, Sofia is a great doctor. With her training complete it is now time for her to find a speciality. Frankly, I think she could probably turn her hand to almost anything in the medical profession; but from what I see she is like Tanya in that her methodological mind means that she can come up with a logical way of solving just about any problem.'

Tanya glowed. She approved of Jim. Obviously a brilliant surgeon, but he also had a knack of saying just the right things. He would make anybody feel at ease in his presence; a man who could use the power of persuasion to get people to do as he bid, and for them to feel glad about it. It was true that he was a little older than Sofia but she needed a more mature man – Tanya could never have seen her daughter with a mere boy. Jim could not really be described as handsome, tall yes, maybe six feet, but slightly stooped and rather heavy-jowled. His eyes twinkled though.

Jim carried on. 'So being a GP will give her the opportunity to make the best use of her skills. Patients arrive with problems, most of them will be quite small but nevertheless important and troubling. Sofia can sort out the small problems, but importantly diagnose the big ones and explain clearly the sequence of events which will need to be followed to deal with whatever issue they face. Most people can't do that.'

'Anyway,' continued Sofia, 'the NHS are crying out for GPs and the surgery at Richmond is very pleased to have me there.'[148]

It seemed to Tanya that if the NHS could be thought of as a machine then using the best quality components for each part of the process maximised efficiency. If Jim said that Sofia's skills would be best utilised as a GP, then Tanya approved completely.

But Jim was still speaking and now he looked across the table at Sofia and winked.

'And given that I've been renting a flat in Holborn I thought I might buy a house now, and so I, well *we* actually, have just agreed to buy a house in Richmond; a few streets away from Sofia's surgery…'

That stopped the dinner conversation! So Jim continued, 'Well, the thing is, I'm sorry that Pasha isn't here this evening, because I went to see him at Kew earlier this afternoon…' he paused '… to ask his permission to marry Sofia. And I'm so pleased to tell you all that he agreed!'

Jim said all this staring across at Sofia – the two of them were grinning like children. Then Jim reached out his hand across the table and Sofia touched his fingertips with hers.

---

148 The British National Health Service (the NHS) was created in 1948 as a 'free at the point of use' healthcare provision for the people of Britain. During the first 25 years of its existence there was a 12% rise in British population coupled with an 80% rise in hospital admissions. The number of NHS employees in hospitals – doctors, nurses, administrative and clerical staff – more than doubled, but over the same period the number of GPs increased by only 16%.

'Don't worry...' she said, '... he had already asked me first – and I said yes too!'

There was silence just for a second while this news sank in – then everyone yelled all at the same time, shouting, kissing, hugging and laughing.

22

MISHA CHESHIRE

Richmond, South West London, 1970 to 1991

S OFIA AND JIM MARRIED IN THE SUMMER OF 1964 AT Chelsea Town Hall – they became Mr and Mrs Cheshire. Greta paid for dinner after at Choy's Chinese Restaurant, just a little way along from the Pheasantry in the King's Road, although Baba Tanya got frustrated trying to eat with chopsticks and declared them less than efficient! Jeremy had borrowed a camera and Tanya was proud to add some new photos to the mantlepiece. Secretly she had wanted her daughter to marry at the Russian church but the old St Philip's in Victoria, where she and Sofia had first met Father Michael Polsky, her Batioushka, in 1946, had been demolished during the 1950s to make way for a coach station and the new church didn't hold the same memories. Anyway, Sofia and Jim wanted a small wedding without any pomp.

The following year, when Mama was 29 and Papa 49, I was born – Michael Cheshire – named after Father Michael, of course.

Papa was a senior surgeon. Mama continued as a GP, practising in Richmond. Both were highly respected; they worked long hours and adored their respective jobs. Each morning Papa would walk to the Underground and Mama would set off on her bike to the surgery. But it didn't matter if they weren't at home because Russian rules applied and in Russia if a child is not at kindergarten then it is the duty of their grandparents to take care of them. This was a role which Baba Tanya took to her heart. She stopped volunteering at the Russian church so she could be there for me in the mornings, walk me to school, and then be at the gates to collect me in the afternoon. If Mama had patients to see in the evening then Baba would cook as well. In the school holidays I would walk down to the Botanical Gardens to spend the day playing in the grounds and helping the gardeners, usually breaking off to have sandwiches and cold milk with Dyeda Pasha at lunchtime.

By the early 1970s Dyeda had stopped going for meetings in Whitehall although he still pottered around his laboratory at Kew and wrote complicated scientific papers which I didn't understand. He officially retired in 1972 but they still allowed him to retain his desk. Everyone always said hello to Dyeda Pasha; everyone loved him.

Most weekends we would head off into London to see Aunt Greta or Uncle Jeremy. I remember riding round Chelsea in Peabody the green Rolls-Royce, which really was very old by then. Sometimes we would go to see Jeremy in a play, and a couple of times we went to the cinema to see him in a film. Aunt Greta always had nicer biscuits than we were allowed at home, and I liked that.

Papa had bought a fine new car in 1970 made by a small British maker called Bristol Motors.[149] On delivery from the Kensington showroom Baba made a thorough inspection and pronounced it 'good'. High praise indeed. It was large, and sky blue, with four good-sized seats, and I remember sitting in the back all the way to Devon where we went on holiday to the Grand Hotel in Torquay. Baba and Dyeda came down on the train to join us and looked after me on the beach while Mama and Papa motored out into the countryside.

Family life was a happy, undemanding routine.

It was the accident that changed everything, of course. I just didn't realise it at the time. Sometimes in life a seismic shift takes place. Your course is set and understood, and then something quite unexpected happens, to change your circumstances for ever. The change can be monumental affecting many, even millions, of people, just like Dyeda and Baba experienced when the Nazis invaded Russia – a sudden and unexpected shock which led to them heading to the West. Or the seismic shift can be quite localised, affecting just one family but nevertheless creating the most profound impact.

Thankfully Papa had been at home when the policeman knocked at the door. The driver of the lorry turning left at the traffic lights hadn't seen Mama on her bicycle in his mirrors.

---

149 Bristol Cars was created in 1945 as an adjunct to the much older Bristol Aeroplane Company. Aircraft orders fell off at the end of World War II and the motor company had the rights to remanufacture old BMW designs obtained by way of wartime reparations. From the 1960s onwards they specialised in large two-door, four-seat, grand-touring cars powered by Chrysler V8 engines, sold from a showroom on London's Kensington High Street. The company hand-built less than a hundred cars a year until 2011 when it fell into administration.

Honestly, I wasn't sure how I should feel. I would never see my mama again. I was ten. It was devastating, everyone said so. I knew that boys weren't supposed to cry like girls could.

When I had been younger, Baba Tanya would say, 'Misha don't be like silly Dyeda, you are a Kuban Cossack, not a crybaby!'

But now I was told it was all right for me to cry over this. This was said, very knowingly and earnestly, by all sorts of people, like my teacher at school, and the lady who lived next door at Richmond, and the doctor from Mama's surgery who came to see us with a card. But I wasn't really sure what crying would achieve. Was I supposed to cry for myself or for Mama? Would it help me to cry? If so then it really wasn't clear how. Or was it expected of me by other people – would they think less of me if I didn't cry? If that was the case, then how long was I supposed to cry for?

I tried crying, but it just made me feel upset, so I stopped. I did feel empty though. And there was the physical pain. I couldn't understand why there was pain as I hadn't fallen and hurt myself, but my chest ached and my stomach churned. I couldn't really eat anything and my trousers grew looser around my waist. I seemed to spend a lot of time on the loo. The other kids at my school were nice – I think they had all been spoken to.

They say that time is a healer, but that isn't correct. Nothing can heal the loss of a parent. It can't be cured. It is a permanent disability, like losing an arm. But the passage of time does allow you to begin to live with and cope with the disability. The difference here is between adults and children. As an adult the mechanism you develop for coping with the grief – for now I recognise that grief is what it all was – is a supplement to your existing personality. It is a coat that you wear – it's still you underneath. But as a child the coping mechanism informs your personality as it is developing, it becomes part of your very being. You cannot remove this coat or even unbutton it.

Maybe that's why I think that children make the best of a loss. Around me everyone was numb but did their best not to show it. They could have done though. I wouldn't have minded, I understood as well as any of them what they were going through. Occasionally I would wake up in the middle of the night and could hear Papa crying. But he would always be his usual self at breakfast the next day – he had put on his coping mechanism coat so that he could face the day. So he could face me.

It was Dyeda who took it worse than any of us. The twinkle in his eyes vanished the moment he learned about Mama, and it never returned. I know he loved us all. I knew he loved me, but now looking back, I realise that he no longer loved life. He died a little over a year after Mama. I think the official cause was a cancer of some sort but, in reality, there could be no doubt that it was a broken heart that did for my Dyeda Pasha.

Papa carried on with his work ever more fervently, and now his blue Bristol car could often be seen parked in London's Harley Street[150] where he would see private patients in addition to continuing with surgery for the National Health Service. Baba now looked after me exclusively.

I'm not sure when the spare room at our home in Richmond officially became Baba's room. I cannot exactly recall when it was that she sold up the flat she had owned

150 Harley Street is a street in the Marylebone area of central London, noted for its large number of private specialists in medicine and surgery since the nineteeth century.

with Dyeda in Kew. But it was efficient for her to come to live with us permanently and Baba always did everything efficiently. It wasn't strange to be brought up by grandparents. Baba was my grandparent and in all honestly Papa could have been. He was only six years younger than Baba, they both continued to wear their respective wedding rings, and as time went by most people thought they must be married to each other. In a sense they were; as in choosing Papa as her husband, Mama could not have found a man more like Dyeda Pasha; whilst the only true difference between my Mama and Baba Tanya had been their age, as in looks, personality and intelligence they were precisely the same.

Please understand there was never anything more between Papa and Baba than their mutual love for me, but it suited us all to live together. People would refer to Baba as Mrs Cheshire rather than Mrs Zayky and she would never correct them. There was no need.

We only spoke Russian at home, and poor Papa struggled. Years later he told me that back in the late 1970s he actually employed a Russian language teacher to come to see him in Harley Street a couple of times a week, just to help him try to keep up with us. But he was never very good.

Reading Chekhov and Pushkin at Richmond was compulsory.[151] When I was younger Baba would lightly rap me across the knuckles with a wooden ruler if I stumbled or mispronounced a word, but as I grew older we would read

---

151 Anton Chekhov (1860–1904) was a Russian playwright and short-story writer, considered to be among the greatest writers of short fiction in history. Alexander Pushkin (1799–1837) was a Russian poet, playwright, and novelist of the Romantic era – possibly the greatest Russian poet and founder of modern Russian literature.

together out loud just for fun. Even when Aunt Greta and Uncle Jeremy would sometimes join us for tea on Sunday afternoons, I would read them passages pulling silly faces to make them laugh.

Baba would command, 'Misha! Stop being stupid, you must respect the great Pushkin!'

And Papa would complain, 'Tanya, I do wish you would call the boy by his proper name: Michael.' He would smile and make a thing out of rolling his eyes but I knew he didn't like me being called Misha.[152] But I didn't mind. There were several boys at school called Mike but nobody else was called Misha and so the name stuck.

Some days Baba and I would chat for hours, in Russian, about the Great Patriotic War, what had happened and what part they had played. She loathed the Soviets for the pain and suffering they had inflicted on the brave Kuban Cossacks – the famines induced by farming collectivisation which killed millions and the purges of the 1930s when so many good and intelligent people had been plucked from their homes in the middle of the night seemingly for no reason, never to return. But she hated the Nazis with a passion for the terror they had wrought when they had invaded her homeland, and for the ethnic cleansing and genocide which had been uncovered at the end of the war; even though she accepted that it had been the German invasion which had created the opportunity, that seismic shift, to allow them to escape to the West.

But her praise was always fulsome for the British, her new adopted homeland, who had taken them in, her Dyeda

---

152 Misha is a short form for the Russian name Mikhail (Michael) and a common Russian colloquialism for a bear.

and Mama, as if they had all been orphaned children. And where in Kenya, during the twilight years of its proud Empire, British rule had exemplified justice, tolerance, and expertise. And she would tell me her stories about flying the Knight, of course.

Conversations about the war always ended with her bringing out the old cigar box to show me the old dog-eared certificates and Mama's old passport and then going through the family photos on the mantlepiece – each picture, one by one, solemnly explaining who was who and when and why, and on and on, even though I knew already as she had explained it all a hundred times before. Her voice would crack and her words would choke. Just a little.

'I never cry,' she would say, as she rubbed her eyes and looked up to the mantlepiece where all the other pictures stood in their gilt frames; pictures of me in school uniform, Mama and Papa on their wedding day, and that picture of a little boy and girl by the river – fishing. That picture was the most yellowed and crumpled one but, for some reason, also the most treasured.

I attended the local primary school in Richmond but when it came to senior school Papa wanted to send me either to his old school, Charterhouse, or possibly to Eton College at Windsor. They easily had the money to afford the fees but Baba would not countenance me boarding and living away from home.

'We had to do it for your mama, Misha, there was no other choice in Kenya, she had to board at the High School in Nairobi; but it was horrible, well, it was difficult for your mama, I think... anyway I would hate it, you being away from home...'

In the end I went to Westminster School, which is a public school in central London but does allow day boys as well as boarders.[153] I just about scraped through the entrance exam and caught the Underground there and back each day. I'm not sure that any child actually enjoys school but I suppose that, for me, it was a relatively benign experience which at least allowed me to hone my language skills, adding French, German and Latin to my roster. Homework was always a trial though. The boarders had set prep periods whereas I had to work at the kitchen table under Baba's watchful eye.

'Misha, come on now, concentrate! This essay needs to be excellent just as your mama would expect. For her sake, please.'

Every Orthodox Easter Baba, Papa and I would go to the Brompton Cemetery to lay flowers on Mama's and Dyeda's graves. *Radonitsa*; 'A day of rejoicing,' Baba would say. It never felt like rejoicing to me, just dreadfully sad to see those we loved reduced to headstones – two dull grey standing stones rising up out of the ground; but Papa and I knew that Baba felt she had to go and she wanted us there with her.

Papa and Baba always expected me to go on to university, but despite my love of languages I was never really that academic. I could have easily read Russian somewhere but other than the kudos of actually obtaining

---

153 With origins before the twelfth century, Westminster School is an independent school located within the precincts of Westminster Abbey. It is one of the original seven public schools as defined by the Public Schools Act 1868. The school has around 750 pupils and most are 'day' pupils rather than 'boarders'.

a degree I wasn't really certain how my Russian language skills could be improved. That sounds a little pompous and probably typical of somebody who didn't have the skill to go on to university in any event. But having gleaned a crop of mediocre exam passes from school I felt that further education was rather futile. I was ready for something new and to be fair it was Papa who recognised that.

'Michael, I was speaking to a patient of mine today. I mentioned you, and that you were at a loose end, and he said that you might want to apply for a summer holiday job at his bank, where he works in London. It's actually a Swiss firm called Credit Suisse.[154] He gave me the address of where to write. Said that if you mention his name he will put in a good word for you.'

In those days most jobs were secured by some sort of back-scratching. You got the job through who your parents knew – usually through the old boys' school network – one of the reasons that Papa had originally wanted me to go to his old school. But a contact through his private medical practice seemed to work just as well and Papa took me to his tailor's to be fitted for a new suit.

If I got the job through back-scratching, then I learned quickly that holding onto the job was down to me. It was 1984 and I was nineteen. Plenty around me got fired for various misdemeanours, but plenty of others made lots of money. There were no second chances in banking in the mid-1980s –

154 Credit Suisse was founded in 1856 in Zurich, Switzerland, as Schweizerische Kreditanstalt to fund the development of Switzerland's rail system. Its operations remained within mainland Europe for most of the twentieth century and it only expanded to become a global bank during the 1980s.

you placed your bet – you won – and you rolled your money into the next wager. Win again and you were a hero – muck it up and you were out. It was so much better than school but I worked out fast that you needed a sharp wit, the ability to think on your feet, and lots of charm to survive. A thick skin was helpful too. Happily, they all seemed to be qualities in my possession, and the summer holiday job converted to a full-time role. University was put on indefinite hold. I would occasionally bump into old school friends who had gone on to Oxford or Exeter and realised that our interests had diverged.

I carried on living at Richmond although the money I earned from Credit Suisse was good and most people said that I was mad not to buy a place of my own. But I knew that Baba would not be at all happy about me moving out of home, and Papa might struggle to manage her without my help. I mentioned the possibility of moving out one day but, as I suspected, Baba was less than keen and made her feelings known.

'Well, I can't think why you would want to disrespect Papa and I by moving out! Can we not satisfy your home-life? What is wrong with us all of a sudden? Maybe that job of yours has given you such big ideas that you can't bear to live here with us, like you always have done. I am sorry that we make you so unhappy!'

And I had to spend the following hour assuring her that I was very happy, and that moving out of home was, indeed, a silly idea.

As a young boy you have childlike, almost feminine, looks and looking back at photos of me when I was about ten I can see that I looked like my mama. But during my late teens my face and physique altered. Baba would gaze at me.

'Oh, Misha, you look so like my Pasha, just as he was when I first knew him. So handsome...'

Sometimes I would walk down the stairs into the living room and she would turn and start speaking but I would have no idea what she was talking about. It would all be in Russian of course. She would start to refer to all sorts of people and places that I had never heard her mention before like Blockleiter Hiltze, Paul Pleiger, Salzgitter, Gathigiriri. I would try to respond and say I didn't understand, and she would look at me, puzzled. And I realised that she wasn't speaking to me – she was speaking to Pasha. That began to happen more regularly.

Occasionally she would forget a word. We all do that from time to time and it's very frustrating when the word you want to use is on the tip of your tongue but your memory just can't place it. But when you notice somebody forgetting words like 'kitchen' or 'bus' then you do wonder. Baba would speak and slip from Russian into English and then German all within one sentence without realising. Papa and I ignored it, probably for much longer than we should have done.

Dementia is a cruel disease, perhaps even more cruel to those you love than to you as the one afflicted. By the end of the 1980s it was me recounting the stories of exploits in the Knight to Baba as I sat visiting her in her nursing home in Richmond every Sunday afternoon. By then she had forgotten most words but still she seemed to understand me. She would place her gently shaking hand against my cheek and smile as I spoke. I knew that, in her heart, she was with her Pasha once again, and perhaps her hero Pyotr too. My Baba Tanya slipped away in 1990 just a few days short of her eightieth birthday.

They had all gone by then. Angus McGrath had died shortly before Dyeda in the mid-1970s. Aunt Greta made it to the ripe age of eighty-five. I remember going to see her at Tite Street towards the end where we would gorge on Swiss roll washed down with milky tea. She was a very fine lady, always as bright as a button; her voice loud and sonorous right to the end. She died quickly after a stroke.

Uncle Jeremy was clearly ill by the late 1980s. He was weak and thin. His dashing looks had gone and his once wonderful blue eyes had receded into his skull. The acting jobs had dried up some years earlier but Greta still had a little money put by.

I don't know how much she knew or realised, but she was no fool, and during the last years of the 1980s the TV ran constant stories about the epidemic.[155] Nevertheless, I was pleased that poor Jeremy outlived her, albeit only for a year or so.

So in the end then it was just Papa and me at Richmond. He was well into his seventies by the start of the 1990s, the record player in the St George's operating theatre having

_____

155 The term AIDS (acquired immune deficiency syndrome) was first used in 1982 to describe the final stage of HIV (human immunodeficiency virus), which gradually breaks down, and finally destroys, the body's natural defence against illness. The disease is thought to have started in Africa in the early twentieth century but came to prominence in the 1980s. At the start of the 1990s over 307,000 AIDS cases had been officially reported with the actual number estimated to be closer to a million. Between 8–10 million people were thought to be living with HIV worldwide. The scale of the fear generated by the disease during the 1980s is hard to imagine now, but ignorance created worldwide hysteria causing massive stigma against the gay community. In the 1980s AIDS created panic, paranoia and discrimination as well as a media frenzy.

been packed away long since. On most days, however, you would see his sky-blue Bristol car parked up in Lincoln's Inn Fields outside the Royal College of Surgeons where he would be sitting on committees working to improve and regulate medical excellence.[156]

I was still at Credit Suisse, but the 'roaring 1980s' had come to an end with a bump and by 1990 the Western economic system was moribund, all stuck in recession. All the fun had gone out of banking.

But things seemed to be looking up to the East. The Soviet Union – that seventy-year-old political experiment – was shaking with old age. In the south, the regions were breaking away from Moscow's control and to the west the satellite states, who had been such loyal and fervent Communists since the end of the second war, were now seeking independence. The Iron Curtain was falling. During 1989 in an 'Autumn of Nations' a wave of revolutions took place in Poland, Hungary, East Germany, Bulgaria, Czechoslovakia and Romania. They all broke away from their former Soviet masters. Had this occurred in the 1950s or 60s, during the peak of the Cold War, then Russian tanks would have filled the streets of the various capital cities, but now the mother state was so weakened that it merely shrugged and let them all go.

In August 1991 hard-line Soviet Communists, from within the army, staged a coup d'état in Moscow whilst Mikhail Gorbachev, the General Secretary of the Soviet

---

156 The Royal College of Surgeons, located at Lincoln's Inn Fields in London, is an independent professional body and registered charity promoting and advancing standards of surgical care for patients and regulating surgery in England and Wales.

Union, was away on holiday in the Crimea. He was placed under house arrest whilst the coup leaders issued an emergency decree suspending political activity and banning most newspapers.

The leaders of the coup had expected popular support but found public opinion against them. Instead, Boris Yeltsin, who had come to prominence as a rebel and who had been elected by a popular vote as president of an independent Russia within the USSR a few months earlier, rallied opposition by making speeches from the top of a tank. His words brought thousands of Muscovites onto the streets. The coup failed and Gorbachev was reinstated; but his political power had been drained.

After that the Soviet Union collapsed with dramatic speed during the last quarter of 1991. On the evening of 25 December, at 7.32pm Moscow time, when Gorbachev left the Kremlin, the Hammer and Sickle flag was lowered for the last time. The USSR no longer existed.

All of this unfolded on the TV screens of the West. The BBC showed pictures of the unfolding coup – Yeltsin on his tank – and later on, Gorbachev's departure from office. I was glued to every TV news report. I moved my chair close to the screen to study the faces of the people – their smiles of joy brought by the freedom from totalitarianism. I could feel their happiness, their optimism was palpable.

The Nazis' Third Reich had been expunged in 1945, the British Empire had been given away by the 1960s and now, in the final decade of the twentieth century, the Communist empire, the once great and terrible USSR, had grown infirm and died as well. If only Baba could have lived to see it.

As soon as he was in power Yeltsin wasted no time. For years across the ideological divide he had watched the West grow ever richer, especially during the free market reforms of the 1980s – the years of 'Reaganomics'.[157] Now he wanted Russia to share in the wealth of nations. In an economic 'shock therapy' he oversaw the privatisation of 225,000 state-owned businesses, the release of price and currency controls, the withdrawal of state subsidies, and full trade liberalisation.

All these new private businesses needed investment and that provided a banking opportunity. The good times were back! But now it was all happening about 1,800 miles to the east of London, and I could speak the language.

---

157 Reaganonmics refers to the economic policies promoted by US President Ronald Reagan during the 1980s. These policies are commonly associated with supply-side and free-market economics. The four pillars of Reagan's economic policy were to reduce the growth of government spending, reduce tax, reduce regulation, and tighten the money supply in order to reduce inflation.

EPILOGUE

H E KNOCKED AGAIN, WAITING; LOOKING DOWN AT
the cracks in the concrete with the dandelions growing
through.

Arriving in the city of the Kuban Cossacks at 10am
following a sleepless twenty-four hour journey, Misha,
dishevelled and unshaven, had found a café near the station
for morning coffee, before setting off on his trek through the
streets – asking the passers-by and policemen for directions
to the grey block of flats on the outskirts of the main centre.
When he had left Moscow he couldn't have been certain
that the flat in Krasnodar would still have been there, but as
soon as he had got off the train he had known that his search
would be successful. One glance at Krasnodar in 1993
revealed that very little had changed from the Soviet-era
picture as described by Baba Tanya. The city was as if it had
been caught, complete, within a time capsule. It was only
the dandelions revealing themselves through the concrete
that were new – nothing else had changed in sixty years.

'There is nobody there. What do you want, young man?'

He looked round to see a woman marching down the
outside landing toward him. He judged her to be late fifties,
short, very stocky, beige cardigan, brown skirt, bare legs, and
clumping brown men's brogue shoes. She wore a headscarf

but it was pulled back on her head so that her hairline was revealed – thick, dark, almost black hair with a streak of white running from the front to under the scarf. Her face was wide and Slavic with long hanging lines either side of her unsmiling mouth which looked almost as if they were the gills of a fish. He realised that she was the block manager, the caretaker. Most apartment buildings in Moscow had an old woman who ran the building, obviously the same was true in Krasnodar.

She looked him up and down, suspiciously, in his Western anorak and jeans.

'Yes?'

Radonitsa had been the day before, the second Tuesday after Easter, but he had been travelling. Somebody might have been at the flat then, but now the woman had obviously emerged to tell him to clear off. He thought back to Baba Tanya's treatment of travelling salesmen who had dared to ring the doorbell at Richmond. Well at least he wasn't trying to sell anything.

He was not at all the confident Moscow banker now. He could feel his heart beating.

'Well… forgive me turning up like this, but my mother, well… and my grandparents… used to live in this flat. Years ago. Before the war. My Baba told me about it, and now I live in Moscow so I wanted to come to see it.'

'You're not from Moscow though…'

'Oh no, I'm British, my grandparents and mother moved there.' He hesitated – how much should he say? 'But I work in Moscow now for a bank.'

'And who are your grandparents?'

'Pavel and Tatania Zayky…? And my mother was Sofia

Zayky. They lived here. I'm sure this is the flat. But they have all passed away now.'

Was there a slight crack in her impassive face? Perhaps just the smallest movement in the fish-like gills covering her cheeks to indicate some recognition, or even empathy, over the passing of Misha's family. But her suspicion remained plain.

'Why have you come now? After all these years?'

'Well in England I would visit the graves of the departed at *Radonitsa* with Baba and so coming to Krasnodar seemed right.'

There was a little further mellowing in her expression now.

'So, what were they, your Baba and Dyedushka Zayky? What did they do here in Krasnodar, before the war?'

Was this a test?

'Well Baba Tanya was an engineer and worked in the food-processing factory, but Dyeda Pasha was originally from Saratov and became a botanist at the university.'

She nodded, she had known that already. Misha's heart leapt.

'Did you know them? Have you always lived here?'

'I know of them, yes. And yes, I have always lived here but I'm not that old. My parents knew them, but my understanding was that the family Zayky all died during the war.'

'No, no, they left here afterwards... They ended up in England. That's where I was brought up. It was my Baba Tanya who taught me Russian.'

The woman looked at him, a long hard stare, her gills twitching. Was he telling the truth? His story seemed fantastic but why would he lie? She cocked her head to one side to signify the next test.

'And what of your uncle?'

Uncle? He had no uncle, although for just a moment Misha thought she must be speaking about Uncle Jeremy, before realising that was ridiculous. He looked puzzled and so she continued.

'Your great-uncle. Your Baboushka's brother?'

Ah yes, now he understood. 'Well he died, after the war, very sadly.'

'What was his name?'

'His name was Pyotr... but he is dead; long ago.'

She examined his face.

'But why do you knock at this flat?'

'Well, I told you, this is where my family used to live. My Baba told me about it in stories during my childhood and I simply wanted to see it... I am so sorry to just turn up like this but there was no way I could pre-warn you that I wanted to visit, you see.'

'Wait here.'

And with that she turned on the heel of her brown brogue shoe and marched away in the direction from which she had come, leaving Misha standing on the first-floor landing, by the firmly closed door of the old flat, and wondering what to do.

But waiting seemed sensible and there was really nothing else for it. Eventually his patience was rewarded as the woman marched back into sight.

'Follow me,' she said and strode off again. Misha did as he was told. She led him back down the concrete steps and around to another block precisely the same as the last, but rather than going up the steps she paused by the front door of a ground-floor flat and knocked. There was a shuffling from inside and the door opened a crack.

'Pyotr Ivanovich, this is the man I told you about.' She paused. 'Should I stay?' she continued.

Now the door opened fully to reveal a tall but elderly man, certainly in his late seventies but perhaps older still. Despite his advancing years his large frame filled the doorway. Decades earlier, when he had been a younger man, people would have described him as a bear; but now his hair was snowy white, as was his beard; although his whiskers remained long and luxuriant, albeit slightly yellowed near his mouth from a lifetime of smoking.

He put out his hand; a huge if slightly quivering palm, which took Misha's and held it firmly.

'Pyotr Moroz,' he said to Misha and then continued, 'no thank you, Ludmilla, I'm sure we shall be fine.'

Ludmilla, the caretaker, took one further long look at Misha, just slightly narrowing her eyes at him, before turning on her heel once more.

'Come in, come in…' boomed the old man. 'I so rarely get visitors these days, and certainly not a smart Western man such as yourself. Please sit down; I have just made us tea. Ludmilla tells me that perhaps your parents knew my sister and her husband before the war.'

The apartment was small, tiny in fact, and the old man seemed physically much larger than the room he was in, rather like a giant moving around in a doll's house. There was a table and two upholstered easy chairs, slightly threadbare. An old television set, on a stand, was positioned against the wall. Straight ahead was the doorway to a bedroom – the only other room. In the corner stood an electric cooker and fridge and next to them a wood-burning stove, although there was no fire that day in late April. Above the stove was a shelf upon which stood numerous framed photographs and Misha noted an icon located in the corner diagonally opposite the front door. It seemed that, in an effort to make the tiny apartment seem even smaller, it had been filled with a lifetime's worth of possessions; boxes, trinkets, newspapers, jars, books, and ornaments occupied every available surface.

There was a window but the adjacent apartment block had been built so close by that there was virtually no natural light. A single electric bulb in the middle of the ceiling fitted with a crochet shade provided dim illumination, and highlighted palls of cigarette smoke hanging in the atmosphere.

Misha moved a small alabaster figurine from the seat of one of the upholstered chairs and placed it carefully on the floor alongside. As he sat down so the chair gave a loud creak in protest and Misha ended up rather lower than he had expected. The old man didn't notice and continued to make tea, ladling in a generous spoonful of honey and stirring vigorously.

'So tell me, how did your parents know my sister?'

Misha was confused. Moroz had been Baba Tanya's family name before she had married Dyeda – and this man had introduced himself as Pyotr. Coincidence?

But Misha retold his story, and why he had come to Krasnodar, just as he had to Ludmilla, the caretaker. The old man listened carefully, but shook his head.

'No no, young man, you are quite wrong. You are suggesting that you are a Zayky; but that is impossible. My sister, her husband, and my beautiful niece were all killed at the end of the war.'

Very carefully, Misha put down his teacup next to the alabaster figurine and stood. Gingerly stepping over the various other possessions placed elsewhere on the floor he went to the shelf above the stove. Across all the detritus of the room, all the knick-knacks, the keepsakes and junk, something had caught his eye; something familiar. Reaching up, he took down a small dark wooden frame, battered and scratched, much handled over the course of a lifetime, and looked down at the yellowed photograph held behind the thin glass. He knew that picture well.

Two children fishing in a shallow stretch of river. A skinny boy in shorts, no shoes, grinning as he turned to the camera. His line was dangling in the water and his face, caught in dazzling sun, was slightly overexposed. Next to the boy was a girl, slightly taller, in a summer dress. She was bony and with frowning dark eyes was carefully adjusting the wire on her rod. It was a day that had been so clearly described to Misha, so many times, that he might almost have been there too.

He turned back to the old man, still holding the framed picture, although now it was Misha's hand that quivered, just slightly. Quickly, he drew his other hand up to his face, pinching at the bridge of his nose, to wipe away moisture from the corners of his eyes.

'This is my Baba Tanya, and this is you, in the summer of 1925. You were fishing on the Kuban. You were there all day, dangling your lines and your toes in the water.'

He was held by coal-dark eyes.

'But you didn't catch any fish.'

Pyotr smiled. 'No,' he replied. 'Not a single one!'

APPENDIX

THE MAU MAU INSURGENCY

The Mau Mau were eventually completely put down by the British. Unsurprisingly the term 'concentration camps' was never used but detaining an entire tribe in prison or within secure villages had the desired effect. The formal state of emergency ordered by Sir Evelyn Baring in 1952 continued until 1959 but the war had been won by British colonial efficiency and brutality by 1956.

The curiously named Carruthers 'Monkey' Johnson went on to work in military intelligence, and John Cowan – the Gathigiriri prison officer who formulated 'Operation Progress', beating suspects into submission – got a job at the Bank of England. Terence Gavaghan was eventually awarded the Order of the British Empire medal by the Queen for his successes during the Emergency Period.

However, by the end of the 1950s details of British atrocities began to emerge. In 1959 a revelation that eleven inmates had been beaten to death at a camp called Hola on the Tana River and that the administration had then tried to cover it up, caused shock waves in Britain. Questions began to be asked and it became obvious that things were going to change. Nevertheless, it took over fifty years and the threat of legal action before the British administration were prepared to acknowledge the extent of their barbarism. Even then their words could be considered by some as mealy-mouthed.

On 6th June 2013, the Foreign Secretary, the Right Honorable William Hague MP, addressed the British Parliament:

With permission, Mr Speaker, I would like to make a statement on a legal settlement that the Government has reached concerning the claims of Kenyan citizens who lived through the Emergency Period and the Mau Mau insurgency from October 1952 to December 1963.

During the Emergency Period widespread violence was committed by both sides, and most of the victims were Kenyan. Many thousands of Mau Mau members were killed, while the Mau Mau themselves were responsible for the deaths of over 2,000 people including 200 casualties among the British regiments and police.

Emergency regulations were introduced: political organisations were banned; prohibited areas were created and provisions for detention without trial were enacted. The colonial authorities made unprecedented use of capital punishment and sanctioned harsh prison so-called 'rehabilitation' regimes. Many of those detained were never tried and the links of many with the Mau Mau were never proven. There was recognition at the time of the brutality of these repressive measures and the shocking level of violence, including an important debate in this House on the infamous events at Hola Camp in 1959.

We recognise that British personnel were called upon to serve in difficult and dangerous circumstances. Many members of the colonial service contributed to establishing the institutions that underpin Kenya today and we acknowledge their contribution.

However I would like to make clear now and for the first time, on behalf of Her Majesty's Government, that we understand the pain and grievance felt by those who were involved in the events of the Emergency in Kenya. The British Government recognises that Kenyans were subject to torture and other forms of ill treatment at the hands of the colonial administration. The British government sincerely regrets that these abuses took place, and that they marred Kenya's progress towards independence. Torture and ill treatment are abhorrent violations of human dignity which we unreservedly condemn.

In October 2009 claims were first brought to the High Court by five individuals who were detained during the Emergency period regarding their treatment in detention.

In 2011 the High Court rejected the claimants' argument that the liabilities of the colonial administration transferred to the British Government on independence, but allowed the claims to proceed on the basis of other arguments.

In 2012 a further hearing took place to determine whether the cases should be allowed to proceed. The High Court ruled that three of the five cases could do so. The Court of Appeal was due to hear our appeal against that decision last month. However, I can announce today that the Government has now reached an agreement with Leigh Day, the solicitors acting on behalf of the Claimants, in full and final settlement of their clients' claims.

The agreement includes payment of a settlement sum in respect of 5,228 claimants, as well as a gross costs sum, to the total value of £19.9 million. The Government will also support the construction of a memorial in Nairobi to the victims of torture and ill-treatment during the colonial era. The memorial will stand alongside others that are already being established in Kenya as the country continues to heal the wounds of the past.

And the British High Commissioner in Nairobi is also today making a public statement to members of the Mau Mau War Veterans Association in Kenya, explaining the settlement and expressing our regret for the events of the Emergency Period.

Mr Speaker this settlement provides recognition of the suffering and injustice that took place in Kenya. The Government of Kenya, the Kenya Human Rights Commission and the Mau Mau War Veterans Association have long been in favour of a settlement, and it is my hope that the agreement now reached will receive wide support, will help draw a line under these events, and will support reconciliation.

We continue to deny liability on behalf of the Government and British taxpayers today for the actions of the colonial administration in respect of the claims, and indeed the courts have made no finding of liability against the Government in this case. We do not believe that claims relating to events that occurred overseas outside direct British jurisdiction more than fifty years ago can be resolved satisfactorily through the courts without the testimony of key witnesses that is no longer available. It is therefore right that the Government has defended the case to this point since 2009.

It is of course right that those who feel they have a case are free to bring it to the courts. However we will also continue to exercise our own right to defend claims brought against the Government. And we do not believe that this settlement establishes a precedent in relation to any other former British colonial administration.

The settlement I am announcing today is part of a process of reconciliation. In December this year, Kenya will mark its 50th anniversary of independence and the country's future belongs to a post independence generation. We do not want our current and future relations with Kenya to be overshadowed by the past. Today we are bound together by commercial, security and personal links that benefit both our countries. We are working together closely to build a more stable region. Bilateral trade between the UK and Kenya amounts to £1 billion each year, and around 200,000 Britons visit Kenya annually.

Although we should never forget history and indeed must always seek to learn from it, we should also look to the future, strengthening a relationship that will promote the security and prosperity of both our nations. I trust that this settlement will support that process. The ability to recognise error in the past but also to build the strongest possible foundation for cooperation and friendship in the future are both hallmarks of our democracy.

In 2015 a new memorial was unveiled in Nairobi depicting a Mau Mau fighter with his home-made rifle accepting food from a villager. Their faces are turned away from each other so that one cannot reveal the identity of the other if caught. The cost was met by the British Government.

https://www.bbc.co.uk/news/world-africa-34231890

ACKNOWLEDGEMENTS

Paul Beaver, Michael Beckman, David and Zan Blundell, Sue Carpenter, Martyn Carrington, John Church, Louise Corcoran, Pam Forbes, Bella Hoare, Tom Hopewell, Dr Peter Cirenza and all at LSE's Economic History Dept, Dr Joanna Lewis, Mike Metcalfe, Fraser Morris, Vic Norman, John-Paul Rowe, Tanya Smith, Dr Olga Sobolev, Dr Judy Stephenson, Jaroslav Ton, Dr Angus Wrenn

My thanks to you all!

BIBLIOGRAPHY AND FURTHER READING

Russia and the East:

Owen Matthews – *Stalin's Children*, 2008

Andrei Makine – *A Life's Music*, 2001

Nina Lugovskaya – *The Diary of a Soviet Schoolgirl 1932–1937*, 2003

Alan Clark – *Barbarossa*, 1965

Simon Sebag Montefiore – *Stalin: The Court of the Red Tsar*, 2003

Mary M. Leder – *My Life in Stalinist Russia*, 2001

Robert Forczyk – *The Caucasus 1942–43: Kleist's Race for Oil*, 2015

Bruce Chatwin – *Utz*, 1988

Valentina Bogdan – *Students in the First Five Year Plan*, 1973

Germany:

Klaus Neuman – *Shifting Memories*, 2000

Eric Lichtblau – *The Nazis Next Door*, 2014

Anthony Beevor – *Berlin*, 2002

William L. Shirer – *The Rise and Fall of the Third Reich: A History of Nazi Germany*, 1959

Kenya:

Daniel Branch – *Defeating Mau Mau, Creating Kenya*, 2009
Jeremy Murray-Brown – *Kenyatta*, 1972
J.B. Carson – *Sun, Sand and Safari*, 1957
Caroline Elkins – *Britain's Gulag: The Brutal End of Empire in Kenya*, 2005
Derek Franklin – *A Pied Cloak: Memoirs of a Colonial Police (Special Branch) Officer*, 1996
Billy Hopkins – *Going Places*, 2003
Elspeth Huxley – *Nellie: Letters from Africa*, 1973
Beryl Markham – *West with the Night*, 1942
C.S. Nicholls – *A Kenya Childhood*, 2011
Robert Ruark – *Something of Value*, 1955
Hilary Sunman – *A Very Different Land: Memories of Empire from Farmlands of Kenya*, 2014

London:

Christopher Birchall – *Embassy, Emigrants, and Englishmen: The Three Hundred Year History of a Russian Orthodox Church in London*, 2014
Ray Desmond – *The History of the Royal Botanic Gardens Kew*, 1995
George Orwell – *Down and Out in Paris and London*, 1933 and *1984*, 1949